The
Traitor's Mark

Also by D.K. Wilson

The First Horseman

... in the last days shall come parlous times. For the men shall be lovers of their own selves, covetous, boasters, proud, cursed speakers, disobedient to father and mother, unthankful, unholy, unkind, truce-breakers, stubborn, false accusers, rioters, fierce despisers of them which are good, traitors, heady, high-minded, greedy upon voluptuousness more than the lovers of God, having a similitude of godly living, but have denied the power thereof ...

– The Second Epistle of St Paul to Timothy, in the 1534 translation by William Tyndale

... certain of the council ... by the enticement and provocation of his ancient enemy the bishop of Winchester, and others of the same sect, attempted the king against him, declaring plainly, that the realm was so infected with heresies and heretics, that it was dangerous for his highness further to permit it unreformed ... the enormity whereof they could not impute to any so much, as to the archbishop of Canterbury, who by his own preaching, and his chaplains, had filled the whole realm full of divers pernicious heresies.

– John Foxe, *Acts and Monuments of the Christian Religion*, 1563

Prologue

10 June 1540

He ran up the steps – a man in a hurry. Thomas Cromwell, Earl of Essex, Lord Great Chamberlain, Vicegerent in Spirituals, the most powerful person in England under the king, mounted the long flight of stairs to the Whitehall Council Chamber two at a time. He was late for the meeting and, though he was not troubled by the thought of keeping his fellow councillors waiting, tardiness, in itself, was a thing he abhorred. It was a mark of disorganised, inefficient or blatantly lazy minds and Cromwell prided himself on not being prey to any of these vices.

There was good reason for his delay on this occasion. He had spent the six hours since dawn organising the carefully accumulated evidence that would strike down his enemies, led by Stephen Gardiner, Bishop of Winchester, and Thomas Howard,

Duke of Norfolk. For months he had been galled by the open hostility and covert intrigues of the men trying to undermine King Henry's confidence in him. These conservative elements, these dullards, these visionless men had set themselves to stop England's development towards a truly Christian commonwealth, independent of Rome, purged of clerical corruption and illumined by the newly Englished word of God. The need to defend himself and organise his counter-attack had taken up valuable time – time that could more profitably have been employed in continuing the legislative programme revolutionising the kingdom. But now he had all the evidence he needed. Lord Lisle, Governor of Calais, was, at last, in the Tower and revealing to his interrogators the antics of the brood of papist vipers causing havoc in the English port under his command. With Bishop Sampson of Chichester and the royal chaplain, Dr Wilson, also under investigation for illicit communication with Rome, the long, secret campaign was over. He could now strike at his conciliar enemies before they were ready to strike at him. Cromwell bustled through the anteroom and its throng of petitioners. At his approach, the door to the Council chamber was hastily thrown open.

As soon as he crossed the threshold he knew something was wrong. His colleagues were not seated around the long table, awaiting his arrival in order to commence the day's business. They stood around the room in groups of two and three. At one side, by the oriel window, stood the captain of the guard and three of his men. Cromwell took in the situation at a glance. Scarcely pausing, he strode purposefully towards his chair at the head of the table.

Norfolk blocked his path. 'You are no longer a member of this board!' His eyes glared the hatred he had only rarely troubled to conceal.

Cromwell scowled. 'Stand aside, My Lord.'

'A Howard does not yield place to an upstart.' The duke raised his hand to Cromwell's chest and pushed.

Cromwell struggled to retain his self-control. 'So now we see you clearly for the arrogant papist you are. Guard, arrest this man. I have evidence here of his treasons.' He held up the sheaf of papers he was carrying.

The captain looked anxiously from one to the other. It was Bishop Gardiner who turned to him and ordered sharply. 'Why do you wait, man? You know your duty. You have your warrant. Execute it.'

The captain walked around the table and stopped two paces from Cromwell.

'My Lord of Essex, I am here with his gracious majesty's warrant to arrest you and take you into custody on charges of high treason.'

'I? High treason? Who dares to charge me, the king's most devoted subject . . .' Cromwell was trembling with rage and fear. 'It is not I who have betrayed the king's trust.' He brandished his evidence.

Norfolk snatched the papers from him. 'Too late,' he sneered. 'His majesty has been fully informed of your disloyalty.'

'He knows how you have been usurping royal power these last years.' The speaker was Sir Thomas Wriothesley, one of the king's secretaries.

Cromwell frowned. 'So, they have corrupted you, have they, Thomas? How soon you have forgotten who raised you to your present position.'

Gardiner added his taunt. 'His majesty now knows who is the biggest heretic in England.'

Cromwell watched as all the others gathered round in a

circle. He was politically astute enough to know that his enemies had grasped the initiative. The neutrals on the Council would now fall into line behind them. He could only stand trembling with impotent rage, as the captain seized him by the arm.

'Wait,' Norfolk ordered. With a leering smile of triumph, he stretched out a hand to grab the gold chain of office round Cromwell's neck. Cromwell's fingers fastened round his wrist. For a long moment the two rivals glowered at each other. In that moment the fate of England was decided. Norfolk broke free, seized the symbol of Cromwell's authority and tugged with such force that one of the links snapped. Wriothesley – if there was treachery in the room it was, surely, his – was instantly on his knees unfastening the Garter insignia from Cromwell's leg.

'Take the heretic!' Gardiner ordered.

Rough hands grasped the Earl of Essex's arms. He was marched from the room. For ten years Thomas Cromwell had virtually ruled England. His destruction had taken fewer than three minutes.

Chapter 1

In God's name, Master Thomas, come and get me out of
this hell-hole. The woman will tell all.
    Your servant,
    Bart Miller

The words were scrawled in what appeared to be charcoal on
a crumpled scrap of paper, roughly folded. I looked up at the
messenger who stood before me in my parlour. She was, I
guessed, about eighteen, simply but tidily dressed, her clean
apron covering a brown woollen kirtle. But her clothes were
awry. Strands of dark hair had escaped from her plain linen
coif. Her brown eyes were reddened with crying and she kept
dabbing them with a kerchief. She had also been running, for
she was sorely out of breath.

'Please sit down,' I said as calmly as possible. 'What's your
name?'

She lowered herself on to a joint stool. 'Adriana, an't please you, Master, but people call me Adie.'

'Well, Adie.' I gave what I hope was a reassuring smile. 'What is all this about? What has befallen my servant?'

'Oh, the poor man! It was terrible. I thought at first he was dead, like George.' Her voice tailed away into a sob.

Bart close to death! Now I shared the anxiety of this unexpected visitor to my house in Goldsmith's Row. I poured a little ale into my own beaker and handed it to her. 'Drink this,' I said. 'Take your time.'

As she sipped, I prompted. 'I sent Bart out this forenoon with a message to a house in Aldgate, close by the Saracen's Head.'

The woman nodded. 'Aye, for Master Johannes.'

'He arrived safely, then?'

'Ye-s. I suppose so.'

'You don't seem very sure.'

'I was upstairs with the children. When all the noise started, I shut the door. I was frightened.'

'What noise?'

'Shouting, banging – like several men arguing, fighting.' She was on the verge of tears again. I had to wait while she took some deep breaths and regained control.

'And this happened in the house?' I asked.

She nodded. 'Yes, in the inner room, close by the stairs. That's why it sounded so loud. Perhaps I should have gone down.' She sniffed and rubbed a hand across her nose. 'But I was scared for the children.'

'Of course. I'm sure you did the right thing . . . And then?'

'Well, Master, I waited a long time . . . till everything was quiet. Then I went down the stairs . . . very carefully . . . and looked. It was terrible. Blood everywhere . . . I didn't know . . .'

'Whose blood?' I demanded quickly, before the girl could be overwhelmed by fresh weeping. 'Has Bart . . . '

'Oh no, Master. It was young George . . . Master Johannes' prentice . . . or assistant . . . or pupil. I don't know what you'd call him. Master Johannes found him at one of the printers what works outside the City. He said the boy had talent . . . Oh, poor George! Lying on the floor, he was . . . all acrumpled . . . blood on his tunic. I didn't know what to think . . . or do. I turned to go back upstairs . . . fetch the children . . . get them away. Then the other man – your man – called out to me. Slumped against the wall, he was. Groaning. Holding his head. "Help me," he said. "For the love of God, help!" But I daren't move. Well, I didn't know what to think. If he'd had a fight with George and . . . done that to him . . . '

'Bart wouldn't harm anyone,' I said.

Adie took a long gulp of ale, followed by a deep, sighing breath. 'Yes, Master. He tried to explain what happened. Said he and George had been attacked by four strangers. Said they'd beaten George all over . . . then stabbed him because he wouldn't tell them where Master Johannes was.'

This time I let the tears gush. I brooded about Bart Miller. If there was one man in London sure to discover trouble wherever it was lurking, that man was my business assistant. I could not call him my apprentice because he had not joined my household to learn the goldsmith's craft, but he had a quick head for figures, was diligent in keeping the books tidily and was very reliable – when he was not getting himself into unnecessary scrapes.

'What happened next?' I asked, when the sobs and sniffs had subsided. 'Where is Bart now?'

'Locked up in Aldgate gatehouse, thanks to our stupid constable!'

'Then we must get back there quickly. You can tell me the rest of the story as we go.' I pushed aside the papers I had been working on, went to the door and called for my man, Will. It was mid-July – plague time. The house was quieter than usual because I had sent most of the staff down to my estate in Kent, where I intended to follow as soon as Bart and I had concluded most of my outstanding business. When Will hurried in from the kitchen I told him to have one of my horses saddled and the donkey cart harnessed.

While we stood in the courtyard waiting for all to be made ready, I pressed the girl for more details. 'What were you saying about the Aldgate constable?'

Adie scowled, the flush on her cheek now one of anger. 'I'd just helped your Bart to his feet. "We must get the constable . . . raise the hue and cry," he said. Only there wasn't no need. A crowd had gathered outside and someone had already sent for Peter Pett.'

'Your ward constable?'

'Yes, but to hear him you'd think he was lord mayor. He's a braggart and a bully. "Peter Pest" people call him. He stood there asking stupid questions and making . . . suggestions.'

'What sort of suggestions?'

Adie lowered her head. 'About me and your man,' she muttered. 'He said that since we was the only ones there, we must have been up to something. Then, George must have found us and we'd all had a fight and your Bart must have pulled a knife . . . Oh, the man's a flap-mouthed jolthead. He wouldn't listen to me and he wouldn't call the hue and cry. Just said he was going to put both of us in irons till the magistrate came. He would have, too, if some of our neighbours hadn't spoken for me. It was Goodwife Mays, next door, who made him see that I'm nurse to Master Johannes' children. Then your man said he was servant to an important merchant and there'd be trouble if they harmed him. Well, that made the Pest think. He wouldn't let Bart go but he did say I could bring you a note. We found a stick of Master Johannes' charcoal and a bit of old drawing paper. Bart wrote the note and I left the children with Goodwife Mays. Then I ran all the way here as fast as I could.'

When Walt, my ostler, had the cart ready, he hauled himself into the driving seat and held out a hand to hoist the girl up beside him. 'Where to, Master Thomas?' he asked, waving a hand at the crowd of flies that buzzed around the donkey's hindquarters.

'Aldgate,' I replied. 'The gatehouse. It seems that our Bart has managed to get himself locked up there. You'll have to bring him back.'

His face creased into a black-toothed grin. 'He'll be right enough, Master Thomas. He's used to taking rough knocks – thrives on 'em.'

'Well, we must see what he's walked into this time.' Golding, my grey, was led out of the stable and I climbed into the saddle. 'I'll go on ahead and see you there.'

I turned out of the yard and set off along West Cheap, eager to get the journey over, yet anxious about what I would discover at its end. What Walt said about Bart Miller was true. When he had come to work for me six years before he was a hothead of less than twenty, always on the lookout for a cause to uphold and ready to use whatever means came to hand. He had lost an arm fighting with the northern rebels in 1536. Marriage had somewhat sobered him. His wife, Lizzie, was a strong-minded woman, tough enough to curb his enthusiasms and clever enough not to let him know that he was being 'handled'. Even so, Bart still saw himself as an adventurer.

Like the knights we hear of in the tales of King Arthur, he could not help looking for dragons to slay. Anyone with a story to tell of injustice or cruelty or exploitation found in Bart Miller a ready listener.

When I sent him out that morning with a message for the German artist, it never occurred to me that he could get involved in a murderous brawl. I simply wanted to know why my old friend Johannes Holbein was keeping me waiting for some tableware designs. I needed them urgently and it was unlike him not to have them ready on time. It was all very aggravating. The work was for an important – and wealthy – client. If I could not show him some designs within days he would, most assuredly, take his business elsewhere. Much as I was concerned about Bart, I was also bothered by what the girl had told me about her master. Could it be that the artist had deliberately 'disappeared' – gone into hiding from enemies who would not stop at murder? But who would want to kill a foreign artist who enjoyed the king's favour and was patronised by most of the fashionable elite?

It was mid-afternoon – hot and humid, warning of a storm to come. The City was quiet, many people seeking the shade – if they had not already escaped the plague-haunted streets to pass high summer in the country, something I was impatient to do. It was annoying having to waste more time trying to locate Holbein or extricate Bart from whatever he had got into. In the West Cheap narrows by the Conduit a large wagon was being loaded causing some congestion. I waited for the donkey cart to catch up in order to ask Adie more questions.

'Do you know where your master has gone?'

She fussed with wisps of hair, tucking them back under the cap. 'He's often away days at a time. Doing what he calls "sittings".'

'Making portraits of fine lords and ladies?'

'Oh, yes, he's much in demand. Everyone wants a likeness by Master Johannes, what with him being the king's painter and all.' For the first time she showed a slight wistful smile. 'He did a picture of me and the children – a year ago, before the little ones died. It wasn't a painting, of course, just a drawing. He's ever so quick. There was I trying to make the two boys sit still. Little Henry's a great wriggler. But it didn't matter. Master Johannes was so quick.'

'And you've no idea where your master has gone this time?'

Adie shook her head. 'He went off first thing Tuesday, as he often does, with all his gear on a packhorse.'

'Is there no way you can get a message to him – a warning?'

Again the doleful, almost resigned, shake of the head.

'What about you and the children – and their mother?'

Adie scowled. 'Oh, she's been up and away long since. Packed her bags and left Master Johannes with four bearns, and one not yet weaned. Said she was tired of his comings and goings. Said she was for better things than bearing babies and looking after them. Slattern!' She spat out the word.

I rode on and was soon at the City wall.

There was only a trickle of humanity passing to and fro through Aldgate. A few people stood beneath the rusted prongs of the raised portcullis, finding some coolness in the shade, where a half-hearted breeze shifted through the archway. I tethered Golding to an iron ring in the wall and announced myself to the duty guard. He was seated at the toll table just inside the open door of the guardhouse. He appraised me with an expert eye.

'Good day, Master Treviot. We was expecting you.'

'Good. Then I can take my man off your hands?'

'Ah well, now, Sir.' He stood up – a tall fellow in a leather

11

jerkin who had the courteous demeanour of an official who knows that politeness is not a weakness when backed by authority. 'I'm afraid I have my orders. The prisoner is to stay here until the coroner arrives to question him.'

'And when will that be?'

'Constable Pett has gone to fetch him. They should be back soon.'

'Well, I hope they are. I can't wait all afternoon. May I see my man, now? I gather he's been injured.'

The guard gave a deferential nod. 'Certainly, Sir, if you'll step this way. You'll see he's taken quite a beating but I shouldn't worry yourself too much on his account. I've seen many a broken head in this job. His looks worse than it is.'

I was glad of the warning. The sight that met me when the inner door was unlocked and I stepped through into the narrow cell would otherwise have shaken me badly. A truckle bed stood against one wall. Bart was half-lying on the bed, his upper body propped up in the corner. A grimy rag was tied round his head and his face was streaked with dirt and dried blood. The right side of his face was badly swollen and the eye almost completely closed. He squinted at me and winced as he eased himself off the bed. 'Master Thomas! Thank God!'

'I came as fast as I could. What in the name of Mary and all the saints ...'

'I'm sorry, Master Thomas. I didn't want to trouble you but it honestly wasn't my fault.'

'So I gather. The girl you sent with the message told me something about it but I'd like to hear an account from your lips.'

Bart grimaced and sank back on to the bed, rubbing his hand gingerly over his ribs. 'Jesus, but that hurts! I came to the painter's house, like you said, and asked for Master

Johannes. There was only this young lad there and he said his master was away. Well, I was obviously not the only one looking for him. Three men came in and started . . . '

'Three men?'

'Well, actually there were four. One stood in the doorway as a lookout.'

'Can you describe them?'

Before Bart could reply there were noises in the outer guard room.

I turned to see the small space filling with people. Walt had arrived with the girl. As they stood in the outer doorway another man pushed past them and strode into the cell. He was a burly fellow in a greasy jerkin and red cap set at an angle atop untidy dark hair. He went straight to Bart, grabbed him by his open doublet and yanked him to his feet. Bart yelped with pain.

'Shut your snout, hedge pig! You've to come with me back to the scene of your crime. The crowner wants to hear what you've got to say. Can't think why. The truth's as plain to see as a strumpet's tits.'

I placed myself between the bully and the door. 'Just a moment,' I said, as calmly as I could. 'I take it you're the ward constable.'

'That I am.' He glared as though inviting contradiction. 'And you, I take it, are this rogue's master.'

I was in no mood to bear with the arrogance of this minor official. 'Is this how you behave to your betters?' I demanded.

'Only when they try to get between me and my duty to protect my neighbours!' He pushed past, dragging a shuffling Bart behind him.

It was only a few yards to Master Johannes' house. The three of us followed the constable. There were four or five people standing round the door. Doubtless there would have

13

been more if the street's throbbing heat had not smothered their curiosity and sent them in search of shade.

We went inside and found a room furnished with a table, benches and stools. The fireplace had been cleaned out. An open cupboard to one side held pots, pans and pewter plates – all tidily arranged. Everything suggested a well-ordered household. The scene that faced us when we went through into the inner room was very different. The first thing I was aware of was the noise, the buzzing of a myriad of flies. The second impression was of vivid colours. Reds, greens, yellows – they were everywhere – splashed on the walls, streaking the floor rushes, leaking from broken dishes. The artist's canvases had, similarly, been thrown about the room. A large easel lay facedown beside the window. The few items of furniture were overturned. Poor Johannes' studio had been wrecked, either deliberately or in the course of a very violent fight. In the middle of the room, sprawled on its back, was the body of a young man, lying in a pool of his own blood, on which the flies were hungrily feasting. Sudden anger welled up in me – anger and anxiety for my friend.

The only living occupant of the room was a small, spare man in a lawyer's black gown. He turned as we entered. 'Nothing to be gained here!' He held a pomander to his nose and motioned us back into the outer room.

We stood in a circle. No one seemed to want to speak. No one, that is, except Constable Pett. 'As requested, Your Honour, I've brought the culprit. And this' – he gave the slightest disdainful nod towards Adie – 'is the person as found the body. Or so she says.'

The coroner nodded and turned to me. 'This citizen I recognise. We have met before, I'm sure. Where was it, now – Gray's Inn revels, last Christmas?'

'Yes,' I said. 'I remember. My name is Thomas Treviot.'

'An honoured name in the City. I am James Corridge. What brings you to this sorry scene, Master Treviot?'

'My assistant, Bartholomew Miller, has been mistakenly detained by the constable. I'm come to explain his presence here. He was on a matter of business for me and became the unfortunate witness of this appalling crime. He was certainly not its perpetrator.'

'So he says!' The constable, who was keeping a tight hold of Bart, took a step forward, almost thrusting himself between the coroner and me.

''Tis God's truth!' Bart pleaded. 'I had no hand in that man's death.'

Pett gave a snort of laughter. 'You don't want to trust what this villain says, Your Worship. Why, you've only got to look at the man—'

'Thank you, Constable. I will decide who is best believed and who not.' Corridge wafted the pomander beneath his nose and edged away from the man, who reeked of sweat, stale ale and onions. 'What other witnesses do we have?'

'None,' the constable replied promptly. 'Very convenient for the murderer. He obviously knew when best to strike – when his victim would be alone.'

'Witnesses?' Bart's angry response was more a frightened whine than a shout. 'Oh, aye, there were witnesses – four of 'em. They were the bloody knaves who did this thing.'

'Well, that should be easy to determine, Constable. I take it you've made enquiry about these men. You've asked all the neighbours.'

'I'd as soon spend my time searching for hobgoblins. There were no four men, Your Worship. This is just a tale to confuse the issue. Here's your murderer!' He thrust Bart forward. 'Just give me an hour with him and I'll get him to confess the truth.'

'I have told the truth, Your Honour,' Bart shouted, his face creasing with pain at the effort. 'This fellow only wants to beat a confession out of me because he's too lazy to do his job properly.'

With a roar, Pett swung his right fist at Bart's face and caught him a glancing blow.

'That will do, Constable!' Corridge asserted himself, not before time. 'We will conduct this investigation in the proper manner. There will be a full inquest in seven days' time. And I will expect you to present there anyone who may have seen or heard anything that might be relevant. Until then, keep this man in custody – and make sure he has a physician to tend his wounds. If I hear that he has been ill-treated in your care . . . ' He left the sentence unfinished as Pett, muttering under his breath, pushed his prisoner towards the street door.

Corridge looked distinctly relieved. 'There's little more to be done here, Master Treviot,' he said. 'I must await the doctor to examine the body – though there can be no doubt how the poor fellow met his end.'

'Well, I can assure you that my man had nothing to do with it. By all the saints, Master Corridge, you've seen him. Could a one-armed man really have been responsible for the violent chaos of that room? The girl here will tell you she heard several men shouting and arguing.' I turned to Adie. 'Is that not so?'

The coroner allowed himself a wistful smile. 'Constable Pett is, perhaps, a mite over-zealous.'

I thought, That is not how I would describe him. I said, 'If you will release Bart into my care, I will answer for his appearance at the inquest. I give you my word—'

At that moment the street door burst open. Peter Pett stumbled in, his face red with fury.

'Gone, Your Honour! Fled!'

'What do you mean?' Corridge responded. 'Calm yourself. Explain . . . '

''Tis the prisoner. We were at the gate. I took my eyes off the knave for no more than a moment. He loosed Master Treviot's horse. Before I could grab him he was in the saddle and off down Fenchurch Street at the gallop. Did I not say he wasn't to be trusted?'

Chapter 2

We had scarcely begun our return journey when the threatened storm broke. Heavy rain cascaded upon us. The donkey cart was crowded. I could not leave Adie and the two small boys in the house of violence or entrust them to the 'protection' of Constable Pett so I had decided to take them back to Goldsmith's Row. Quite what arrangements I would make for them there I could not think. Deciding that would have to wait, I had a more pressing problem to solve. Walt whipped the donkey into a fast trot while the rest of us huddled together against the downpour. By the time I jumped down at the corner of Milk Street, I was soaked to the skin and ready to tell Bart exactly what I thought of his irresponsible behaviour. Any sympathy I felt was – temporarily, at least – obliterated by the humiliation his sudden departure had caused me. I ordered Walt to get the others back to my home as quickly as possible and show them where they could dry their clothes and await my arrival. I ran the few yards along Milk Street to the narrow house where Bart and Lizzie lived. It was a timber structure wedged in-between two substantial merchants' residences.

I hammered on the door and stood back to avoid the water gushing down from the eaves. There was no immediate answer. Though the rain had eased, I had no desire to be kept waiting in the street. I knocked again and began to wonder whether Bart had collected his family and taken them into hiding with him. Then the door opened and Lizzie stood there with little Annie, her two-year-old, in her arms.

'Jesu Mary! Thomas, you do look a sight! Come in the dry.'

There was an intimacy between Bart's wife and me that onlookers found strange. The adventures we had been through together six years before had removed any formalities that differences of social status would otherwise have demanded. Lizzie was handsome, rather than pretty. A stiffened band of white linen, bordered in scarlet, covered the crown of her head and her dark hair was drawn back and hung down to her shoulders. Her figure was still slim, despite her two pregnancies. She stood aside for me to pass, a faintly mocking smile about her lips, her brown eyes smiling but appraising.

'Get that wet doublet off,' she ordered. 'I'll put it by the fire.'

As soon as she set Annie down, the child toddled straight to me, arms upraised. I took hold of her hand, smiling despite myself. 'Not now, Annie. I'm all wet.'

When Lizzie returned from the inner room, she handed me a cloth to dry my head and face. Then she scooped up her daughter. 'Is she being a nuisance? You've only yourself to blame. You spoil her. Wait till you marry again and have little brothers and sisters for Raffy; you'll soon realise . . . '

'Still determined to find me a wife?'

She laughed. 'Oh, you don't deserve a wife but Raffy needs a mother.'

'Lizzie, enough of this nonsense. I must see Bart. It's serious.' I stood in the middle of the small living room, feeling slightly less bedraggled. 'Where is he?' I demanded.

'Who?'

'Bart, of course. Is he here?'

'Well, I suppose he might be.' She giggled. 'We'd better look. You search downstairs and I'll go through the upper chambers. Oh!' She put a hand to her mouth as though she had been struck by a sudden thought. 'Perhaps he's hiding in the coffer over there by the stairs.'

'This is no laughing matter, Lizzie,' I said sharply. 'I must find him urgently.'

She frowned, suddenly serious. 'Isn't he at the shop?'

'No, he's—'

'Then, where in the name of all the saints is he? If you don't know he must have had an accident.'

'Not exactly,' I said. 'I'm afraid he managed to get himself into a fight.'

'He's hurt!' she said quickly, sitting on a stool and setting Annie on the rushes beside her.

'Not badly.' I tried to sound reassuring. 'But I do need to speak with him.'

'I don't understand. If you know he's been in a fight, why don't you know where he is?'

I had long since learned that it was impossible to conceal anything from this clever young woman. I pulled another stool to the table and sat facing her. Then I gave her a brief account of the events at Aldgate, leaving out as many as possible of the more vivid details.

Many young wives would have gone into tearful panic at the news. Not Lizzie. She had grown up in a hard school in which survival meant relying on her wits and not letting practicality get stifled by sentiment. 'Well, if he's decided to disappear you'll not find him. He obviously thinks he's got to go huggering to escape the law.'

'But he's wrong!' I almost shouted. 'He can only make things worse for himself by running away.'

'Oh, Thomas, Thomas, are you still so innocent?' Lizzie looked at me with a grim smile. 'If this poxy constable has marked my Bart for the gallows he'll be hell-set on making him swing. I know his sort. There were many of that scelerous, lying breed always sniffing round the brothel when I was there. They passed themselves off as public servants, keeping the streets fit for respectable citizens, but they only wanted one thing – and they wanted it free.'

'But ...'

'There are no buts, Thomas. Suppose you found Bart and took him back to face the coroner's court, do you think any of the jurymen would turn down their local constable's version of events? Those who weren't scared of him would support him out of loyalty. No, Bart's done the right thing.'

'That's nonsense! He's committed no crime. Why should he become a penniless runagate, leaving you and the children ... and me ... Anyway, I think you're wrong about the law and its officers. There may have been a time when poor men could get no justice, but this is 1543. There are ways to establish an accused man's innocence. If not in the magistrate's court, then at King's Bench. If he found himself in want of a good barrister—'

'I know, I know,' Lizzie interrupted. 'You'd pay for any help he needed. No, Annie, not through there!' She jumped up to collect the little girl, who was pushing open the door to the inner room. She held the child's hand, led her back towards the table and gave her a wooden spoon and pewter plate to play with. The rest of our conversation was accompanied by a rhythmic, metallic banging.

'I know my Bart,' Lizzie continued. 'At this moment he'll be thinking about me and the children; trying to work out what to do next. When he can't work out an answer to that question he'll find some way to get a message to me.'

'When he does, be sure to tell me,' I insisted. I stood up. 'Now I must go and sort things out at home.'

The storm had passed over and as soon as my clothes were reasonably dry I made my way back to Goldsmith's Row.

It was not difficult to find a chamber to lodge Adie and the two young boys in her charge, especially as the household numbers had been reduced by the evacuation of several servants to Hemmings, my estate in Kent. I told the girl that she was welcome to stay as long as necessary and suggested that she would be wise to remain beneath my roof until we had located Holbein.

Finding the artist was now urgent – for Bart's sake and in the interests of my own business. During my absence that afternoon a message had been delivered, sealed with the impressive arms of the City. It was brief and to the point.

Master Treviot, this to advise you that I still await the initial designs for a parcel-gilt cup and cover which you undertook to supply in March of this year. As I explained, this is an exceedingly important commission. I intend to present the cup to his majesty to mark my tenure of office. You are aware that my successor will be appointed at Michaelmas and that, by then, the work must be in hand. If I have not the designs for my consideration within the next seven days I shall place the order elsewhere and think not to do further business with Treviots.

John Cotes,
Lord Mayor

Building a reputation is a long and arduous process. Losing it may be achieved in the space of a few days or even hours. Thanks to the industry and skill of my forebears, the Treviots have prospered. We make fine jewellery and tableware for an exclusive clientele. We buy precious items from customers in need of ready cash. We smelt gold and silver and either refashion it or sell it to the royal treasurer for minting into coin. An increasing part of our business in recent years has been lending against security to trusted clients. My father had a saying, 'Kings come and go but gold is always sovereign'. It was he who acquired the prestigious property at the sign of the Swan in Goldsmith's Row, West Cheapside, which accommodated both the workshop and spacious living accommodation. I took over the business – unprepared and unwilling – at the age of twenty-three. Unwilling, not because I disliked my trade, but because I only acquired it by my father's death. Then within months I lost my wife in child-birth. These calamities drove me to the pit. How I drew back and regained my wits is a long story. With the aid of friends and a loyal workforce I took control of myself and of Treviots. Once more the business was one of the most successful in the City. I could not, would not, risk damaging Treviots' good name.

I sent for Adie and questioned her further.

'We must find your master urgently,' I said. 'Do you know any of his friends who might have some idea where he has gone?'

She looked thoughtful. 'There was always foreigners coming to the house.'

'Foreigners?'

'Yes, Sir, you know ... men that spoke Master Johannes' language ... from the German House.'

'German House? Do you mean the Steelyard?'

'That's right, Sir.' Her face brightened. 'The Steelyard, down by Cosin Lane.'

'Thank you, Adie. That's very helpful.' I realised I should have thought of it myself. It was only natural that Master Johannes would have friends among his own compatriots in the German merchant community. The Steelyard was their staple, their centre of operations. There they stored their goods for import and export and had their offices. 'Is there anyone special he knows there?' I asked.

Again the girl's face donned a frown of concentration. 'There is one who comes more often ... a merry little man, full of jokes. He likes to play with the children. He always brings them sweetmeats and toys.'

'His name?' I prompted.

'Well, 'tis the same as the master's – Johannes.'

'Just Johannes? 'Tis a common enough name among the Germans. You know no more about him?'

She shrugged. ''Tis hard to understand all they say. They speak funny, don't they? Master did talk about him sometimes. Now what was it he called him ... Johannes ... Fonant ... something like that? Sorry, that's not much help, is it?'

'Well, 'tis a start,' I said. 'I'll go down to the German wharf tomorrow and see if I can find out any more. There must be several men there who know your master.'

'Do you think anything's happened to him, Master Treviot? I can't stop thinking about poor George. Those men were looking for Master Johannes. If they find him . . . '

'You must not think the worst, Adie. Whoever these murderous rakehells are, they haven't found your master. We must pray they don't.'

'Do you think he knows about them?' Her dark eyes searched mine, seeking reassurance. 'Perhaps that's why he went away – hiding. Oh, Jesus Mary, what am I to tell the boys?'

'That their father is away on business – which is probably the truth,' I said firmly. 'What you must not do is think the worst. They would soon sense that something was wrong. You go on looking after them as usual and leave me to discover what I can about their father.'

It was mid-morning of the following day that I rode along Thames Street past the imposing walls bounding the premises of the Hanseatic League's headquarters. 'Heretics', 'Lutheran pigs' – these and other daubed slogans spattered the stonework. Much as the City authorities tried to stop Catholic sloganeers defacing this building, the protests continued, encouraged by the more conservative clergy. The massive wooden gate stood half-open, permitting pedestrians and horsemen to enter in order to state their business at the porters' lodge. I went through and dismounted. There were a dozen or so visitors waiting for admission and I soon realised that we were being divided into three categories: those who were known to the official on duty or who could produce suitable credentials were waved through an inner barrier; those who did not survive scrutiny were turned away; the remainder were asked to wait while enquiries were made about them. When my turn arrived I gave my name and explained that I was looking for Herr Johannes Holbein.

The guard – a man whose sombre habit was strangely in contrast to an enormously exuberant beard – was a person of few words. '*Ja*, we know him. He is not here.'

Perhaps there might be some friend of Master Johannes with whom I might speak?

He did not think so.

Would it be possible for some enquiry to be made – it was important that I should locate Master Johannes urgently.

The guardian of the gate looked at the queue forming behind me. He shook his head. I must be good enough to leave. If I wished I might come back another day.

I raised my voice to protest. The guard remained unimpressed and the people behind became restless. Someone called out to me to move on and there was a murmur of support. I was about to turn when another man appeared from the gatehouse. He was obviously superior to the official who stood in my way, with whom he entered on a brief conversation in his own language. He turned his attention to me.

'You are looking for Herr Holbein?'

'Yes.'

'May I enquire why?'

'Certainly. I believe his life is in danger.'

'You have good reasons for this suspicion?'

'His assistant was murdered yesterday by men looking for his master.'

He frowned. 'You are sure of this?'

'Very. I saw the poor young man's body. He was beaten and stabbed.'

We had now become the centre of a circle of curious onlookers – not a state of affairs welcomed by the Hanse official, whose demeanour changed dramatically.

'Well, Sir, Master Holbein is not of our company but he is well known to us and much respected. We would certainly not want any evil to befall him. Perhaps you would care to tether your horse over there and wait in the wine house opposite. I'll see if I can find someone who might be able to help you.'

I did as he suggested and entered a large room furnished with several rows of tables and benches. At this hour there were few customers and I soon had a corner and a jug of Rhenish all to myself. I looked around at the early drinkers. There was never any mistaking these wealthy merchants from North Europe, with their wide hats or bonnets with turned-up brims, their short fur-lined capes and their bushy beards. Here in the Steelyard, where they had long been welcomed to live by a government that needed the trade they brought, they had created their own little Germany. This mercantile citadel, protected by high walls and vigilant officials, was, of course, regarded with mixed feelings by the good burghers of London: some loved to hate the Baltic merchants; others hated to love them. Some made no secret of their opposition and justified it on religious grounds. These Germans were all tarred with the Lutheran brush and the conservative clergy feared – not without reason – that the Steelyard was a breeding ground for English heresy. They made no secret of their desire to see the mercantile ghetto closed down and the Hanse trading privileges revoked, but here the Germans had been for longer than anyone could remember and here they would undoubtedly stay.

It was after I had been waiting about half an hour that a

rotund little man with a ruddy, clean-shaven face entered by a corner door and made his way to my table.

'Master Treviot? Good day. My name is Andreas Meyer, pastor to the community here. It is a privilege to meet someone whose name is held in such esteem among those of the true faith.'

'I did not think I was so . . .'

'Oh, but you are. That terrible business of Master Packington.' Meyer spoke in excited short bursts that came in rapid succession. 'He had many friends here. Many friends. Merchants involved in spreading the truth in those evil days when Bibles had to be smuggled into England. Evil days. And you tracked down Master Packington's killer.'

'Well, I . . .'

'No need for modesty. You were tenacious in your quest. Tenacious. And were hounded for it by the Catholic curs. We of the Steelyard would have helped but 'tis difficult for us. Politics. You understand.'

'It was a long time ago,' I muttered.

'An important time. Lord Cromwell's time. Without him there would be no official English Bible. We would still be smuggling them in our bales of cloth and barrels of wine. He was truly a Christian martyr. Done to death by the enemies of the Gospel. A great loss. A great loss.' He paused for breath – but only briefly. 'Now how can we help you? Our guard captain said you were enquiring about Johannes Holbein.'

'That's correct. I understand . . .'

'Holbein! Why do you seek him here?'

'I understand he has friends here who might know his whereabouts.'

Meyer eyed me cautiously. 'He visits us from time to time.'

'Please,' I said, with all the urgency I could muster, 'if you know anything of his whereabouts tell me. I must speak with him urgently.'

'In that case, Master Treviot, you had best call at his house in Aldgate.'

'Have you heard nothing about the murder at Holbein's house? The news is all over town by now.'

Meyer looked startled. 'Murder? No. Our walls are stout. It takes London gossip a long time to penetrate. What happened?'

'Violent men looking for our friend killed his assistant. Now you can see why I must find Holbein.'

Meyer shrugged. 'I really wish I could help you, but . . .'

I tried another approach. 'Can you remember when you last saw Master Johannes?'

Meyer pondered the question. 'It must be two or three weeks since. Strange that, now I come to think of it. The Steelyard is his second home. He's usually here several times a week.'

'Tell me, Master Meyer, if he wanted – for any reason – to hide . . .'

'Would we help him? Certainly. He would be safe from prying eyes here. We could even get him on to a ship and out of the country.'

'And you're sure this hasn't already happened?'

He stood abruptly. 'Come, let me show you something.'

We left the wine house by the door through which Meyer had entered, crossed a narrow alley and entered what was obviously the merchants' guildhall, a lofty building whose panelled walls reached upwards to an elaborate arrangement of rafters. Light entered through large windows opposite the entrance but much of the remaining wall space was occupied with portraits of Hanseatic merchants past and present.

'You want to see how close we of the Hanse are to Master Holbein?' Meyer waved a hand to right and left.

Two long frescoes faced each other. Each represented a procession of numerous figures in vivid, glowing colours. Men, women, horses, wagons and chariots paraded from right to left. The paintings were amazingly detailed and lifelike.

'Magnificent,' I exclaimed.

'Indeed, indeed.' Meyer, anxious to show off the treasures of his community, waxed eloquent. 'On the right you see an allegory of riches. On the left, poverty. They remind us of the vanity of earthly wealth. It illustrates the motto you can see over the doorway behind us.'

I turned and gazed up at a long Latin inscription.

Meyer, obviously very familiar with the role of guide, translated. '"He who is rich fears the inconstant turning of Fate's wheel. He who is poor fears nothing, but lives in joyful hope."'

'A noble sentiment,' I muttered – and wondered how much 'joyful hope' was felt by the beggars squatting in alleyways outside the walls close to where we stood.

Meyer was now in full flood, pointing out details in the paintings – the industry and honest toil of the smiling, contented workers, contrasted with the frenetic pursuit of gain pictured on the opposite wall. Most of his eulogy passed me by; I was captivated with the exuberance and sheer scale of the two cavalcades. It was difficult to believe that this was the work of the same man who produced for my workshop intricate designs for table salts, chains of office, medallions and other items of jewellery. 'Truly a genius,' I observed, rather tamely.

'Indeed! Indeed! We're very proud of Master Holbein's work. He has also made portraits of some of our recent masters.' My guide led the way along the hall, pointing out the depictions of solemn-looking merchants holding the tools of their trade – scales, money boxes, bills and seals.

'So,' Meyer said, as we completed the tour, 'you can see we are much indebted to Herr Holbein. If ever he was in trouble he could come to us. We would not fail him.'

'But he has not recently come to you for succour?'

The little pastor shook his head.

'And yet,' I ventured, 'if he had you would probably not tell me.'

For once Meyer had no words. He simply smiled.

We returned to the wine house. By the outer door the pastor extended his hand. 'I fear I have been of little help. I most sincerely hope that your anxieties are groundless. God grant you success in your quest.'

'Thank you. If you see Master Holbein perhaps you would be kind enough to let him know I am looking for him.'

I stepped out into the passageway as Meyer held the door for me. Then, turning, I said, 'One more question if I may. I understand Master Holbein has a particular German friend called Johannes Fonant ... or something like that. Am I right?'

Meyer's rubicund face creased in a frown. 'Fonant? No, it is not a German name.'

I thanked him again and stepped across to where my horse was tethered. I mounted my bay mare and turned her head towards the gate. I was just passing under the arch into Thames Street when I heard my name called. Meyer came bustling up to me.

'Could the man you mention possibly be Johannes von Antwerp? He is not German but he is often here. And he is a friend of Herr Holbein. You may know him.'

Johannes von Antwerp. John of Antwerp as he was known

to members of the Goldsmiths' Company. Did I know him? Oh, yes and heartily wished I did not. As I threaded my way along the busy street I pictured the burly Flemish scoundrel. If he was, indeed, the friend whose name Adie had imperfectly remembered, I could expect little help from him.

I was reflecting gloomily on my wasted morning as I turned into the yard of my house in Goldsmith's Row. The first thing that I lighted upon was my missing horse.

Chapter 3

Golding stood contentedly in a corner of the yard having his mane brushed by Walt. I dropped from my saddle and hurried across.

'When did he come back?' I demanded. 'Is Bart here?'

The groom shook his head. 'Lizzie brought the horse, Master. She's inside.'

Bart's wife was in the kitchen, talking with Jane, my cook, who was plying Annie with tid-bits from the larder. Her baby son, Jack, well swaddled, lay on the wide kitchen table, close to where Lizzie sat. She stood as I strode in.

'Come to the parlour,' I said brusquely, crossing to the inner door. 'The children will be happy here for a few minutes.'

As soon as the door was closed behind us, I turned. 'What is he up to?' I demanded.

'This will tell you.' Lizzie handed me a folded sheet of paper.

I sat to read it and motioned Lizzie to a chair across the table. The note was carefully composed and written in Bart's surprisingly neat hand.

My duty to Your Worship remembered, I heartily thank you for speaking for me to the magistrate. Marvel not, I pray you, good Master, that I chose sudden flight above your protection. I dared not trust Constable Pett. The man is known for a double-tongued ruffian, as runs with the hare as well as the hounds. He will not seek out the murderous villains who killed Master Johannes' man. I am the only one as can do that. I have seen them. By Mary and all the saints, I mean to find them. When I do I will come back. Until then I beg that you will not try to find me.

Your Worship's assured servant,
Bart Miller

I threw the note down on the table and leaned back in my chair. 'Jesu! Where was that husband of yours when the good Lord handed out brains?'

Lizzie pouted. 'What else can he do? We've discussed the matter hours without end. This is the only way he can stay safe.'

'The way *he* can stay safe? And what of you and the children? Do you think the villains will not come a-visiting when they learn that Bart is on their trail?'

She tossed her head in defiance, sudden colour in her cheeks. 'We can shift for ourselves.'

'That you cannot!' I thumped the table. 'Mother of God,

I thought you had enough wit for both of you. Now I see you're as addle-pated as Bart.'

'A woman must stand by her husband,' she said stubbornly.

'Even at the cost of her infants' lives? Think for a moment, Lizzie. These men Bart has got tangled with are vicious murderers. Probably well-paid experts sent to take or kill Master Johannes. God in heaven knows what that poor artist has done to warrant it but, sure as hellfire's for sinners, someone means him harm and will do anything to lay hands on him. When word's out that Bart is at liberty and going about asking questions, where will be the first place they come?'

Lizzie was sullenly silent for several moments. From beyond the casement there came the sound of Paul's clock striking ten.

'I'm trying to find Master Johannes,' I said. 'That must be the best way to identify his enemies. But 'twill take me some time. Meanwhile we must make sure that you and the children are safe.'

She glanced up, scowling. 'And why should you take that on yourself?'

'I'm sorry you ask that question. I'll pretend I didn't hear it.' I stood abruptly. 'Wait here. There's someone I want you to meet.'

I hurried from the room. When I returned minutes later, Lizzie was standing at the window, looking out into West Cheap. 'The pestilence is getting worse,' she said. 'Two houses in our street are shut up now, by order of the council.'

'All the more reason not to stay. Come to Kent with us.'

She shook her head firmly. 'I must be where Bart can find me when he needs me.'

'But there's no need for Annie and Jack to be exposed.'

She turned suddenly, anger and frustration in her voice. 'Thomas, do you suppose I haven't thought of that? What am I to do?'

There was a soft knock at the door. I opened it and ushered in Adie, accompanied by her two young charges. They were remarkably different. Carl, who I supposed to be about seven, was dark-haired, already tall and constantly looking around him with enquiring eyes. Henry, younger by some two years, was squat, with reddish hair and seemed less self-assured. He was clinging tightly to his nurse's apron.

'Thank you for coming down, Adie. I want you to meet someone.' I made the introductions. 'And now I'm going to leave you to get to know each other.' I went out into the yard to check that Golding was no worse for his little adventure. I hoped that, in my absence, what in women passes for reason might prevail.

When I returned some half an hour later, I saw that Lizzie's children had joined the party. Even my own eight-year-old, Raphael (known to everyone as 'Raffy'), had come to cast an appraising eye over our visitors. The boys seemed to be play-ing some form of hide-and-go-seek with Annie, and Adie was cradling the baby. 'They're enjoying themselves,' I said, pointing to the older children. I hoped they were forming a bridge between the women.

Lizzie treated me to a wry smile. 'Not as much as you enjoy organising other people's lives.' She turned to Adie. 'You'll find he's very good at that.'

'I simply think it makes sense for you all to come to Hemmings till the plague has passed and this other business is sorted out.'

Lizzie turned back to the window. 'I can't be that far away from Bart. I must be where he can find me easily.'

'Very well, but at least let the children come. Adie is bringing the boys down. She has the sense to realise that they can't go back to Aldgate until Master Johannes returns. She'd be happy to take care of your bearns, too. Isn't that so, Adie?'

The girl gave a shy smile by way of acknowledgement.

Lizzie made no further argument. It was arranged that I would set off into Kent three days later with my augmented household. While the servants completed the work of closing up the house and workshop and loading on to wagons the furniture and other goods which had to be taken into the country, I tidied up my business affairs.

I also had a visit to make.

I rode out next morning, Friday 4 September, through Ludgate and over the Fleet Bridge. Turning left into narrow Bride Lane, I had only a few yards to go before dismounting in the shadow of the high walls bordering the precinct of old Bridewell Palace. A row of quite substantial houses clustered by the boundary, as though enjoying royal protection. Three of them belonged to alien goldsmiths, a little nest of foreigners who could stare out from their casements at the City wall, mere yards away, and disregard the Guild rules binding honest London craftsmen. They could take on and train their own apprentices (usually of their own ilk), attract their own customers and charge their own prices. Theoretically the Worshipful Company exercised control over the quality of the interlopers' merchandise. All gold items had to pass through our assay office, which authenticated the purity of the precious metal. But many of the foreigners (and there were more than a hundred of them working in and around London) ignored the regulations. In practice, we were powerless to prevent them stealing our markets. We were obliged to compete

37

with them for quality – and some of them were hellishly good. This was bad enough but at least the distinction between us and them was clear. There were, however, a few who deliberately blurred that distinction; who had cunningly worked themselves into a position of being able to enjoy the advantages of life on both sides of the wall. One such was John of Antwerp.

He had run this workshop on Bride Street longer than anyone could remember. He was a fine craftsman – of that there was no doubt. He attracted custom from the highest in the land and he had prospered – really prospered. He married an Englishwoman. He reared a family. But he remained staunchly a Netherlander. He had another home in Antwerp and spent months there every year. That, of course, was his privilege. But a few years ago he had sought to be made a freeman of the Goldsmiths' Company. That led to fierce arguments among the members. It split us into rival factions. But John of Antwerp had friends. Rich friends. Powerful friends. He secured his election. Well, he might have won the right to sit at our board, to worship in our chapel (despite his Lutheran opinions), to vote at our assemblies, but few of us could accept him as one of us. His presence in our midst remained an irritant.

A notice was pinned to the door of the largest of the three houses. It informed callers that Master Jan van der Goes (he did not even accept the Englishing of his name) had closed his workshop until the plague abated but that prospective clients could find him most mornings between ten and noon at the sign of the Red Hand in Fleet Street. I turned Golding's head and a few minutes later tethered him outside the prestigious inn frequented by barristers of the inns of court, visitors with business at Whitehall Palace and gentlemen attendant on the great men whose nearby fine houses on The Strand overlooked the river.

There were not many people in the fashionable inn. August and September were always quiet in this locality. The royal household was on progress and the law courts were not in session until Michaelmas. Students and teachers at the law schools usually took the opportunity to go into the country between terms. Even so, it was unusual to see most of the tables in the Red Hand's large hall empty. However, even had the room been all a-bustle and crowded with customers, it would have been easy to locate John of Antwerp. His booming voice could always be heard at a distance and he was seldom to be seen without a throng of sycophantic admirers. Today his attendants had been reduced to three in number. They sat at a table by an open casement, taking advantage of the slight breeze that whiffled through the room.

'Brother Treviot,' the Fleming bellowed as I approached. 'This is an unexpected pleasure. Simon, fetch a flagon for our distinguished guest.' This instruction was given to an apprentice who immediately rose and hurried about his errand. John was a heavily built man in his fifties who affected the manners and dress of someone twenty years his junior. Today he sported a yellow doublet and a shirt open at the neck. His cap was pushed back on his bush of brown hair and his thick beard completely encircled his ruddy features. He waved me to a seat on the bench opposite and introduced his companions. They were Reynold, a slim young man in royal livery, and Sir Tobias Harriday, a priest from Worcester.

'Reynold is a messenger come hot-paced from court,' John explained. 'And Sir Tobias is here to order a new set of altar plate.'

'For our Prince Arthur chantry chapel,' the fresh-featured cleric added.

'Chantry chapel, Brother John?' I said, unable to resist the taunt, 'I thought you did not approve of prayers for the dead and what you call "popish superstition".'

The Fleming was unfazed. 'His majesty wishes to honour his late brother's memory with a magnificent gift of gold plate for the tomb chapel. I'm honoured to help this pious and charitable act. But tell me, Brother, what brings you to the Red Hand? I thought you had left the City.'

'I'm only here briefly. I have to collect some designs from Master Holbein.'

'Will that be for the Cotes Cup?'

I nodded and just managed a smile. The foreigner seemed damnably well informed about my affairs.

'Johannes told me he was working on it,' he explained.

'Do you happen to know his whereabouts at the moment?' I asked. 'He seems to be from home.'

Simon returned and set a full tankard before me. I raised it to my lips, watching John over the brim.

He took his time over the reply, obviously thinking carefully what to say. 'I heard there was some trouble at his house recently.' His tone was nonchalant.

'Yes, Wednesday. Some ruffians broke in and killed his assistant.'

'What? Young George? How terrible.' His pretence of shock and surprise was not convincing. He obviously knew more than he wanted to admit. I began to think I was wasting my time with the fellow.

'Indeed. It was fortunate Master Johannes was not there. You have no idea where I might find him now?'

'When I saw him last, a few days ago, he was on his way to

court. He was talking about some commission he had for the new queen. I suppose he is still there.'

'Perhaps Master Reynold, here, may have seen him.' I turned to the messenger. 'Where is his majesty keeping court now? Do you know if our artist friend is there?'

The young man was glad to air his knowledge. 'The court's at Ampthill Castle, near Bedford. It's small for the whole court but his majesty vows he'll not come a mile nearer London as long as the plague lasts.'

'Ampthill – was that not where Queen Catherine was kept?' the priest asked.

'Aye, that she was,' Reynold replied.

'God keep her!' Harriday crossed himself. 'The kingdom has gone from bad to—'

'So,' I interrupted impatiently. 'Is Master Holbein there?'

'Was,' the messenger replied. 'Her majesty commanded him there to paint likenesses of the king's children. The princesses are travelling with the court but Prince Edward lives nearby at Ashridge.'

'So, the artist is no longer there?' I prompted.

'I think he left at the beginning of the week.'

'To come back to London?'

Reynold shrugged. 'I suppose.'

I looked at the Fleming. 'And he has not been in touch with you since then?'

John shook his head.

'Then it seems he never reached the City.'

'Perhaps he was headed somewhere else,' John suggested. 'Another customer. Another commission.'

'And you've no idea where I might seek him?'

'Johannes is a quite solitary man – secretive even. I do not

41

think he confides his movements to other people. Certainly not to me.'

'A pity,' I said. 'I have important news for him about his children. They are safe and in my care. Should you ever stumble across Master Holbein,' I said sarcastically, 'perhaps you would be kind enough to let him know where to find his family.'

Soon afterwards I bade the company farewell. As I rode back to West Cheap I reflected grimly on my wasted morning. Yet, perhaps not totally wasted. Was it just because I disliked the man that I felt convinced John of Antwerp was determined to stop me making contact with his friend?

Over the next couple of days the work of closing up the house continued. I sent Adie and the children on ahead in my coach with the loaded wagons and most of the remaining staff. Because the roads were in such a sorry state due to the heavy rain, it was obvious that the journey would take them at least a couple of days. My plan was to leave twenty-four hours later with three mounted and armed servants and arrive at about the same time. Before I could go I had to reply to the Lord Mayor's letter. All I could say was that I had failed to contact Holbein and, thus, must regretfully decline the commission. It was the bare truth. It made both me and my friend appear incompetent but I could not add to it. That would only have encouraged speculation about Holbein's disappearance and set tongues wagging around the City. For the hundredth time I racked my brains to think what could have happened to him. I had been farming out design work to him for some three years and had never had cause for complaint. He always produced his drawings promptly and they were always of the highest quality. Holbein had a knack of divining exactly what the customer wanted and his invention was breathtaking in its originality. He also understood the techniques of metalworking and gem-setting, which meant that he never posed problems impossible for my craftsmen to solve. I remember him telling me once that he had actually practised as a goldsmith in Basel, where he lived before coming to England. Holbein was more than a good craftsman; he was a pleasant man to deal with – inclined to be solemn, even morose, but always agreeable company. If he was in trouble, I would like to be in a position to help him. The fact that his friends were keeping his whereabouts secret from me could only mean that he was in grave danger.

My concern was, if anything, heightened by what happened on Monday morning. After breakfasting simply and early, I assembled my little group of riders in the yard, ready for our departure. We were about to mount when a ragged, bootless boy ran in from the street. He came up and touched his cap. 'You Master Treviot, the goldsmith?'

'I am.'

He thrust a small package at me. 'The man said you'd give me a penny.'

'What man?'

'Man what gave it me.' He smirked at his own cleverness.

I took the flat parcel and fished a coin out of my purse. 'Stay here while I see if there's a reply,' I said.

But the boy shook his head. 'He said I wasn't to wait.' Pausing only to scrutinise the penny, he turned and darted out of the yard.

The offering seemed to be wrapped in several layers of thick paper. Scrawled across the front was my name and the legend, 'Haste. Haste.' I took it into the kitchen and unfastened it on the table. With a gasp I instantly recognised

Master Johannes' impeccable draughtsmanship. On five crisp sheets were the cup and cover designs I had been waiting for. The artist had supplied two complete drawings and some detailed studies of the more intricate elements. The two designs were almost identical but the variations offered the client a choice. I was sure that either would delight the Lord Mayor. The cup was magnificent. A stem of two female figures supported a bowl chased with twined foliage and above it the motto FIDES ET INTEGRITAS ('Loyalty and Trustworthiness'). The fifth sheet had obviously been included by mistake. Although it was also a design for a cup and cover, it was simply carved with a coat of arms and was nothing like the object ordered by Sir John Cotes. I stuffed it into my purse, folded the others carefully and placed them into Golding's saddle bag. He was all ready for our departure but that departure would now have to be delayed. I sprang into the saddle, told the others to await my return and set off briskly for the Lord Mayor's house on Walbrook.

Fortunately, Sir John was at home. He was not altogether pleased to see me but he was relieved to discover that his gift to the king would, after all, be the creation of the royal painter. This and his approval of Holbein's drawings was sufficient for him to forgive the inconvenience he had been caused. We spent some time discussing the finer points of the design and it was mid-morning before I was able to return to Goldsmith's Row and set out for Hemmings.

At last there was nothing to keep me in London. I had been able to satisfy my customer. I also knew that Master Johannes was safe – or, at least, alive. What was disturbing was that he was still in hiding. If I could not find him I would have no means of helping Bart in his quest for the murderers and his innocence. There was one other source of information I could try. One other person whose contacts among the lower levels of society were extensive and who just might have heard something. As my little group made its way along Cheapside, Lombard Street and so, down Fish Street Hill, to the bridge, I decided to risk another delay. I would stop in Southwark and seek out my old friend, Ned Longbourne.

Chapter 4

Calling on Ned did not take us much out of our way. He lived in the shadow of the great abbey church of St Mary Overie where he plied the trade of an apothecary. Ned's grizzled pate covered a storehouse of wisdom – wisdom born of varied experience and much suffering. He had spent most of his life as a monk. Then, King Henry closed the monasteries and, like his brethren, he had been forced to earn a living in the world of ordinary mortals. He had fetched up in another, rather unlikely, 'convent', the bawdy house at the old St Swithun's inn in Southwark. Here he had ministered to the medical needs of the whores, pimps, lorrels and ribalds who congregated within its walls. But two years previously he had been rendered homeless again. In one of the government's occasional purges St Swithun's had been closed down. Of course, this did not stop harlotry; it simply dispersed the brothel's inmates. Ned had had to find his own lodgings. But that was not his only misfortune. He had a 'companion'; a well-favoured, athletic young man called Jed. Just at the time that Ned needed his support, Jed had formed another attachment and left. It was quite shocking to see how much this desertion aged my friend. Fortunately, his skills and his amiable disposition had won him the affection of many Southwark dwellers and he had little difficulty in finding new accommodation. Now he occupied his time ministering to the needs of the local community among whom he enjoyed a considerable reputation. I was in no doubt that he could have amassed a considerable fortune – or, at least, managed to live very comfortably – through the sale of potions and simples and the performance of minor surgical operations. Heaven knows there are mountebanks a-plenty who gull huge fees out of people with evil-smelling hell broths, incantations and pretended knowledge of astral motions. By contrast, I suspected that Ned all too often provided his services free of charge to those who were too poor to pay (or who feigned poverty).

He welcomed me with his usual effusiveness and I stooped to enter the room that served as living space, shop and work area. He led the way through to the small garden which was his particular delight. Here, sheltered on one side by the wall of the old abbey and on the other by neighbouring houses, Ned cultivated the herbs, flowers and plants from which he concocted his nostrums. He settled me on a bench and brought out two horn beakers containing an amber liquid.

''Tis a tincture of honey, rose buds and *aqua vitae*,' he explained. 'Most of my customers prefer it to hippocras and it is excellent good for expelling the damp humours.'

I sipped it appreciatively. 'Ned,' I said, 'I must not tarry long. I'm on my way to Hemmings. I wanted to have a word with you about—'

'About our unfortunate friend Bart Miller?'

I could not suppress a chuckle. 'They say, "bad news rides a fast horse", but I had not thought you would have heard so soon.'

'An evil business. Poor young man.' Ned stroked his long grey beard.

'You know that he's gone into hiding; become an outlaw; a suspected murderer on the run?'

Ned nodded.

'He seems to think he can only clear his name by discovering the real criminals.'

'That could prove more arduous than the Grail quest. The kingdom is over full of desperate men. Without taxing my old brain too hard, I could name you half a dozen boot-baler gangs who have sold their immortal souls for a handful of transient silver.'

'You think we are looking for hired hacksters, rather than the regular retainers of some great man?'

Ned looked up sharply. 'You said "we", Thomas. I hope that does not mean you intend to plunge yourself into the cesspit of villainy again. Did you not see enough of that world back in thirty-six?'

'A just rebuke, old friend. No, I was young and headstrong then – as you told me often enough. Now, even if I had the time, there would be little I could do to extricate Bart from his predicament, but ...'

'I feared there would be a "but".'

'Well ...' I hesitated, watching the bees hovering round the hive at the end of the garden. 'You know Lizzie ... Who'd have thought seven years ago that she and Bart could have made a good life for themselves.'

Ned nodded. 'Indeed. I still thank God for them in my prayers.'

'And now they have the two bearns ... To see all that thrown away just because Bart found himself in the wrong place at the wrong time ...'

'But you must not blame yourself for that, Thomas.' Ned fixed me with that earnest gaze I always found disconcerting.

'Oh, I don't. Of course not.'

'Are you sure?'

'Well ... I could have thought more before sending Bart to Aldgate. It was so out of character for Holbein to keep me waiting for his drawings. I might have guessed that something was wrong. I should have gone myself. What happened was ...'

I briefly explained the sequence of events.

Ned listened attentively, nodding occasionally. At last he said, 'Back in the monastery one of the biggest problems we faced was false sins. Some of the brothers were so intent on pursuing holiness that they invented sins to confess. They punished themselves for things God had no intention of punishing them for.'

'And you think I'm doing the same?'

'You could not possibly have foreseen what would befall Bart in Aldgate.'

'So you're suggesting I should shrug my shoulders, say, "It's not my fault", and leave him to his fate?'

Ned sighed deeply. 'No, we must, of course, do all we can.'

'We?' I smiled.

'Is that not why you have come – to enlist my help?'

'You did say you knew at least half a dozen gangs of ruffians who might have committed this crime.'

He nodded wearily. 'I will make some enquiries – very, very discreetly. It is not wise to appear too inquisitive.'

The Kent Road was inches deep in mud and very busy. Twice we were obliged to stop and help other travellers ease their mired vehicles on to firmer ground. We made slow progress and had to stay the night in one of the better inns. I hoped that the rest of my household had not fared so badly, and was relieved to find everyone safely installed at Hemmings when we arrived late the following morning.

There was, as always, much to be done in and around the estate – steward's accounts to be checked, tenants' complaints to be heard, building repairs to be assessed and, where necessary, set in hand. I never forgot about Bart and Lizzie's plight. Every day I hoped that I might hear some positive news: that Master Johannes had come out of hiding to save my friends; that Ned had identified the real assassins; that someone from the alien community might offer a clue about the artist's enemies. I even allowed myself to imagine that John of Antwerp might experience a twinge of conscience and break his oath of secrecy to a friend in the interests of wider justice. But these thoughts were pushed to the back of my mind by my many responsibilities as a landowner.

And by my concern for the children. As I watched Carl, Henry and Annie explore their new surroundings, I was amazed by their remarkable resilience. Adie was extremely good with the tiny ones. By the time I arrived she had already found a wet nurse for little Jack and she knew many games and stratagems to keep his older sister occupied. After a couple of days, little Annie stopped crying for her mother. The boys were enjoying exploring the woods and parkland. Cheerfully accepting Raffy's leadership, they were always off on some new adventure. It was something of a revelation to watch my son at play with other children. As an only child he was accustomed to entertaining himself – and to having his own way. He was spoiled by the servants and, as I realised if I was honest, also by me. Now, in play with Carl and Henry, he expected to be deferred to. I must be firmer with him, I told myself – a decision confirmed by an event that occurred one Saturday morning. On the first Friday of our stay several of us went to the fair in Ightham. Raffy had been boasting to the Holbein brothers of his prowess as an archer and when they saw a bowyer's stall with several weapons suitable for various ages they clamoured for their own bows. The next morning the boys dragged me – not unwillingly – to Long Meadow, where I and others of the household practised archery. Our visitors had not drawn a bow before and I spent some time showing them how to handle their new weapons. I was somewhat rusty myself and glad of the practice. We chose a row of tree stumps as targets and I gave a brief demonstration. Fortunately, I managed to quit myself reasonably well. Then we moved forward to shorten the range. Raffy was determined to show his prowess. With five arrows he managed to hit two of the stumps. Carl was the next to try. I had noticed that he was not only tall but broad of shoulder. It was not a surprise that he quitted himself very well. His first shaft overshot but he intelligently adjusted his aim and three of his remaining four arrows struck home. Raffy was not pleased. 'You've got a better bow,' he shouted, and made a grab for it. Carl put out a hand to fend him off and, quite unintentionally, struck Raffy on the nose. That was the end of our practice. Instantly the two boys were rolling on the ground, pummelling each other. With some difficulty, I separated them and was on the point of delivering a couple of blows of my own when I heard my name called. I turned and saw two men in helmets, breast-plates and blue livery striding across the meadow.

'Master Treviot, we're here to deliver a warrant from his grace of Canterbury,' one of them said, holding out a sealed letter.

I read the message. It was very brief. The archbishop required my presence in his palace at Ford.

I was stunned. I sat on a tree stump and read the secretary's neat lines two or three times. What could Cranmer possibly want with me? All I could think of immediately was to try to gain time to give the summons further thought.

'Thank you,' I said. 'Please present my respects to his grace and tell him I will be delighted to call upon him tomorrow.'

The retainer shook his head. 'We are instructed to take you with us now.'

'Now?' I protested. 'What is the urgency? Is this an arrest? I've done nothing to displease his grace.'

The man was impassive. 'He doesn't explain his actions to us. He just gives us orders and our orders are to return with you immediately.'

I was about to argue but then I looked at the boys. They were standing in a line, eyes wide with fear. Raffy broke ranks and ran across to put his arms round me. He glared at the soldiers. 'Go away,' he shouted. 'My father's a good man.'

I hugged him briefly. 'It's all right, Raffy,' I said as calmly as I could. 'Just some goldsmith's matters I have to discuss with the archbishop. I won't be gone long. Take your friends indoors and tell Will that I've been called away on urgent business.'

Within half an hour I was mounted and on the road to the archbishop's summer residence, flanked by two of his guard. Our fifty-mile journey was fast and uncomfortable. My escort rode their horses hard, spattering through puddles, scattering other travellers who were in our way, drawing shouts of protest from villagers as we raced through their streets, careless of the inhabitants, their children and their animals. I had little chance to question the guards about my arrest but it was clear that they either knew nothing or would say nothing. At least the speed of our progress allowed me little time to worry about my predicament; I was too busy keeping up with the guards and avoiding obstacles. Only as we crossed the moat of the archbishop's ancient fortified manor house and passed under the gatehouse arch did real anxiety grip me. The walls were high and strong. The windows overlooking the courtyard were old and narrow. On one side there were two pairs of stocks. Both were empty. Was one of them being kept for me? Was I about to find myself in some cramped, lightless cell being interrogated about some supposed offence I had given his lordship? How long would it be before I might be able to leave this formidable building?

The courtyard was busy with servants and visitors going about their business. No one paid us any attention. When we had dismounted and handed our horses to the stable staff, I was taken into the main range of the house. When I had been to the garderobe and also done my best to remove mud from my boots I was shown to an anteroom. I did not have to wait long before the door half-opened and a small priest – presumably the archbishop's clerk or chaplain – sidled in. He beckoned and, in quiet, reverential tones, indicated that his grace was ready to receive me.

I entered a large room with panelled and tapestried walls, not knowing what to expect. Before that day I had only seen Thomas Cranmer at a distance, officiating in the cathedral or carrying out visitations in neighbouring parishes – an austere figure, separated from ordinary mortals by social status and the holy theatricality of his office. Any knowledge I had of him beyond that was a mixture of gossip and partisan rumour. Some regarded him as a brilliant theologian and religious politician who had shown King Henry that the pope had no legal jurisdiction in England and was now, boldly and bravely, purifying the teaching and practices of our church. Others despised him as the mere tool whom Henry had used to prise himself loose from 'good Queen Catherine'. Then there were the ale-house prattlers who told scandalous stories about the archbishop. He was secretly married, they confidently asserted, and carried his wife about concealed in a coffer. Only one thing was beyond dispute: like him or loathe him, since the fall of Lord Cromwell, the fate of the English church lay entirely in the hands of Thomas Cranmer. For my own part, I preferred to leave as much distance as possible between myself and powerful men. As the door was closed quietly and discreetly behind me, I braced myself for confrontation. It was, therefore, disconcerting to look around the chamber and to discover that it was empty.

That, at least, was my first impression. Late evening light still entered through tall windows and the lamps had not yet been lit. The room had its shadows and dim corners, into which I peered. It was some moments before I became aware of shuffling sounds coming from behind a large table on which stood a stack of books. Drawing closer, I came upon the Primate of all England on all fours beside a coffer and unloading more volumes which he added to the pile.

After some moments he looked up. 'Ah, Master Treviot, my apologies. I'm looking for my copy of Jerome's *Dialogus contra Pelagianos*. My roguish servants at Lambeth Palace never pack my books properly. Every time I move it takes hours to locate everything I need.' He stood up and held out his hand across the desk. I stooped to kiss his ring.

'Thank you for coming so promptly,' Cranmer continued.

I thought but did not say, I had no option. Instead, I responded, 'I am anxious to know the reason for Your Grace's urgent summons.'

'Grave matters. Grave matters.' He shook his head. He took his seat behind the desk and for some moments seemed distracted by solemn thoughts.

His brow was care-lined, his eyes searching and cautious. Then, with a sudden change of mood, he smiled. 'You have come from Ightham, have you not? Who's the vicar there? Ah, yes, Stimson, isn't it. The man's an idiot. Now, let me see, have you eaten?'

'Not since breakfast, Your Grace.'

'Then we must attend to that first.' He rang a handbell. The obsequious little cleric entered immediately. 'Take Master Treviot to the hall and see him properly fed,' Cranmer ordered. To me he said, 'One should never discuss matters of state on an empty stomach.'

When I returned to the archbishop's study an hour or so later, replete with venison, carp, marchpane cake and muscadel, I was no less confused or anxious than when I first arrived. Apparently I was not to be accused of some unwitting offence and detained at his grace's pleasure but his talk of grave affairs of state was unnerving. By now the candles had been lit and a good fire blazed on the hearth. The archbishop sat to one side of the chimney in a high-backed chair and bade me be seated opposite. Between us was a low table on which were letters and other documents.

Cranmer gazed at the burning logs. 'Would you go to the fire for your faith, Master Treviot?'

I knew not how to answer such an unexpected question and eventually made some sort of protest about believing what the Church said and not being guilty of any heresy for which I needed to fear being sent to the stake.

He looked up with a smile that somehow was not a smile. 'There are men who would like to burn the Archbishop of Canterbury.'

'Merely a few unrepentant papist traitors who would have the king bow his neck again under the pope's authority,' I suggested.

Cranmer shook his head. 'Not few and, by no means, only those who owe secret allegiance to the Bishop of Rome.'

There was a long silence before the archbishop spoke again. He seemed uncertain about how to proceed, like someone outside a house looking for the entrance. At last he sat back and said, 'You are familiar, I believe, with Master Johannes Holbein, his majesty's painter.'

I replied cautiously. 'He has done design work for me – jewellery, tableware, altar furnishings – that sort of thing.'

'To be sure, he is a fine craftsman.'

'Beyond doubt,' I agreed. 'In my opinion there is none better.'

There was another long silence.

'Would you go so far as to call Johannes Holbein a friend?'

My reply was carefully considered. 'I think I would, Your Grace.'

'Then you will know that he is in some danger,' Cranmer said, watching closely for my reaction.

My hopes rose. Perhaps from this unexpected source I might be able to learn who the painter's enemies were or gain some other information that would help Bart. 'I thought as much,' I said. 'I haven't been able to make contact with him recently and, a few days ago—'

'You are about to tell me about the unpleasant incident at Holbein's house.'

'Do you know who was responsible for it, Your Grace? Is that why you have summoned me here? I shall be most grateful for any information—'

He held up a hand to interrupt me. 'What I am about to tell you must not go beyond these walls. Will you swear to keep silence?'

I nodded. Cranmer went to his desk and returned with a large, heavily bound book. It was easily recognisable as the English Bible, the one commonly known as 'Cromwell's Bible'. He set it on the table between us. 'Place your hand on it and make your solemn oath.'

It was with a feeling of rising apprehension that I did as the archbishop insisted.

'Good. God keep you true to your word.' Cranmer resumed his seat. 'You do not need me to remind you what happened, three years ago, to Lord Cromwell. There was a plot against him and he was brought down by men opposed to what they sneeringly called the "New Learning". A foolish expression. What he ... what we ... stood for was a new commonwealth, a godly commonwealth. And we had begun to see the realisation of our dream. We had got rid of the pope and replaced his authority with that of the word of God.' He tapped a finger on the Bible. 'Old learning, Master Treviot. We closed down the abbeys, those bastions of papal error, and began the assault on superstition. *Para kurion egeneto aute*: "This was the Lord's doing and it was marvellous in our eyes".'

Cranmer's caution had fallen away from him; he was speaking with a preacher's fervour. 'Of course, there were those who could not or would not share our vision. They spun a web of lies. They produced paid informers. They managed to persuade his majesty to abandon the most faithful minister he had ever had, or was ever likely to have. They had him shut up in the Tower and, once there ...' Cranmer shrugged. 'Perhaps I should have stood by him; urged the king to clemency.' He sighed. 'But I fear to say that I am not the stuff of which martyrs are made. Of course, I visited my friend in prison. He urged me to continue the work and he gave me this – in strict secrecy.' The archbishop indicated a folded sheet of paper.

'What is it, Your Grace?'

'A list of men Lord Cromwell knew to be faithful to our cause; men who, in various ways, had served him and served the Gospel. One name on that list is "Johannes Holbein".'

'Even so, Your Grace? Holbein? I know he has Lutheran friends and tends in that direction but he is a mere painter. How could he have been of service to Lord Cromwell?'

Cranmer smiled wistfully. 'A mere painter? Yes, that is the point. Think for a moment. Everyone wants to be portrayed by him. He is in fashion ... though, perhaps, not as much as he was. Anyway, the point is that he was welcomed into the houses of the greatest in the land. He made some charcoal sketches or set up his easel in a corner and worked away silently. All the time his keen eyes took in every detail of his surroundings. He went to the kitchen and had meals with the servants. They talked in friendly style of this and that. No man guarded his tongue strictly. After all, this gruff little German was only a painter.'

'I see. And he passed any useful information on to Lord Cromwell. He was, in a word, a spy.'

'Let us say, rather, that he was a trained observer. He

certainly gathered much useful information. He discovered what Lord Cromwell's enemies were planning. Unfortunately, he was too late in conveying this intelligence to his lordship.'

'Even so? Then I begin to see why Your Grace is concerned for his safety. You fear that this "spy", or whatever you wish to call him, has been unmasked by people intent on taking their revenge.'

'No, we are not dealing with petty-minded men whose eyes are fixed on the past. Those who wish to silence our mutual friend are very much concerned with the future. You see, Master Treviot, the struggle – or, rather, let us call it the war, for in very truth that is what it is – the war continues. Many men – powerful in the Church and in the royal court – will stop at nothing to extinguish the light of the Gospel and return us all to popish darkness.'

'Surely, Your Grace,' I protested, 'things are quieting down now. For the last couple of years there have been fewer public protests by partisans of different religious camps, fewer angry sermons denouncing "papists" and "heretics". Most people want nothing but to be allowed to get on with their lives in peace.'

'What most people want, Master Treviot, is of little con- sequence. Decisions are made by King Henry. Therefore, the only people who matter are those who influence the king. Now, his majesty – whom God long preserve – is a sick man. For those of us who knew him in his prime it is sad to see him as he is now. Just to move from one room to another he needs to be supported by two strong servants. As to stairs ... well, I need not go into details. The important point is that he sees fewer people now and relies increasingly on the members of his Privy Chamber and a handful of others – like myself – whom he trusts. That is where the war is being fought now –

in the king's inner circle. Those who wish to suppress the truth know they must remove us – just as they removed Lord Cromwell.'

'Who are these men and how are they working against Your Grace?'

'That is precisely what I, aided by such as Master Holbein, intend to discover. Our friend continues to work for me. That is why his life is in danger.'

I was at a loss to know where this conversation was headed. I said, 'Thank you for explaining this, Your Grace. You may be sure I will redouble my prayers for his majesty and for yourself. I wish it was in my power to do more.'

'It is, Master Treviot. It is.' Cranmer unfolded the sheet of paper. 'Lord Cromwell's list has been very helpful to me. His assessment of potential agents is incisive. He was a fine judge of character. This is how he describes one young man: "He is tenacious, intelligent but not quick-witted, transparently honest and, above all, fiercely loyal".' The archbishop stared at me intently. 'That is the kind of man I need now. The kind his majesty needs. The kind England needs.'

Chapter 5

I was without words. Almost without breath, as though I had been punched in the stomach. When I did find my voice I could only mutter and mumble. What I tried to impress upon the archbishop was that, while I had briefly been employed on confidential business for Lord Cromwell, that had been several years before. I protested that I had no training as a spy. 'And to be honest, Your Grace, I have no taste for it,' I said.

'Then we are alike in that, you and I,' Cranmer replied. 'I am a simple scholar at heart and frequently wish I had remained so. It was his majesty who summoned me out of the university and set me to the game of intrigue. I had no option but to learn its devious rules and follow them as best I could. It is easier to be a spectator but the game must be played and sometimes reluctant participants have to give up the luxury of merely looking on. Believe me, Master Treviot, there are things that need doing and only you can do them.'

'Your Grace, I beg you to excuse me. I am not the man for—'

'You are if I say you are!' For the first time this gentle-spoken cleric raised his voice. Then, as suddenly, his tone returned to its usual volume. 'You have yet to hear what I require of you. As I explained, the future of our godly commonwealth rests, in large measure, with his majesty's more trusted companions.'

'I'm sure he leans heavily on Your Grace's advice.'

'I thank God that he does.' Cranmer paused. Then, watching closely for my reaction, he said, 'There was a time when his majesty leaned heavily on Lord Cromwell's advice.'

'And you think . . .'

'I do not think, Master Treviot. I know. I am the major obstacle in the enemy's path. The only way I can be removed is by convincing his majesty that I am a heretic – as they did with Cromwell. That is why I need to be kept informed of their plans – by faithful friends like Master Holbein and your-self.'

'But I do not move in court circles,' I protested.

'No, but you are a leading member of society here in Kent.'

'Yes, but . . .'

Cranmer ignored the interruption. 'The conspiracy against me is like ripples on a pond. It spreads out from the centre to lap against the distant banks.'

At that moment there was a tap at the door and the obse-quious little priest appeared again. He coughed apologetically.

'Time for mass already, Martin?' Cranmer stood up. 'Master Treviot, it seems we must continue our discussion later. Martin take our guest to the chapel. Have a chamber prepared for him. He will be staying tonight. Master Treviot, be so good as to return here after supper.'

Once again the priest preluded his words with a discreet cough. 'Your Grace has letters which Your Grace might consider urgent – including two from his majesty.'

Cranmer sighed deeply. 'You see why I yearn for the scholar's life, Master Treviot. Very well, Martin, I will dictate letters after supper. In the morning I wish to be left alone with our guest directly after early mass. Nothing is to disturb us. Do you understand – nothing.'

I took my leave of the archbishop and accompanied my guide to the chapel. It was laid out collegiate-style – stalls facing each other, north and south, across a narrow chancel. The choir and clergy occupied the seats closest to the altar. As I took my place, my mind was still on the unfinished conversation. At least I would not be distracted by the worship. As a mere layman I would only be expected to observe the clergy performing their ritual, aided by the singing men and boys of the archbishop's fine choir. Or so I thought. I was, therefore, surprised to be handed a card on which parts of the mass were printed – in English – and to discover that the whole congregation was expected to recite them with the priests. If this was an example of the kind of innovation Cranmer wanted to introduce in the Church as a whole, I could see why those wedded to the old ways might consider such novelties heretical. I noticed that even here, in his grace's own domain, not a few clergy and lay people kept their mouths tight shut during the recitation of the English passages.

Afterwards, at supper in the great hall, I sat at one of the long tables among members of the household. Some were curious to know my business with the archbishop but, remembering Cranmer's admonition and my own vow, I returned only vague answers. I was aware of – or thought I could detect – an atmosphere of divided loyalties or fractured trust. I told myself at the time that I imagined it; that the fragments of backstairs gossip and differences over domestic trivia were no more than one might encounter in the entourage of any great lord, whether spiritual or temporal. Yet it was difficult wholly to avoid the impression that cautious glances were being exchanged across the board and tongues carefully guarded.

The sombre-faced man sitting opposite, though friendly, seemed more reticent than his companions, so I was slightly surprised when, at the end of the meal, he suggested we might loosen our limbs with a walk around the cloister. I had recognised him immediately as one of the archbishop's singing men and he had introduced himself as John Marbeck. He was, I guessed, in his mid-thirties, though his face bore the lines of a man somewhat older. As we strolled slowly round the cloister, torches in the walls threw across the flower beds long shadows of the columns supporting the roof of the square walkway. The evening was not cold but, after a few paces, Marbeck drew up his hood. I had the distinct impression that there was more to this gesture than a desire to protect his head from chill air. This was confirmed when, after a few inconsequential pleasantries, he became suddenly serious.

'May I ask what brings you to Ford?'

'I have been summoned here on confidential business.'

'You are, then, a close friend of the archbishop?'

'No, but his grace has indicated that he trusts me.'

'He needs men he can trust,' Marbeck muttered gloomily.

He fell silent for several moments. I could not see his face but his whole demeanour – the slumped shoulders and shuffling footsteps – was that of a deeply troubled man. I felt awkward and after another half-circuit I said, 'If you'll excuse me, Master Marbeck, I've had a tiring day and am more than ready for bed. Tomorrow I will be in conference with the archbishop. He will expect me to be well-rested and have my wits about me.'

Marbeck clutched my arm. 'Then you must speak to his grace for me, for I cannot gain audience. You must warn him!' The light from a flaring torch accentuated the sharp lines on his anguished features.

'In God's name, what ails you man?' I gasped.

'I must tell you my story. I shall go mad if I can make no one listen. When I've done, you must decide what to say to his grace.'

I groaned inwardly but did not have the heart to refuse. Marbeck launched into his alarming tale.

'I was born in Windsor. Spent all my life in the shadow of the castle. Married there. Three children. I got a position as singing man and sub-organist in the royal chapel and thought myself the luckiest man in the world. I taught the choristers, played for worship, wrote some music myself. Never wanted anything else. No ambition, you see, no ambition. Some men dream of making their mark in the world. Not me. Not till Cromwell had the new book put in all the churches.'

'The English Bible?'

'Yes. It was a revelation to me. I read it from cover to cover. It was wonderfully exciting – actually to have God's word in my own hands. Then – Lord forgive my presumption – I thought how useful it would be if readers could have a concordance – a list of Bible words with all their references. The more I thought about it, the more I thought, I could do that. So I set to work.'

'Was that not rather a dreary task?'

The musician's eyes lit up. 'Oh no! It was a joy. My friends encouraged me and so did some of the king's courtiers. They even lent me books and gave me money to buy more. I'd never been happier. Then, one night last March . . .' He broke off and wiped the back of a hand across his eyes.

I tried to grasp the opportunity to disengage myself. 'This is obviously distressing for you. Perhaps we should talk more tomorrow . . .'

'No, no, Master Treviot, in Jesu's name hear me out, I beg you! It was the middle of the night. Black as soot. No moon. There comes a hammering on the door. My wife went to open it and was pushed aside by three of the king's guard. They rampaged from room to room, grabbing up all my papers and books. They ignored my protests and the children's cries. When they'd done, they bound my arms and marched me off to the town jail.'

'They took you for a heretic? But why?'

'It seems that some of the books I'd been lent were banned. I swear I did not know it. They were just commentaries written by foreign scholars about various books of the Bible. Well, I soon discovered I wasn't alone. The guards threw me into a cell with Robert Testwood – my friend and a fellow choirman. And there were two others, Robert Bennett, a local lawyer, and Henry Filmer, who kept a tailor's shop in Peascod Street. The door was locked and there we stayed for a couple of days.'

'Were these other men heretics?'

'No more than I, I'm sure. But that's little to the point. Once you're marked for the fire nothing can save you. They go pestering friends and neighbours, looking for people who will testify against you.'

'And who are "they"?' I asked.

'The Bishop of Winchester's men, as I later discovered.'

'You're sure.'

'Oh, yes. He had us taken to the Marshalsea prison in Southwark, close to his palace so that he could interrogate us in person. He kept me there for four months. Twice he had me to his own house, shouting insults and threats at me.'

The Marshalsea! An image of that stinking, vermin-infested, overcrowded hovel came into my mind. As a prison it was, by some people, feared more than the Tower. The lees of the criminal world were habitually swilled into it. Highway robbers, murderers, rebels and other desperate men were shut up there to await trial (often indefinitely) and were known to beg for their appointment with the hangman, in preference to spending another day in the Marshalsea. The thought of this gentle musician having been incarcerated there was an affront to reason and certainly an affront to justice.

'How appalling!' I said.

'I wouldn't wish it on any human soul – Christian or heathen. Everything was done there to make me confess my supposed heresies and provide the names of others. Terrible things. They still haunt my dreams. By the time I was released my wife was hard put to recognise me. My body was black from the beatings. I could scarcely hobble because the irons had chafed my ankles.'

'I'm so sorry for your ordeal,' I said. 'But one thing puzzles me – why was Bishop Gardiner personally interested in the opinions of a humble singing man?'

'Exactly!' Marbeck stopped in his tracks to emphasise the point. 'A thousand times and more I asked myself the question, "Why me?". Then I realised that they cared not a farthing for what I believed. I could roast in hell as an unrepentant heretic for all they cared. What they wanted from me was names.'

'Names?'

'Aye. "Who aided you in your pernicious studies? Who seduced you with heretical books? You are no scholar; you could not have undertaken your wretched concordance unaided. You were set to it by your betters; men of the royal court. Who were they? Give us their names and we may yet save you from the fire."'

'And did you tell them what they wanted to know?'

'Never. Though I thank God they didn't put me to the torture. What I might have falsely confessed if they had racked me ...'

'But if you didn't do their bidding how did you escape burning as an unrepentant heretic?'

Marbeck halted again and this time sank on to a stone bench. He shook his head and sighed deeply. 'Oh, Master Treviot, it isn't over! It isn't over!' The torchlight glistened on tears creeping down his cheeks. 'I wish to God that it might be over; that I could go back to my family and bolt our door firmly against them. They're too powerful, too clever, too relentless.' He brushed a hand across his face.

I sat beside him. 'I'm afraid I don't understand ...'

Marbeck grabbed my wrist, his grip almost painful. 'The twenty-eighth of July was wet ... but not wet enough. They burned Filmer and a local priest and Robbie Testwood in Windsor marketplace. Robbie was scarce more than a boy, a merry lad, always joking.' Marbeck's frame was now shaking. The tears flowed freely. Unchecked. 'We were all of us guilty – according to the trial. *Trial?* Ptah!' He spat violently. 'The bishop's man told the jury what verdict to bring. And we were *all* found guilty, *all* of us! The others burned. But not Bennett and not me. *Why?*' Marbeck turned his anguished face towards me. And now he was gabbling, words pouring out like rain from a waterspout. 'Do you know what Gardiner said? He petitioned the king for a pardon because it would be a pity his majesty should lose "such a fine musician". Lying, double-tongued hypocrite. He did it to buy me. To buy me! I must now be one of his ears around the court, listening for murmurs against the king's laws and whispers of heresy. If I fail fresh charges will be brought against me. That is why I am sent here to his grace of Canterbury's house. Officially I come with messages from Windsor, from the odious dean, Dr London. He's thick with Winchester. They mean to destroy any of the king's friends not of their party. Especially the archbishop. My real mission here is to learn all I can about him and those around him. I beg you, Master Treviot, if you are in his grace's favour, warn him. He must have a care. He must guard himself against traitors. He must be sparing with his trust. He must not trust me!'

Marbeck stood abruptly and stumbled off along the cloister.

Comfortable as my allotted quarters were, I slept little that night. The hideous images Marbeck had conjured up recurred unbidden every time I tried to rid my mind of them. And the personal implications of his story for me were frightening. What was I being dragged into? Part of me was shouting, 'Get yourself out of this.' But there was another – a whisper, though insistent – which said, 'You must do what you can to stop such villainy.'

When Cranmer summoned me back to his study the following morning I reported my conversation with the distracted choirman.

'Poor John,' Cranmer said. 'I must see him and try to offer some comfort. At least his testimony seems to have been more persuasive than mine. I think you understand more clearly now the situation in which I am placed.'

'Surely, Your Grace, if you were to report the Bishop of Winchester and his associates to the king, he would soon put a stop to their schemes.'

'It is not so simple. His majesty will require proof. Just as Stephen Gardiner goes about to prove me a heretic, so I need to gain evidence of his stratagems. As I remarked yesterday, I have no alternative but to play the game of intrigue by the rules. The good bishop has a network of agents, as you have heard from the unfortunate John Marbeck. Master Holbein has been gathering information about this organisation and was on the point of discovering something vital. If he has been unmasked and forced into hiding, that is deeply worrying. Gardiner's people are not only in Windsor. They are located throughout the land – in the royal court, in London, here in Canterbury, in many shires and certainly in Kent. There are leading men in this county who are against me – parish clergy, magistrates, townsmen, landowners. I, too, must have local people working for me. That is why I want you to discover all you can about your Kentish colleagues.'

'You wish me to spy on my friends and neighbours?'

'In a word, "yes". I understand your reluctance. It does you credit. But reflect on this: any information you can gather about the plot against me may bring you closer to unmasking the villains who killed Master Holbein's assistant.'

'You think they were working for Bishop Gardiner?'

Cranmer frowned. 'Stephen would never condone such an appalling crime. Of that I am sure. But is he able to control all those who work for him? That is a more open question. Now to practicalities. I have appointed a commission – on his majesty's authority – to inquire into preaching throughout the diocese. It is headed by Sir Thomas Moyle, whom I'm sure you know.'

'Yes, he's one of the parliament members for the shire.'

'That's right. A good man. Thoroughly reliable. One of Lord Cromwell's protégés. I'll instruct him to add your name to the commission. That way you'll be able to go round asking questions without raising suspicion. But, of course, you will report anything of interest directly to me.' He drew a ring from his finger. 'This will always ensure direct access to me, any time, anywhere. As far as possible you should report to me in person. If you need to put anything in writing do so under heavy seal and have it delivered directly to me or to my secretary, Ralph Morice.' The archbishop rose from his chair. 'For the moment there's nothing more to discuss. You will find my guards ready to escort you back to Hemmings. Now kneel and I'll give you my blessing.'

Chapter 6

It was an uncomfortable journey. The rain clouds had blown over, at least for the time being, and a sickly sun glimmered dimly, veiled in high haze. But it was not the weather that depressed my spirits. My thoughts were dominated by the task I had accepted and the problems of approaching old friends and neighbours as a covert information-gatherer. Yet even my personal predicament did not fully account for my sombre mood. We seemed to be clattering through a broken land. Waterlogged fields skirted the road, covered with flattened, unharvested and unharvestable crops. In some better-drained places farmers were already ploughing the rotten wheat back into the soil. Listless villagers sat outside their cottages. In Chilham and Charing the stocks and pillories were fully occupied with men and women arrested for vagrancy. The bodies of thieves and other felons swung from most wayside gibbets.

As we passed through Maidstone a group of young men – scarcely more than boys – threw stones at us and disappeared down a narrow alley where we could not give chase.

'Why are they angry with us?' I asked my escort captain.

'They blame the archbishop and we wear the archbishop's livery.'

'Blame him for what?'

'I doubt whether they know,' he replied. 'Their bellies are empty. Their shops lack customers. They have to blame some-one.'

''Tis the preachers who put them up to it,' another of the guardsmen said. 'They tell the people his grace is leading the king deeper into heresy and God is punishing the land with plague and dearth. I've heard them myself.'

'Then they should be arrested for treason.'

'Who's going to do that? Most of the magistrates are on their side. I tell you this, Master Treviot. Have a care for you and yours. The country all around is ready to break out in open rebellion.'

Such doom-laden prophecies seemed to be supported next day when I called on my neighbour, Sir James Dewey. His estate at Hadbourne was some five miles from Hemmings. Though he was a few years my senior, we had been friends ever since we had trapped conies on our fathers' lands and gone fishing together in the local streams. I found him in his orchard supervising the collecting of the crop.

His welcome was warm. 'Glad to see you, Thomas – glad and relieved. When your people came down from London without you I was worried that you'd fallen prey to the contagion. Things are obviously bad in the City. People have been flocking down here to escape.' He linked his arm in mine and we walked together towards the house.

73

'Has that made things difficult?'

'Difficult? That is not the word I would choose. 'Tis my ill fortune to be JP again this year. Scarce a day passes when I'm not called on to give judgement on vagrants, market thieves, cutpurses, dicemen and I know not what. This summer alone I've sent five villains to the quarter sessions for robbery on the highway or breaking into houses. And, of course, for every felon we catch there are a score who go on their evil way.'

'Do you know of any gangs of hucksters selling their services to wealthy patrons?'

'There are always desperate men who will do anything for instant coin.' James looked at me quizzically. 'But you, I hazard, have a particular reason for asking.'

I told him about the Aldgate murder.

By the time I finished we had reached the house. James ordered wine and led the way up to the first-floor solar. When we were settled in the window embrasure, overlooking the land towards Mereworth Woods, he said, 'Thomas, I'm so sorry to hear your terrible tale. I wish I could say I am surprised to hear it. But these are evil times. Everything seems to be coming . . . unstuck.'

'Unstuck?'

"Tis the only word I can find. You know what I mean. If it was just foul weather spoiling the crops and putting the price of bread beyond many men's purses, we could pray and tell each other things will be better next year. But much more is amiss. The king is sick to death – between us I can say what would be a Tower of London offence if uttered in public – and we shall have a child to rule us, governed by who knows who? For all the laws against vagrancy made by the parliament, jobless men wander the realm making themselves a nuisance wherever they go. And nowadays no one knows what the

74

word "religion" means. Preachers stand in the pulpit and tell us whatever takes their fancy.'

'As to that, I can tell you that the archbishop is determined to restore order. He has appointed me to a commission inquiring into what truths and untruths are being proclaimed throughout the diocese.'

'Ah, yes, Cranmer's famous commission. I, too, am a part of it.' James frowned. 'I am sorry to hear you are involved, Thomas.'

'Why so?'

'Because it is unpopular.'

'I can understand that the clergy do not welcome it, but, surely . . .'

'I don't mean the clergy. 'Tis the landowners, the magistrates, the gentlemen. As if we had not enough to do in these troubled times, we must now turn theologians and weigh fine points of doctrine.'

'I don't think that's what the archbishop has in mind. His concern is for religious unity.'

'Well, there's many would say his cure is worse than the ailment. I have no desire to examine preachers or encourage people hereabouts to turn informers.'

I did not tell James how much I agreed with his sentiment. I changed the subject. 'You've no idea, then, where I might go in search of the murderers?'

'I hardly think you will find them here, Thomas. Do you not think they are more likely to be hiding in London's labyrinth?'

'Unless, like so many others, they've quit the City for fear of the plague.'

'I will keep on the alert for any information but I must say I think you are looking for a needle in a bottle of hay.'

James's depressing words echoed around my mind as I rode home. He had starkly expressed the truth that I had been trying to hide from myself. The task I had taken on *was* an impossible one. The chance of my locating the real murderers was remote. I could not help Bart and my efforts to do so had merely sucked me into the dangerous world of high politics. As one of the archbishop's spies I now risked becoming unpopular in the county. More than that, I could be placing myself at serious risk. Supposing Cranmer lost his 'war' with the Bishop of Winchester and his powerful colleagues? Would there not then be a purge of all those known to be associated with him? Marbeck's tale was a vivid warning of the methods used to track down and exterminate supposed heretics. Years before I had spent several days incarcerated in the Bishop of London's prison and had but narrowly escaped death as an enemy of the Church. Some of the powerful clergy I antagonised then had long memories. There could be little doubt they would grasp any opportunity for revenge eagerly. It was ironical that I had mentally censured Bart for blundering into a quarrel that was none of his concern and now I was doing exactly the same.

However, my dark mood lightened somewhat when I strode into the hall at Hemmings. In my absence, Raffy was sitting in my armed chair and playing host to a visitor. He and Ned Longbourne were seated at table, dining off pottage and manchet, and, judging from the laughter echoing from the rafters, enjoying a lively conversation. That was no surprise; my old friend was very good with children. I drew up a stool and joined them, happy to relax briefly. After the meal, when Raffy had been sent off to join his playfellows, I leaned across the table.

'What news, Ned? Have you heard anything about the killers?'

For some moments, he stroked his grey beard in silence – a gesture I knew well. It meant, I am reluctant to speak; please don't press me. At last he said, with as much caution as he could load on to the words, 'There is a name. It may be quite wrong, but it comes from two, independent sources.'

'Yes?' I urged.

'You're sure you want to pursue this, Thomas?'

'By all the saints, Ned, you've not ridden all this way for nothing! Tell me the name!'

The answer came as a murmur, scarcely audible: 'Henry Walden.' The old man looked at me closely, as though expecting a response. When I did not react, he continued, 'You have not heard of him?'

'I don't think so. Should I have?'

'He is more commonly known as "Black Harry". There's folk believe the name was bestowed by the devil in person who baptised him in hell-water.'

'Then, I'm glad to say I have never come across him.'

'You do well to be glad.'

'So, who is he?'

Ned shrugged. 'There are many stories about him – usually confused and often mutually contradictory. As far as I can piece together anything coherent, it goes something like this: once there was an honest sailor, one of a crew that traded across Biscay with Bordeaux and ports on the Castilian coast. One day they decided that piracy was a more profitable vocation. They became notorious as ruthless, pitiless cut-throats. At last justice caught up with them. They were captured, tried and sentenced in a Spanish court. But Harry persuaded his captors that he was more use to them alive than dead. The Inquisition is always on the lookout for unscrupulous men in its unending purge of society. When I was in the monastery two of the brothers made a pilgrimage to the shrine of St James at Compostela. They brought back horrific tales of outrages committed in the name of God. Crown and church sanction any action against people suspected of being secret Jews, Muslims or Lutherans. Holy Mary and all the saints will bear witness that I have no love for heretics but torture, rape, burning – I cannot make these agree ...'

'Of course not.' I tapped the table impatiently. 'But what of this Black Harry?'

'It appears that he went too far even for the fathers of the Holy Office. I do not have the details but it seems that, a couple of years ago, he and his merry band were obliged to leave Spain in a hurry. What would they do back in England? They only know one trade. They are now for hire by any patron determined enough or desperate enough to want their services.'

'So, who are they working for?'

Ned sat back, holding up his hands. 'I have told all I know. They and their employers obviously cloak their activities in secrecy.'

'Then how can we find them?'

'We cannot.' Ned glared at me. 'And we should not try. We are facing something truly diabolical. When someone who believes anything is justifiable in the service of his cause sanctions the activities of someone prepared to do anything as long as the price is right, the result is inhuman acts of unrestrained horror.'

After the silence that followed, Ned leaned forward again. He spoke softly. 'There's one thing I should add about this band of devil-spawned copesmates; they have a good intelligence system. If you go looking for them they'll know it before you set foot outside your house. You should not be concerned about how to find *them*; just pray they do not find *you*.'

'If that is the case,' I said, 'poor Bart is as good as dead. The gang must know he is looking for them.'

Ned sighed. 'Thomas, I may be wrong. Perhaps Black Harry is not the villain responsible for the death in Aldgate.'

'And perhaps he is. So what should I do? Sit here in Kent and wait?' I stood up and paced the hall, trying to force my thoughts and fears into a pattern that might suggest some course of action. I flung words out almost at random.

'Bart is in danger. He may be able to hide from the magistrate. But from the criminals? What of Lizzie and the children? Won't Black Harry seek them out in order to get to Bart? Where does Cranmer's trouble fit into all this?'

'Cranmer?' Ned looked puzzled.

I gave him a brief account of my visit to Ford.

'Mary and all the saints!' Ned exclaimed. 'What morass have you waded into now?'

'Whatever it is we must make sure no one else gets trapped in it. Ned, we must keep everyone safe that we can. Please, go back to London. Bring Lizzie here. She won't want to come but bring her – bound and gagged if necessary.'

'I'll try, but—'

'No, don't try; succeed! She can't stay on her own in London. Here I can defend her and the children.'

'Pray God you can. But what will you be doing the while?'

'I don't know. I must think. We have to assume, for now, at least, that our enemy is Black Harry. That means we have to act urgently. I don't want to hustle you but could you set out straight away? I'll send a couple of my men with you to bring you and Lizzie back safely.'

As soon as Ned had gone I took precautions for the safety

79

of everyone at Hemmings, especially Adie and the children. I set up a twenty-four-hour guard rota so that the estate was patrolled constantly by armed servants. In order not to alarm everyone I told them the caution was necessary because of the disturbed state of the countryside. Since there were bands of hungry and desperate men abroad, breaking into houses and barns, I explained, all householders needed to take special measures. I urged everyone to be on the alert and report to me immediately they saw or heard anything suspicious.

The next thing I had to do was contact neighbouring landowners in order to carry out the archbishop's commission. I sent messages informing the recipients that I intended to call upon them during the next week. In the event, I was forestalled by a letter which arrived two days later, on 16 September. It was from Sir Thomas Moyle, member of parliament for Kent, justice of the peace and probably the richest gentleman in the county. It summoned me to a meeting together with all the principal landowners of northern Kent on the forthcoming Saturday, the eighteenth, at Moyle's house, Eastwell Court. I was curious to see the mansion that others referred to as one of the most splendid in the county. Although I was fairly well acquainted with the man, I had never visited him. His rise to wealth and influence had been rapid. As an associate of Thomas Cromwell in bringing down the abbeys, he had acquired several parcels of monastic land throughout southern England. The money with which to make this investment had come from his marriage to the daughter and heiress of Edward Jordeyne, one of the leading London goldsmiths. It was through this connection with the Worshipful Company that I got to know him. I was glad Cranmer spoke well of him and regarded him as an ally. This gave me some hope that he might bring his influence to bear in the search for my quarry.

I made an early start on Saturday but not before going round Hemmings and satisfying myself that all the walls, gates and buildings were secure and well-guarded. I and my men joined up with James Dewey's party and we took the Dover road, avoiding the more direct route through the low-lying and sodden country to the south. We had just passed through Chilham and were on the last leg of our journey when we came up with Edward Thwaites, whose home was nearby. He was one of the senior gentlemen of the shire and also one of the most conservative. He certainly did not seem pleased with his summons to the meeting.

'You'd think Sir Thomas would know we have better things to do,' Thwaites grumbled. 'I've never known the country so unstable, not even at the time the monasteries were being pulled down. The more troublemakers I hang, the more are lining up to take their places.'

'I believe the archbishop is hoping our commission will ensure that preachers stick to official doctrine. That ought to make our job easier.'

'Hypocrite!' Thwaites exploded in cynical laughter. 'Cranmer's the biggest heretic in England!'

'That is foolish talk,' James protested. 'I've heard slack-brained ploughmen say that sort of thing after four jars of ale, but Cranmer speaks for the king and has the backing of parliament.'

'For the moment,' Thwaites muttered.

'What do you mean by that?' I asked.

'No matter.' Thwaites waved a hand. 'All I know is that most of the pulpit pounders and Bible bashers round here claim to have Cranmer's support. Let me tell you about the

81

worst of the brood. He's a snivelling little rabble rouser called Richard Turner, Vicar of Chartham, and he's been rampaging around these parts for the last couple of years. He preaches inside the churches and out. He stirs young men to all sorts of vandalism. My grandfather left money – a lot of money – in his will for a statue of the Virgin for Chilham Church. Three months ago, one of Turner's mobs hauled it down – sacrilegious, degenerate traitors! Don't tell me his majesty sanctions that sort of behaviour!' Thwaites's face was red with fury.

'You have the power to arrest such villains,' James observed mildly.

'Aye, and there's the point of it. Twice I've had Turner clapped in jail and sent him up to the archbishop's court. What happened? His grace says he "finds no fault" in the man. So Turner goes on his way, bolder than before. Well, this time I have him. He's in irons waiting to go before the assize judges at Michaelmas. Cranmer won't rescue him from the gallows this time.'

'That was well done, Edward,' I said. 'I trust you are as hard on gangs who are paid by papistical bishops to go around maiming and killing folk not of their faith.'

'What do you mean by that?' the old man asked.

'No matter,' I replied, with a wave of my hand.

Eastwell Court was as impressive as popular rumour had led me to expect. The original courtyard had been extended westwards and a large workforce was occupied in erecting a balancing range of buildings to the east. Sir Thomas received us in his great hall where several guests were already assembled and were talking in small groups. Everything about Moyle impressed and was meant to impress. He wore a doublet of grey silk with a gold chain stretched across his ample stomach. He shook hands and shared a few words with each newcomer in turn. He clearly enjoyed holding court and was well practised at it. Having received his words of greeting, I moved towards the fireplace, before which a small group were engaged in debates.

'Bishop Gardiner says he would give six thousand pounds to pluck down the archbishop. I have that on good authority from a friend on the Privy Council.' The speaker was an austere man with lank black hair. I immediately recognised Sir Anthony St Leger of Ulcombe, a man high in the king's confidence and but recently returned from acting as viceroy in Ireland. I joined his group.

'How does Gardiner intend to achieve that, do you think?' I asked.

'Oh, I keep clear of religious infighting,' St Leger replied. 'I leave that sort of thing to my brother, Arthur. He's a prebendary at Canterbury.'

Someone else said, 'I gather all the prebendaries and senior clergy at Canterbury heartily wish to be rid of Cranmer.'

'But again I ask, how are they going to do it?' I persisted. 'Brave talk is easy but I understand that Cranmer stands very high in his majesty's affections.'

'I agree with Thomas.' Peter Flett, from Hadstead, near Tonbridge, like me, was one of the younger members of the gathering. 'When there was all that trouble at Windsor, a few weeks back, everyone was saying that the archbishop would be caught up in it, but nothing has happened.'

'As far as you know,' St Leger suggested. 'It matters not what "everyone" is saying; 'tis what is being said and plotted in secret that is important. When Cromwell was brought down who could have foretold it? For all the world knew, he stood high in his majesty's affections. Yet, within a few hours, the upstart's reign was over. My guess is that it will be the

83

same with Cranmer. He is much unloved by people who matter. They will not suffer him to remain at the king's right hand much longer. Anyone who is wise will be careful not to get too close to our dear archbishop. When ships sink, little boats can get caught in their wake and founder also.'

At that moment, a bell sounded and we were called to dinner. This had been laid out on a long table in the upper part of the hall. As the company took their seats, I had the distinct impression that they were dividing into two sections. St Leger, Thwaites and others of a similar disposition seemed to be settling around the right end of the table. Those who might be considered to be well disposed to Cranmer occupied the other end. Moyle, of course, took his place in the centre, facing down the hall. He was backed by a huge tapestry of some allegorical scene. On his right was a man wearing a clerk's gown. I was careful to fill one of the gaps almost opposite our host. If he wanted to gauge my allegiance I would not make it easy for him.

The dinner was impressive – at least seven messes – and Moyle seemed in no hurry to conclude it and bring us to our business. When at length he did so, he spoke in the confident tones of a man well versed in chairing meetings.

'Gentlemen, I thank you for coming. As you know, we are gathered to consider the best ways we can assist the archbishop in putting an end to religious discord. I have asked his grace's secretary, Ralph Morice' – he indicated his neighbour – 'to be present in order to report on our deliberations to the archbishop in person.'

'This is a religious matter,' someone to my right said. 'Surely the clergy should be dealing with it.'

'By your leave, Sir Thomas, I'll answer that.' Morice, a fair-complexioned man of middle years, directed his gaze up and down the table. 'This body carries his majesty's commission as head of the Church. Doctrine, as defined by the king in council with his bishops and parliament, is now enshrined in statute law. The king – and the archbishop – simply require that you enforce the law.'

There were murmurings to my right and left but no one spoke. Moyle resumed control. 'His majesty has set forth true Christian doctrine in the manual published last May and commonly called the *King's Book*.'

'Are we supposed to commit it all to memory and examine our parish priests on every detail?' another man wanted to know.

'Certainly not,' Moyle assured him. 'We simply have to make sure the clergy swear to teach from it and from nothing else. If we hear that anyone is preaching something unauthorised, we are to take testimonies and send them with the offenders to the quarter sessions. Once example has been made of a few disobedient clergy, I'll warrant we shall have little more trouble.'

I don't think anyone was convinced by Moyle's assurances but, in the presence of the archbishop's representative, no one was prepared to give voice to criticism. We spent another half-hour or so exchanging information on possible troublemakers and dividing the county into smaller regional units for more effective united action. In mid-afternoon the meeting was formally closed and members drifted away. Through the windows high in the old walls we could all see the grey-black clouds crawling across the sky and we were anxious to start for home. However, I wanted to have a word in private with our host and lingered by the outer doorway, waiting for an opportunity. It was then that Ralph Morice came across and, taking me by the arm, steered me outside.

As we stood on the broad steps leading up to the entrance, watching members of the party mount their horses, assemble their servants and ride off towards the gateway, Morice said, 'So, Thomas, which of these men can be trusted?'

'I'd be loath to speak ill of any of them,' I replied evasively.

'A charitable answer, but not a wise one. We both know that some of our neighbours are set in their old-fashioned ways. Some are protecting clergy who long to refill their churches with popish paraphernalia. Some have friends in high places and will be hastening to report to them on today's meeting. Some are ready to distribute arms to their tenants and lead them in what they would call a war against heresy. So, I ask again, who can the king and the archbishop rely on and who must we watch carefully?'

'Well, I have no evidence of rebellious intent but, if you press me for my suspicions ...' I mentioned half a dozen names, including those of Thwaites and St Leger. Then I saw Moyle come out of the house. 'Excuse me,' I said, 'I need to have a quick word with our host.'

'Very well,' Morice replied quietly, 'but don't forget your oath to report anything suspicious.'

As I approached the elegant figure standing proprietorially before the massive oak door of his splendid house I heard a murmur of distant thunder.

'I fear you may be in for a wet ride, young Treviot,' Sir Thomas said as he shook my hand.

'Indeed, Sir Thomas. I must not delay my departure, but I wanted to have a quick word in confidence.'

He nodded gravely. 'Then let us go back inside.'

When we were standing in the hall once more, close by the outer door, he said, 'Please, speak freely.'

'I have heard of a group of men – desperate men – who are

in the pay of the archbishop's enemies and are intent on his ruin. They will stop at nothing – including murder.'

Moyle frowned. 'That is a very serious thing to say. Is it any more than country rumour?'

'Two weeks ago a young man was stabbed to death in Aldgate.'

'At Master Holbein's house? Yes, I heard something about it, but what has that to do with the archbishop?'

'I discussed it with his grace and we are both convinced the assassins were trying to prevent him receiving from Master Holbein information of a plot against him.'

'If that is true, these men must be found.'

'Exactly, Sir Thomas, that is why I thought you might be able to help. You have wide interests in and around London. I beg you to tell me if you have heard anything about this gang.'

'Can you describe them?'

'We believe their leader is a savage hellhound by the name of Henry Walden, though he prefers to be called Black Harry. I've been obliged to offer protection to Holbein's children. They are safe in one of my cottages at Hemmings.'

'I'll certainly make enquiries. Be sure to let me know if you hear any more. We must rid the realm ... '

'Good even, Sir Thomas. I'm taking my leave now.' The speaker, emerging from the shadows beside the door, was Edward Thwaites. 'Will you ride with us?' He smiled at me. 'I think your friend and neighbour, James Dewey, is already fetching your horses from the stable yard.'

Within minutes we had collected our party together and were on our way northwards. The sky was growing steadily darker and, before we had travelled more than five miles, the storm crashed violently all around us. Lightning jagged the sky. The rain was more like a waterfall.

Thwaites pointed to a cluster of buildings close to the road-side and we spurred our horses towards the only visible shelter. Our refuge was three cottages and a tiled barn. Thwaites took instant command. He sent the servants into the barn for shelter with the horses, then ran towards the nearest cottage, with James and I following, our cloaks held tight around us. Thwaites kicked the door open and we tumbled into the dim interior. A young woman sat spinning by the light of a small lamp. Two small children sat close to her on the rushes and looked up frightened as we burst in.

Thwaites removed his cloak and shook it vigorously, showering water all over the floor. 'Good day, Mistress. Seats for me and my friends and set our clothes by the fire to dry.'

Wordlessly, the woman vacated her stool and indicated a bench close to the wall. She took our sodden garments and busied herself arranging them on hooks by the hearth. The infants retreated to a corner where they sat huddled together, staring at us with wide eyes.

'When you've done that, fetch us some ale.' Thwaites lowered himself on to the stool and stretched his legs before him. 'Dear God, what weather!'

We gazed out through the still open doorway into what appeared to be an opaque wall of water. I turned to watch the woman impassively obeying her instructions. It brought back memories. One was very recent: my arrival, well-soaked, at Lizzie's house and the cheerful willingness with which she made me comfortable. The other – a painful childhood recollection but just as salutary – was of a sound thrashing I had received from my father when he caught me insolently giving orders to one of our servants.

'What do you think, Thomas?' I was aware that James was speaking.

'Sorry, I was daydreaming.'

'Edward is offering us his hospitality.'

'We're not far from my house. You must spend the night there,' Thwaites said.

'That's good of you, Edward,' I replied, 'but I must get home today.'

'What! Through this? You must do no such thing. I won't hear of it. If you try to travel on, you won't reach home by nightfall and like as not you'll be stopped by another savage tempest and lucky to find even a hovel like this for shelter. No, when this rain eases you'll come to Chilham. We'll see you well supped and rested and set you back on the road tomorrow as soon as the weather is fit for Christians.'

'I'm concerned for my people at Hemmings,' I protested. 'I ought—'

'If they've any wits, your people at Hemmings will be well bolted in,' Thwaites persisted. 'They won't need you to show them how to keep the weather out.'

James said, 'He's right, Thomas. We'd be churls to reject Edward's offer. I've certainly no stomach for riding on through this.'

I could see the sense of what they were saying and, despite my anxieties, I accepted Thwaites's hospitality. An hour or so later we made the short journey to his house at Chilham, where he was as good as his word. I certainly felt refreshed by the time our little party was back on the road soon after dawn on Sunday morning. Still our progress was slow. The storm had left showery weather in its wake, as well as roads that were deeply mired. Twice we had to stop while workmen cleared trees that had fallen across the highway and near Allington a swollen river had taken away the bridge, forcing us to ride downstream until we found a fording place. Noon was passed before I bade goodbye to James and headed along the wooded road to Hemmings.

My man and I had not gone another mile before we saw a rider coming rapidly towards us. Seeing us, he reined in and I recognised Andrew, one of my stable hands. He was in great distress.

'Master Treviot, is that you? Oh, praise the Lord! I've been sent to look for you. I thought not to find you so soon. You must come! You must come! Something terrible!'

Chapter 7

At Hemmings everything was in a state of shocked confusion. Women were crying. Men were either sullenly silent or noisily blaming each other. Only out of Walt did I manage to obtain a coherent account of what had happened. Standing in the doorway of the long barn, he gave me his report.

'It was soon after cock crow, Master; not fully light. It was time to change the guards. We assembled here in the yard. I went with Andrew to the south gate. I was taking over there and he was supposed to be patrolling Long Wood. When we came to the cottage where Adie and the children were, I stopped to check with John Thatcher, the man I had set to do the night watch. I found him on the floor lying in a pool of blood.'

'God in heaven! Was he . . . '

'Dead? No, Master, praise be, but he'd taken a bad blow to

the head. We've got him abed now and the physician from Ightham has been in to bandage him up.'

'And Adie and the children?'

'Gone, Master – all save the baby, who was crying as though he would burst open. This was fixed to the door.' He handed me a scrap of paper. Its scrawled message was brief: 'THE GIRL AND THE BEARNS FOR THE PAINTER LONDON BRIDGE THREE DAYS'.

The words were like a blow to the stomach. 'Curse me for an idiot! This is Black Harry's work. I should have been here. How did the rogues get past our guards?'

"Twas cleverly done, Master. Devil knows how they got into the grounds. What I think is that they had a good look round under cover of darkness. When they saw John guarding the cottage they must have realised that was where our visitors were staying. The doctor said John hadn't lost much blood, so he couldn't have been lying there long before we found him – perhaps half an hour. Long enough to bind and gag young Adie and the children or terrify them into silence then leave the same way as they came. We found evidence that horses had been tethered in a thicket close to the east gate. I sent out search parties along all the roads leading from here ... but ... nothing.'

'They would have gone cross country. A group of horsemen carrying children would have been too conspicuous riding through villages and hamlets.'

'We have had one report. Some woodmen clearing storm damage on the Tonbridge road near Mereworth saw them travelling along forest tracks.'

'Going east then.'

'Yes.'

'I wonder ...'

'Master?'

'Where are they heading for? They'll have to hide somewhere, and soon. They must know where to go; where to find someone who will shelter them. Who is it?'

'Impossible to say, Master. We could search the country for weeks and never find them.'

'You're right, of course. Oh, how stupid, stupid, stupid I've been! This was the one thing I wanted to prevent happening.'

'So what's to be done, Master?' Walt looked to me for a decision, and several others stood nearby waiting to hear my answer.

What was I to say? I was too stunned by what had happened to give my people the lead they expected of me but I had to do something. With a confidence I certainly did not feel, I gave my orders. 'I'll write letters to the magistrates and all the gentry. Get together whatever men you can spare and have them ready to ride all over the shire. If we alert as many landowners as possible we should be able to discover where this gang is hiding.'

I went to my chamber and called for ink and paper. I had scrawled no more than three messages when the door burst open. Lizzie marched in with Ned Longbourne a few paces behind her.

'You cackbrained clotpole! What have you done?' She stood before me, hands on hips, dark eyes flashing. 'You get this old man to bring me here for "safety" and what do I find as soon as I arrive, my children taken by a gang of cut-throats. I'll never see them again.'

Ned stepped forward. 'It seems the baby is safe and in good hands,' he ventured diffidently.

'Close your maw, you old fool!' Lizzie raged. 'I'm thinking of my little Annie. She'll be frightened to death – if she isn't already dead.' She turned away and paced the room. 'There are three witless gulls here. You two haven't a brain to share between you and I've been lunatic enough to listen to you.'

I stood up and took a step away from the table. 'It's good that you're here, Lizzie . . .'

'Don't you soft-talk me!' She raised her hands, fingers outstretched like claws and lurched forward.

What she would have done if Ned had not stepped between us I know not. He took hold of her arms and guided her to a chair. 'You are right,' he said. 'We've all been foolish. But now we share the same grief and anger. What we must do is channel our feelings, pool our folly and see if we cannot, between us, find a few grains of wisdom. Thomas, can you tell us exactly what has happened? We have had only garbled accounts from the servants.'

He settled on a stool beside Lizzie while I outlined the sequence of events from my departure the previous day to my arrival home again.

Ned looked puzzled. 'Why do these desperate men think you know where Master Holbein is hiding?'

'It must be because they know I'm looking after his children. Their safety is my only concern. I'm just writing letters to all the main landlords,' I concluded. 'I mean to alert the whole shire. That way we should hear news of these villains.'

Lizzie glared at me across the table. 'More folly!' she shouted. 'What's the first thing they'll do when they know they're being tracked?'

Ned and I exchanged glances. We both knew Lizzie was right. To be sure of avoiding capture the murderers would not hesitate to get rid of their hostages.

'What else can we do?' I asked.

Lizzie answered promptly. 'Give them this man they're looking for.'

Ned shook his head. 'But we don't know where he is, Lizzie.'

'Then try harder.' Lizzie stood up, tight-lipped. 'I'm going to take my baby.'

For some moments after she had gone Ned and I stared at each other in helpless silence. 'So the children are doomed whether we act or whether we do nothing,' I said at last.

Ned nodded. 'We are in what the mystics call the dark forest of fear. Yet, what makes our case worse is that we are not the only ones lost in it.'

'Your meaning?'

'Well, for sure Black Harry (and it must be him we seek) lives in dread of the hangman. Adie and the children must be suffering from we know not what terrors. Poor Bart and this Master Johannes you tell me about are frightened into hiding.'

'Aye, and it stops not there.' I told Ned of my meetings with Cranmer and Marbeck. 'All these things must be connected. For example, I believe I may know why this raid was made today.'

'Tell me.'

I wandered to the window and gazed out across an overgrown patch of lawn where water had gathered in the depressions. 'I have been very careful not to mention the name "Black Harry" to anyone I do not trust completely, because I do not know who might be among his patrons. Yesterday afternoon I'm fairly sure someone overheard me speak the name.' In my mind I saw again the figure of Edward Thwaites emerging from the shadows in Moyle's hall. 'That same person is a sworn enemy of the archbishop. Later he pressed me – very hard – to stay the night with him.'

'To keep you away from Hemmings?'

'I think so.'

'Because he knew the children were here?'

'I think he must have overheard that, too.'

'Even if you are right about this fellow 'tis not information you can use. Lizzie's judgement is sound: we dare not let Black Harry and his associates think we're on his trail. You see what I mean about us all blundering around in the same darkness. Not only do we need to find our own way out; we have to avoid bumping into each other.'

'Mary and all the angels, what a mess! I suppose Lizzie is right. We must find Master Holbein. 'Tis the only way.'

'How, if he will not be found?'

'I know someone who is a party to his plans; I'm sure of it.' I told Ned about Jan van der Goes. 'I'll seek him out tomorrow.'

'And you think you can persuade this man to betray his friend and then persuade Master Holbein to surrender himself to the assassins?'

'Perhaps. Once he knows that his children are in mortal danger, he might do the right thing.'

'Is it the right thing? What of his importance to Cranmer ... and your own solemn oath? Heaven knows, I'm no lover of our archbishop but you are sworn before God to serve him. Will you so lightly put your immortal soul in danger?'

'Don't preach at me, monk!' I glared across the room. 'I need no one to draw the cords of conscience tighter than they already are. If you've nothing more useful to say, you'd better be away back to Southwark.'

The party that set out for London the next morning was in a sombre mood. Lizzie, as was her wont, rode astride and she had baby Jack well swaddled and strapped to her chest. I had chosen fresh horses for her and Ned. Several of those in my stable were tired, having been ridden hard along treacherous muddy tracks the previous day in search of the abducted children. We were accompanied by six of my strongest men. After the events of the weekend I was taking no chances for the safety of myself and my friends. I set as brisk a pace as the conditions would allow. Although the weather had brightened, the highway was still badly rutted and pitted. Some of the parishes along the way had taken their statutory responsibilities seriously. Groups of workers were out with spades, picks and carts of stone, filling holes and smoothing the surface. There was less wheeled traffic than usual, presumably because carters were wary of wasting long hours freeing their vehicles from the mud. That, at least, made travelling easier for horsemen. I had hopes that we might reach the City by day's end and could set about our quest for the painter early on the morrow. Keeping up a good speed while, at the same time, watching for hazards ahead, left us little time for conversation. We were only able to discuss our plans in spaced-out, disjointed episodes.

'I should come with you when you go to Bart,' I suggested to Lizzie.

'Why?'

''Tis my fault his daughter is in jeopardy.'

'Like as not he'll blame himself for starting all this trouble.'

'That's another reason for me to see him. I want him to know that I don't reproach him. He stumbled quite innocently into matters of high state. He couldn't have known of the dangers involved. Probably he still doesn't.'

'Well, I certainly don't.' Lizzie scowled. 'What's it all about, Thomas? If I'm on the point of losing my husband and my child, I'd rather like to know what cause they're being sacrificed for.'

'Lizzie, as long as there's blood in my body, I'll do all I can to save them – both.'

'We know that's not possible.'

'You mustn't think that.'

'Mustn't?' she snapped. 'I've been thinking of nothing else all night. If we save the children by giving this Black Harry you talk about what he wants, he'll remain at liberty and Bart will still be an outlaw wanted for murder. But if we track down the gang in order to clear Bart's name they'll kill their hostages. So, don't give me empty promises. Just explain what higher purpose this is all supposed to be serving.'

'Oh, Lizzie, I wish I could. I don't fully understand it myself. It's all about ...'

'Politics?'

'Yes – politics and religion.'

'Dear God, the games these kings and great men play, using us for their cards and counters.' Her angry bluster was an outlet for her anxiety, just as mine had been the previous day when I snapped at Ned.

We were coming into a small village. A little family group stood at the roadside – a mother and three young children, barefoot and ragged. They held out their hands to the passing travellers.

Lizzie found her purse and threw down some coins. 'Do you think they care about kings and popes and archbishops?'

'Probably no more than kings and popes and archbishops care about them,' I said.

'Then, in the name of all the saints in heaven – or wherever they are – why should we put everything at risk to keep one single nobleman or bishop in power or bring down

98

another nobleman or bishop? Can you honestly tell me that this wretched business matters – I mean, *really* matters?'

In simplified terms I tried to explain that Cranmer and his enemies could not agree about the kind of church life England should have, that each was passionately attached to his understanding of truth and that for them, and many others, it was a matter of life and death. I don't think I convinced her.

Sometime afterwards I brought my gelding alongside Ned's horse. We had scarcely spoken since the previous afternoon.

'I spoke rashly yesterday,' I said. 'Please put my foolish words down to worry.'

The old man smiled his usual calm smile. 'We read in the Book of Proverbs, "A man of discretion controls his anger; it is his glory to overlook wrongs". You were under great strain. You had to shout at someone. I'm glad it was me.'

'I wish I had your placid nature. You never lose your temper.'

He chuckled. 'Oh, don't you believe it. There are times when I swear more colourfully than a London drayman.'

'Who do you swear at?'

'Oh, God, usually.'

'Doesn't he mind?'

'I comfort myself with the thought that he's heard it all before. Now, what about our problem? Have you had time to lock away your fears and start thinking clearly?'

'There's not much to think really. The man we have to see is a close friend of Master Holbein by the name of Jan van der Goes. When we last met he said he did not know where the painter is hiding but I'm sure he was lying.'

'His friend is obviously in great danger. He would hardly reveal his whereabouts to a stranger. And what you're asking him to do now is much more serious.'

99

'Yes, to deliver his friend up to certain death. All I can do is tell van der Goes, or John of Antwerp as most people know him, that Holbein's children are in mortal danger. If he explains that to the artist, perhaps he will come out of hiding. It is asking much but I think few fathers would sacrifice their sons for a cause, however important. I know I wouldn't.'

Ned smiled grimly. 'It has been known,' he said. 'Have you given any thought to your commitment to the archbishop?'

'Yes, you were right to remind me of that obligation. If Holbein will trust me with the information he has gathered I will pass it on to Cranmer. With any luck Black Harry won't suspect anything.'

'That could be dangerous but I'm sure it is the right thing to do. Now, to more immediate matters. Where do you plan to stay while you are in London?'

'I'll go to Goldsmith's Row.'

'But the house is shut up and the servants gone.'

'I can manage for a couple of days.'

'More sense for you to stay with me. If you are to keep your wits about you, you will need good food and a well-turned bed.'

It was agreed that we would make the Southwark house our headquarters and I passed this on to Lizzie a little later.

'Could you, please, bring Bart to meet us there,' I urged.

She looked doubtful. 'He made me swear not to take anyone into my confidence, not even you.'

'Things have changed a lot since you made that promise. I need to speak with him. If he's been trying to identify the murderers, he may have discovered something useful.'

'I don't know. I don't see him often and when I do he tells me nothing. He says it's safer for me to remain ignorant.'

'Well, now it's time to pool our knowledge. Any scraps of information could prove helpful.'

When we parted company outside St Olave's Church in Southwark in the deepening dusk of that September day it was in the knowledge that the morrow would bring events that would change our lives and, whichever way things went, would probably result in death for someone.

Chapter 8

It was still dark on Tuesday when Ned roused me after a night of very heavy sleep.

'There's cheese and ale downstairs and two visitors,' he said.

I dressed quickly, refreshed myself with cold water and descended the narrow stair. In the room below, Lizzie was seated at the table with Ned. Between them, to my immense relief, was Bart. He jumped up as I entered.

'Master, I'm so sorry. Everything's going wrong and 'tis all my fault.'

I grasped his hand warmly. 'We'll have no more of that talk. I'm so pleased to see you safe.'

I looked at Bart closely. He was a sorry sight. There was little sign of the boisterous, carefree man I had known so long. His clothes were crumpled. His chin wore several days stubble and his red-rimmed eyes suggested that he had been crying.

'Safe? Aye. Would I were not. I'd give anything to have little Annie standing here instead of me. Oh, God in heaven, what have I done to put her in such danger. We will save her, won't we, Master?' He drew a hand across his cheek where fresh tears were flowing. 'When Lizzie told me . . . '

'Come and sit again, Poppet.' Lizzie put an arm round him and led him back to his stool. 'Such talk doesn't help. We've plans to make.'

'She's right, Bart,' I said. 'We have to find Master Johannes and persuade him to come with us to London Bridge tomorrow. We don't have a moment to waste on blaming ourselves or bewailing the past. Has Lizzie explained everything to you?'

'Yes,' he muttered. 'It seems such a complicated mess.'

'Yes, it is rather. That's why we need cool heads to untangle everything.' I spoke with a confidence well above anything I felt. Trying to boost Bart's morale gave the impression that I was optimistic of the outcome of the day's activities. 'Now, first, have you anything to tell us? What have you been doing this last three weeks? Have you discovered anything about the murderers?'

'It's been difficult. With the magistrate's men looking for me and, probably, the gang as well, I haven't been able to move about much. The watchmen are on the lookout for a one-armed man. Difficult to disguise this.' He patted his empty sleeve. 'I go about mostly at night. I've visited just about all the more disreputable ale houses, especially the ones down by the river. Can't ask too many questions. Folk are very quick to get suspicious.'

'So, have you found out anything?' I asked.

'Well, 'tis the Black Harry gang that butchered that poor lad, as you've already worked out. There's many a tale told about them. They're ... well, if half the things folk say are true London's never seen anything like them. They're not just violent; they're ... evil.'

'What does that mean; that they love violence for its own sake? They don't kill and maim in order to get power or vengeance or money?'

'Oh, they like money well enough but that's not what drives them.'

'I can tell you what motivates them,' Ned said. 'It is hatred – and hatred of the worst kind.'

'What's that?' Lizzie asked.

'Fanatical hatred, spiritual hatred, if you like. *Satanic* hatred.'

'You've heard the stories about Black Harry, then?' Bart asked. 'Children murdered in front of their mothers; men slowly roasted ...'

'No. I don't need to.' Ned scowled. 'I know enough of his career to recognise a phenomenon any student of theology is familiar with – evil of the most concentrated kind ... the very essence of evil. You see my alembic over there by the fire. If I could nicely measure out portions of the seven great sins, put them in my apparatus and set it to the fire, what would be distilled would be unadulterated, terrifying, irredeemable evil. All the great saints have encountered it in their conflict with the forces of hell. I, thank God, have only met it once. Then, I saw the devil looking out at me through human eyes and knew the soul within lived for nothing but dissolution, decay and destruction of every good, merciful, generous, holy impulse. The creature before me was possessed of a blind, obsessive malice which was oblivious not only to the good of others but even to its own good. I fear that is what we are facing here.'

We listened motionless, scarcely breathing, to Ned's impassioned, yet calm and measured words.

Bart said, 'Well, that certainly explains things I have heard about Black Harry. Folk say he doesn't just enjoy cruelty; he lives for it; feeds on it.'

'Yes,' Ned agreed. 'And that means we must be absolutely on our guard in our dealings with him. We must not make the mistake of thinking that we can reason with him, trust him, believe anything he says. We must be on the watch for any deceit, any lies, any treachery that he may fancy serves his purpose.'

Lizzie stared aghast. 'Do you mean that he might promise to hand over the children, then kill them anyway?'

'I think that's exactly the kind of thing he might do unless we set up the exchange in such a way that prevents any such trickery.'

I turned to Bart. 'Have you managed to find out who this monster is working for.'

'Surely,' Lizzie protested, 'no decent man would pay such a creature to do his bidding.'

Ned said, 'As I've already explained to Master Thomas, Black Harry worked for the Inquisition in Spain and carried out some of their worst atrocities.'

'But that sort of thing doesn't happen in England,' she said.

'Three men were sent to the stake in Windsor a mere few weeks ago because they believed the wrong things,' I said.

'That's not the same thing at all,' Ned observed. 'I deplore the burning of heretics. It's bad theology and it doesn't work. It only creates martyrs. But, at least when the Church hands unrepentant, misguided people over to the magistrates for

105

execution there has been an open process of law. What powerful patrons use Black Harry for is work done in secret: removing obstacles from their path, silencing noisy opponents, disposing of critics.'

'Yes,' Bart agreed, 'that's exactly what people say Black Harry does. Dr Banfry, the vicar at St Thomas-in-the-East, was fished out of the Thames just after Easter. He had preached mightily against religious images and attracted large crowds. The bishop couldn't drag him into his court because he had preached before the king and his majesty liked his style.'

'So was it the bishop behind the Aldgate murder?' I asked.

'Possibly. There are various rumours but no one really knows. There's one person I've heard talk of, but I only remember him because of his name – Dr London.'

'London,' I exclaimed. 'Yes, I've heard of him. He was behind the Windsor burnings, though he's only a tool in the hands of more powerful men. But all this high politics is not to the point. We're here to save Adie and the children from someone who is a complete stranger to morality and human decency. Bart, is there anything else you know about Black Harry; any information that will arm us against him?'

Bart's brow wrinkled in concentration. 'Folk say his gang is small – men who've been with him a long time. He doesn't trust newcomers. There's scapegraces as would like to join him, but he'll have none of them. Apart from that I don't know ... Oh, yes, one other thing: his base is somewhere in Essex.'

'Then that's where they'll have taken their hostages,' I said. 'Not that it helps us much. We don't have time to mount a search. All we can do is make sure we get Holbein to the bridge tomorrow. He is our bargaining counter – with him we can force Black Harry to do a deal. Ned, can you come with me to see van der Goes? We'll escort Lizzie safe home on the way. Bart, you had better stay here now that it's light. Keep out of sight and don't answer the door if any of Ned's customers come calling. So' – I stood up – 'the time for talk is over. Let us go – and pray God our mission is successful.'

Half an hour later Ned and I were riding along Bride Lane. When we reined in outside the goldsmith's house we received the first of the shocks that day was to bring. There was a bundle of straw hanging from the door jamb.

'Plague!' Ned exclaimed. He fumbled a medallion from his scrip, kissed it and held it out to me. 'The Fourteen Holy Helpers,' he said. 'Beg their protection.'

I followed his example but was more interested in a written note pinned to the door frame. Jumping down, I read the brief message. 'No entry. One pestilence victim within. Master van der Goes continues his business at his house in Chiswick.'

'Curse this delay!' I muttered. 'We'll have to go upriver. It will be quicker than riding against the incoming traffic. Ned, find us a boatman while I lodge the horses.'

I led our two mounts to the Red Hand inn and left them with the ostler. By the time I returned Ned was seated in the stern of a wherry moored at Bridewell Dock. As I stepped down into the boat, he said, 'The waterman says he only does cross-river ferrying. I've had to pay him extra to go to Chiswick.'

'These fellows know their business,' I muttered. 'They can spot a customer in a hurry and know how to turn it to their advantage.'

It was a long haul against the current for our waterman and I fretted as Westminster, the noblemen's waterside mansions and then the open fields slid slowly past. After what seemed hours we disembarked at the landing stage and walked into Chiswick village. We asked the first passers-by for directions and soon found ourselves before a recently built house set in its own garden.

'Your van der Goes must be a wealthy man,' Ned observed.

'And grown so by stealing business from honest English tradesmen,' I growled.

When we were shown into his presence, John of Antwerp was his usual over-boisterously hospitable self. He settled us in a pair of elaborate, padded armed chairs and offered refreshments. Dry though my mouth was, I declined.

'No time for pleasantries,' I insisted. 'We're here on very urgent business. Where is Master Holbein? We must see him.'

Our host shrugged. 'You still haven't found him, then? I'm sorry ...'

I raised my voice. 'Please don't keep up this pretence of ignorance. I know your friend is in trouble and forced to hide from his enemies. I am not an enemy but I must see him. Four lives depend on it.'

'Four lives?' Van der Goes raised his eyebrows in seemingly genuine surprise.

'Yes, including his two sons.'

That shook him. 'Carl and Henry? What has happened to them?'

'They've been captured by the men who are looking for Holbein. They're being held to ransom.'

'Holy Mother of God!' He crossed himself. 'That is terrible. Johannes will be appalled to hear it.'

At last I had driven a wedge into the Fleming's secrecy and loyalty. I hammered it home. 'The children's salvation lies in his hands.'

'His life for theirs?'

'There is no other way.'

He sat in silence for several moments, stroking his bushy beard. Then he said, 'You place me in a difficult position. Some days ago Johannes came to me in great distress. He had been attacked on his way home from the royal court by men intent on murder. He was lucky to escape. He asked me to hide him. Of course, I agreed. That is what friends do. He didn't tell me who his enemies were and I didn't ask. All he would say was that he had an important message for someone of high rank and that he didn't know how he was going to deliver it with assassins on his trail. I offered to take it for him but he wouldn't hear of it. He said it was too dangerous and that I would be safer knowing nothing about the business.'

'If our friend gives himself up, I will personally see that his message is delivered. You have my solemn word,' I said.

'After his death,' van der Goes muttered grimly, 'you can decide whether or not to keep your promise.'

'I can't force him to give himself up,' I said. 'But I must give him the choice. The children deserve that – and so does he.'

Our host shook his head. 'He loves those boys dearly. He has a family in Basel but they mean little to him compared with his English sons. They are excellent lads.'

'Indeed they are. I would be proud to be their father and, if I were, I think I would do anything for them.'

'Anything? 'Tis a word easy to say.'

There was another agonised silence. Eventually he looked straight at me. 'Master Treviot, what would you do in my position? If I came to you with the story you have just told me, would you lightly break your oath to an old and very dear friend and deliver that friend into the hands of violent enemies?'

'I certainly would do no such thing *lightly*. I would want to

satisfy myself that you were utterly trustworthy and not someone in league with my friend's enemies. I would hope that I
could be confident of the honesty of . . . a brother goldsmith.'
The last words almost stuck in my throat.

Van der Goes stood up. 'Very well, this is what I will do. I
will take you close to where Johannes is and I will speak with
him in private. If he agrees to see you, I will bring you to him.
So, let us go. We must travel back downriver. I have my own
little barge.'

He called for his boatman and we returned to the landing
stage. On our arrival I had noticed a sleek boat with a cabin
in the stern fronted by a brightly coloured curtain. Now, as we
boarded and settled on the cushions within, I could not help
reflecting on the vulgar showiness of alien tradesmen who
loved to flaunt their success before their English neighbours.

The downstream journey in a superior craft took half the
time of our trip to Chiswick. As we approached the stage from
which we had departed, the chime of Paul's clock signalled
noon.

The Fleming stepped nimbly ashore. 'I will return as soon
as I have spoken with Johannes. My boatman will pull out
into mid-stream, just in case you feel tempted to follow.' He
disappeared down an alleyway between the warehouses.

'This is scarcely necessary.' Ned fretted as we sat helpless in
the middle of the river.

'No, clearly his trust of a "brother goldsmith" does not run
very deep.'

In fact, we had little time to wait. After a few minutes van
der Goes reappeared on the quayside and waved. When we
stepped from the boat, he looked at us grim-faced. 'Bad news,
I'm afraid. Come with me.'

He led us along the narrow walkways between the high-walled, riverside storehouses. In a dark corner he unlocked a door. Inside, he preceded us up a narrow staircase. On the first floor he unfastened another door. The room we entered was lit by barred windows high in the walls. An external door between them was obviously intended for loading goods on to the quay. The storage space, however, was not occupied with any commercial merchandise. In one corner there was a truckle bed the coverings of which were piled upon it in a heap. A stool and table made up the rest of the furnishings, save for an easel, on which stood an unfinished painting. There was evidence of a partially consumed meal on the table. Empty canvases, painted canvases, sheets of paper with sketches on, rags, brushes and bowls containing coloured pigments were scattered everywhere.

My eyes probed every corner of the space. 'Where is he, then?' I demanded.

For of Johannes Holbein there was no trace.

Chapter 9

'I don't understand,' the Fleming said. 'We agreed that he would not leave here until we knew it was safe for him to do so. He and I have the only keys. I come every couple of days to bring food and remove night soil. It is not a comfortable refuge, as you can see, but Johannes felt safe here and had no desire to move. As long as he could paint and draw, he was reasonably content.'

I stared at him and he read my thoughts. 'You think I warned him of your coming and he has run away. I give you my word that this is exactly how I found the room.'

Ned was examining the doors. 'No one has forced an entry here,' he said. 'Master Holbein must have let himself out.'

Van der Goes shook his head. 'I'm sure he wouldn't have gone anywhere without letting me know.'

'Have you looked for a note?' I asked.

'Yes. There's nothing.'

'When did you last see him?'

'Yesterday. It's been difficult since one of my people caught the plague and I had to move everyone out of my house along the street, but I have kept up my visits.'

Ned sank wearily on to the stool. 'What do we do now?'

'We wait,' I said. 'If this really is his only refuge he must come back to sleep.'

'And if he doesn't?'

'Then all is lost.'

The painter did not return. We waited until late in the evening, our depression deepening with every passing minute. At last we abandoned our vigil and returned to Southwark.

Bart went into a frenzy of despair when we reported the day's events. 'Then Annie and the others are as good as dead!' he wailed.

Ned was busy preparing a kettle of pottage. 'They certainly are if we give way to the evil humours,' he said, setting bowls on the table.

Bart and I said we were not hungry but the old man glared at us. 'Good wits need feeding and if ever we needed good wits it is now. So eat,' he ordered.

'What can we do?' Bart asked. 'Black Harry will not release his hostages until he has his hands on Master Holbein.'

'We'll return to Bridewell Dock at first light,' Ned said, 'and just pray that the artist has come back.'

'Yes,' I agreed, 'but we must have a reserve plan in case he has not.'

'How is the exchange supposed to be made?' Ned asked.

'Black Harry's note didn't say. We were just ordered to be

at the bridge with Master Holbein. No time was mentioned, nor any other details.'

'He's sure to have men watching. He'll know the moment Holbein appears.'

'That's true, Ned. He's met Holbein. He knows what he looks like. He'll have to wait until the painter comes.'

'That's right,' I said. 'Holbein is the only one he'll recognise. He doesn't know us, just as we don't know him.'

'I know him,' Bart said, 'and his copesmates. I'd recognise that evil crew anywhere.'

'Of course. For once we have a slight advantage. If Bart comes with us – suitably disguised, of course – we'll be able to spot Black Harry and his men before they have any idea who we are.'

'Just how does that help,' Bart asked.

'I don't know. Let's think it through. The gang will come to the bridge with their hostages.'

'Perhaps. They may well play us false.' Ned emphasised the point with his spoon.

'True, but the bridge will be crowded. If the villains tried to grab Holbein and make off with him with us in pursuit, they'd stand little chance of getting away. I think they'll have to produce at least one of their hostages to convince us the deal is on.'

'How will they get Adie and the children there?' Bart asked.

Ned and I replied in unison. 'Wagon.'

'Of course,' Bart said. 'There'll be plenty of covered vehicles going to and fro.' His doubtful frown returned. 'But I still don't see . . .'

'Nor do I – yet. We've got to take it step by step. So Black Harry comes to the bridge. He walks around looking for Holbein. He'll have to have his wagon with the captives at one end or the other. There's too much traffic for him to leave it standing in the middle of the roadway.'

'And that would attract attention,' Ned commented.

'Now, while he's looking for us, we're looking for him. As soon as Bart recognises him I introduce myself and ask him where Adie and the children are.'

'And he'll say, "Where's the artist?".'

'That's right, Bart. Then I say we have him in a nearby house.'

Ned frowned. 'Do you mean here?'

I nodded.

'No,' the old man said, 'he is far too wary for that. He'll suspect a trap. He won't go anywhere without his men.'

'And we'll have ours. I can bring half a dozen of my people here to be waiting for them.'

Ned still looked doubtful. 'If I were in his position, I'd want the exchange done out in the open where there was no risk. 'Tis hard to trick a trickster.'

'That's a valid point,' I agreed. 'Let's see if we can think of a way round it.'

After several moments of silence it was Bart who said, 'Why don't we have a wagon, too? We say, "The artist's inside. You bring your vehicle next to ours and we can make the swap right here in the open street." Only, our wagon's full of our men.'

Like many of Bart's ideas, this one revealed more enthusiasm than wisdom but, however much we discussed its detail, we could not arrive at anything better.

''Tis a risky plan – for all concerned,' Ned said. 'I can think of a dozen things that could go wrong. We could end up with a bloody brawl and nothing gained. Let us pray that we find Master Holbein and don't have to put it to the test.'

*

The following morning I was at Bridewell Dock before dawn. A river mist swirled around me as I let myself into the warehouse and, holding a lantern, climbed the stairs. Holbein's lair was exactly as we had left it. I sat shivering in the large room as light slowly filled it. Sometimes I paced to and fro to warm myself. I strained my ears listening for a footfall on the stairs. With mounting impatience I waited until nine o'clock. I waited in vain. The former occupant did not return. The conclusion seemed inescapable that he had decided to disappear, telling no one, including the friend who had succoured him. I could not help feeling, as I locked the door behind me, that Holbein now fully deserved whatever fate befell him. He had left me without a bargaining counter. I would have to carry through what would now be an extremely precarious bluff. There was a heavy weight of apprehension in my stomach. As Ned had rightly observed, it was hard to trick a trickster. I rode to Goldsmith's Row and discussed the proposed events of the day with my servants. There was only one covered wagon fit for the brief journey we had planned. It was old and much repaired, which was why we had not taken it to Hemmings. Walt harnessed one of the horses to it and put in place a much-patched canvas cover. At least, we agreed, its rickety appearance would attract no attention among the hundreds of vehicles passing to and fro across the bridge. We managed to pack six men inside, well-armed with a variety of clubs and cudgels. Then Walt climbed on to the box and cracked his whip.

I rode on ahead and joined my friends at Ned's house. Bart was unrecognisable. He was wearing an old grey habit, a relic saved from Ned's monastic days. This made him indistinguishable from the scores of poor people who wandered the streets clad in items salvaged from the abbeys by dealers in old clothes. Wisps of straggled hair had been applied to his chin, culled, I soon realised, from Ned's now-shortened beard. We set out on foot. Ned lingered by the drawbridge, occasionally passing the time of day with friends and customers, while Bart and I threaded our way through the slow-moving pedestrians, horses and vehicles crammed into the twelve-foot-wide carriageway.

It was on our third crossing that Bart said suddenly, 'There he is!'

We were close to the centre of the bridge, by the Becket Chapel. It was easy to see why our quarry might have chosen his professional name. He was tall with thick black hair. His doublet and hose were of the same colour under a short grey cloak. He strode purposefully through the crowd looking to right and left. He was followed, a few paces behind, by one of his henchmen, a burly fellow with whom I certainly would not wish to pick a fight. Bart and I followed at a slight distance.

Black Harry emerged from the shadow of the great south gate, slowed and surveyed the roadway that opened out beside St Olave's. Well, I thought, this is it. I took a deep breath and came up behind the ruthless murderer.

'Master Walden. I believe we have some business to conclude.'

He turned to face me. His associate stepped forward to place himself between us, drawing a poniard from his belt as he did so. He was not quick enough for Bart, whose hand clamped over his wrist. The blade dropped to the pavings and Bart kicked it well away. The man spun round, fist raised.

'Please explain to your friend that we are here for business and not a fight,' I said, trying to project a calm I certainly did not feel.

Black Harry motioned to the other man to step back. He glared at me with contempt. 'You have what I want?'

'Indeed.'

He looked around. 'Where?'

'Within a few paces of where we stand.'

He looked at the people passing to and fro. His gaze passed over the wagon but did not rest there. 'I don't see him. You're lying!' He beckoned to his man. 'Go and look!'

I felt a sudden twinge in my stomach. If the villain looked inside the wagon all would be lost. I thought quickly. 'I don't think your half-witted friend is likely to recognise Holbein beneath the disguise we have provided for him.'

Black Harry looked unsure of himself, probably expecting a trap. I pressed home my slim advantage.

'You have some items to deliver to me. Where are they?'

'At the other end of the bridge.'

'Now, suppose I choose to say I think you're lying. Then we'll both be wasting our time.'

Behind his sneer I could sense his mind working, calculating rapidly. 'Come with me and I'll show you.'

'Oh, I think not, Master Walden.' I laughed and hoped it did not sound nervous. 'This will be a satisfactory place for our transaction.'

'Don't try to dictate terms to me. If I give the signal, the bearns die.'

Now who was bluffing who? My mouth was dry as I tried to calculate the possibilities. If Black Harry had brought the children, I had to make him convey them to my side of the bridge. If he had not brought the children, he would try to force me to show my hand. In that case the only thing I could do would be to get him close enough to the wagon for my men to grab him. We stared at each other, like wrestlers manoeuvring for a hold. I continued the verbal bout, my face, I hoped, not revealing my uncertainty.

'Master Walden, I'm a simple merchant. Unlike you, I do not conduct my business by shouts and threats. I work on the basis of mutual trust. I am here to conclude a deal. If you've decided not to trust me, we have nothing further to discuss.' My gaze flickered to Bart. He shook his head slightly, obviously horrified at the way I was speaking to this frightening man. But suddenly to me he was not frightening. I had been racked by so many emotions in the last few days that something inside me was shouting, 'Stop'. It was as though I had broken through a fear barrier and my mind was numb. For the moment, at least, I could stand up to this monster whom Ned likened to absolute evil personified. 'If you have lost interest in the painter,' I told him, 'say so and we can both get on with our lives.' I paused before adding, 'Although I imagine your paymasters will not be happy about that.'

There was a shimmer of uncertainty in the man's eyes. I guessed he was not used to people standing up to him and he was, temporarily, disconcerted. 'Have you lost interest in the children?' he countered.

I shrugged. 'They're not my children. Frankly, they're a nuisance. I'm sure you've discovered that. Why don't you just send your minion here to fetch them. Then they'll be off your hands.'

'Don't you tell me what to do,' he snarled. Then, he turned abruptly. 'Wait here!' he shouted and walked back across the bridge with his subordinate.

I moved forward a few paces until I could see Ned watching from beside the gate. I nodded and he followed the two men at a discreet distance. Only as I turned back to speak to Bart did my limbs begin to shake.

'What now?' Bart asked, as we crossed the street to where the wagon was standing.

'As soon as Ned reports that the gang are on their way with the hostages, we'll prepare our reception. You and Ned must concentrate on freeing Adie and the children. Get them to Ned's house. The rest of us will try to keep Master Walden and his friends occupied.'

'They'll put up a vicious fight.'

'I'm sure of it, but they won't want to attract a crowd. Black Harry can't afford to have any of his men arrested. He's only useful to his paymasters as long as he keeps clear of the law.'

Walt jumped down from the box. 'We're all ready, Master. Looking forward to a brawl. There's a score to be settled.'

'Be careful. They won't fight clean. Any sign of unsheathed steel, and you back off. Is that clear? I don't want anyone wounded or ... worse. The plan is for you and the others to get yourselves between the gang and the hostages. That should enable Bart and Ned to get Adie and the children away.' Put like that it sounded simple. I knew it would not be.

It was several minutes before Ned reappeared, puffing and wiping his brow. He sat thankfully on a stone mounting block. 'We were right,' he said. 'They have a wagon ... quite large. I couldn't see inside but I'd say it was big enough for Adie and the children and probably three men to guard them.'

'Good, that means the odds are on our side.'

Ned shook his head. 'The bad news is they're not unloading their cargo. They're bringing the wagon over the bridge.'

'Devil take the double-dealing rogue! He doesn't intend us to see whether he's brought the hostages or not! For all we know his wagon may be full of armed men come to take Holbein by force. What's to do now?'

'Nothing for the moment,' Ned replied. 'The traffic is build-ing up. It will take quite a time for them to get through.'

Waiting was the worst of it. We watched the cavalcade of people, vehicles and driven beasts coming away from the City, our nerves growing more jangled every minute. Ned took up his position again by the gate, peering within.

At last he walked briskly back. 'They're coming. Black Harry's a-horseback, riding ahead and trying to clear the way.'

'Right. You and Bart stand over there by the wall and wait for your chance.'

Moments later the gang leader clattered down the slope from the bridge. He rode a magnificent horse. It was, pre-dictably, as black as night. He reined in where Walt and I stood in the middle of the roadway. 'Here are your whelps.' He pointed to the wagon, which followed, yards behind. 'Where's my German dauber?'

I indicated our vehicle. 'Pull up your wagon behind ours,' I said. 'But first show us the children and the girl.'

Black Harry scowled down at us. For a moment his right hand drifted towards the pistol in his saddle-holster and it seemed he would defy us. Then Walt strolled over, brandish-ing his stout stave and the rogue thought better of it. He yanked at his rein and went across to the wagon, which was coming to a halt at the roadside. He said something to the men inside. The rear curtain parted and a bundle was handed out. It was Annie. He took the girl, held her on his pommel and walked his horse back. 'Satisfied?' he asked.

I had no chance to reply.

Several things happened at once. Bart cried out, 'Annie!' and rushed forward. Black Harry drew his gun and cocked it. Walt struck at him with his staff. The weapon fell to the ground and discharged with an alarming bang. My men spilled out of the wagon and ran to surround the other vehicle. Before they could reach it, its rear curtain was pulled aside and five of Black Harry's men tumbled out. With shouts and screams, the two forces fell upon each other. They filled the roadway. Other travellers ran panicking in all directions. In the midst of the mayhem I rushed to the gang's wagon. Ned was there before me, peering inside. He turned and shook his head. 'They're not here,' he called.

I ran back across the road. The horse was skittering around as Black Harry tried to hold it steady, while drawing his sword, hampered by his burden.

'Where are the woman and the boys?' I shouted.

'You think to make a fool of me! I will send you the boys – in pieces! The woman? Well, my friends and I can find a use for her.' He threw Annie down roughly, called out an order to his men and spurred away down Long Southwark. His followers scrambled back into their wagon and set off in the same direction at a swaying trot.

Bart grabbed up his screaming daughter and hugged her to him. Calm spread back across the street. The whole incident had lasted no more than a few seconds. What had it achieved? For the life of me I knew not.

Chapter 10

'How is she? I asked, as Lizzie descended the stair.

'Asleep at last. She was clinging desperately but I think I've managed to calm her. I just hope she'll be able to forget.'

'I'm told children are amazingly resilient,' Ned suggested, 'but I can't back that with personal experience.'

Lizzie, Bart and I were supping at Ned's house that evening. I had sent the others back to Goldsmith's Row and despatched a message to Bart's wife, who had hurried to join us.

We sat around the table in a state of anti-climax.

'At least she's safe,' I said.

'Do I sense a "but" coming?' Ned asked.

'I'm just angry with myself for bungling everything. Of course it was all worth it to get Annie back but, apart from that, we're no further forward. Bart's still wanted for murder. The only witness who can give evidence against Black Harry has disappeared without trace. Worse than that, we've probably forced the gang to butcher their captives.'

'Do you really believe all that talk of sending the children back in pieces?' Bart asked.

Ned stared down at his trencher. 'I fear Black Harry is not the sort of man to make idle threats.'

'The boys are such lively mites.' Lizzie sighed. 'I keep thinking that our Jack will be like them in a few years. And Adie is so nice. To imagine what those brutes . . .'

We ate in silence for a long time.

It was Lizzie who broke it – in her usual emphatic manner. She threw down her spoon and declared, 'We must do something.'

'What do you suggest?'

'You're supposed to be the one with brains. Come up with a plan. You won't be able to marry Adie if you don't rescue her.'

'A plague on your confounded matchmaking, Lizzie. This is nothing to do with marriage. I've extended my protection to Adie and her charges. I didn't want to and sometimes I wish I'd never . . .'

'Oh well, in that case, you'd better leave her to her fate.' Lizzie pouted – an expression I always found annoying.

'I didn't say I don't care what happens to Adie and the boys. I just don't see what else we can do for them.'

'Perhaps we could start,' Ned said, 'by thinking about what we know of Black Harry's movements. Where will he be headed for right now?'

'He has powerful supporters in Kent,' I said.

'And a base in Essex,' Bart added.

'That would enable him to travel to and fro across the estuary quite easily. You don't know whereabouts in Essex his place is, I suppose?'

Bart frowned in concentration. 'Well, the information came from a pedlar who travels all over the eastern parts. He said he knew things about Black Harry as could get him killed if ever he told them. So I bought him some more ale, and then some more again, and eventually he blurted out about a gang that has a big house on the Essex marshes. He said it was near somewhere called . . .' He closed his eyes and hammered his fist against his brow. 'No, it's no use; I can't remember. It was some place I'd never heard of, so I didn't take a deal of notice.'

'Pity. The marshes cover a wide area – though I would guess the gang's boss can't be all that far from the crossing at Tilbury.'

'Are you thinking we should go there and look for him?' Ned asked. 'We could ask in the ale houses. Someone must know something.'

I thought hard. 'No, it would be too big an area for us to search and he'd know we were there before ever we found him. I suppose it might be worth . . . We've probably got enough . . . Oh, I don't know! I must think.'

What I was struggling to decide was whether to alert Archbishop Cranmer. I had promised to send him any information that might help him against his enemies and there was no doubt that he would relish the opportunity to interrogate Black Harry and his associates. Well, now I could give him some indication of where to find the gang's hideout. But would it really be of any use? Suppose Bart's drunken pedlar was simply hawking tall stories for free ale. Or what if Black Harry was not to be found in his lair? If Cranmer's men went

125

tramping around the Essex marshes that would send the hell brood deeper into hiding.

'If there's the slightest chance of saving Adie and the boys you know you must take it.' Lizzie's words broke through my doubts.

'Any search that stood a chance of success would demand many more men than we have at our disposal. Unless we can narrow down . . .'

'Flitching! No, that's not it!' Bart had been pacing to and fro but now suddenly stopped. 'Flitcham? No.'

'Don't cudgel your brains, Bart,' Ned said. 'I find sleep to be the best thing for a cloudy memory. You'll probably find in the morning . . .'

'Fletcham!' Bart shouted. 'Yes, Fletcham, Fletcham. I'm sure that's it!'

Lizzie went over and threw her arms round him. 'There's a clever boy.' She turned to me. 'Well, then?'

I sighed. 'Yes, if Bart's right I could take a few men and spy out the land. If the girl and her charges are there we'll find them.'

Ned said, 'Then God speed. I pray you'll not be too late.'

The sun's rays had just touched the top of Paul's spire when I rode briskly through the cathedral yard and turned into West Cheap. I jumped from the saddle in my own stable yard and called loudly for Walt. He emerged from the outbuildings, rubbing the sleep from his eyes.

'I want everyone horsed and ready to leave in ten minutes,' I ordered.

When we were assembled I led the way through the waking City down to the waterfront below the bridge. At Custom House Wharf half a dozen coastal vessels were unloading or taking on cargo. After a few enquiries I found one captain who was ready to consider a charter. There then followed the necessary haggling before he allowed us to go aboard with the horses. By the time sails were hoisted and we were moving slowly past the Tower the river ahead of us was a broad pathway of shimmering gold.

With nothing to do but wait upon the favours of wind and tide I had plenty of time to explain my plan to the others. 'Dick, we're going to drop you off at Gravesend. You're to ride as hard as you can to the archbishop's house at Ford. Give him this letter. If you have any difficulty gaining access to his grace, show this ring.' I handed him Cranmer's jewel. 'As soon as you've done that you are to ride on and deliver this other letter to Sir Thomas Moyle. His grace or his sec- retary will give you directions. The letters are appeals for mounted men to be sent to assist us. The rest of us will be taken across the river to Tilbury. From there we'll try to locate Black Harry's lair.'

'Do you know whether we'll find our black friend at home?' Walt asked.

'No, but I hope we may have got ahead of him. The last time we saw him he was probably heading for Kent Street. He has friends in the county with whom he can rest so I doubt whether he would be in a hurry to get to the ferry. We may be able to check on that when we reach Gravesend. To answer your question more fully, Walt, I don't know what we'll find when we get to Fletcham. I suspect all we'll be able to do is spy out the land and wait for reinforcements. For now I suggest we all find somewhere to rest. Life may get hectic when we go ashore.' I found a corner where I could wrap myself in my riding cloak and curl up by the bulkhead. Fitfully, I slept.

When, at length, we were set ashore the afternoon was well spent. At Tilbury no one had, apparently, noticed a party of mounted men coming from the ferry that day. However, whenever I mentioned a rider on a black horse I noticed that people looked at me warily or exchanged anxious glances. We easily obtained directions to Fletcham and discovered it to be a hamlet on rising ground some five miles further along the coast. It was a scattering of very simple dwellings and there were few people about. Since we had to assume we were in enemy territory we asked no questions. We divided into pairs and split up to explore the surrounding countryside. When we reassembled it was Walt who brought information of what seemed to be the only house in the locality substantial enough to serve as a base for Black Harry and his band.

He led us to a high-walled estate. A chained gate denied access to the short drive leading to the manor house.

'What now, Master?' he asked.

'Let's find a way in,' someone said. 'We've come this far; why stop now?'

'That's right,' another agreed. 'They broke into Hemmings. Let's see how they like it.'

'I'd be happier if I knew how well guarded the place is,' I said. 'Anyway it might not even be the right place.'

As I spoke I edged my mount forward for a closer look at the gate. On one of the stone pillars I made out a carved coat of arms. I peered closely. 'I've seen this before,' I said.

'Where?' Walt asked.

'I can't remember. It wasn't carved.' I concentrated all my attention on the simple heraldic device. 'It was ...' I removed my gauntlets and fumbled with the strings of my purse. 'I think it was ...' I reached my hand to the bottom and found a crumpled piece of paper. I smoothed it out and squinted in the fading light at the drawing of a cup and cover. 'Yes, it *is* the same. Look.' I handed the paper to Walt. 'A chevron between three animals of some sort.'

Walt agreed. 'Yes, you're right, Master, but what . . . '

I explained. 'This was sent to me by Holbein. I assumed it was just a mistake. But now I think it was a deliberate message. He hoped I might show it to someone who could make the connection.'

The others were now crowding closer, trying to get a look at Holbein's design. 'What connection, Master?' one of them asked.

'The connection between Black Harry and whoever is supporting him. He knew that the men who attacked him on the road and who murdered his assistant were sent by whoever wanted to prevent his information reaching the archbishop. He knew I was trying to find these men. Perhaps he sent the drawing as a clue – or a warning. Since he dared not go to Cranmer in person, he hoped I might be in contact with his grace and would show him the picture. If I'd thought about it properly, I certainly would have done so.'

'This is the right place, then,' someone said. 'What are we to do, Master?'

'The first thing,' I said, 'is to find out who's at home. Walt, you take John and Simon and go round to the left. The rest of us will follow the wall to the right. When we meet we'll compare notes.'

Some twenty minutes later both groups had come together on the far side of the walled grounds.

'Not very large,' Walt commented. 'Not half the size of Hemmings. In good order, though.'

'Yes,' I agreed. 'The walls are well kept and the only small door we found was securely bolted. Did anyone hear any noise inside?'

'All very quiet, Master.'

'Not a sound.'

'I heard nothing.'

'Well,' I said, 'we mustn't assume too much from that. We'll climb the wall and everyone keep your wits about you.'

'We passed an ideal spot,' Walt said. 'There's a copse comes right close to the wall. We can leave the horses there, well hidden, in case anyone comes by.'

We found the location and dismounted. I delegated Simon, the youngest of our party, to stay with the horses. He protested. 'Let John stay outside. I'm better in a fight than him.'

'All the more reason why we need you out here. Stand near the gate. If you hear anyone coming, get yourself over the wall and come and warn us. If there's any fighting – which God in heaven forbid – we'll need someone who can go for help. If we're not back here within the hour ride like the wind to Tilbury and wait for the men that Cranmer and Moyle should be sending. The rest of you remember we are just spying out the ground. If you see any of Black Harry's men inside make sure they don't see you. We've come to find out if the hostages are here. That's all. If there's any fighting to be done it must wait till we have reinforcements. As soon as we've found out what we can we'll all make our way back to the horses. Good luck, everyone.'

Inside the grounds we again split into two groups cautiously approaching the buildings from different directions. A three-quarter moon came to our assistance. I felt excited and fearful. I was not afraid of another confrontation with Black Harry's men. The anxiety that gnawed at me was that we would find nothing; that there would be neither gang members nor hostages in this house; that the whole expedition would prove to have been a waste of time and effort; that I would be no nearer the conclusion of the wretched business by this night's end than I had been at its beginning.

My two companions and I approached from the south side, cleared the undergrowth and reached the edge of a lawn badly in need of scything. The black bulk of the house reared before us, with not a lighted window to be seen. As we moved further round there was still no sign of life.

'The place is deserted,' Walt said, when we eventually met up again. 'We've missed the slippery hacksters.'

'There's only one way to make sure. We'll go to the stable yard. If they've taken the horses, you'll be right. Either they'll have fled or they haven't got back yet.'

Quietly we moved to the rear of the house. The gate to the yard stood open. As we entered, no animal noises greeted us and when we looked in the stables, every stall was empty.

I sat on the edge of the water trough. 'God's body, what a wasted day we've had. The hostages aren't here.'

'Like enough he's killed them,' someone muttered. 'God grant I get my hand on the murderous villain.'

'Don't let's be too sure,' Walt said. 'He boasted that he'd still got them. I reckon he'll keep them as long as they can be any use to him.'

'Pray God you're right,' I said. But I remembered Ned's analysis of the kind of man we were up against – a man who took a positive delight in causing suffering and pain; the sort of unnatural creature who would look on with fiendish pleasure while his men hacked defenceless children to pieces. 'He'll be angry because we made a fool of him in London. He might vent his spite on the hostages.'

The others stood around in a semicircle, waiting for me to

make a decision. 'Well,' I said, standing up, 'there's nothing we can do here. Let's go back to Tilbury and wait for the men Cranmer and Moyle are sending. Perhaps we can organise a wider search tomorrow.' They turned, dejected, towards the gate, knowing, as I did, that the suggestion was born of despair, rather than hope.

'Wait!' Walt spun round.

'What is it?' I whispered, my hand going to the dagger at my belt.

'I heard something.'

We all strained our ears, alert now to a possible trap.

'Over there,' Walt said softly, pointing to the door of the hay barn.

I motioned everyone to form a line and we moved forward, clutching whatever weapons we had. Now, I could hear the sound also – a shuffling and bumping, It was probably an animal but I was not prepared to take any chances. When the others were in place, I reached out a hand and drew back the bolt. Instantly the large door crashed open and the sharp end of a hay fork passed within inches of my stomach. I grabbed the haft and tugged. My assailant slithered and tumbled out, screaming like a pig about to be slaughtered, and fell at my feet.

My first thought was that some inmate from Bedlam had escaped and taken refuge in this lonely place. The creature was scantily clad in grimy, blood-daubed clothes. Its hair was long and tangled. Its face in the moonlight was pale and its eyes gleamed like those of a cornered animal.

It looked up, ready, as I thought, to spring at me. Then it spoke. 'Master Treviot? Is it you?'

'Adie!' I gasped in relieved yet horrified recognition and helped the young woman to her feet.

'Praise God! Oh, praise God!' She fell into my arms, sobbing. But abruptly she stood away. 'What am I thinking. The boys! Find the boys. They're at the back.'

Two of my men rushed into the barn. Moments later they reappeared, each carrying one of Holbein's sons, tied with thick cord. Walt took his knife and severed the bonds.

I stepped across and knelt beside them as they were set on their feet. 'Are you all right?'

Carl stretched his limbs and stood up straight. 'Henry was a bit frightened,' he said. 'But I said you would find us.' He looked straight into my eyes. 'It took you a long time.'

At that point my relief and the lad's bravery got the better of me. I hugged the two boys to me and wept.

'Best be moving, Master,' Walt said. 'The sooner we put some country miles between us and this place, the better.'

'You're right. Get a couple of the others to carry the boys. I'll help Adie.'

She was sitting on the horse trough, dipping her sleeve in the water and wiping her face. I took out a kerchief and soaked it. 'Let me help.' I gently bathed her brow. 'Adie, I'm so sorry about this.'

She managed a slight smile. 'All's well, now, Master. I told the boys you'd come for us – and here you are.'

Once more I was on the verge of tears. 'Are you badly hurt? We must get away. The hellhounds may be on their way here. Do you know anything of their plans?'

'They went away to London a couple of days ago. They said they wouldn't be back soon.'

'That's good,' I said. I thought, Our skirmish might have made them change their minds.

I helped Adie to her feet and half-carried her across the long grass. It took three of us to get her and the boys over the wall. As soon as I was mounted Adie was handed up and I settled her astride before me. When Carl and Henry were similarly seated we set off. The journey was slow, uncomfortable and was made worse by a thick river mist rolling in over the marshes and obscuring the moon. At least there was no one else on the road and for that I was thankful.

Then, when we were not far from the ferry, we heard the clopping and jingling of a group of horsemen coming towards us. My immediate thought was that this must be Black Harry returning to his lair. I softly called urgent orders to the others. I steered my horse off the road into the cover of the mist. Walt and John, who were carrying the boys, followed.

As the other travellers drew level a gruff, authoritative voice called out, 'Who's that? Show yourselves!'

I recognised the speaker and urged my mount forward. Sir Thomas Moyle, well-wrapped in furs, peered at me. 'Treviot? That you? What's going on? I got your note and came straight away. I thought I'd better come in person. What's all this about someone called Black Harry?'

'Sir Thomas, I'm much relieved to see you.' I explained, in as few words as I could, the day's events. 'And now,' I concluded, 'we must get this poor woman and the children somewhere dry and warm. They're exhausted.'

Moyle grunted. 'You'll find nothing of that sort this side of the river. This is a God-forsaken country. There's reasonable lodging to be had in Gravesend. We must get you there.'

He ordered his men to turn round and we all rode back to the ferry jetty. If Moyle had not been with us that is probably where we would have had to spend the night. The ferrymen would have refused the four crossings necessary to convey us all to the Kent side. But Moyle's bluff authority and, doubtless, his gold overcame their reluctance. By mid-night we were lodged in a moderately comfortable Gravesend inn and even provided with food. Moyle sent most of his attendants home but also spent the night at the inn. 'I want to get to the bottom of this business,' he said.

But we both had to wait until the following morning to hear Adie's harrowing story.

Chapter 11

Sir Thomas had procured a private room for us to break our fast and there, the following morning, while we were waiting for Adie to join us, I gave a full account of the last few days' events.

'If what you tell me about this Black Harry is true, the sooner we have him kicking his heels in air, the better,' Moyle said.

'We shall hear from Adie the sort of rogue he is and why he is a danger to the realm.'

'Tell me about this "Adie". Strange name for a young woman.'

'She tells me it is short for "Adriana".'

'Adriana who?'

'Imray – a foreign name. I know nothing about her family.'

'So what is she exactly?'

'A nurse employed to look after Master Holbein's children.'

Moyle frowned and grunted.

'Is that a problem?'

'I was just imagining her giving evidence before a court. You tell me this Black Harry has friends – important friends – in the county. If they were to speak up on his behalf, I wonder whether a jury would believe them or a hysterical serving wench.'

I winced at his description of Adie but said, 'Do you mean we need the evidence of more "respectable" people if we are to bring this gang to justice?'

'What I mean, young Treviot, is that we have a long way to go yet before we can be sure of putting a stop to their activities. You tell me that they work for some highly placed patrons.'

'So Archbishop Cranmer believes.'

'Has he named these influential supporters?'

'He believes that Black Harry is in Bishop Gardiner's pay. I've heard also that Dr London, Canon of Windsor, may be a link in the chain that connects to the gang.'

'If his grace's suspicions are well founded, you see what we are up against. I, too, am often at the royal court. I am proud to have enjoyed the support and confidence of Lord Cromwell. I saw at close quarters what happened to him; the subtle schemes of unscrupulous enemies who gained his majesty's ear just long enough to pour in poisonous lies.'

'Are you saying, Sir Thomas, that we should not do all in our power to bring these murderers to justice?'

Moyle looked genuinely shocked. 'By no means, Master Treviot! No, I take your word for it that they are the kind of knaves the kingdom must be rid of. I simply counsel caution. In this matter we could find ourselves walking on political ground, and that is something that is forever shifting. If only we had evidence connecting Black Harry with his protectors – something more substantial than mere suspicion . . . '

'I gather that is exactly the kind of evidence Master Holbein had gathered for the archbishop.'

'You said in your report to his grace and me that this painter fellow had disappeared.'

'Yes, he's probably overseas by now.'

'A pity.'

At that moment Adie came into the room. She had tidied herself as best she could and, with hair combed and face washed, she looked more like the young woman I knew, but her torn, grimy clothes were still evidence of her ordeal. She curtsied to Sir Thomas and stood mute with downcast eyes, her hands clasped in front of her.

'Now, young . . . er . . . Adie,' Moyle said. 'We know you've had an unpleasant few days but we need to discover all we can about these men who abducted you. You must tell us everything you know. First of all, what is your name?'

'Adriana Imray, Sir.' She spoke quietly but seemed in control of her feelings.

'And what is your father's trade?'

'He's dead, Sir, and my mother.'

'Ah, hmm. No other relatives?'

'My brother Ignatius is falconer to Lord Graves, Sir.'

'Really?' Moyle looked impressed. 'I've met his lordship through my work in the Court of Augmentations.'

I smiled inwardly. Augmentations was the royal body that handled the sale of ex-monastic property. Moyle was Chancellor of Augmentations and, as such, much courted by ambitious landowners, of whom Lord Graves was probably one. I leaned forward and whispered something to Sir Thomas.

'What?' he spluttered. 'Oh, very well.' He returned his attention to Adie. 'You may sit,' he said. 'There's a bench over there.'

After another curtsy, Adie took her seat by the door.

'Now then,' Moyle continued, 'Master Treviot and I have been put to much trouble rescuing you and your charges from this brigand who calls himself Black Harry. You must tell us about him.'

'Yes, Sir.'

'Well, go on, then. We're listening.'

Adie explained how she and the children had been dragged from their beds in the night.

'They gagged the bearns to stop them screaming and one of them held a knife to my throat. He said if I caused any trouble they would kill us all. They put us on their horses and rode fast with us until it was full light. We came to a big house and they took us to a small, empty room. We stayed there all that day.' She spoke with eyes downcast, holding her feelings in check. Her composure was extraordinary.

'Do you know whose house it was?' I asked.

'No, Master Thomas, but I did see him . . . in the hall, just as we were leaving. I don't think he was pleased that I saw him.'

'You'd recognise him again?'

'Oh, yes, Master Thomas.'

'What happened next?' Moyle demanded.

'They put me and the boys in a covered wagon, bound hand and foot. We jolted and banged about most of the night.'

'You've no idea what route you took?'

'No, Sir. Most of the time I was trying to calm the boys. At last we came to another big house and the men threw us into a barn for the whole day.'

'It seems Black Harry has several wealthy supporters – willing accomplices in his crimes,' I said.

Moyle grunted. 'Go on, girl, what happened then?'

'Next evening we crossed by the ferry and ended up in the place where you found us, Master Thomas. I was never more glad to see anyone.'

I laughed, wanting to lighten the atmosphere. 'You very nearly skewered me with that pitchfork, Adie.'

'I'm right sorry for that, Master. I thought you were—'

'Yes, yes,' Moyle interrupted. 'So you arrived in that Essex place, when? Must have been Tuesday, three days ago?'

'I suppose so, Sir. It seemed a lot longer.'

'How did they treat you?' Moyle asked.

Adie looked away. She raised a kerchief to her eyes. 'I'd rather not say what they did to me, Sir. You're a respectable gentleman but I expect you can imagine—'

I interrupted. 'Do we need to press her on that matter, Sir Thomas?'

He ignored me. 'And they all used you thus?'

Adie nodded, biting her lip to hold back the tears. 'Most of them. They said they'd do things to the children if I didn't . . . I was more concerned for the bearns.' This time she failed to stem the tears. 'The poor dearlings!' she muttered between sobs.

Sir Thomas pressed on regardless. 'Now, then, girl, all the time you were with them did you hear anything of their plans?'

'Do you think we might take a break, Sir Thomas?' I asked. 'Mistress Imray is obviously distressed.'

He scowled. 'I don't have all day, Master Treviot. If we're

to track down these criminals we need information and we need it now.'

''Tis all right, Master. I can answer your questions. We didn't see much of our captors because we were locked in a room by ourselves.'

'Are you saying these monsters never talked to you, even when they were . . . using . . . you?'

'Oh, they talked to me, or, rather, they tried to make me talk. They wanted me to tell them where Master Holbein was. They beat the boys in front of me. They said they would go on beating them till I told them what they wanted. Only I couldn't because I didn't know. I couldn't tell them, not even to save the children. I couldn't . . . I couldn't . . . I couldn't.' She began sobbing again.

'God in heaven, Sir Thomas, what sort of monsters are we dealing with here? What drives them to such evil?' My mind went back to Marbeck's story.

I went over and laid a hand on Adie's shoulder. 'You did all you could to spare the boys' sufferings. Of that we're sure. I swear to you that these villains will pay ten times over for everything they've done to you and the children.' Trembling rage swept over me. 'Jesus, Mary and all the saints, I will make them pay, whatever it costs.'

Adie recovered a little. It was between sniffs that she continued her story. 'They came to our room very early on Wednesday – before dawn. They'd come to fetch Annie. I asked what they were going to do to her. Black Harry just laughed. "We're going to do something terrible to her," he said. "We'll leave you to imagine what." Then he stood by the doorway talking to one of his men . . . well, arguing, really and I listened as hard as I could. Black Harry said they were meeting Master Treviot in London and he hoped you'd managed to find Master Holbein ... He really is desperate to find my master. He said, "We'll take the girl just to put extra pressure on him." The other man said, "What about the woman and the boys?" and Black Harry replied, "We'll kill them before we go." That's what the argument was about. The other man didn't want to do it and Black Harry got very angry with him. In the end, he said, "Since they mean so much to you we won't cut their throats. We'll tie them up and leave them here. That way they'll starve to death slowly instead of having a quick end. No one will find them here."'

'They weren't planning to return, then?' Sir Thomas asked.

'No, I'm sure of it. They tied us up, threw us in the barn and left us. I spent two days struggling to get free.' She held out her hands to show us the bruises and deep rope burns. 'I worked at it on and off till I felt my strength failing. Then I rested and started again. I only succeeded by gnawing through the cords. I'd just got free and started to untie the boys when I heard voices outside. I thought the gang had come back after all. I was terrified. I couldn't believe it when I saw Master Treviot.'

'I suppose you didn't hear where the gang were planning to go next,' I said.

Adie wrinkled her brow in concentration. 'It was just as they were closing the door ... Black Harry said something like, "We'll take the German to Rook's and interrogate him." I suppose that can't be right, but that's what it sounded like.'

Moyle turned to me with a shrug. 'Not very helpful, I'm afraid. Obviously the girl misheard. She was under a lot of strain. I'll make sure the whole county is alerted. A gang like that can't go unnoticed for long. As for you, young Treviot, you deserve a rest. You've done a splendid job.'

''Tis Mistress Imray and the children who are the real heroes, but, yes, we all need some time to recover.'

Shortly afterwards Sir Thomas set out to return to Ashford. Before he left he insisted on paying the inn bill for all of us. When I had made sure that Adie and the boys were ready to travel, I put them in the charge of Walt and told him to see them safe home to Hemmings.

'Are you not coming, Master?' the groom asked.

'I must report to the archbishop,' I said. 'He ordered me to keep him informed personally. I hope to be back tonight but if his grace cannot see me straight away I may be delayed.'

I reached Ford soon after noon but it was a couple of hours before Cranmer summoned me to his presence.

'Come,' he said, 'let us walk in the orchard. Now that the weather has turned we should take advantage of it.'

Warm sunshine and a soft, caressing breeze gave the first intimation of autumn as we strolled among the trees where gardeners were busy gathering apples and pears in baskets.

'I was highly alarmed to receive your note from Essex,' the archbishop said. 'I was ready to send a party of my own guard to your aid this morning when I had news from Sir Thomas Moyle that the crisis was over. I thank God that our prayers have been answered for the safety of Holbein's boys. Now, tell me everything in detail.'

He listened intently to my report, sometimes stopping me to check a detail or clarify a point. His scholar's mind would not permit of any vagueness or inaccuracy.

'Clearly, it is of the utmost importance now to track down this Black Harry. Praise God he has not found Master Holbein.'

'Has the painter made contact with you, Your Grace?'

'Not a word.'

143

'Then, I fear he may have fled. He has loyal friends at the Steelyard who would not hesitate to help him quit the country.'

Cranmer sighed. 'That would be understandable. And yet I think better of him than that. He has proved himself very loyal over several years, first to Lord Cromwell, then to me, sometimes at no small danger to himself. I cannot believe he would flee without passing on the information he has for me.'

'Perhaps, like Your Grace, he knows not who he can trust.'

'Solomon the Wise warns us, "He who hates deceives with his lips: when he speaks graciously believe him not." That is a lesson for all who live in kings' courts – or in bishops' palaces. There is so much hate abroad in England now that I sometimes hesitate to call it a Christian country.'

We walked a while in silence. Then Cranmer continued in the same vein. 'I used to love this part of Kent – the orchards, the shallow, gentle hills, the oak woods. Now the serpent has entered Eden and nowhere seems safe or sacred.'

I felt the need to say something reassuring. 'Your Grace's commission will surely root out much of the evil. Saturday's meeting at Ashford was useful. We have a plan of campaign for silencing inflammatory preaching.'

'Yes, Ralph spoke well of it. Sir Thomas, I think, is a man who is strong-minded and industrious. I am already receiving reports from some of your neighbours and will be summoning certain clergy here in the next few days to give account of themselves. But there are still some who are protected by family and friends among the leaders of society. There is a league . . . yes, I think we may call it a league . . . between some of the cathedral officers and the county gentry. You must have formed some of your own suspicions. Whatever your reluctance to provide information about neighbours you've known for years, I beg you not to keep silent.'

I recalled Adie's account of the conversation she had overheard. 'It is possible that Black Harry may be seeking refuge with someone called Rook but I'm not very sure of the name. It is not one I recognise.'

Cranmer looked round sharply. 'Could that not be Sir Andrew Rookwood?'

'Now that Your Grace mentions the name I do recall hearing it. Does he not live in the south of the county?'

'Yes, near Hawkhurst. He is related to the Duke of Norfolk and even more stubbornly conservative than his lordship. I know his chaplain for a troublemaker. If he is now harbouring murderers . . .' Cranmer turned abruptly. 'Come, we must act quickly.' He walked and half ran towards the house, calling to a servant to have his secretary sent to him immediately.'

Minutes later Ralph Morice and I were standing in front of the archbishop as he sat at his desk. Briskly, he gave his instructions.

'I want summonses made out for Sir Andrew Rookwood and Gervase Honey, his chaplain. Bring them to me for signing and have a troop ready to deliver them straight away. Thank you, Thomas. This may be an important turning point. If we can catch . . .'

But I was not listening. My attention had been caught by one of the letters on Cranmer's desk, or rather by the large seal with which it had been fixed. The sender had impressed an image of his own shield in the red wax.

'Excuse me, Your Grace, might I ask whose heraldic device is on that letter?'

Cranmer picked it up. 'This – a chevron between three moles? Terrible heraldic pun, isn't it?'

'But whose is it?' I demanded with rising excitement.

'Why, 'tis Sir Thomas Moyle's,' the archbishop said.

'But, Your Grace,' I gasped, 'that is the shield on the gate post at Fletcham.'

Chapter 12

'No, Thomas, you are clearly mistaken. One heraldic shield can look much like another. You must have been deceived by the poor light.' The archbishop sighed. 'The times are treacherous and uncertain but we must not allow insidious suspicion to turn us against our friends.'

I rummaged in my purse and took out the cup and cover design in the artist's exquisitely precise hand. 'Your Grace, Master Holbein sent this to me from his hiding place. I had no idea why but some impulse made me keep it.' I placed the crumpled sheet of paper beside Moyle's letter.

Cranmer looked from one to the other. He handed them to Ralph Morice, who also scrutinised them closely. 'They certainly seem to be the same,' the secretary said, 'but 'tis not possible . . . '

'Are you really sure you saw the identical shield carved on the gate at Fletcham?' Cranmer asked.

'The truth is easily proved,' Morice said. 'Sir Thomas has properties in Essex. It will be easy enough to discover whether he owns Fletcham.'

My mind was working fast. 'It all becomes clear to me now. It must have been Moyle, not Thwaites who informed Black Harry that Adie and the boys were at Hemmings. Then, when he knew I had been to Fletcham, he could not come fast enough to see what I had discovered. Small wonder he was so keen to question Adie.'

The archbishop sat back in his chair with a hand to his brow. 'No, no, this is ridiculous. I have known Sir Thomas for years. He has no reason to wish me ill. I cannot believe he is a covert papist. He worked closely with Lord Cromwell to bring down those little Roman nests, the abbeys.'

'So did Dr London,' Morice observed softly, 'and now who is the chief hunter of so-called heretics?'

Cranmer was still struggling to be convinced. 'What does this signify?' He pointed to the drawing. 'Why did Master Holbein send it to you, Thomas?'

'If he guessed he was being watched, he would not have been able to communicate directly with Your Grace. He knew of my interest in tracking down the Aldgate murderers; though, at that time, I had not identified Black Harry. He wanted me to know there is a connection between the gang and one of the most important men in Kent. Perhaps he hoped that somehow, at some time, I might show this to you.'

'No, no, Thomas, this is slender reasoning. He must know the chances of your seeing this as some sort of clue are remote.'

'He is probably desperate enough to take any chance,' Morice said. 'He is like a cony trapped in its own burrow, with the hounds waiting outside. He can never be free until Black Harry is caught.'

'I also know him to be a great lover of cyphers, codes and hidden meanings,' I said. 'It amuses him to put puzzles in his paintings and we have sometimes discussed secret messages for jewels that will please our patrons. I know the way his mind works. Looking back, I suppose that is why I kept the sketch.'

Cranmer shook his head wearily and I have seldom seen a man look more miserable. 'Who can I trust? Among all the swirling treacheries and deceits of Kentish society Sir Thomas is one of the few rocks I have clung to. Am I to believe now that he is a supporter of felons who slaughter women and children?'

Morice said, 'Perhaps, Your Grace, the time has come to take Master Treviot more fully into our confidence.'

'Yes, yes.' Cranmer waved a hand. 'Take him to your office, I need to think.'

Morice's 'office' was a tiny room adjacent to the archbishop's, which was almost filled by a standing desk, two stools and a large coffer.

'His grace seems much distressed,' I said.

'More than he shows. He carries a heavy burden. 'Tis my job to lighten it as much as possible. That means that I must do things he cannot or will not do.' He stood at his desk. 'I think better on my feet and we've a knotty problem to unravel, but please do take a seat.'

'What is it his grace chooses not to do?' I perched on one of the stools, resting my back against the wall.

'He lacks ruthlessness. He always thinks the best of people. Sometimes I fear it may prove his undoing.'

'I know he has powerful enemies but as long as he enjoys the king's favour ...'

'You have put your finger on the problem. There are three points you need to understand.' Morice enumerated them clearly, like a grammar teacher rehearsing the rules of Latin declensions. Indeed, I felt as though I had returned to the schoolroom, with this austere figure looking down at me and explaining everything, as though to a sluggardly pupil.

'Point one: God's truth is enshrined in his written word . It is to this that his grace is committed above all things. Point two: there are those who seek truth elsewhere; in Rome, in the doctors of the Church, in the traditions of men. Point three: his majesty's truth is something of a chameleon. Its hue varies according to political or diplomatic necessity. Do you understand what I am saying?'

'I think so.'

'For example,' Morice went on, like a long-suffering pedagogue, 'when his majesty needs to be on good terms with the Emperor, he is almost as Catholic as the pope. When he needs the support of the Lutheran princes, he is a vigorous reformer.'

'And which camp is he in at the moment?'

'His ambassadors have been instructed to back the Emperor in his conflict with France.'

'Then that is not good for the archbishop.'

Morice frowned. 'If only it were that simple. The partisans at court jostle for power ceaselessly. They watch the political situation and try to take advantage of every twist and turn but the king is not easily manipulated. He seems to be like a slumbering lion and they tiptoe around him, carefully laying their plans. But he knows what they are doing and he may suddenly fling out a paw with vicious talons. He understands well who he can trust, who he can use – and who he can destroy.'

'As he destroyed Lord Cromwell?'

Morice scowled. 'That was a bad business. For a while it seemed that all was lost. The likes of Bishop Gardiner and the Duke of Norfolk had the upper hand. They would have had the king launch an English version of the Spanish Inquisition. Several of our friends were arrested but we knew well enough who the real target was.'

'The archbishop?'

'Of course.'

'But they failed.'

'They failed three years ago. That doesn't mean they have given up. You have heard what happened at Windsor – three good Christian men burned to death for confessing Christ. But that was only meant to be the first chapter in their cruel book. Dr London, Gardiner's personal inquisitor, was aiming to catch in his net men of the Privy Chamber, close to the king. That was why the good bishop had poor Marbeck imprisoned and mercilessly interrogated.'

'But again they failed.'

'And again I say that they failed *then* but have not abandoned their crusade.'

'Well, I am glad I do not move in court circles,' I said.

'Don't be naive, Thomas,' Morice snapped, the verbal equivalent of a teacher lashing out with the birch. 'You are involved in this business now, whether you will or not.'

'How say you so?'

'Because the battleground has moved from the court to the country. Some weeks ago the reactionaries went ahead with a plan they had long been brewing against the archbishop. "Your Majesty," they said, "look at your county of Kent; it is a very vipers' nest of Lutherans and fanatics of all kinds. We really should have a commission charged with examining all the clergy and rooting out all who are not dutiful preachers of the religion set out in Your Majesty's book." And the king agreed.'

'But I thought this new commission was his grace's idea.'

Morice allowed himself a slight smile. 'Oh, no, what really happened is this. A couple of weeks ago he summoned the archbishop to join him for a trip along the Thames in the royal barge. "Aha," says the king, as soon as they were alone and no one to hear them, "I have discovered who is the biggest heretic in Kent." "Name him," says his grace, "and I'll have him straightly arrested." Why," says his majesty, "it is you, My Lord Archbishop, or so I am informed."'

I gasped. 'Yet Cranmer was not straightly arrested?'

'Fortunately, it was his majesty's idea of a joke.' Morice smiled grimly. 'The lion growled but kept his claws sheathed. He said, "My Lord Archbishop, we must do something about the spread of false teaching in your diocese. I have agreed to set up a commission to examine all your clergy. I have here a list of suspects diligently drawn up by the Bishop of Winchester and his associates. I hereby appoint you, My Lord Archbishop, to head this commission. You may choose whoever you wish to assist you in this task but see that it is done swiftly and thoroughly."'

'So now his grace can use his powers to remove all those tainted with Catholicism.'

'Yes, but the commission is meant to be even-handed, rooting out Bible men, as well. Therefore, we do have to tread very carefully. We thought we had made a wise move when we appointed Sir Thomas Moyle as deputy commissioner. It seems we made a grave mistake.'

'What's to be done now?'

'Thanks to you,' Morice said, 'we have discovered Sir Thomas's true colours. Once we have apprehended this Black

Harry, I doubt whether it will be difficult to persuade him or one of his mercenary crew to give evidence against Moyle. Then it should be only a matter of unravelling the string of treachery until it leads us to the *fons et origo*. It will be very satisfactory to see Gardiner, Norfolk and London caught in the snare they had set for the archbishop.'

By now I felt very uncomfortable – hemmed in as much by events as I was by the walls of the closet-like office. Like a press-ganged soldier I was involved against my will in this war Morice was describing – and I was not acquitting myself well.

'Would that I had known all this ere today,' I muttered, avoiding Morice's eye.

'Why say you so?'

'This morning, before I suspected anything of Sir Thomas's link to Black Harry, I gave him a full account of my own activities and discoveries.'

'Devil take it!' Morice thumped the desk with his fist.

'I'm sorry, I . . .'

''Tis not your fault. As you say, you did not know then. Unfortunately, this has given Moyle a head start. No doubt his messengers are already on the road to warn Black Harry. The best we can do is circulate a description of the gang as widely as possible. I'll attend to that straight away. At least we can now neutralise Sir Thomas. I'll have him taken off the commission – along with anyone else we have reason to suspect. Now, then, what else can be done?' Morice closed his eyes in concentration and tapped his forehead.

'Is there anything I can do?' I offered tamely.

He made no reply, wrapped in his own thoughts. 'We need some big artillery. I'll send to our friends in the Privy Chamber and have them obtain a warrant to send Thomas Legh to us.'

'"Lank" Legh?'

'Yes, you know him?'

'Who doesn't? He's one of the most notorious men in England. Folk say he bullied the abbots into resigning their houses and those he couldn't bully he tricked.' I conjured up an image of the fat lawyer whose mocking nickname referred to his enormous bulk.

'Indeed. Not the handsomest or most likeable man his majesty has ever employed. The archbishop certainly has no love for him. But he is the man for a crisis. He's an advocate in Chancery and one of the finest legal brains in the realm. I've watched him question strong men in court and reduce them to whimpering mice. We will have him replace Moyle. That will give us proper control of the commission.'

'Might it not make the archbishop unpopular?'

Morice stared at me, once more the stern schoolmaster. 'Shall I tell you some of the things our enemies have done in their efforts to undermine his grace? Twice I have caught cathedral clergy in his study, going through his papers. I have collected up and destroyed a libellous pamphlet accusing the archbishop's sister of bigamy. Two months ago I had a man and his wife stood in the pillory for spreading a rumour that his grace committed acts of buggery with one of his kitchen boys. The hatred of our foes knows no bounds. In May we laid to rest the body of Dr Champion, one of the archbishop's most long-standing friends. As the coffin was being lowered one of the cathedral staff jumped down and scattered hot coals over it from his incense thurifer, screaming, "Burn in hell, heretic!" Now, Master Treviot, what say you? Should we not use whatever weapons we have against such people and those who set them on?'

'His grace told me he was involved in a war but I did not think ...'

'A war indeed, and on several fronts. Did you know that the Duke of Norfolk gives a sumptuous banquet every 28 July to celebrate the execution of Lord Cromwell? That is to remind all his important guests of the supposed heresies the country has been delivered from. And, of course, he and Bishop Gardiner have set up their own commission, under Dr London, to seek out Bible men in the capital and elsewhere. Our satanic foe is like the Hydra, many-headed and deadly. We have to be constantly on the watch to see where he will strike next – and there is so much at stake. Only the archbishop stands between the devil's henchmen and the collapse of all we have gained since his majesty expelled the pope. He does, indeed, carry a crushingly heavy burden.'

By the time we finished talking, the day was late and I grate-fully accepted an invitation to spend another night at Ford. Morice was very busy organising groups of the archbishop's guard to set off in search of Black Harry. His energy and effi-ciency were admirable. He prepared written instructions for each captain, as well as letters to be delivered to the gentle-men and senior townsmen through whose territory they passed. I watched as he addressed his little army, for all the world like a general launching a military campaign. If anyone could locate Black Harry and have him brought back in chains, I thought, that man would be Ralph Morice. But the difficulties of the operation were formidable. His men had a large area to cover and I had seen for myself how unwelcome the archbishop's men were in many places. In the morning the secretary had another brief word with me before I set off with one troop who were to accompany me most of the way to Hemmings. Once again he exhorted me to keep alert to any news that could be useful to the archbishop and to make frequent reports.

It was a relief to arrive back at my own home and an even bigger relief to observe the members of the household, outwardly at least, going about their lives as if nothing untoward had recently shattered the peace of Hemmings. On enquiry I discovered that our three guests had slept long and late. My steward had called in a local physician to examine them and apply salve to their various cuts and bruises. He reported that the Holbein boys were more subdued than usual but seemed otherwise none the worse for their ordeal. Adie, he said, spent all her time by the kitchen fire and was only relaxed in the company of other women. I wanted to find her and see for myself how she was but realised that the sight of me might bring back painful memories. Instead, I busied myself for a couple of hours with some of the outside workers, discussing estate matters and then retired to my chamber. There was a small pile of letters on the table, most of them routine. One, however, was addressed in a hand I did not recognise. I broke the seal and read it by the light of a lamp.

> Master Treviot, I greet you and trust that my messenger
> will find you in Kent, having received directions from
> your servants in West Cheap. I write with urgent news
> of Master Holbein, who came to me in Chiswick this
> day. I told him that you had called to see him to bring
> the sad news that his sons were captured by the men
> seeking his own life. He was much distressed to hear it
> and prayed I would assure you he desired above all
> things the safety of his children. The reason he was not
> at Bridewell when you visited was that he had departed

secretly for the Steelyard, having purposed to obtain
passage for himself and his family on a Hanse trading
vessel. Having agreed with a captain from Bremen, he
was anxious I should make enquiry for the whereabouts
of the boys. He was greatly distressed to learn that he
was too late and his sons were captured. His anguish,
Master Treviot, was distressing to behold and his resolve
now quite changed. He declares that he wishes to
surrender himself to his enemies in exchange for the
children and begs me to ask, if you know how to reach
the abductors, that you will convey his wishes to them.
Master Holbein also says that he would like to meet you
in order to give into your hands certain information he
is desirous you should pass to a third party. Thus, Master
Treviot, it is with a heavy heart that I do the office of a
friend and beseech that you will come to Bridewell at
your earliest opportunity.

From Chiswick, this 22nd day of September
Your worshipful brother,
Jan van der Goes

The twenty-second! That was three days ago! It seemed more
like three weeks, so much had happened. And here was news
of a distracted father planning to give himself up to a gang of
murderers in exchange for his sons, not knowing that those
sons were now safe. I had no choice about what I should do.
I would have to hurry back to London without delay.

But what would I find? The Fleming would be concerned
not to have received an answer to his letter. Every day that
passed without my responding to his urgent summons would
be like dagger blows of despair to the agonised Holbein. What
might distraction not move him to? I tried to imagine what I

would be driven to if evil befell young Ralph and I believed I was the cause of it? I thought of the draughty, drab warehouse where the painter was forced to live – and of the swift Thames running past it.

I would have to take to the road yet again first thing in the morning. I prayed earnestly that I would not be too late.

Chapter 13

The news of my imminent departure was received with disquiet by most of my people at Hemmings. Their routines had been repeatedly upset of late and they had had enough excitement to last them for at least another year. Word rapidly spread – and grew in the spreading – that the master was about to plunge headlong into fresh dangers. If recent events were any indication of what might befall me in the plague-ridden City, they had reason to be anxious. Walt took it on himself to mention the household's misgivings the next morning, as we set out once again on the London road, the dawn shadows stretching before us on the furrowed highway. I had chosen him to be one of my three companions, because he was both strong and level-headed. He had given long service to me and to my father before me and, of all my servants, he was the one who came closest to being a confidant.

'I hear there's no sign of the pestilence abating in London,' he said. 'A pedlar who came past a couple of days since says it's quiet as the tomb there. Not even a stray animal to be seen; all slaughtered for fear of contagion.'

''Tis only in the City, Walt,' I said. 'My information is that it's not spread far. Even Southwark seems to have missed the worst of it. We'll spend the night at Master Longbourne's.'

But Walt would not be denied his gloom. 'They say most of the churches are closed and mass graves are being dug out at Moor Fields. It must be a terrible thing to die unshriven and nothing to mark the spot.'

'I daresay much of this talk is exaggerated, Walt.'

'Well, I know for a fact that the vicar of St Michael at Querne has fled. He was already gone when we were there a-Tuesday. You'd think the priests would be the last ones to leave, wouldn't you, Master, being shepherds of the flock and all that? No one I've spoken to can remember anything like this plague.'

'As I say, Walt, we should not be too worried. It's keeping itself within the walls. My meeting is at Bridewell but I shan't need you and the others. You can wait for me at Ned Longbourne's if you wish.'

Walt was determined to fend off reassurance. 'What I want to know is, why London? There must be a curse on the City.'

'And what do you think London has done to deserve it?'

'God alone knows, Master Thomas.'

'Exactly! And we do best not to try to fathom his thoughts.'

The groom was silent for the next couple of miles, though I could tell he was struggling with his thoughts. At last he gave voice to what was really worrying him. 'Heaven forbid that anything bad should happen to you, Master Thomas, but these men we're dealing with . . .'

'Yes, Walt?'

'Well, if anything were to go wrong . . . if this Black Harry found you . . . Well, he has a score to settle, hasn't he?'

'What you mean is, he might kill me.'

'Well, yes . . . and then there's the plague.'

'What you're trying to say is that I'm needlessly endangering my life and you're worried about what would happen to you if I got killed.'

'It's not just me, Master. There's everyone in the household and the workshop to think about. And now we seem to have taken on responsibility for Mistress Adie and the two young lads. If you had to leave everything to Master Raffy, and he only a boy, what would become of the business?'

Walt's concern was obviously something shared by his colleagues and, doubtless, had been much discussed by them in recent days. They were fully justified in worrying about their futures, which I had put at risk. I did my best to offer reassurance. But was I really trying to convince myself and banish my own guilt?

'As to the boys and their nurse, I hope to see them reunited with Master Holbein. That's why we're going to look for him now. I rather think he will take them back to his own people in Germany. If anything happened to me, Raffy would be looked after by the Goldsmiths' Company. They would see to his training in the craft until he was able to take over the business. But, Walt, try not to worry about what could go wrong. Nothing is certain in this world. We might ride round that bend up yonder, be set on by highway robbers and all left for dead. What I can tell you is that I've no intention of getting myself killed but that, if the worst should happen, Treviots will stay in business. Now, the ground seems firmer here; let's give the horses a canter.'

If you had to leave everything to Master Raffy, and he only a boy, what would become of the business? The words echoed around in my head throughout the rest of the journey. But not in relation to my own situation. This was the question in very many minds as they thought about England and its future. We had a king who was sick and ageing rapidly. Some said it was only the unbending oak of his stubborn will that defied the angel of death and kept him at bay. I had vivid memories of royal Henry as I had seen him in my youth. Word would spread that his majesty was to ride through the City, or that he had organised a Whitehall tournament or a river pageant. My friends and I would rush to find a vantage point where we could get a glimpse of our sovereign. And the sight never disappointed. Massive, regal, splendid in silks and jewels, he paraded before his subjects, the very embodiment of kingship. It was impossible for us not to feel a surge of pride. But now he seldom ventured beyond the walls of his palaces and when he did so even his sumptuous wardrobe could not conceal the over-fleshed body or the occasional winces of pain he failed to suppress. And this ailing, failing monarch only had a child to succeed him, a son two years younger than Raffy. There was, of course, no question of either of the two princesses assuming their father's crown. Women were not made by God to rule kingdoms. What then would become of the 'business' of England?

This was the concern that underlay all the political manoeuvring in which Cranmer, Gardiner, Norfolk and all our leaders of church and state were involved. They were fighting for the future of England. Rather, they were fighting to control the future of England and the destinies of all Englishmen. Shaping our religion was only a part of the conflict the archbishop spoke of. Foreign alliances, war and peace, taxes and the use to which they were put – all matters of state would be in the hands of the men who would exercise the real power when Prince Edward became our king. Of course, they could not say so. Even to speak of his majesty's death was treason, punishable by hanging, drawing and quartering. But power, total power, ultimate power was the prize for which they were all contending. And it was this struggle in which I had become embroiled.

Holbein also was a player in this dangerous political tourney in which any fall was fatal. The difference between us was that he had chosen his role and I had not. He possessed information that could destroy Cranmer's enemies and he was intent on passing it to me. What use the archbishop would put it to I could only guess but whatever its importance to his feud, it was unlikely to solve my own problem, that of rescuing Bart from the gallows. There was still only one way to achieve that. As we drew closer to London and what I hoped would be my meeting with Holbein, I knew I had to do two things: become the courier of highly dangerous information and make sure that Black Harry was captured. On reflection, Walt was probably right to be worried.

It was mid-afternoon when we reached Ned's house in Southwark. He refreshed us with one of his celebrated cordials and wanted to hear all our news.

'God and the saints be praised!' he exclaimed, when I related the rescue of Adie and the boys. 'I fear the news here is as bad as yours is good. Matters are grown much worse since your last visit only a few days ago. People are streaming over the bridge to escape the plague. The authorities have placed guards at both ends in an effort to stop poor, infected souls from leaving. Sufferers are ordered to stay within doors. If they have to venture abroad they must carry a white stick so that others can avoid them. Of course, many choose not to do so, but mingle with the fleeing crowds. That increases the spread of the disease and also panic. That's why the soldiers are there to examine everyone. It does little good; plague victims simply leave the City by boat. The Michaelmas law sittings at Westminster have been postponed to stop plaintiffs and defendants carrying the pestilence upriver and thronging the hall. Not very good for lawyers' business.'

'No,' Walt said gloomily, 'and it will reduce the number of cases to be heard when the courts do reopen.'

'How so?' I asked.

'Well, think of all the prisoners who will die in the stinking overcrowded jails.'

'What brings you back?' Ned asked. 'You would do well to stay away until a change in the weather clears the hot and moist humours.'

'I shan't venture inside the City,' I explained. 'I will take a boat to Bridewell Quay in the hope of seeing Master Holbein and giving him the good news about his sons.'

I explained about the letter I had received from John of Antwerp.

'What a sad muddle,' Ned said. 'The poor man must be distracted with grief.'

'Indeed. That's why I must get to him as soon as possible. By your leave, Ned, I will go now and, I hope, be back in an hour or so.'

'God's speed,' the old man said. 'I pray you will be able to bring that poor fugitive some cheer.'

Sadly, Ned's supplication was not answered. When I reached Bridewell I found Holbein's door open. His room was deserted and in chaos. Everything lay strewn about the floor – bedding, food, dishes, papers, canvases, brushes, all littered in confusion. Vivid paints were spread everywhere, as though they had been deliberately poured over the debris. I found a stool, wiped it over with a torn sheet, sat down and tried to work out what could possibly have happened. Clearly, I was too late. Black Harry must have received from Moyle the details of Holbein's hiding place that I had foolishly revealed. There was something astonishing about the man's persistent vigour. Ned would have called it diabolical. He would probably have been right.

I stood and wandered around the room, picking up items, turning over others, in the vain hope of finding some clue to what might have happened to the painter. I set the easel squarely on its feet and picked up the last painting he had been working on. I saw now that it was a self-portrait. I gazed at the familiar features – the fringe of dark beard in the German fashion, the serious, almost severe set of the mouth, the penetrating eyes that appeared more searching of me than I of them. Not for the first time, I marvelled at the skill of this remarkable craftsman, who could capture a likeness with such awesome precision. It struck me that I was looking at his last piece of work. Johannes Holbein must, by now, surely be dead. I could not imagine that Black Harry and his ruffians would have wasted any time before killing him. I tried to picture the horror this place must have recently witnessed. I imagined the sadistic attackers inflicting as much pain as possible upon the victim before removing his body, perhaps in a sack to be disposed of later or slipped unobtrusively into the refuse-laden river.

After a last look round, I let myself out. As I turned the key in the door, something suddenly struck me as odd: why had I found the room locked when I arrived? If the gang found Holbein here and took him away – dead or alive – why would they waste more time getting the key off him and locking the door behind them?

'What will you do now?' Ned asked when I returned to Southwark.

'I must send word to Cranmer. Then I'll go to Chiswick to call once more on the Fleming. I must tell him about his friend, if he does not already know. But these things will have to wait until tomorrow. I'm weary now – to the very depths of my soul.'

The following morning – Monday 27 September – I despatched one of my men to the archbishop with my report. That done, I hired a boatman to row me up to Chiswick. If my discovery at Bridewell had been a shock, what met me at the elegant house of van der Goes was almost as disturbing. Two burly men with heavy clubs guarded the door and demanded my business. Only when this information had been relayed within was I admitted. The sombre atmosphere inside was immediately apparent. I was shown into a small anteroom, where the goldsmith's English wife sat attended by two female attendants. She had obviously been crying and she still clutched a kerchief in trembling fingers.'

'Whatever has happened?' I demanded.

'Oh, Master Treviot,' she wailed. 'Do you know aught of this business? My John has done nothing to deserve what those men did to him. Who are they? I thought they would kill him.'

I was gripped by terrible foreboding. 'Was the leader a tall man with black hair?'

'Yes, yes! In heaven's name, who is he? Why did he force his way in here at first light? What grievance can he possibly have had with John?'

'Mistress, I am deeply sorry for your distress but 'tis vital I see your husband. May I go to him?'

She looked doubtful. 'He is very weak ... but if it will help to catch these wretches.' She motioned to one of her companions who silently led me up the stairs to the main bed chamber.

The curtains of an impressive bed were drawn back. Van der Goes lay partially propped on the pillows. His head was bound with a cloth which bore traces of blood and his face was bruised and swollen. I seated myself on the bed. 'Dear God, what have they done?' I muttered as much to myself as to the recumbent merchant.

He partially opened his lids and, with evident difficulty, focused on me. 'Brother Treviot, is that you?'

'Yes, what has happened here?'

'It was those enemies of Johannes Holbein. They came looking for him.'

'Today?' I was confused. Or, more likely, it was van der Goes whose mind was fuddled.

The sick man nodded and winced with the pain. 'Very early. I had scarcely risen.'

I pictured Holbein's lair as I had last seen it with its broken and scattered furniture. 'But the ruffians were at Bridewell yesterday. I was sure they must have found Holbein.'

'No. Their leader – a tall brute – said they spotted Johannes and followed him to Bridewell but he escaped them.'

'How could he do that? There's only one way in and out.'

'He has a key to a small store room next door and it has a trapdoor to the floor below. That was one of the reasons Johannes chose the place for his secret studio.' Van der Goes closed his eyes again and I feared he was lapsing into unconsciousness.

'Why did they come here?' I asked. 'Why did they do this to you?'

Van der Goes moaned. 'They were angry – very, very angry about losing Johannes again.'

'But why come to you?'

'They discovered that I own the warehouse and let out the space. They thought I'd know where Johannes has gone.'

'But you don't?'

'If Johannes is not at Bridewell, I know not where he is,' the injured man said, with great difficulty.

'You don't suppose . . .' I could hardly bring myself to mention the fearful question that occurred to me. 'He must have been terribly distressed to know that his sons had fallen into Black Harry's clutches. Is it possible he might have been overwhelmed with remorse. Could he have . . .'

'Taken his own life? I don't like to think it . . . Yet . . . He was very broken when he heard about the children . . . Poor Johannes! Is there anything to be done?'

'I can try the Steelyard. Someone there might know something.'

'Yes,' van der Goes said, 'that is our only chance. Pray God you find him there or hear news of him.' His head fell back against the pillow.

I stood up. 'I must let you rest. Take care of yourself. You have been a good friend to Holbein. I would not want to see you suffer more for him than you already have.'

'Thank you,' van der Goes muttered weakly. 'You, too, have tried to help him, Brother Treviot. Perhaps if I had trusted you more at the beginning.'

'Please, do not think like that. We have both made mistakes. I pray God grants us wit and time to put them right.' I crossed to the door. 'I promise to send you any news I have.'

As I was rowed back downriver I tried to make sense of the latest turn of events. Holbein must have had enough warning of the gang's approach to slip into the neighbouring room and make his escape. But where to? I went straight to the Hanse wharf. I climbed the stair in the shadow of the great crane which was busily hoisting bales of wool on to the quay. I asked the guard for Andreas Meyer and he sent a boy in search of the Steelyard's pastor. A chill autumnal wind was now blowing across the river and I began to get cold waiting on the open wharf. It was some minutes before the rotund figure appeared but when he did come bustling through the archway from the residential area, he was all affability.

'Master Treviot, how good to see you again, though I imagine your errand is not of the happiest.'

He led me through the complex of buildings to All Saints Church, the Hanse community's chapel. We passed through the building with its austere interior of white walls bereft of statues and pictures. A door close by the large pulpit led to Meyer's house and we were soon seated in his small study overlooking Thames Street. He called for beer and the taste of this beverage, still frowned on by many of my own countrymen, brought back memories of my visit to Antwerp some years before.

'Once again I come to you in search of Johannes Holbein,' I said.

'And once again I have to tell you that he is not here,' the pastor replied.

'But he has been here since I called.'

'Oh, yes. In fact, you have only missed him by a few hours.'

'He is still alive, then.'

Meyer nodded gravely. 'Alive, yes, but deeply troubled. I have spent much time counselling him. As you know too well, his two boys have been abducted by the desperate men who have been pursuing him.'

'Yes, I'm anxious to find him to tell him that his sons have been found and are safe.'

Meyer's face lit up in a broad smile. 'Oh, I'm so glad to hear that. I've been praying constantly for them. Oh, that is good news.'

'So where can I find Holbein to tell him?'

'I do not know, Master Treviot. I genuinely do not know. Perhaps it would be best if I explain to you from the beginning how I came to be involved in Johannes' complicated and troubled life.' He sat back in his chair and closed his eyes in an effort of memory. 'It is very difficult because he has only ever told me what he thinks it necessary for me to know. Whenever I press him for detail he replies that my safety lies in ignorance. I have no idea what he is involved in. I've only pieced together his story from scraps of things that he has said.'

'Perhaps you could tell me – briefly – what you do know, so that I may continue my search.'

'Of course. Well, it all began almost a month ago. I recall it was the first day of September. That was when the plague really began to affect us. We always have a feast on St Augustine's Day – that's the twenty-eighth – but we had decided to cancel it—'

'Yes, yes, Pastor Meyer,' I interrupted. 'If you could just give me the facts. Every minute might be vital.'

He nodded, but continued with his leisurely narrative. 'Indeed, indeed. Well, Johannes arrived all hot and begrimed. He looked terrible. He said he'd been waylaid on the road back to London from the royal court, somewhere east of the City. I assumed he had been attacked by highway robbers but from other things he let slip I realised there was more to it than that. He wanted asylum for a few days and, of course, we were happy to help. He was very agitated. He believed enemies were close on his trail.'

'Yes, yes. I know all this. Did he name his pursuers?'

'No. He was more concerned for the safety of his children and their nurse. He begged me to give them shelter also. Of course, I went immediately to his house – in person ...'

'You were presumably too late.'

'Indeed, the neighbours told me about the horrible crime and ...'

'So you told Holbein,' I prompted.

'Poor Johannes. He was distraught at the news. He was convinced evil men must have taken his boys. He shut himself away here and would see no one. I had no chance till later to tell him that people had come here looking for him.'

'People? I was not the only one, then?'

'No, another came that very afternoon.'

'A tall man with black hair?'

'Oh, no. This man was of average build, a gentleman ... very well dressed ... some might say overdressed.'

'Did he give his name?'

Meyer frowned. 'He did not. He was a haughty fellow ... thought I should be impressed by his talk of coming from the royal court. Popinjay! I made certain to tell him no more than he told me.'

'So when I called on 2 September, Holbein *was* here?'

'Yes, I'm afraid I was a little less than wholly honest with you. But he did leave again that very night. He said to stay here would put his friends' lives in danger.'

I sat back with a sigh of exasperation. 'If only you had let me see him so much tragedy might have been avoided.'

Meyer was crestfallen. 'I'm sorry. I really am but you can see why I was cautious, can you not? I didn't know who was looking for poor Johannes; only that he was very afraid of them. The only thing I could do was feign complete ignorance. However, I did, as you will recall, direct you to Master van der Goes, who is Johannes' closest friend. Was he not able to help you?'

'So you've really no idea where Holbein went after leaving here?'

'No. Later I worked out from odd things he said that he had two or three secret refuges but he would not tell me where they were. He had a powerful obsession about being hunted. If he was here in this room now, he would be repeatedly going to the window and peering down into the street. Once he snatched the door open in the middle of our conversation, convinced there was an eavesdropper outside. I tell you, Master Treviot, our friend lives in a very strange world; a world of secrecy, subterfuge and violence.'

'Master van der Goes told me that Holbein has been here again more recently.'

The pastor smiled. 'Simple people in my country believe in the *wichtel*, a fairy creature who comes and goes, appears and disappears at will. Johannes has something of the *wichtel* about him. We never know when to expect him. He was here ... it must have been two weeks ago. He said he'd found his boys and was looking for a shipmaster to carry the three of them secretly across the German Sea. That was not easy to arrange. Hanse merchants are very wary of getting into trouble with your government. If they are caught carrying the king's enemies out of England, they have their vessels and cargoes confiscated. However, a deal was struck. But then, last Wednesday, he was back again to say that he would not need a passage after all.'

'And that was not the last time you saw him?'

'No, he was here, just for a few minutes this morning. He was in a terrible state; almost out of his wits. He came to make his confession. You will understand I cannot go into detail about our discussion. Let me, instead, pose a theological question – hypothetical, of course. If a man surrenders himself to an enemy in the certain knowledge that that enemy will kill him, is he, thereby, guilty of the sin of suicide?'

'Hmm, I see.'

'I'm sure you do. I pray for him and I beg that you will do so too.'

'Of course. And if he "appears" again, in God's name tell him that his boys are safe with me and that I must talk with him. Urgently!'

Chapter 14

That evening Ned and I sat until late examining from every angle a situation that was becoming more complex by the day. I reported my conversation with Meyer.

'He had little to say, then?' Ned asked.

'Oh, he had a great deal to say but very little to tell. Heaven grant I never have to listen to one of his sermons. He did, however, make clear his great anxiety for Holbein. He fears our friend may rush headlong into some desperate deal. That's a concern I share.'

Ned was replacing one of the guttering candles. 'One thing that has occurred to me,' he said 'is the hurry everyone is in – or perhaps panic would be a better word. When I lived in the cloister, everything was regulated. Prayer, worship, work, silent meditation – all things had their allotted places. Life followed a measured, calm routine. That was the beauty of it.

When I came out into your world my first impression was one of mad, headlong rush. It took me several weeks to realise that it was an illusion. Very few people, in fact, move faster than they need to move. The seasons come and go, so do feast days and fast days, market days, wash days, baking days. Folk love the unhurried pattern. They avoid frenzy. So when I see people madly rushing to and fro, it makes me wonder why.'

'You mean like Black Harry?'

'Him, certainly. He is in London, then he's here, then in Essex, then back to London. But he's not the only one. Your Johannes Holbein moves rapidly to and fro across the City, never resting more than a day or two anywhere. And now, here you are, caught up in the same delirious rampaging around the country.'

'Not of my own free will, I can assure you.'

'Exactly!' Ned said with a tone of triumph. 'Now, if not your will, whose?'

'I'm not sure I follow.'

'Then let me catechise you. What turns a trickling stream into a raging torrent?'

'A greater volume of water coming from upriver.'

'And what causes the greater volume of water?'

'Well, storms, unusually heavy rain.'

'So what is the storm that is turning so many lives into a tumbling, raging fury?'

When I hesitated to reply, Ned answered his own question: 'Fear. Black Harry provokes fear in Holbein but only because he is afraid of someone behind him – upriver, to continue our analogy. Now who can strike fear into the heart of this God-less fiend?'

'His paymasters.'

'Yes, he is well protected by powerful men and, presumably, well paid also. But what if he fails to satisfy them?'

'No more protection and no more gold.'

'Exactly. His patrons will not hesitate to abandon him if he does not give them what they want. And then?'

'The great Black Harry becomes just another desperate outlaw, heading almost inexorably for the gallows. That's all very interesting, Ned, but I don't see how it helps us.'

'It always helps to know your enemy, especially his weaknesses. Just bear in mind that yours is vulnerable. One day that knowledge may come in useful. I also counsel you to cultivate the art of reflection.'

I laughed. 'Would you have me become a recluse, a holy hermit?'

But Ned was quite serious. 'I would have you stay alive, my friend, and you are more likely to do that if you can stand back from your problems. Rush and hurry begin in the mind – or the soul – and may gallop us unheeding to the precipice. One of the mystics tells us, "The man who lives in contemplation will not err in his worldly affairs".'

'Easily said if you live in a monastery,' I said. 'Now, talking of fear, I'm very worried about Bart and Lizzie. They and the children ought not to be in the City while the plague is raging.'

'I agree, and—'

'Then there's Bart's impetuousness. As long as he plays the lone hunter, trying to corner a beast like Black Harry, he's in constant danger.'

'Yes, that's why—'

'We must try to find some safe refuge where we can keep a check on their activities.'

Now it was Ned's turn to laugh. 'You prove my point most

eloquently, Thomas. While you've been rushing from anxiety to anxiety, I have made the necessary arrangements. A friend of mine – ex-abbess of a Poor Clare convent – has her own house not far away. She will be delighted to take in Lizzie and the children. I've also persuaded Lizzie to let Bart stay here with me. If he has to go out we can arrange a suitable disguise, as we did the other day, and I may just possibly be able to exert a calming influence.'

I muttered something to cover my embarrassment.

'And you,' Ned continued, 'what are your plans?'

'I'll leave messages for Master Johannes with his friends in the hope of arranging a meeting. For the next few days I shall be busy in Kent on the archbishop's commission.'

'Have you thought of trying to work your way back upstream?'

'Upstream?'

Ned chuckled. 'Forgive me. I was carried away by my own metaphor. What I mean is, since all these misfortunes have their origins in the royal court, do you have any contacts there who might be able to help with information or advice?'

'I have done work for some members of the Privy Chamber. In fact, only a few months ago my workshop made a magnificent astronomical clock for Anthony Denny, his majesty's Groom of the Stool. A gift for the king. It was designed by Holbein – a most elaborate piece: clock, hourglass, sundial and compass all in one. It stretched my workmen to the limit. Master Anthony was delighted with it.'

'Could you not have a word with him? Perhaps there might be a way to dam the flood upriver or divert its channel.'

'He will be with the court. I believe they're all out in Berkshire somewhere.'

'No more than a short day's ride.'

'I thought you disapproved of my galloping round the country.'

Ned turned on me his familiar deceptive smile which gave the impression he was a rather simple old man, and concealed his guileful wisdom. 'It seems to me there is much difference between following a trail and laying one.'

As I took my candle and hauled myself wearily up to Ned's guest chamber my head whirled. All this talk of rivers and trails! Would I ever again find an even and well-signposted road beneath my feet?

Any thought of taking Ned's advice was put from my mind when I arrived back at Hemmings. Among the messages waiting for me was one from James Dewey, my friend and Kentish neighbour, suggesting an itinerary for our investigation of local clergy. However, more urgent was the summons to serve on the jury at the Canterbury quarter sessions. There was also a letter from Ralph Morice in response to my reports to the archbishop. The cumulative effect of these documents was worrying in the extreme. I sat in my chamber with them spread before me, looking from one to the other, trying to form a coherent impression of the situation that was developing in the county.

The summons stressed the importance of the forthcoming judicial proceedings:

There is much more business than usual. The postponement of the Michaelmas sittings at Westminster has led to some cases being referred to the quarter sessions. More pressing is the growing unrest in the county. Jails are full with offenders awaiting trial. Until these are dealt with and space made to detain other malefactors, magistrates will find it difficult to place in custody the noisome preachers and popular agitators who are everywhere disturbing his majesty's peace ...

The notice instructed jurors to make provision for spending several days in Canterbury to deal with the crisis.

James's letter listed seven churches that, in his opinion, warranted our urgent attention.

... Information has been laid against the Vicar of Bremley, that he is sluggardly in setting forth the king's supremacy, utters saucy words against his grace, the archbishop, and has removed the Bible from his church. At St Margaret's, Settringham, there has been much stirring caused by the parson, Edmund Styles. People complain of statues defaced by his order and of his preaching in the marketplace. He seems to have built up a large popular following of hotbrained young men who talk of using force to – as they say – rid the realm of popery ...

The letter from Ralph Morice was longer and slightly rambling, which was strange, coming from someone who had an orderly mind.

His grace thanks you for your endeavours and regrets that they have yet to bear fruit ...

No mention of Holbein's name. Perhaps Morice feared his letter might be intercepted.

... The information is more important than ever ... His grace's enemies among the cathedral clergy and shire gentry have met in secret, as they suppose, to plan their campaign.

Their immediate target is Richard Turner, vicar at Chartham, a true Bible man and a zealous preacher. They have arrested him and purpose to bring him before the sessions. The reason is, not so much his godly teaching – though that they abhor – but that he stands high in his grace's favour. If they can once indict Turner for preaching against official doctrine and have him brought to trial, they hope to tear from him recantation of the truth and words they can twist and use against his grace and sundry of our friends who stand by the king's supremacy and the reformed religion. His grace dares do nothing for the poor man's delivery save that he sanctions me to approach our friends at court to inform his majesty of the wicked deviousness of these papists ... His grace is in his manor at Croydon and waits to receive any new information you have ...

New information? Heartily did I wish that I had *any* information – anything that made sense to me, any facts that were firm beneath my feet, instead of the shifting sands of feuding factions, clashing religious convictions, personal rivalries and violence which knew no limit. It was now the end of September and I was no closer to finding Holbein, saving Bart from the gallows or obtaining justice for a poor young man butchered in Aldgate than I had been the first day of the month, when my involvement in this wretched business started. Nor, I realised, would I find my way to solid ground while I was embroiled in the rivalries and hatreds of Kent's political life. Ned was right; I would achieve nothing as long as I continued to let events propel me along a twisting lane leading I knew not where. It was time to do some of the pushing myself. But not yet. For now I was caught up in the cumbersome machinery of the English legal system.

These thoughts occupied my mind for much of the next day's journey to Canterbury. James and I travelled together with our own escort and spoke little.

'Do you know anything about this Turner troublemaker we have to deal with at the sessions?' I asked the question as we sat in the inn at Lenham, where we had stopped for dinner.

James carved himself another slice of cheese. 'This is very good,' he said. 'Turner? I only know what Thwaites and others say. They've been trying to silence him for a couple of years. Every time they send him up to the archbishop's court he comes back with his grace's blessing.' He grinned. 'Frustrating for them. Personally, anything that upsets Thwaites is sweet music to me.'

'Has the archbishop appointed Turner to speed up the pace of reform?'

'Not so much Cranmer; more his secretary, Ralph Morice. It was Morice who instituted Turner to the living at Chartham. I don't think even Morice can save him this time.'

'Because he's being brought to the secular court?'

James nodded. 'Violation of Statute of Six Articles, 31 Henry VIII number 14.'

I laughed. 'I didn't know you were a lawyer. Do you have all the laws of the realm at your finger ends?'

'Not many,' he replied with his mouth full, 'but this one's particularly useful.' He swallowed, cleared his throat and recited: '"In the most blessed sacrament of the altar, by the strength and efficacy of Christ's mighty word, it being spoken by the priest, is present really under the form of bread and wine, the natural body and blood of our Saviour Jesu Christ, conceived of the Virgin Mary, and that after the consecration there remains no substance of bread or wine."'

'So, you are a theologian as well as a lawyer.'

'No, I don't understand all the stuff about "substance" and "real presence". The beauty of this statute is that I don't have to. All we magistrates are called on to do is recite the words and ask the prisoner, "Do you believe it?" If he says no, he burns. Of course, very few do say no. I've only ever sent one man up to a higher court for the death sentence.'

'I think that would worry me.'

'What?'

'Sending someone to the stake for what he believes.'

He shrugged. 'Life was easier for magistrates when we didn't have to get involved in such cases but since his majesty has extended the scope of common law we have no choice. You've no idea how much the burden of our work has increased in the last few years. Anyway, most of these heretics recant under pressure and then lose credibility among their own followers.'

'So when I cast my vote in the jury hearing Turner's case I will be expected to find him guilty so that he'll be persuaded to recant?'

James frowned at me over the rim of his tankard. 'You know your duty, Thomas.'

'I know nothing. I just need to understand what will be expected of me as a juryman.'

'Turner will be indicted for preaching against the Six Articles. You have to decide if he's guilty.' James pushed his trencher to one side. 'Now we should be getting back on the road.'

I did not move. 'And if he's pronounced guilty the arch-bishop's enemies will accuse him of supporting heretics.'

He stood and set his cap on his head. 'I really don't know ...'

'James, we've been friends for too long. I can tell when you're trying to hide something from me.'

'There are things it would be better if you did not know.'

'Then let me guess. Magistrates are under pressure to uncover any information that can be used against Cranmer.'

James hesitated for several moments, then said, 'All I can tell you is that certain men – powerful men – feel the archbishop is trying to force change too quickly and that it encourages rebellious spirits.'

'By "certain men" you mean Sir Thomas Moyle and his friends.'

But James was already walking to the door.

As we rode our horses out of the inn yard and turned along the short village street, James pointed to a group of men and women emerging from one of the larger houses. 'In my opinion, the law would be better occupied keeping an eye on them.'

'Why? Who are they? They look peaceable enough.'

'Cloth workers. There's a tribe of them in this area. Aliens mostly. They work for lower wages than their neighbours. You can imagine what feelings that stirs. More importantly, they bring their own religious ideas with them.'

'Lutherans?'

'Aye, and others. There's all sorts of foreigners who've left the pope's church to follow I don't know what weird opinions. The trouble is, they spread their ideas to others.'

'What sort of ideas?'

'Oh, I don't know. I've got tired of arguing with the simpletons. You and I know, don't we, that religion is priests' business. So if the Church says, "This bread and wine is now flesh and blood because the priest has said some words over it", we believe it. Not these people. "It still looks like bread and wine, so it is bread and wine," they say. Well, what's the point of trying to reason with that sort of simple-minded nonsense?'

I thought, but did not say, 'Tis not clear to me exactly who is being simple-minded.

The Shire Hall was a scene of constant movement. People were coming and going all the time. Witnesses and other interested parties arrived early, not knowing when their cases would be called. Thus, while some of the throng in the body of the hall were involved in the proceedings and pressed forward to the bar to follow what the lawyers and court officials were saying, others were waiting and talking among themselves. Frequently the Clerk of the Peace had to call for silence. Magistrates, who took turns to preside over the quarter sessions, hurried the day's business forward as quickly as they could. More than once an impatient chairman glowered at the jury and demanded to know why we were taking so long to reach our verdict.

The jury occupied a bench to one side of the upper hall. Most members served for at least a day, though twice someone from among the casual observers had to be sworn to make up numbers. My colleagues were yeomen farmers or tenants of the area's major landowners. When a verdict was called for we huddled together in the nearest corner, each man stating his opinion while very aware of the court officers' impatience to press on to the next case. Thus we made short work of a succession of men and women charged with theft, highway robbery, fraud and treasonous words.

It was mid-afternoon when Richard Turner was brought in. I studied him carefully as he stood, manacled, beside a constable. Thin, pale, straggle-haired and with wisps of straw from the prison floor stuck to his overgown, he did not look an imposing figure. It was when he spoke, answering questions without hesitation and declaring in a forthright manner what he believed, that I came swiftly to the conclusion that here was a man not come hither to recant.

Sir Thomas Moyle had been elected, as senior magistrate, to take the chair for this case and he called for the indictment to be read. Clearly, Cranmer had, as yet, taken no action against him.

'You are charged that, on Passion Sunday last past, you did preach in Chartham Church against the doctrine of the Church, as defined in the Statute of Six Articles. What say you to the charge?'

'That I am not guilty,' Turner replied so quietly that I had to lean forward to hear his words.

'Well,' said Moyle, 'we shall see. Here are witnesses who will declare otherwise. Master Sanders and Master Brown, stand forth to be sworn.'

Two men in the dress of simple husbandmen shuffled into the area beneath the raised platform on which the chairman sat. They took their oaths.

'As good Christian men, you attended mass in your parish church upon Passion Sunday, did you not?'

'Yes, Master,' the witnesses replied in unison.

'And was the vicar, Richard Turner, preaching upon that day?'

'Yes, Master.'

'And, to the best of your recollection, what did he say in his sermon?'

There was laughter in the court as both men tried to answer at once. Moyle tetchily told Sanders to give his evidence first.

'He said that the mass was nothing worth; that Our Lord did give his body and blood on the cross and that no living person, be he priest or layman, can add to that sacrifice.'

'That seems clear enough,' said Moyle. 'Master Brown, is your recollection in agreement with that?'

Brown nodded, seeming suddenly tongue-tied.

Moyle turned to the prisoner. 'What say you to that?'

'I say it is not in contradiction of the Act,' Turner replied. 'That Christ's sacrifice is sufficient for all men at all times no Christian would disagree. I do not debate how that sacrifice is represented in the mass.'

At that moment a young man in a lawyer's gown stood and approached the bench. 'May it please, Your Honour, my name is Ralph Symons of Gray's Inn. I have been engaged to represent the prisoner.'

'Engaged? Who by?' Moyle did not look pleased.

'By Master Morice, on behalf of his grace of Canterbury. With your permission I would like to ask one or two questions of the witnesses.'

The chairman nodded.

So, I thought, Cranmer is taking a hand in this affair? Would Moyle, I wondered, take note and modify his hostility towards the accused?

Symons smiled at the two Chartham men, who appeared bewildered and had obviously not expected this development. 'Good day to you, Masters. How do you fare? These are hard times for honest husbandmen. I know not how you manage to produce sufficient yield to feed your families.'

''Tis indeed a struggle, Sir,' Sanders replied.

'I presume you go to market every day possible to sell your surplus.'

The witnesses readily signified their agreement, presumably relieved that they were not facing a difficult interrogation.

'Were you at Wye Fair this year?'

'Yes, Sir.'

'You always make a point of attending this major event.'

'Yes, Sir, never miss,' Brown agreed.

'That takes place upon St Gregory's Eve, I believe.' Symons picked up a book and opened it. 'Now, the feast of St Gregory is 12 March, is it not? So the eve is 11 March. Well, here's something interesting in my almanac. It seems that Passion Sunday this year fell upon 11 March. Now, Masters, answer me truthfully, do you practise witchcraft?'

The witnesses were dumbfounded. They muttered and spluttered their denials.

'We are all relieved to hear it. That being the case, I assume you have not mastered the diabolical art of being in two places at the same time. If you spent the day at Wye Fair, you could not have heard Master Turner preach in Chartham.'

Moyle now intervened angrily. 'This is nothing to the point, Master Symons. We are here to decide whether the prisoner teaches dangerous heresy.'

'Your Honour, the indictment is very specific. It charges the prisoner with uttering words against the Six Articles Act on Passion Sunday of this year. No witnesses have yet been brought forward who can help the jury decide the matter.'

Moyle was now red-faced with fury. 'Mere technicality!' he shouted. 'I'll have no more of this nonsense!' He glowered at my colleagues and me. 'Men of the jury, consider your verdict – and make haste.'

Chapter 15

We quickly shuffled into our jurors' huddle.

'Guilty?' our foreman enquired and there was a general murmur of assent.

'Surely not,' I protested. 'The lawyer's point was a strong one. Turner has not defied the law as stated in the indictment.'

'But Sir Thomas says that is a mere technicality,' a burly man – and one of Moyle's tenants – said.

'We have heard no evidence about Turner's preaching,' I urged. 'The witnesses were not in church on Passion Sunday.'

'They know what they heard,' the foreman insisted. 'The date hardly matters.'

'Aye,' said another, 'we all know the stirs made by the likes of this fellow.'

'And for that you would burn him, without evidence?' By now I was shouting and people were staring.

'Master foreman, what's to do?' Moyle bellowed. 'Are we to have your decision today?'

'Indeed, Your Honour. I beg Your Honour's pardon for the delay. We find the accused guilty.'

I jumped to my feet. 'I do not!' I glowered at my colleagues. 'As for you, perjure yourselves if you will to please whoever is paying you.'

Now there was commotion in the court. The clerk's demand for order could scarcely be heard.

Only Moyle's voice carried over the hubbub. He was on his feet and shouting. 'Master Treviot, you will behave yourself in my court or I will have you arrested.'

'*Your* court, Sir Thomas? I had thought it was the king's court and, by God, his majesty shall hear how you abuse his justice. I want no more of your court.' I turned and strode down the hall.

'Arrest that man! Guard! God flay you; where are you? Arrest him, I say!'

But no one laid a hand on me as I elbowed my way through the crowd.

I went straight to my inn, collected my bag and my escort and rode out of Canterbury. Not until we were jogging along the London road did I think about where we were going. A fresh westerly breeze did something to calm my temper and make me reflect on my actions. Was it just Moyle's high-handedness that enraged me or was I beginning to take sides in the religious war that was starting to divide the country so bitterly? Whatever my motive, I had done something very foolish. In my hot-headedness, I had threatened to complain to the king – a threat I was in no position to carry out. Yet, if I did nothing, I would have made a powerful enemy for no good reason. Moyle was not the sort of man to overlook my behaviour. How would he go about exacting his revenge? Clap me in jail for aiding a heretic? Put me on trial in his sham court? Or, perhaps, set Black Harry on my trail? If I was to escape his wrath I would have to act first – and quickly.

Walt brought his horse alongside mine. 'That was well spoken back there, Master. I don't like troublemakers but that Turner was poorly treated.'

'I shouldn't have let my anger get the better of me.'

'You've shown there's at least one honourable man in Kent. Where to now, Master? Back to Hemmings?'

'Not yet,' I replied. 'We have a call to make in Croydon.'

The early sunshine softened the austere outline of the arch-bishop's venerable palace. The large building, partly of stone and partly of brick, was certainly impressive but the gentle eastern light gave it a warm, almost welcoming appearance. We had arrived in Croydon on Thursday evening and obtained lodging in a pleasant inn. The following morning I rose early in the hope of meeting Ralph Morice before he became embroiled in the day's affairs. When my presence had been announced, I was led through several rooms and up a staircase to a first-floor long gallery. I had heard of this archi-tectural fashion for a special space where the residents could take indoor exercise but had not before encountered one. As I waited, I slowly paced the length of the room, pausing occa-sionally to admire the view through its many south-facing windows. These overlooked extensive gardens and offered an excellent prospect of wooded upland beyond.

'What a beautiful day.'

I had not heard Ralph Morice's approach. Turning to shake his hand, I said, 'Yes, and an excellent vantage point.'

'This is his grace's favourite house. He's spent considerable sums on improvements over the years. Lambeth Palace is appallingly damp and Ford is too close to Canterbury for comfort. I gather you've just come from there.'

'Yes, and was glad to be quit of the place.'

As we paced up and down the gallery, I recounted the events of the last few days.

Morice listened attentively, occasionally interrupting to ask a question. 'Poor Richard,' he said at last.

'Can you do anything for him?' I asked.

'I hope so.' He walked on a few paces, head forward, hands clasped behind his back. He stopped and turned. When he spoke it was with a new gravity and urgency. 'Thomas, you are already a long way into this business. May I ask you to go even further?'

'Will it help me keep my friend from the gallows?'

'It may. His fate has become tangled with matters of greater import.'

'Then, I will do whatever I can . . .'

'It will be dangerous – more dangerous than even I can guess. The people we're up against are driven by forces that I don't hesitate to call demonic. As soon as they know you're probing their affairs . . .'

'Ralph, for God's sake, will you tell me what all this is about? I've picked up bits and pieces, hints and suggestions, suspicions and accusations. I can't fit them together. I don't even know if they do fit together.'

'Thomas, you are closer to the truth than you know.' Morice breathed a long, shuddering sigh. 'Come sit.'

We moved to two large panelled chairs by a window and Morice continued. 'The pieces do *not* fit. If they did that would suggest that there is a scheme, a pattern, a plan, something governed by coherent principles. In England today no

191

such intelligent arrangement of facts, ideas, policies exists. All is chaos.'

'I don't begin to understand.'

'No, and it would be better, safer, for you to continue in ignorance. But, if you want to save your friend and, God willing, also the archbishop, you must open your mind to the unpleasant truth.' He paused. 'There is pain that is so intense it can drive a man out of his wits. Our king is a victim of such pain – in his legs.'

'Are you saying his majesty is . . .'

Morice put a finger to his lips. 'We may think it but must never say it. He is not afflicted all the time. When his ulcerous sores are opened and drained, or when he has been bled, he has a measure of relief. Then, we get glimpses of the old Henry – affable, approachable, rational. At other times . . . Well, I prefer to think 'tis the devil that possesses him. Then no one can guess what he will say, what he will do, what he will order to be done.'

'If what you say is true, how is England governed?'

'It isn't. Not properly. Not this last three years.'

'Since Cromwell's fall?'

'Aye. He was a political genius – and a man of God. He understood what ailed his majesty. He could ride the king's moods, handle complex affairs of state, give England a political direction – and a spiritual one. He had a vision for the building of a godly commonwealth. He could speak plainly to the king. I've seen his majesty box Cromwell round the ears and Cromwell walk away smiling. He knew how far he could go; what he needed to do to keep the king's trust.'

'Until the day he lost it.'

'Aye, and since then England has been like a ship adrift.'

'But surely the Privy Council . . .'

Morice snorted his contempt. 'Worse than half-brewed ale! They're frightened of the king and each one is concerned only for his own security. That is why they squabble among themselves.'

'And it's the Duke of Norfolk and Bishop Gardiner who are heading the attack on the archbishop?'

'Foxy Gardiner is the one to watch. Old Norfolk is all oaths and bluster. He lacks the wit for conspiracy. I wonder he's survived to three score years and ten. His influence is largely based on family ties and the power of the ancient nobility, especially in the remote areas away from London. Gardiner is canny and he has a large section of the Church behind him. He really does head a "party", a "faction", a far-reaching "web". He has friends among all those who hanker after the old days of papal Antichrist, whether in parliament, among the parish clergy or the shire gentry. You've heard Marbeck's story. You've seen for yourself the campaign against Turner. I could name a baker's dozen of other good Christian souls who have been embroiled in Wily Winchester's plots this last year alone.'

He stood up. 'Let's walk a little more. My legs become stiff with too much sitting.'

As we turned to pace the gallery again, the secretary resumed his tale. 'This business in Canterbury is the most dangerous yet.'

'Because it aims to unseat Cranmer from his position at the centre of the diocese?'

'Yes, the real power there lies with the prebendaries, the senior clergy. Most of them have been in place several years and are reactionary to a man. In order to limit their influence, his grace established a new body, the Six Preachers, whose task it is to maintain regular Gospel preaching. Richard Turner is one of them.'

'Really? I did not know that.'

'The two groups and their supporters are locked in conflict and their quarrel extends into the parishes and the manor houses of Kent. This you know. What you probably do not know is that the prebendaries take their lead directly from the Bishop of Winchester. The link is Germain Gardiner, the bishop's nephew and secretary. He travels constantly between the court and the cathedral.'

'Why doesn't his grace take strong action to deal with these subversive elements?'

Morice sighed and lifted his gaze heavenwards. 'Because he disdains intrigue. Because he thinks he is not called to play worldly politics. Because he believes God will support him against the machinations of evil men. Because he is sure that truth will prevail. In short, because he is too much the saint and too little the archbishop. So I must play the Machiavel, make the deals, conceive the strategies, do the best I can with the cards his grace has been dealt.'

'And what kind of hand is that?'

'We are very strong in one suit. Please God, it may win us the game but we will have to use all our skill – and time is running out.'

'Ralph, it would help if you spoke plain and not in preacher's analogies.'

'Very well. Who do you suppose controls the government of England under the king?'

'The Council.'

'No, the members of the Privy Chamber. If you want to know who it is helps his majesty to make up his mind on matters of state you should look to his doctors, to his intimate servants who change the bandages on his painful legs, to the companions who ease his sleepless nights by playing at cards or dice, his fool who can make him laugh, his musicians who remind him of earlier, happier days. And, of course, we must not forget the queen. Such people are with the king all the time, whether at Westminster or Greenwich or when he travels on summer progress. The Council, by contrast, is stuck at Whitehall. Our enemies are well represented on the Council but we have many friends in the Privy Chamber. Ironically, the plague has done us a great favour by extending the progress longer than usual but this advantage must end soon. When the court returns for the winter Gardiner and his associates will be able to pour all manner of evil counsels into the royal ear.'

'What exactly is it you want me to do?'

'Go to the court. Seek out those of our friends closest to the king. Give them your first-hand account of Moyle's misbehaviour. Ask them to petition his majesty for a royal pardon for Richard Turner. That would send a very strong signal to his grace's enemies in Kent.'

'I had already planned a visit to Master Anthony Denny in connection with my search for Holbein.'

'Excellent! There is no man better. As Groom of the Stool, he is the king's closest attendant and much trusted. I will give you letters to take to him and to Sir William Butts, his majesty's physician. Gardiner's agents are, of course, always on the watch for messengers from his grace but they will have no reason to suspect you.'

I gazed out over the gardens. The sun had retreated behind black clouds depriving the trees and hedges of their radiance. The first leaves of autumn drifted across the mown lawns and gravelled walks. 'This, then, is how innocent men get drawn into intrigue,' I said.

*

195

Morice had told me that the court was now to be found at Woodstock, beyond Oxford, and Walt and I set out early the next day, Saturday, hoping to reach our destination by Sunday evening. The journey was without note, save what transpired when we halted to hear mass in a village not far from Windsor.

As we rode along the straggling street, people – many people – were making their way towards the small, squat church at its northern end.

'I see we're in for a sermon.' Walt pointed out some villagers who were carrying stools.

'We can't afford the time for that,' I said. 'We'll stand at the back and leave before the pulpiting starts.'

There were a number of reasons why this did not happen. The church was well filled when we entered and several more members of the congregation pressed in to stand behind us. Pushing our way out was always going to be difficult. Then, just before the start of the service, a well-dressed lad of about twelve years wriggled through the throng and addressed me. 'Good day to you, Sir. Father begs that you will be pleased to sit with us.' He turned and led me to the front of the nave where three private pews stood. They were occupied by members of the most important local family. A tall fresh-faced man who was obviously lord of the manor greeted me warmly and introduced himself as Richard Greenham. 'We can't allow visitors of quality to stand with the commons,' he said. I thanked him and cursed inwardly at the time his invitation was causing us to lose. I suspected that we would be very lucky to escape without being urged to stay for dinner. Provincial 'grandees', in my experience, usually grasped every opportunity to scrape up acquaintance with visiting social equals and superiors.

The liturgy followed its familiar pattern and was briskly completed, much to my relief. When the priest ascended the pulpit, my host whispered to me, 'John Sturt, my chaplain, excellent man, Oxford.' There was a sound of shuffling and, gazing round, I had the distinct impression that the congregation was settling to what they regarded as the main part of the proceedings.

The preacher was an unprepossessing man of about forty but there was nothing commonplace about his message or its delivery. From his first few sentences he had his listeners' rapt attention.

'"Not all they that say unto me, Master, Master, shall enter into the kingdom of heaven, but he who does my Father's will, who is in heaven". You have heard the words yourselves read from the Gospel of Saint Matthew; words that came from the very lips of our Lord. Hear again his solemn response to those who call upon him "Master, Master, have we not in your name prophesied, and in your name cast out devils, and in your name done many miracles?": Then, will I say unto them, "I never knew you; depart from me you workers of iniquity."'

Sturt made a long pause and glared round the congregation, his bushy eyebrows almost meeting. 'Now, who was our Lord speaking about? He tells us in this same chapter. He warns us against false prophets; dissembling wolves who come among us in the guise of sheep. "See my godly works," they say. "I can absolve sins; I can pray for souls in purgatory; I can make Christ on the altar." Believe them not. Do not listen to their words; rather pay heed to their actions, for our Lord says, "You will recognise them by their fruits." Do they take money from you to say masses for the dead? That is a bitter fruit. Are they more concerned for their tithes and fees than for the spiritual needs of their people? More bitter fruit. Do they make you bow down to carved and painted statues? That, too, is bitter fruit. Do they burn your body to ashes if you disagree with their devilish doctrine? Oh, what bitter fruit our dear friends in Windsor were made to taste on that evil day in July.' The preacher's words brought murmurs of agreement from the congregation and these became louder as he warmed to his subject.

Afterwards we hastened to be on our way. I managed to avoid the expected invitation and also to impress the Greenham family by telling them we had urgent business at the royal court. After a couple of miles I noticed my men, riding ahead, were arguing among themselves. When we stopped at a stream to water the horses, Dick, the youngest of them, edged close to me. 'Master Thomas,' he said as he washed mud from his mare's legs, 'do you think he was right?'

'The preacher?'

'Yes.'

'Why do you ask?'

'He seems to have made Walt very angry. He says the clergy are God's ministers and we should respect them.'

'And you?'

'I had a great falling out with our priest back home when my mother died. The priest talked my father into paying for several masses and making an offering at St Ippolyt's shrine. He took everything the old man had – money that should have come to me and my brother.'

'That was wrong of him.'

'Aye, and when I told him so he got right angry. Said he'd heard I was a Bible-reading troublemaker and if I didn't seek his absolution, he'd see me in the bishop's court as a heretic.'

'And that was why you left home and came to London?'

He nodded. 'Now I daren't go back for fear of what he

might do. Walt says I should. He reckons God made priests and laymen, masters and servants, and we do well to give all honour to our betters. I say I want proof that a man *is* my better before I doff my cap to him. Like the preacher said, "by their fruits you shall know them". Walt says we shouldn't listen to such Bible-toting men because they undermine what he calls the "natural order". Is he right, Master?'

I tried to weigh my response very carefully. 'I think we live in troubled times and probably sermons like the one we've just heard don't help.'

Dick frowned and I guessed my answer was not what he wanted to hear. To console him I added, 'But change – reform – there must be, partly because there are parish priests like yours around. If God gave us priests, he also gave us the Bible, and I don't see how the two can be in conflict.'

We all remounted and as we rode on I mused about the clashing authorities of magistrate, priest and Bible. I realised more clearly than before that these things which were the concerns of kings, councillors and archbishops also troubled the minds of ordinary people. Now, they were beginning to trouble me.

Chapter 16

It was almost possible to calculate how close we were to Woodstock from the prices charged for food, drink and lodging at the inns. The increased demand created by the large royal household and travellers having business with the king enabled local suppliers to double or even treble their normal charges. It was obvious we would have difficulty finding somewhere to stay, so I despatched two of my men to scour the countryside in search of accommodation while Dick and I rode to the imposing ancient palace set on rising ground above the town.

'Shall we see the king?' Dick asked eagerly as we approached the gatehouse.

'I shouldn't set your hopes on it,' I said. 'I understand his majesty seldom ventures outside the Privy apartments.'

So it proved. The central bastion housing the royal quarters was like a fortress within a fortress. Guards denied access to all except chamber staff and visitors who could present permits. Everyone else was obliged to wait in the main courtyard or adjacent chambers designated for hopeful suitors. I did manage to waylay a royal page and give him a quarter sovereign to carry a message to Anthony Denny but I did not know whether he faithfully carried out my commission.

But luck was with me. A little before noon on Monday I saw Denny emerge from the royal quarters, deep in conversation with an older, white-haired man. When I approached Denny regarded me uncertainly. Then came recognition. 'Master goldsmith, is it not? What brings you to court?'

I fell into step beside him as he and his companion walked briskly across the courtyard. 'I come with messages from My Lord Archbishop of Canterbury.'

The two men stopped and exchanged brief glances. 'From Cranmer? How fares his grace?' Denny asked. His tone conveyed more than casual politeness.

'In good health, 'I responded, 'though much careworn.' I produced letters that had been entrusted to me by the archbishop and his secretary.

Denny introduced his companion. 'This is Dr William Butts, his majesty's senior physician. We would gladly hear more of the archbishop but cannot stay now. Perhaps you would care to join us later. His majesty will be spending the evening with the queen in her apartments. Come and sup with us in my quarters. I will inform the guard captain. Until later, Master Treviot.' He nodded and he and Butts hurried on their way.

The chamber I entered that evening was narrow and high-ceilinged, like many in ancient buildings. Much of the bare stonework was covered by tapestries and other hangings.

Torches set in sconces lit the space well and a good fire blazed on the hearth. Two servants were engaged in setting silver dishes close to the burning logs to keep warm. Other utensils and platters were set on a small buffet and reflected the flames. Denny and Butts were already seated at the table looking over the letters I had brought.

From my earlier commercial dealings with the courtier it did not surprise me that Denny insisted on getting straight down to business.

'Ralph Morice has given a remarkable account of your recent activities, Master Treviot. He assures us you are a man to be trusted. As for us, you may speak freely here. My servants are well chosen for their discretion.' He spoke in rapid sentences, his forked beard fluttering as his chin rose and fell. 'Now, first of all, this business of Richard Turner. The man is somewhat troublesome. I have already obtained a pardon for him once.'

'His enemies seem extremely persistent. Perhaps, they hope by bringing repeated charges they may convince his majesty that the man really is a heretic,' I suggested.

A smile lit up the doctor's dark, intelligent eyes. 'If they believe their steady drip, drip will wear down the stone, they do not know our Harry.'

'How is Turner's preaching received in Kent?' Denny asked.

'I gather he has a large following in Chartham and the surrounding area.'

'How do you judge the mood of the shire as a whole?'

'It seems there are pockets where reformed teaching prevails and others where the preference is for a stubborn traditionalism.'

'Do you have a list of the more active papists among the gentry?' Butts asked mildly.

'No. Doubtless his grace's commissioners will reveal who the most difficult landowners are.'

'Then let us hope they make haste,' Denny said acerbically.

'I'm sure Morice understands the urgency of the situation. He impressed upon me that if the opposition is not silenced within days or weeks his grace's enemies may prevail,' I said.

'He is right, though not entirely for the reasons he thinks. The problem is wider and deeper.'

Several moments of silence followed. I was aware of unspoken communication between the other men. Then Denny dismissed the servants. 'Master Treviot, we believe you have been brought here by Providence and we have decided to share with you things that no one outside our very tight circle knows.'

The words were ominous. I had grown very wary of being made party to dangerous confidences. 'Master Denny, I doubt—'

'We are at the political centre,' Denny continued, ignoring my protest. 'We can see much of what is happening. But not all. You have the advantage of being able to move freely about the country.' He moved aside several of the dishes. 'As you will see, there are aggravating gaps in our knowledge. We want those gaps filled by whatever you can discover. The first thing you should know is that our king intends to go to war – possibly in person.'

'War?' I gasped. 'But I thought he was a sick man. I had heard he was offering friendship to the Emperor – but war!'

Butts said, 'Would you like to tell his majesty he is too old and too ill for charging around on battlefields? He has decided to send troops to France and to lead them in person. It might kill him. It will certainly bankrupt England. But he will do it.'

Denny took up the tale again. 'Now the man who has

talked him into this folly is the imperial ambassador, Eustace Chapuys.' Taking a silver table salt, he spooned a small mound of the contents on to the bare boards. 'This policy has the support of some members of the Council, principally Bishop Gardiner.'

'Because he sees it as one step in reuniting England with Catholic Europe?'

'Precisely, Master Treviot. His ultimate objective is to restore our bondage to the pope. So, here we have Gardiner, working closely with Chapuys.' He put another pile of salt on the table and with the spoon made a white line between the two. 'Gardiner is hard at work to put a stop to the reformation of the English Church. His biggest obstacle is Cranmer. So, as you have seen, he is working hard to undermine the archbishop. As he rid the realm of Cromwell, so he plans to dispose of Cranmer and have himself appointed in his place. That explains the trouble he is stirring in Canterbury. Let's put another pile of salt for the prebendaries and a line linking them to the bishop.'

'He uses his nephew to maintain close contact,' I said.

'Yes, Germain; as double-dyed a papist as you would never want to see. Of course, from the cathedral at Canterbury, lines run throughout Kent and the South-east.' He laid some more thin traces of salt. 'We have to find ways to block this activity. I'll come back to that in a moment. Now, at least Gardiner's opposition is in the open. We can trace his network and, by God's good grace, close it down. But there is another network – secret, insidious, unscrupulous and violent.'

'Presumably, that is the organisation Black Harry is part of?' I suggested.

Denny held up a warning finger. 'Don't jump ahead. It is vital to see things as clearly as we can.' He pointed to his first pile of salt. 'Like everything else, this starts with the tireless schemer, Eustace Chapuys. He has connections with the papistically inclined all over the country. However, his most powerful ally is the Duke of Norfolk. So let's put another salty marker for him. His lordship has ample resources for the Catholic campaign – money, estates where his authority rivals the king's, an army of servants ready to do his bidding. But even Norfolk has to tread warily.'

'I'm amazed he has survived so long,' Butts added. 'Twice he's inveigled the king into marriage with his nieces. Both have ended up under the headsman's axe. His majesty watches Norfolk closely now.'

'And that leads us to the big question,' Denny said. He picked up the salt cellar and placed it between the mounds of salt representing Chapuys and Norfolk. 'Who is this?'

We all stared at the pattern marked out on the table as Denny continued. 'In Leicestershire a godly preacher is found drowned in his own fishpond. In Bristol a rich merchant is "persuaded" by a gang of ruffians to stop supporting a congregation where the Gospel is truly preached. In Hampshire a minister, his wife and four children perish in a mysterious fire. There is one mind behind these and other incidents; one monster as well endowed with cunning as he is devoid of morality and human feeling.'

Butts nodded. 'A fanatic bent on opposing the Gospel by all and every means.'

'You mean Sir Thomas Moyle,' I suggested.

The others looked at me in surprise.

'Moyle?' Butts queried. 'The Kentish MP?'

Denny said, 'Whatever makes you suggest his name?'

I told them about Black Harry's activities and how I had discovered that the gang was supported by Sir Thomas.

'You must be mistaken,' Denny said. 'Our mysterious limb of Satan operates from the centre. He is closely connected with the duke; someone familiar with the court. But he also has influence and interests over a wide area.'

I persisted. 'If we assume that Holbein the painter, working for the archbishop, discovered the identity of your salt cellar, he had to be silenced before he could pass on the information. So Black Harry was sent to kill him. When Harry failed he took refuge in one of his patron's houses. We know that house belonged to Moyle.'

The courtiers were still not convinced.

Butts said, 'You are certainly right about Holbein's connection with Norfolk. He has made several likenesses of the duke and other members of his family.'

Denny added, 'We know he used his access to the duke's household to gather information and I'm inclined to agree with you that this placed him in grave danger, but Sir Thomas Moyle . . . I cannot see him as the paymaster of assassins.'

'If only we could make contact with Holbein we would soon know the truth,' Butts added.

'Yes, this is of prime importance,' Denny agreed. 'Do you think you can find him, Master Treviot?'

'The problem is finding him before Black Harry does.'

'Is there anything we can do to help? Do you need more men for the search?'

'Thank you, Master Denny, but if we have too many people asking questions around London that will alarm our enemy. Better we should wait for Master Holbein to get a message to us.'

'Pray God he does so quickly.'

'I'm sure he will as soon as he safely can. He will want to be reunited with his sons. Meanwhile, what can we do to help the archbishop?'

'Make sure his commission works properly is the short answer. Unfortunately, his grace is a stranger to ruthlessness but ruthlessness is what we need.'

Butts said, 'It is his lack of guile that the king finds so attractive. I doubt he would ever be manoeuvred into sacrificing his grace.'

'And there, as you know, William, we disagree. His majesty trusted Cromwell . . .'

'Ah, yes, Anthony, but he did not like him. There's the difference.'

'I grant that Cranmer is the last man the king would throw to the wolves – if he was in his right mind.' Denny stopped abruptly.

'Then is the rumour true that the king is sometimes not in his right mind?' I asked.

Denny was clearly discomfited. 'You must not take me too literally.'

Butts came to his aid. 'No one can appreciate the pressures kings are under. Every day his majesty has to make a hundred decisions: a courtier seeks promotion; a bill must be drafted for parliament, a letter from the Emperor needs to be answered. Age and infirmity make it more difficult to shoulder his responsibilities. They may cloud judgement; affect decisions . . .'

'Such as whether to launch the country into war,' I suggested.

Butts nodded. 'That among other things.'

'We are getting off the point,' Denny said hurriedly. 'We were discussing your commission in Kent. His majesty has agreed to send for Thomas Legh to join you. He is the most formidable lawyer in the country; as a member of the commission for dissolving the monasteries he was invaluable. I think you'll find him more than an equal of the Canterbury clergy and their friends.'

There was a knock at the door and a royal page entered. 'An't please you, Master Denny, his majesty wishes to retire.'

'Then I must go and prepare him for bed.' Denny stood quickly.

'Perhaps I should attend also,' Butts said. 'He might require a sleeping draught.'

I said my farewells and went to the stable yard, where a yawning Dick was waiting. As we rode away from Woodstock towards the inn where we were staying I pondered a question that had often occurred to me before: why would any man in his right mind covet the position of a courtier? Money, power, status? If these things were gained they certainly came at a price – one beyond any I was ready to pay.

Chapter 17

Having crossed the Thames at Kingston and followed the south bank, we reached Southwark after two days' steady riding. I sent two men back to Goldsmith's Row and kept Walt and Dick with me. We sat around Ned's fire, drinking one of his heart-warming concoctions. He and Bart listened intently as I recounted my visits to Croydon and Woodstock but I noticed that Ned looked somewhat perplexed when I finished my account.

'Unfortunate that you upset Sir Thomas,' he said. 'I imagine he could make life very difficult for you in the county.'

'Not as difficult as I plan to make his life when I expose his connection with Black Harry.'

'You are sure about that?'

'That's the one thing in this whole complicated business that I am sure about. There's proof, heraldic proof.'

'Well, if you're convinced.' He shrugged.

'Tell me why you're not.'

'I'm just an old ex-monk who's spent most of his life cut off from the real world. I know nothing about intrigues and plots. But it does seem to me slightly odd that Sir Thomas Moyle is, on the one hand, a secret manipulator, hiding in the shadows, and, on the other, a partisan, vigorously and openly demonstrating his opposition to the archbishop's friends.'

'Well, odd or not, that's the sort of man he is,' I said. 'Now, tell me what's been happening here.'

Bart said, with an air of triumph, 'I've found him.'

'Master Holbein? Well done! That's wonderful!'

Ned sounded a note of caution. 'Come now, Bart, be honest. What you really mean is that you have seen Master Holbein.'

Bart grimaced. 'Don't be so dainty-minded, Ned. I know where he is. That's to say, I know where he might be. Two or three places, anyway.'

'Perhaps it would be good if you started at the beginning,' I suggested.

At that moment there was a knock at the door. Ned opened it to admit Lizzie. Dick gave her his stool and squatted beside her on the floor. As I looked round the circle I could not help reflecting that we had become a group of conspirators, perhaps no better than the men we were pitted against.

Lizzie's first question was 'How is Adie?'

'I've been away from Hemmings a week or more and I saw little of her when I was there.'

'She will need much time to recover,' Lizzie replied. 'Perhaps I should go to her.'

'Better for you to stay where you can look after your own,' I suggested.

She gave me one of her intense – and quite indecipherable – stares.

'Your husband was about to tell us of his finding – or not finding – Master Johannes,' I said.

Bart began his story: 'I couldn't stay cooped up here all the time, getting in Ned's way. In any case, I want to put an end to all this hiding in corners. I want to get back to normal; the life I had with Lizzie and the children, and with my work, before this Black Harry turned it upside down. So I went out looking for Master Johannes. Ned helped me with disguises. We've become quite good at it. I can become a begging leper, a bushy-bearded German, a pedlar of potions. With walnut juice to darken my face I can even—'

'Spare us the secrets of your art,' I said. 'Tell us what you discovered.'

'Well, the Steelyard seemed the obvious place to start. I thought Master Johannes was sure to call on his friends there. So I went with my beggar's scrip and found a corner in Thames Street where I could watch the foreigners' comings and goings. First day – nothing. Second day – nothing till noon. Then I realised I was looking for the wrong person. Master Johannes, like me, is in hiding. Therefore, he would also use disguise. From that moment I looked more closely at the faces of the men coming out of the Steelyard. I tried to spot false hair, painted cheeks, large, concealing hoods. After about an hour a man with just such a large hood, stepped into the street, paused, looked each way, then turned eastwards. I followed. He led me to Mark Lane, then Hart Street and so to Aldgate. I was sure I had my man and this was confirmed when he produced a key and let himself into Master Johannes' house. I settled myself opposite, meaning to approach him when he came out. Then, guess who came along? Constable Pett. He stopped and yanked me to my feet.'

'Did he recognise you?' I gasped.

Bart laughed. 'Not he, the blunderhead! He had me worried for a moment, though. Looked at me long and hard, he did. Then he says, "You're new. Well, just you listen to the rules for beggars in my ward. It's half for you and half for me. If you don't like that you get taken to the magistrate for a thrashing." He grabbed my scrip and emptied all the coins into his purse. "I'll take this for an earnest", he says. "I see you a-trembling," he says. "You do well to be afraid. All your sort tremble before Constable Pett." Empty-headed churl! If I was shaking, it was with laughter. Trouble was, while this villainous braggart was shouting in my face, Master Johannes came out of the house and hurried along the road. I got away from Pett and set off in pursuit. Master Johannes went down an alley by the Saracen's Head but when I reached it there was no sign. It was another two days before I found out anything else. I thought he might go back sometime to the place you'd spoken of in Bridewell Lane. So I hung about the quay there for a couple of days. I asked the dock men if they'd seen anyone answering Master Johannes' description. This time I was a lawyer trying to find a witness in a fraud case. No luck there – not when they realised I wasn't paying for information. But I did learn that I wasn't the only one asking questions about a foreigner who sometimes came to the quay. Someone else is looking for him. Must be Black Harry. The rest of the week was a waste of time. It wasn't till yesterday that I saw him again. I decided to take horse and spend the whole day visiting the locations where I'd seen him. Just before dark I spied him coming out of Bridewell Lane. He turned left, went as far as the Conduit, then turned down

Shoe Lane. I was just in time to see him enter a house on the right but the light by then was too poor for me to be sure of which house it was.'

'Then your conclusion is that Master Johannes has a number of refuges in and around the City,' I suggested.

'Yes, and is constantly on the move.'

I voiced my frustration. 'Why doesn't he make contact? If he's seen Pastor Meyer, he will know the boys are safe and he can trust us to help him.'

'Now that you and the others are back, Master Thomas, we can watch his hiding places,' Bart urged. 'I can show them to you and one of us is sure to see him.'

'That's true,' I agreed. 'Tomorrow you can take us round and show us.'

During this conversation Lizzie had been gazing thoughtfully into the fire. Now she said, 'So you won't be going straight back to Hemmings.'

'No, this business with Master Johannes is too urgent,' I replied.

'Well, you won't need all your men to find him. I'd like to borrow some.'

'What for?' I asked.

'For an escort down to Hemmings. You all seem to be forgetting Adie and the children. Someone has to look after them.'

'They seemed to be recovering when I last saw them,' I said.

'Recovering! By all the saints, Thomas! A few weeks back you called me slack-brained for helping Bart hide from the law. Now you sit there calmly saying Adie and the boys are happily "recovering" from their ordeal. Now who's being empty-headed? Carl and Henry have lost their mother;

their father has disappeared; they have been captured; dragged around the country; tied up and left to die. As for Adie, she's had to support the boys and try to give them courage, while being ravished by Black Harry's men. And you blithely say, "They'll recover". Well, let me tell you about our Annie. Every night she wakes up dreaming about being chased by black demons on horseback. I don't know if she'll ever get those frightening pictures out of her head. You say it's very important to find this painter. Well, I say it's every bit as important to show some compassion to those whose lives have been shattered in the quest. So I'm going to find me a wagon to take me and the children down to Kent and I'd greatly appreciate it if you could provide me with an escort.'

It was in a very sombre mood that the party sat down to supper.

The next morning I put Walt in charge of arranging Lizzie's journey to Hemmings. I was about to set out with Bart on a tour of Holbein's hiding places, when one of my men arrived from Goldsmith's Row. He handed me a letter. 'Delivered about three days ago,' he said.

There was no name on the outside but as soon as I opened it out, I recognised – with huge relief – Holbein's meticulous writing.

Master Treviot, I greet you well.
Pastor Meyer has told me of your recent conversation. Most heartily I thank you for your care of my sons, who are my only joy in this world. I beg you will continue to keep them in your charge until I am free to relieve you of that burden. For now they can only be safe at distance

from their father. I must remain in hiding from those who seek me with untiring diligence. They know I have information that will destroy them and for that reason they will not forbear until either they achieve their ends or they are apprehended. If you will meet me at the place shown you by our Flemish friend on Tuesday evening after seven I will pass on to you what I have discovered, confident that you will know where to deliver it.

Your assured friend,

Johannes Holbein

I handed the letter to Ned. 'Tuesday! He wants a meeting on Tuesday! And now 'tis Thursday! Mother of God, must we be always missing each other?'

'What will you do?' Ned asked.

'I must go straight to Bridewell and wait.'

'Is that wise? The warehouse is being watched.'

'That's true, but we can't miss our chance again.'

'Black Harry's men are sure to recognise you as soon as you arrive in Bridewell Lane.'

Bart said brightly, 'You'll have to go in disguise.'

'No,' I said firmly. 'One lot of disguisings is quite enough.'

Ned looked thoughtful. 'I wonder why Master Johannes suggested meeting at Bridewell. He will know it's being watched.'

I reread the letter. 'He is very specific about the time of meeting: "Tuesday evening after seven",' I pointed out.

'For some reason that time is safe,' Bart said. 'Why, what happens at seven after noon on Tuesday?'

'Or on any day,' I said.

Ned nodded. 'I see what you mean.'

'Well, I don't,' Bart protested.

Ned explained. 'Holbein has had plenty of time to observe the routine of Black Harry's men – watching the watchers. He has discovered that they do not keep vigil round the clock.'

'But why not?'

'They would soon arouse the suspicion of the constable's watch.'

'It may also be that our master fiend does not have enough men for arduous surveillance, all night long,' I added. 'Whatever the cause, it may be safe there once 'tis fully dark. We must try tonight and hope Holbein comes.'

I busied myself with the arrangements for Lizzie's journey to Hemmings and saw her on her way around midday, in the capable hands of Walt and two of my other servants. After that all I had to do was wait – wait and worry. This should be, could be, might be, the day the last, vital piece of evidence fell into place. If Black Harry's men were not there to intervene; if Holbein came to the rendezvous; if his information was as important as he believed; then we could complete the chain linking Moyle and the villains he hired to the Duke of Norfolk and the imperial ambassador. Then I could leave Anthony Denny, Archbishop Cranmer and their friends at court to do whatever they had to do to uncover the whole network of traitors. In the process, Bart would be freed from suspicion. All this hung upon one meeting. But would that meeting take place? What would I do if it did not? Try again the next day? And the next? And the next? I did not want to think about the result of failure. I watched the sky darken over Southwark as rain clouds heralded an early dusk. Ned had prepared a tempting supper but I had little appetite and before six o'clock I saddled the horses myself and, with Dick for company, set out to cross the bridge.

Traffic was light and there was nothing to impede our

progress the whole length of Thames Street. We were at Ludgate well before seven o'clock. Rather than arrive too early and risk an encounter with Black Harry's minions, we turned into St Paul's Yard and ambled round the cathedral until the clock struck. I left Dick at the north end of Bridewell Lane and cautiously made my way past the houses and the high walls of the palace. As I approached the quay two horsemen approached from the other direction. I reined in to let them pass, keeping my hood well over my face.

'Good even to you,' one of them called out, slowing his mount.

'And to you,' I responded lightly.

'Are you going to the quay?' he asked and I was conscious of being carefully scrutinised.

'Yes, are there still boatmen for hire?'

'One, I think,' he replied. 'You'd best hurry.'

'Thank you, friend.' I legged my horse into a trot. I had not recognised either of the men but I felt sure they were members of the gang. Had I satisfied them?

I waited several minutes on the deserted quay before turning and retracing my steps.

'Did you see two men come up the lane?' I asked Dick when I reached him.

'Yes, Master. They turned right, towards the gate. Were they Black Harry's men?'

'I think so. I hope so. Anyway all's quiet now. We'll leave our horses over there at the Red Hand inn and go on foot.'

Minutes later we walked back down the deserted lane. I led the way through the alley and up the stairs, unlocked the door and entered Holbein's lair. With the aid of the last of the light through the high windows we found lamps and lit them. I looked around the large room.

The scene that met my gaze was very different from the one I had left ten days earlier. The place had been tidied up. The floor timbers still bore multi-hued smudges of paint, but the few pieces of furniture were now in place. The bed was covered. Stools stood upright. At the far end Holbein's self-portrait stood on its easel. Brushes and pots of pigment set on a table beside it indicated that the artist was still working on it. And he had obviously been using a polished tin mirror nailed to one of the wall beams.

We seated ourselves on two of the stools. Now there was nothing to do but wait.

I do not know how long it was before we heard footsteps on the stair – probably not as long as it seemed. We jumped up and stepped across to the door. We stood either side of it. My hand went to the pommel of my poniard. The steps stopped outside and we heard the key turn in the lock. The door opened and swung inwards. The figure that entered was well covered in a hooded riding cape. He took a pace into the room, looked around cautiously and closed the door behind him. He threw back the hood.

'Good even to you, Thomas Treviot,' said Johannes Holbein.

Chapter 18

We embraced warmly. 'You cannot know how overjoyed I am to see you, Johannes,' I said.

I stood back and stared at him. My first impression of the artist was that he had aged noticeably since we had last met. Though not yet fifty, his features were lined and his eyes lacked sparkle. He dropped his cloak to the floor and, with a sound between a sigh and a grunt, lowered himself on to a stool. His doublet was unbuttoned and his shirt crumpled.

'Master Treviot, I fear I have put you to much trouble,' he said.

''Tis you who have been in great trouble. I hope I can help you put an end to it.' I turned to Dick. 'Better go outside and stand guard in the lane. We don't want any surprise visitors.'

'The villains won't return till first light,' Holbein said, 'but 'tis as well to be cautious.'

'I believe we saw two of them going off duty. I do not think they recognised me, but . . . '

'Pastor Meyer has told me of some of the difficulties you've faced on my behalf. And you have also taken care of my sons.' Holbein smiled. 'That is a great burden lifted from me. How are they?'

I recalled Lizzie's words on the subject and checked myself from offering a glib answer. 'They have been touched by this business but they are safe now. I think no lasting damage has been done.'

Holbein smiled. 'They are bright boys. Alas, I have seen too little of them.'

'You will have plenty of time to spend with them as soon as this present problem is over.'

'Well, well, we shall see.' He was silent for several moments. Then he said, ''Tis time, I think, for them to be put to a tutor. Do you know someone suitable?'

'My own son is privately taught,' I said. 'Francis Sturn-good is an excellent scholar and wields his birch well, though not too often. I'll arrange for you to meet him, if you wish.'

He raised his eyes towards the rafters, avoiding my gaze. 'We must do the best for them. I have made a will. It is with John of Antwerp, as you call him. There is provision for the boys and their nurse.'

''Tis not time yet to talk of wills,' I protested. 'We will bring your enemies to justice and you can take up your life again.'

He shook his head. 'Does it not alarm you, Master Treviot, how much hatred there is in the world?'

'Indeed it does. Wherever I go – in the City, in villages, in churches, in court rooms, in great men's palaces – people are at odds with their neighbours, friends fall out, the king's subjects seek to destroy one another.'

'Everywhere,' he said wearily. ''Tis the same everywhere.' He paused. 'You know I'm a citizen of Basel – officially. When I settled there, years ago, it was like a haven of peace and common sense. I had many friends. Some called themselves "Catholic"; some had forsaken the old church, but all, I think, were men of generous spirit. Young, of course, and enthusiastic for our own beliefs. We could – often did – argue the night away. But seldom with rancour. Then I came to England, never intending to stay. I made more friends. I was introduced to the king's court. I prospered.'

'You well deserve your success,' I said. 'There is no finer limner in England, perhaps in Europe.'

'They were good years.' Holbein continued with his reminiscence, as though talking to himself. 'Then I returned to Basel. Everything had changed. It wasn't enough, any more, to know what you believed; you had to make everyone else believe the same. That led to mob warfare on the streets. Gangs attacked churches. Pulled down statues. Slashed paintings. The city council gave way. All religious art was banned. No one needed painters any more. So I came back here. Do you know what I found?'

'That things were much the same in England?'

'Yes, like the plague, religious fervour had crossed the water. Even my old patron, Sir Thomas More, had taken to locking men up and having them tortured.'

'Yet you stayed and established a brilliant career.'

He stood and walked over to his easel. Taking up a brush, he began dabbing at the canvas. 'What an artist feels, he must try to bring out of himself; put it into his work. Your great men and women wanted portraits. I made them; tried to show them not just what they looked like, but what they *were*. I don't know if any of them ever realised that the "Oh so *fashionable* German, Master Holbein" was looking into their souls.'

'You must take much satisfaction from your success.'

'Looking into their souls,' Holbein continued, as though he had not heard. 'But *my* soul? What happened to that? The success, the acclaim, the money – they took over. But the soul? I think it shrivelled. I had a wife and children but we drifted apart. I didn't want to go to Basel. They didn't want to come to England. I thought I had found happiness with an English woman. Soon I had a new family. Then my two little girls died. My woman left. All I had was my work, my fame, my clamouring patrons.'

'That would be enough for many craftsmen.'

'Patrons. So generous. So loud in their praise. But they always want more than they give. Even the greatest man in England. Especially him.'

'Lord Cromwell?'

'Yes. I miss him. He was brilliant. I could always talk to him. He understood. And I understood him. He made me see that the troubles England was going through were just birthing pains for the godly commonwealth he was bringing into the world. So, when he asked more of me than just painting, I was ready . . . '

'He wanted you to spy for him?'

'He called it "keeping him informed" about potential enemies.' Holbein laid down the brush and turned to me. 'Do you know I could have saved him?'

'How?'

'I discovered what Lord Norfolk – that haughty, misborn, foul-tempered proudster – was planning. But I did not get the message to Cromwell in time. That will always haunt me.'

'Is that why you are so anxious to have your information passed to Archbishop Cranmer, now?'

'He is a good man and Norfolk is up to his usual foul tricks. But now he is part of something much bigger. We cannot let him and his fellow conspirators succeed this time.'

'This information you have – will it really stop him?'

'Oh yes, if it is correctly used. His grace will know how to use it, if you pass it on to him.'

'But you can give it to him yourself. We'll get you to him safely.'

'No, that won't work. Norfolk and his associates must not know that their plans have been discovered. If they do they will simply disband and wait for another opportunity. They are diabolically persistent. They will go to absolutely any lengths.'

'So I've discovered. They killed your assistant, they left van der Goes half-dead and they'd have let the children starve.'

'The only way to avenge these wrongs is to close down the whole organisation. You will be able to do that, but only if they believe that I have failed in my mission.'

'But that would mean letting them capture you.'

The painter smiled and nodded. Suddenly I recalled Meyer's words about Holbein nursing the idea of suicide. 'You can't do that!' I protested.

'It is the only way, Thomas. I have had plenty of time to think about it. I must admit when I heard what had happened to poor George my instinct was to run away, get on a Hanse ship and escape. But where to? Basel has no charms for me now. My family there are provided for. They're perfectly happy without me. At my age I can't start building a career somewhere else. In any case, I'm too old-fashioned. The demand now is for a debased, exaggerated, "showy" art. I hate it. So my time is over and I am content.'

'My dear friend, this is foolish talk. Your talent is unequalled. You are painter to the King of England.'

He gave a cynical laugh. 'To a king who has no more commissions for me.'

'But—'

'No, Thomas, you waste your breath seeking to dissuade me. I count myself very fortunate. It is not, I think, given to many men to know when their time in this world is spent. I have played my little role and I leave the stage willingly. The play continues, but my part in it will soon be forgotten. There's one important thing left for me to do and, with your help, I can do it.'

'Very well,' I said. 'Give me the information and I'll leave you – but only with a very heavy heart.'

To my surprise, Holbein laughed. 'I've already sent it to you – or part of it, but you must have missed it.'

'The engraved coat of arms on the chalice design?'

'Ah, so you did notice it. It was a very faint chance but the only way I could think of at the time. When I heard you had become involved I tried to think of something that might catch your attention. I recalled our frequent discussions of cyphers and concealed meanings. You know I have a weakness for that sort of thing. That heraldic device will identify the man whose twisted mind lies behind the attack on the archbishop and so much more devilry.'

'Yes, I have discovered him and warned the archbishop.'

'Excellent! Then most of the work is done. But there is more information – times and dates – that will complete the picture. This man – I never knew his name . . . '

'Thomas Moyle,' I said.

'Really? Well, he is the organiser. He has links with important men here and abroad. He came two or three times to see the Duke of Norfolk. The first was when I was at his house in Kenninghall working on a new portrait. The duke was out of favour following the fall of his niece, Queen Catherine Howard, and seething with fury about those who had exposed her and brought him close to ruin. Then, more recently, this man – Moyle, you say? – visited his lordship again in his chambers at Whitehall Palace. They always talked in secret but I managed to overhear a few snatches of conversation – enough to realise their treachery. I memorised the heraldic badge worn by the man's servants. Unfortunately, I was not quite discreet enough. The conspirators were suspicious. They could do nothing immediately because I was with the royal court – a small commission for the new queen. When I left, they sent their pet assassins to waylay me. As you know, I escaped and have been in hiding ever since, trying to think how I could convey what I know to the archbishop or some trusted friend. Thank God, I can now do that. In the morning I'll allow myself to be captured. Now, Thomas, listen carefully. The traitor's visits to Norfolk—'

Suddenly, we were disturbed by the sound of hurried footsteps on the stair. Dick rushed in. 'Someone's coming!' he called out softly.

'Quick,' Holbein said, 'douse the lamps! Stay in the corner!'

In the darkness I heard him move towards the door. He whispered something that sounded like 'Smile'. Then he was gone.

Moments later there was a commotion on the staircase – shouts, grunts, thuds, a scream. Then laughter and the thump, thump, thump of something being dragged down the stair.

I waited several minutes to see if the ruffians would come back, perhaps to search the room. When the silence remained unbroken, I stumbled around trying to find a lamp. I tripped over a stool and just stopped myself falling headlong. 'Dick,' I called, 'where did we put the lamps?'

'I think there's one here . . . ' The words were followed by a large crash and an oath.

'Are you all right?' I called.

'Yes, I think I've knocked his painting over. Ah, here we are. I've got a lamp.'

'Can you get your tinderbox out?'

'Yes.'

Sparks flashed out as he struck the iron. Then a small flame appeared in the darkness. Moments later he had a lamp wick flaring.

I picked up the stool I had fallen over and sat down.

'They've got him,' Dick gasped. 'Must have recognised us and come back. Did he tell you what you wanted to know?'

'No,' I groaned. 'No, no, no, not a word. Nothing we did not know before we came in. That's it – our last chance gone.'

'Will they kill him?'

'Sure to. Though, it seems, he'll not mind that. He just wanted to complete his task first. And he came so close to doing it. A couple more minutes and he'd have told me everything. Now, whatever he knew he'll take with him to the grave – assuming Norfolk's men permit him the luxury of a grave.'

After a while I got to my feet. I picked up the painting and set it back on the easel. 'At least he left us something to remember him by. I'll keep this.'

I peered at the portrait. There was a vermilion streak

running from one corner of the mouth. The paint Holbein had applied only minutes before had been smudged when the canvas was knocked over. It made Holbein's smile look more like a sneer.

Smile! Could it be?

'Dick,' I said quietly. 'Bring that lamp closer.'

Chapter 19

I picked up a cloth from the table and began to wipe it over the wet paint.

'What are you doing, Master?' Dick stared at me as though I had lost my senses.

'Did you hear the last thing Master Johannes said?'

'Not clearly.'

'I think he said "smile".' I gradually applied more pressure to the paint surface. 'When I was here last the expression on this portrait was quite serious. Now, as you can see, it wears a smile. The artist has changed it recently. The paint in this lower section is fresher. It's not yet fully dry. Just possibly . . .' There was a jar of oil that Holbein had used to mix his pigments. I dipped the rag in it and went back to work, cautiously clearing away part of the area around the mouth. 'Pray God I'm not wrong.'

Slowly one side of the lips and the adjacent beard disappeared. 'More light,' I demanded. 'If this reveals only the paint base or the canvas then I'm ... Look!'

We both peered intently at the damaged portrait. What was emerging was a patch of brilliant yellow.

'That's not under-paint,' I said with relief. 'It's part of something else.'

'Perhaps Master Johannes has re-used an old canvas,' Dick said. 'I've heard that poor artists often do that.'

'Yes, that's possible. We'll have to take it away and complete the job more carefully. See if you can find something to wrap the picture in.'

'Here's his riding cloak,' Dick said moments later, picking up the heavy garment from the floor. 'He went without it.'

I spread it on the floor, laid the canvas on it and gently folded the cloth across it. Then I rolled it over to make a tight, bulky bundle. That done, I carried it very carefully to the door while Dick extinguished the lamps.

The occupants of Ned's house had little sleep that night. Bart, Ned, Dick and I stood round the table on which we had laid the portrait. The others watched intently as I continued to work on the paint surface. More of the plain yellow was becoming visible when I was forced to stop. The cloth had become dry and clogged with congealed paint and score marks were appearing on the surface.

I looked up, frustrated. 'We should have brought the oil, Dick. We need more solvent.'

'I think I can help,' Ned said. He went to the shelves where all his jars and bottles were stored and came back with a squat glass container holding a yellowish fluid. 'Walnut oil,' he said. 'I use it in lotions for dressing skin wounds. It speeds up the healing process.'

'Will it work as a solvent?' I asked. 'Might it damage the paint?'

Ned shook his head. 'One of the brothers in the monastery who made our icons used it all the time for mixing his pigments. Though I always felt it tended to make the colours darker, it was certainly effective. But please use it sparingly, Thomas. 'Tis very expensive.'

I returned to the work. What emerged was a heraldic shield. My heart leaped the moment I recognised it. On a yellow ground there was a red chevron and three black moles. 'There,' I said exultantly, 'Moyle's shield.'

Only Ned failed to share the general excitement. 'It seems that our fine painter has never seen a mole,' he said, laughing.

'For that matter, nor have I,' I said.

'They were a plague at the monastery,' Ned replied. 'Always getting into the herb garden. One of the novices used to trap them.'

'We must carry on and see what else is in Master Johannes' hidden message.' Steadily I worked away at the canvas. What emerged was a panel covering the bottom third of the picture. Beside the shield was a white scroll with black lettering – in German.

'That appears to be all,' I said, standing up thankfully, my back aching from hours of bending.

We all stared at the revealed message.

Bart grinned. 'If that describes Moyle's meetings with the Duke of Norfolk we've got them!'

'I think so,' I said. 'We'll get our friend at the Steelyard to translate for us. Then we'll make copies for Sir Anthony and the archbishop. They'll have to decide how to use the information.'

'By all the saints, I hope they make the traitors pay. I want to see Black Harry's face grinning down from a spike on London Bridge and his paymasters swinging on a gallows' tree,' Bart said.

'We owe nothing less to Master Johannes,' I agreed.

It was with thoughts of the painter's sacrifice in my mind that I eventually lay down on my bed in the early hours of Friday morning.

'What time is it?' I asked as I stumbled, yawning, down the stairs later that day.

'Gone nine,' Ned replied. 'I didn't wake you. You needed the sleep. Come and eat.'

Thankfully, I attacked the food he set before me. 'I don't want to waste any more time,' I said, 'now that we've finally found what we wanted.'

'I doubt a couple of hours will make any difference,' he replied. 'It will be too late to start for Woodstock by the time you've concluded your business with your Lutheran friend.' Ned Longbourne was the kindest and most open-minded of men – except when he was speaking of German 'heretics'.

'I've decided to go straight to Croydon. I can reach the archbishop today and leave him to send fast messengers to Sir Anthony.'

'And then you'll go on to Hemmings?'

'That depends on his grace. He might need my help if he decides to proceed against Moyle immediately. However, the first job is to see exactly what Master Johannes' message says.'

'I think, perhaps, I will come with you, at least part of the way. I might be of some use at Hemmings. Like Lizzie, I'm concerned about Adie and the boys. Someone will have to break the news to them about Master Holbein's death.'

I thought I detected a hint of criticism. 'Of course ... I should have ...'

Ned shook his head. 'No need to reproach yourself, Thomas. I will explain things delicately. You are too far into this business to turn aside for personal reasons.'

I took the portrait, now wrapped in cloth, and had myself rowed across to the Steelyard wharf. When I went in search of Meyer I was told that he was busy. I waited for him in the chapel until almost noon and spent part of the time in prayer for Johannes Holbein. I implored heaven for his safety but whether that might be secured in this world or the next I had to leave in higher hands. The pastor eventually appeared and led me to his office, where I described the events of the previous evening.

Meyer sighed deeply. 'I suppose he always knew that there could only be one end to this affair.'

'We must hope for good news until we know for certain what has happened to him. Meanwhile, the best we can do for him is to complete what he began.' I unwrapped the painting and laid it on the pastor's desk. 'This is the message he left for me to pass on. What does it mean?'

Meyer stared at the canvas. 'What an extraordinary ...'

'Please, can you translate?' I urged. 'I'm in a hurry to pass the message on.'

'Yes, of course. Exquisite handwriting. So much talent. What a waste.'

'The translation?' I tried not to shout.

He took a sheaf of paper from a shelf and handed it to me. 'There's pen and ink beside you,' he said. 'If I read perhaps you would like to write.'

The words pastor Meyer dictated were as follows:

Visits of this man to the Duke of Norfolk

15 December, 1541, Kenninghall. Visitor says we are delaying our plans. You must beg forgiveness of his majesty and avoid being arrested like others of your family. We cannot proceed without you

20 May, 1543, Whitehall. Visitor says you must draw his majesty's attention to the Windsor heretics ... Our friends in Canterbury are ready to spring the trap

20 August, 1543, Whitehall. Visitor says everything is ready for the purge in Essex and Kent. My agents need more money. The pope will grant absolution ...

'That is the end', Meyer said. 'Who is this man who gives orders to your duke?'

'Someone who conceals his power extremely well,' I replied.

At Ned's house all was ready for our departure, including a simple meal packed by our host that we could eat as we travelled. The only task we had to perform was to make copies of Holbein's notes and his painting of the heraldic device. As I worked, Ned sat opposite me at the table.

'Strange to think of the Duke of Norfolk taking orders from a social inferior,' he said. 'Such a proud man.'

'They are both in the service of Emperor Charles and the pope. That, I suppose, levels out lesser distinctions of rank. As covert Catholics, I imagine they enjoy your sympathy, Ned.'

'That's an unjust taunt, my friend.'

'I mean no insult by it. I'm intrigued to know what you really think of a man like Thomas Moyle.'

'I have never been able to understand how violence, militancy and treason can be squared with the Christian

233

profession,' he said. 'By all accounts this Moyle has always been a duplicitous creature. In time past he was one of the most virulent enemies of the religious life. He was a chief commissioner in the campaign to close the monasteries.'

'Aye, and a zealous supporter of Cromwell. It was only after Cromwell's fall that he showed his true colours. He knew all about the ex-minister's network and was in a position to sell his information to Eustace Chapuys, the imperial ambassador.'

'So it seems we should not think of him as a good Catholic; just an ambitious, self-serving scoundrel who believes in nothing but his own advancement.'

I laid aside the quill. 'Do you have a sharper pen, Ned? This one is beginning to blotch badly. If Moyle believes in nothing but Moyle, his religion has served him well. He's made a rich marriage with the daughter of one of the leading goldsmiths and his control of the Court of Augmentations must bring him in hundreds by the year.'

Ned signed. 'I have often noticed one characteristic of successful men: however much they have, it is seldom sufficient.'

'Well, this time he has reached for one prize too many. This' – I collected together my notes – 'will bring about his downfall. Let us be on our way to lay the evidence before Archbishop Cranmer.'

Bart begged to be allowed to accompany us and there seemed no good reason to deny him. We rode into the main courtyard at Croydon Palace just as the last sunlight was drenching the tiled roofs. The household was at supper in the great hall and we were bidden to join them. Afterwards I was escorted to Ralph Morice's office.

The secretary listened with mounting excitement as I recounted my meetings at Woodstock and Bridewell.

'Johannes has sacrificed himself in a great cause,' he commented. 'The archbishop will include him in his prayers. He is a lesson to us all in dedication to God's truth.' He laid out my notes on his standing desk and studied them carefully.

'I had no dyes to represent the heraldic shield fully,' I explained, 'but I have written in the colours.'

'Have you brought the painting with you? I'd like to see it.'

I sent a message to Dick and within minutes he came with the wrapped canvas. I unpacked it and set it on a stool placed against the wall.

'There is much sadness in those eyes,' Morice said quietly. Then, more briskly, 'His grace will want to see this. He reads German very well – not that I doubt that this translation is excellent. It will be good to have the shield copied in colour. We have someone here who can do it in water-paint. Let me see if I can recall how the heralds would describe it . . . "On a ground or, a chevron jules, between three moles sable". I think that's right. Personally, I dislike such gaudy, self-glorifying display.' He picked up the portrait and strode to the door. 'His grace should have finished supper now. I'll go and report to him. Please wait here; I know he'll want to talk to you himself.'

He was gone a long time. The last twenty-four hours had been tiring. The lamplight was soft. The fire gave off a comforting heat. My head drooped.

'So, if you're ready, Thomas . . . '

I woke with a start.

'His grace will see you now. He's in the library. Bring the painting.'

Morice led the way to a long chamber with several book presses standing against the walls. Cranmer was sitting in a

235

high-backed chair at one of the tables. I made my obeisance. The archbishop received it with a nod and a wistful smile. He looked weary and there were shadows around his eyes. He motioned me to a bench opposite.

'It is good to see you again, Thomas, and may I say how relieved I am that you are safe and well. Ralph has kept me informed of your activities. I appreciate what you have been doing.'

I made some self-deprecating response but the archbishop was now staring at my notes and seemed not to be listening.

'This is very, very sad,' he said.

'I wonder if "sad" is the right word, Your Grace.'

'You believe I should be angry, indignant, personally offended?'

'I'm sure I would be.'

'Perhaps you won't object if I remind you that Jesus enjoins us to love our enemies.'

I must have looked crestfallen, for his smile broadened and he added, 'Fortunately, our Lord said nothing about loving other people's enemies.' After a pause, he continued, 'I have looked at the painting. Its message is clear: treason. These people wish to overthrow Church and state, as established by his gracious majesty. That we cannot permit. Yet, it dismays me to see a man of Sir Thomas's talent and long years of service to the Crown becoming the agent of a foreign power.'

Morice said, 'He's obviously been concealing his real allegiance for many years.'

Cranmer nodded. 'So it would seem. We have always known that he has a hankering after the old ways but his behaviour up till now has been correct. I was appalled to hear of his treatment of poor Richard.'

236

'Your Grace, a royal messenger arrived this afternoon with a letter from Anthony Denny. He is drawing up Turner's pardon for the king's signature.'

'Good, good. Perhaps we should arrange for Richard to rest for a while. It makes little sense to aggravate discord.'

Morice tugged at his beard and gave a discreet cough. 'With respect, Your Grace, may I suggest that it might be interpreted as a sign of weakness. Thanks to Master Holbein's endeavours, we can now take the offensive against all this subtle and secretive plotting. With the evidence we have, we can arrest Moyle. Denny also reports that Thomas Legh will be with us by tomorrow evening at the latest. With him leading your commission, all the enemies of Church and state will rapidly be brought to heel. The Duke of Norfolk has laid his last plot. When his majesty sees Master Holbein's notes nothing can save him.'

Cranmer frowned. 'Ralph, be careful. If you play the political game you may yet find yourself outmanoeuvred. If the king wished to be rid of his lordship, he has had many opportunities in the past to do so. Norfolk is a survivor, and if we fail to dislodge him . . .'

'Then, Your Grace, at least the king may have his eyes opened to the subversive activities of the imperial ambassador. That could mean an end to this talk of a joint war with the Emperor against France.'

'That would certainly be a great prize,' Cranmer agreed.

'Then shall I proceed with the warrant for Sir Thomas's arrest?'

'The archbishop sighed deeply. 'Yes,' he said.

The following morning, Ned and Dick made ready to depart for Hemmings. We stood in the great courtyard watching

Morice assemble a large troop of mounted guards to ride to Ashford. He strolled across to us.

'His grace has decided that I should go with them,' he said. 'Would you like to keep me company?'

'I must admit it would give me some pleasure to witness Sir Thomas's humiliation.'

He grinned. 'That's a reward you have richly deserved. We'll leave as soon as you are ready. And here is the colour copy of the shield.' He handed me a folded paper.

As we journeyed towards Moyle's mansion at Eastwell we were both in ebullient mood and talked of many things. I asked how long Morice had been in the archbishop's service.

'Since before he was archbishop,' Morice said. 'I joined him fifteen years ago, soon after leaving university. We were both at Cambridge, though he was a fellow at Jesus, when I was a mere undergraduate. Brave days! Brave days!'

'Why do you say that?'

'That was when it all began – the discovery of Bible truth; the changes in the church. You can't imagine how exciting it was. Latimer was drawing crowds to hear him at St Edmund's. Robert Barnes was preaching at the Augustine priory. Salesmen came to the town with books smuggled in from Germany. We students read them in secret, gobbling up the pure Gospel, meeting at the White Horse to discuss forbidden truths, defying the authorities, risking discovery and having our books burned – if not ourselves. Brave days!'

'You think things are less good now?'

'I think when you stir politics into the pot it turns the mixture sour. We're rid of the pope. That is good. The Bible is in English. That is good. But we walk not on a straight path illumined by the Gospel. We are not the godly commonwealth that Lord Cromwell and others gave their lives for.'

'And for which Archbishop Cranmer strives.'

'Of course.'

'Will it ever come, this godly commonwealth?'

'We must believe so and work towards it. Otherwise the sacrifices of people like Johannes Holbein will have been in vain.'

'He did not give his life for a perfect England,' I said. 'He thought the reformed nations had gone too far; that they had their own kinds of violence and oppression and were no better than those where the pope still reigns.'

'I find that difficult to accept. He must have believed in something. No man would risk what he risked without being sustained by faith of some kind.'

I pondered my answer. 'I think he believed in good people. He revered Cromwell. He had a genuine affection for the archbishop.'

'And you, Thomas? What do you believe in this world of confused and conflicting ideas?'

'I don't care much for ideas ... doctrines ... official state-ments of faith. They all make men do strange things – sometimes heroic things but also violent, abominable things. Once, like Holbein, I was impressed by Lord Cromwell – until he did something terrible in pursuit of an ideal. So, perhaps I'm still looking for someone to believe in, someone so obvi-ously good that I want to share whatever it is that he has found. That's not a scholar's answer to your question but it's the best answer I can give at the moment.'

Morice turned to me with a warm smile. 'I think it's an excellent answer and a better one than I've heard many sup-posedly clever scholars give. Hold to it, Thomas, and one day you will find that person you're looking for. He or she won't be perfect. Never make the mistake of seeking perfection. But that person will be genuine, and honest and good-hearted and worthy of your trust.'

With such discussion, as well as talk of trivial things, we passed the journey to Eastwell. Arrived at the impressive centre of Moyle's domain we dismounted, and, leaving the guard in the courtyard, we approached the main entrance. The door opened before we reached it to reveal, not one of the owner's many servants, but the owner himself. He greeted Morice with a smile and looked me over with a less friendly expression. 'I bid you welcome,' he said, 'but why do you come with such a large escort?'

'I bear an urgent message from his grace, the Archbishop of Canterbury and Primate of All England.' Morice spoke in a tone that made the formal announcement sound all the more frigid.

Moyle nodded in acknowledgement and preceded us into the hall. 'We'll go to my parlour.'

The spacious chamber was richly furnished and lined with Flemish tapestries. Moyle waved us to chairs close to the hearth where large logs smouldered. Morice unfastened his purse to take out the warrant. But my attention was focused elsewhere. I stood transfixed, staring at the space above the fireplace. There, in full, exuberant blazon, was the Moyle coat of arms. The shield at the centre of the design, enfolded in extravagant red and white mantling, was comprised of a black chevron and three black moles, all on a white ground.

Chapter 20

'Is this your family coat of arms?' A stupid question spoken out of shock and confusion.

'Of course it is.' Moyle turned to look at the armorial decoration. 'Argent, a chevron sable, between three moles of the second,' he declared with obvious pride. 'What is your interest in it?'

I glanced at Morice to make sure he understood why I had diverted Moyle's attention. I saw him return the archbishop's warrant to his purse. I stumbled for words. ''Tis ... 'tis rather similar to another I came across recently.' Inwardly cursing myself for an idiot, I took out the coloured version of the Holbein painting Morice had given me and showed it to Moyle.

''Tis nothing like,' he said. 'This is or, a chevron jules between three badgers sable.' Clearly, he enjoyed airing his heraldic knowledge.

'Yes, of course, you are right. Now that I can compare the colours ...'

'Tinctures,' Moyle corrected.

'Yes, exactly, as you say, quite different. Do you happen to know whose arms these are?'

'No idea.' He shrugged. 'But I assume you did not come here to discuss heraldry.'

'Indeed not,' Morice said, recovering quickly. 'His grace desires to inform you of new arrangements for his commission. He has nominated Thomas Legh to lead it. I believe you are familiar with Dr Legh and worked with him in the suppression of some of the religious houses. His majesty's approval of this appointment indicates the importance he places on it. His grace wanted you to be the first to hear the news. I assume I can report back your enthusiastic welcome of this decision. It will expedite the inquiries and enable us to deal swiftly with all troublemakers.'

'As his grace pleases.' Moyle received the news with an expressionless face but only with difficulty concealed his displeasure. 'Does bearing this message require such an impressive armed escort? And why is young Treviot with you? When last we met I had occasion to protest against his insolence.'

I grasped the opportunity to provide an explanation for my presence. 'You were right to reprimand me, Sir Thomas. My behaviour was rash and inexcusable. I insisted on accompanying Master Morice in order to offer my apologies.'

Morice nodded sagely. ''Tis important we have no falling out among the leaders of the shire. His grace hopes you will make your peace with Master Treviot. As to the escort, we have another errand to perform of a more difficult nature. Indeed, by your leave, Sir Thomas we must be on our way. We bid you good day.'

As we travelled westwards, the mood of our party was very different from that which had marked our outward journey. Morice and I rode on a little ahead of the guards. I was too humiliated and ashamed to find words. After a long silence Morice said, 'You realise the grave embarrassment you almost caused his grace – to say nothing of the total waste of my time.'

'I'm sorry, but—'

'There are no "buts". You've stirred up suspicion against Sir Thomas, who may have papist sympathies but is certainly no traitor.'

'The evidence I had seemed to point—'

'The only evidence I can see is that you don't know the difference between a mole and a badger.'

'That's unfair,' I protested. 'I'd only seen them carved in stone at Fletcham and drawn very small on Holbein's goblet design. Without colour they did look very like the seal on Moyle's letter to his grace.'

'I believe you saw what you wanted to see because you don't like Sir Thomas. I should have checked your story myself. If I had made enquiries about Fletcham we would have been spared today's indignity. Unfortunately, I was too busy – and I trusted you. My mistake!'

After another mile or so of silence, Morice seemed to have calmed down a little. 'Moyle is a powerful man who sometimes abuses his power and must be watched. But he is, nevertheless, someone his grace has to work with in the county and the diocese and cannot afford to antagonise unnecessarily.'

'I will, of course, make my apologies to his grace in person.'

After another silence, I said, 'At least we do now know how to track down the real ringleader of his grace's enemies.'

'Thanks to Johannes Holbein.'

'Yes, thanks to Johannes Holbein, but I think you might acknowledge that I had something to do with rescuing his information and bringing it to Croydon.'

Morice made no response. He was deep in his own thoughts and muttering almost to himself. 'Affairs in Kent have absorbed all my time. I have the commission to organise. Letters to send all over the shire. I'm never in bed before midnight. Nevertheless, I should have gone to London to consult Christopher Barker.'

'Barker?'

'But then, of course, I couldn't be sure he would be there. Belike he has left for his house at Wanstead.'

'Who is Christopher Barker?' I persisted.

'Garter King of Arms. He can tell us who the *real* coat of arms belongs to. I must gain permission to call on him without more delay.'

'And then we can . . .'

'Then we shall have to embark on a completely new line of enquiry. That will mean *discreetly* examining the movements of the owner of Fletcham. That could take us weeks – weeks we can't afford.'

After this exchange Morice was wrapped in his own thoughts – doubtless calculating all the extra work he thought my blundering had caused him. Darkness fell and we continued our journey. Morice ignored the grumbling of the troops and when I offered a night's hospitality at Hemmings he declined, saying that he could not afford any more delay than I had already caused him. We parted at Ightham and I reached Hemmings sometime in the small hours, cursing Moyle, and Morice, and Black Harry, and the owner of Fletcham manor – but mostly cursing myself.

*

When I came down late the following morning the hall was echoing with commotion and laughter. Lizzie, Adie and the children were playing blind man's buff. Henry Holbein, with a cloth sash tied round his head, was charging around making fierce growling noises, which he seemed to find necessary for his role as the blind man. The others, with much squealing, were scurrying to and fro to avoid him. The boys kept rushing up to within inches to taunt him, like braves at a bear-baiting, while Adie was helping Annie avoid being caught.

'So you've returned to us. How did you enjoy your fine company?' Lizzie came up as I stood by the screens passage, watching.

'I don't think they enjoyed me very much. I managed to blacken my reputation in a certain area. But what's happening here? You all seem to be having a good time.'

'We're trying to keep them occupied.' She nodded towards the revellers. 'Occupied and cheerful, but some scars run deep.'

'Have the boys been told about their father?'

'Yes, Ned managed that beautifully. He talked to them about the heaven where brave men go and hugged them when they wept. He even made me cry. They're sensible children. If you can give them peace and security for a few years, they'll be fine.'

'And Adie?'

'More difficult. She has built a wall around herself. It's the only way she can see at the moment to stop herself being hurt. She spends all her time with the children. She knows she's safe with them. As for the rest of us – she's very polite but always on edge. She can't relax because she can't allow herself to feel that anyone can value her for herself.'

'I suppose she must think that all men are rutting stags.'

'That's only part of it. I know all about the wants and needs of men. I was younger than her when I was put in the brothel. All whores – or all sensible ones – learn to distance themselves from their work. You almost become a looker-on, watching yourself going through the motions. That way you keep your self-respect and persuade yourself that, someday, a man will come along with whom it will be different. Adie feels deep down that she's been spoiled for ever. Someone will have to coax her back into a belief that she's lovable.' Lizzie stared at me long and hard.

'Well, we must do what we can,' I said, and went in search of breakfast.

The next couple of days were an interval of calm. The tone seemed set by the yellowing leaves that drifted down from the trees. Stubbornly, they had clung to the elms which lined the drive and the beeches bordering the nearer fields when blustering tempests did their best to shake them free. Now, of their own volition, they yielded to the changing season. I, too, felt buffeted by the recent days of hectic activity and welcomed the freedom to reflect on the situation of the little society at Hemmings and make my own plans. I rode around the estate, often taking the boys with me, to attend to routine matters. I dealt with correspondence forwarded from Goldsmith's Row by the small staff I had left there. I sent to London for Raffy's tutor. My son had already had an overlong holiday from his books because I had been too distracted to attend to his schooling. Now that it seemed further time would elapse before it would be safe to return to the capital, it was time to establish a routine for Raffy and his new classmates. I also tried my clumsy best to help Adie.

I came upon her one evening after the children were abed, sitting in a corner of the kitchen, sewing a patch on a garment.

'I'm sorry about your master,' I said, drawing up a stool facing her. 'I expect you will miss him.'

She nodded, keeping her eyes on her needlework.

'How long had you been with him?'

'Three years.'

'And he had been good to you?'

'Yes, Master.'

'Have you heard from your brother recently? Would you like to go and see him?'

'I think he is too busy.'

'He serves Lord Graves, does he not?'

'Yes, Master.'

'In Leicestershire?'

'Yes, Master.'

'Tell me about him.'

She shrugged. 'He's tall … fair … He works hard. He's very good with animals.'

'Older than you?' I prompted.

'By two years.'

'And you have no other family?'

'No.'

'Did your father make any provision for you? A dowry?'

She shook her head. 'There was no money. He was falconer to Lord Graves. His lordship allowed Ignatius to take over from him. He found me a position with Master Holbein. He said that was all he could do for me.'

'I think we should go and see your brother. Would you like that?'

'If it please you, Master.'

'No, Adie,' I said, trying not to raise my voice. 'If it please *you*.'

Again, the emotionless shrug.

'Well, shall I tell you what really would please *me*? That would be to see a smile on your face. So, as soon as we can arrange it, we'll make a journey into Leicestershire to visit Ignatius.'

Now she did look up. 'You want to be rid of me!' She dropped her sewing and rushed from the room.

A little later I told Ned about the encounter. 'What did I do wrong?' I asked.

'When a person's humours are so far out of alignment it is hard for anyone to help them. Adie is in a deep melancholy. If I was at home I would be able to put her on a regime of remedies that might restore the balance. Hellebore is good but the treatment is a long process. In the cloister we sometimes had brothers whose melancholy lasted months, even years. There is borage in the kitchen garden here. I will make up a mild purgative with it. I will also prescribe a diet for her – warm, moist foods. That might help. Otherwise the best we can do for now is keep a close watch on her.'

'You mean . . .'

'Melancholy can drive sufferers to desperate measures.'

These and other concerns kept us preoccupied. For a time Hemmings was its own closed little world, in which our problems absorbed us totally. For a time. Not long enough. The rumours – soon to be verified – began to insinuate themselves halfway through the following week: a fire at the priest's house in Radlow had claimed the lives of everyone inside. The vicar at Stepton had disappeared, as had a curate recently installed in Branfield Abbots. On Thursday morning I rode over to Hadbourne to discover what James Dewey knew of these events.

'I like it not,' my old friend said as we sat in his parlour.

'You think these things are connected?'

'There can be no doubt. There have been several accounts of a group of riders seen in the location of every incident.'

'Black Harry's gang?'

'I'd wager a purse of sovereigns on it. And that is not the only thing linking them. All the victims were protégés of the archbishop.'

'I suspected as much.'

'The curate at Branfield was one of Cranmer's chaplains and had recently returned from a year as his representative to various Lutheran scholars in Germany. John Padman at Radlow I've known for many years. To the best of my knowledge no one has ever complained about him preaching novel doctrine but he was widely rumoured to have a wife.'

'Some people say the same of the archbishop. You must have heard the story about him conveying her between his various residences in a specially made chest.'

'That's common gossip. I wonder if the murder of Padman and his household isn't intended to be some kind of warning to his grace: "This is what happens to priests who break their vow of celibacy."'

I laughed. 'And how many clergy do we know who keep their vow of celibacy?'

'True enough.' James's reply was serious. 'But 'tis not the fornication that bothers Rome-faced churchmen. They care not how many priests visit whores or keep concubines but if a man in orders does the right thing by his paramour and marries her, then he is seen to be openly flouting the Church's rules – and that is an unforgivable sin.'

'James,' I said, 'I do believe you're turning heretic.'

'Not I. I leave all that theological stuff to those who can

make sense of it. But I find myself getting increasingly angry with clerical hypocrisy. "Do as I say, not as I do" seems to be their only guiding principle. You know, of course, that they have their own law which keeps them out of my court.'

'You mean benefit of clergy?'

'That's right. A man comes before me for a felony worthy of the gallows and, before I can even hear the evidence, he "claims his clergy" and the matter is taken to the bishop's court. You know what happens there.'

'The bishop says, "Oh, you malapert rogue, go and pay ten pence to St Noddy's shrine, and don't sin again."'

James laughed. 'Quite right.'

'What about the other case?' I asked. 'What happened at Stepton?'

'Men claiming to have been sent by the archbishop ransacked the vicarage and went off with Stephen Garrow and a sackful of his books.'

'Do you think he and the vicar of Branfield have been murdered, too?'

'I suspect not. In both cases the rogues have been seen riding off with their victims bound and tied to a packhorse. If they intended to kill them, why not do it straight away?'

'Interrogation, then?'

'That would be my guess. Interrogation and torture. God's body, Thomas, the Inquisition's come among us! Well, I won't allow it – not in my jurisdiction. We have laws and a system. They may not be perfect but they're all we have. We don't need holy armies and secret tribunals.'

'We know now the organisation behind this illegal activity.' I explained what Holbein had discovered about the leading figures in the Catholic conspiracy. 'In the meantime, how can we stop Black Harry, if that's who it is?'

'I've sent messages to all the leading landowners and townsmen asking them to pass on any information they have. That way I hope we can plot the gang's movements. That may help us to discover their base.'

'They'll know what you're doing. They may go into hiding or move out of the area.'

'Thomas, my first objective is to see these rogues swinging from a gallows but if we only drive them out of the area, I'll settle for that.'

There was a knock at the door and a servant entered. He had a brief quiet word with James, who stood up.

'Excuse me, Thomas. It seems I have other visitors.'

When he returned, a few minutes later, he was followed by two men. The first I recognised immediately. It was Ralph Morice. Behind him a figure trundled in whose vast bulk almost filled the doorway.

'Thomas,' James said, 'permit me to introduce Dr Thomas Legh.'

Chapter 21

It was easy to see how Legh had gained a reputation as a petty tyrant among those who were lovers of the old order and why so many abbots and priors had meekly resigned their convents rather than stand up to his blustering self-assertion. It was not just his size that commanded attention; he exuded authority and intolerance towards all opposition. Within seconds he assumed control.

'I'm glad you're here, Master Treviot. I've heard good things of you. Your name is well spoken of at the royal court. I was mindful to call upon you later. Now I've been saved an extra visit. That's good. There's much to be done and little enough time if we're to rid this shire of all elements hostile to his majesty.'

James gave up his own armed chair to the cumbersome lawyer and sent for cakes and ale. The rest of us sat round the table, waiting on Legh's words. We did not have to wait long. Dispensing with small talk, he presented us with a clear statement of the situation as he saw it and the plan of action necessary to deal with it. It was the polished performance of a seasoned prosecutor presenting his case to the jury.

'A state of affairs has been allowed to develop here which threatens to thwart his majesty's desire for the religious unity of his people. Now, let us be absolutely clear from the outset that anyone who opposes the will of his majesty is guilty of treason. We are not dealing with philosophers' speculation or theologians' debating points. I am not here to enter into discussion with men who would love to draw me into the quagmire of religious argument.' He sneered. 'You know the sort of thing I mean, "Saint Thomas Aquinas says this" or "On the other hand, we must bear in mind the blessed Augustine's words". Pox on all that! Truth is what his majesty says it is and we are here to ensure that nothing else, no subversive papist nonsense, is fed to his majesty's subjects.'

There was a pause as food and drink was set before us. Ralph Morice took the opportunity to provide us with new information. 'Dr Legh is absolutely right to point out the connection between false teaching and treason. Thomas here has been instrumental in uncovering the evil designs of papists who cloak their sedition in religious zeal. There is a well-organised plot being hatched which links the preachers and the leaders of Kentish society with a chain that runs all the way to Rome and Madrid. This is now clear to us from evidence gathered by an agent working on behalf of his grace of Canterbury – evidence, I may say, gathered at great personal cost. Doctor, may I outline our latest information?'

Legh nodded, temporarily engaged in enjoying a saffron cake.

'Have you identified the man Holbein overheard plotting with the Duke of Norfolk?' I asked.

'Yes, and very interesting it is. Garter King of Arms had no difficulty identifying the bearer of the coat of arms Holbein saw. The badgers appear because, in many parts, they're called "brocks". The arms are those of Ferdinand Brooke.'

'Brooke! Brooke!' I cried. 'That completes the connection, then.'

Morice was puzzled. 'How so, Thomas?'

'When Adie – Mistress Imray – was held captive by Black Harry she heard him mention a co-conspirator. She thought the name was "Rook" but she did not catch it clearly. It must have been "Brooke". Saints be praised we were stayed from arresting Moyle. Do you know anything about this Ferdinand Brooke?'

'It seems he's quite a familiar figure in court circles – a persistent satellite.'

'Satellite?'

'A follower, a flatterer, someone always to be seen circling around great men. He's one of those who wheedles his way into favour.'

'Has he attracted Norfolk's patronage?'

'Indeed. The duke welcomes him because of his Catholic sympathies.'

'Ferdinand? That's not an English name,' James suggested. 'It sounds Spanish.'

'Quite correct,' Morice said. 'His mother was one of Queen Catherine's ladies-in-waiting. When the queen fell from grace, the Brookes moved to Spain. Young Ferdinand was brought up by priests and became something of a zealot – more Catholic than the pope. He returned a couple of years ago when his father died, to take over the family estate in Essex.'

My mind was moving fast as I tried to make connections

between what we already knew about the plot against Cranmer and this new information. 'I don't quite understand the relationship between Brooke and Norfolk. According to Holbein, Brooke seems to have been conveying instructions to the duke. That has always seemed odd.'

'I agree,' Morice said. 'What we suspect is that Brooke has been recruited by the imperial ambassador, Eustace Chapuys.'

'Weaselly troublemaker!' Legh spluttered, showering cake crumbs. 'Everyone knows that he's forever scheming with his majesty's enemies.'

'That is so,' Morice continued. 'He maintains a secret organisation pledged to undermine the reform of the English Church by any and every means.'

'Why doesn't the king expel him?' Dewey asked.

'Because he needs the Emperor's friendship. That means we must be constantly on the alert to minimise any damage Chapuys may do. Up until now we haven't been able to connect the ambassador's network to the likes of Norfolk and Gardiner. Now, thanks to Holbein, we have the link – Brooke, or "the Popinjay" as some call him.'

'Because he dresses exuberantly?' I asked.

'Yes, he likes to think of himself as one step ahead of fashion. To my mind he simply looks ridiculous.'

'Then Brooke is the man who went looking for Holbein at the Steelyard,' I said, recalling my conversation with Pastor Meyer.

Morice said, 'I suspect his ribbons and rings and furs may be part of an act.'

'Playing the empty-headed courtier so that no one takes him seriously?'

'Exactly, Thomas. The reality is that he's a dangerous fanatic.'

'Now we know of his connection with Black Harry you can arrest him,' I said, 'and, so it please God, you can bring down the whole organisation.'

Legh having completed his repast was anxious to resume control of the meeting. 'However, we are not here to concern ourselves overmuch with high politics. Our task is to ensure that the king's doctrine is preached in this area and that all enemies of it are presented to the archbishop's court or to the assizes, whichever is appropriate. Now, we will approach this in an organised way. The first step is to summon here, to Sir James Dewey's house, anyone suspected of preaching sedition or supporting those who do preach sedition. The writs have already gone out and I will hold court here on Saturday. His grace is sending a contingent of his guard to convey to Canterbury any who merit closer examination. This will send a very clear message to any covert papists. On Sunday all clergy will read to their congregations a statement of official doctrine. On Monday they will all report here and swear to uphold everything in the *King's Book* and only everything in the *King's Book*. The following day I move on to Maidstone, where I will repeat the same process. Within a month I will have covered the whole of Kent – that is, the dioceses of Canterbury and Rochester – and rid it of papistry. Now, Sir James, perhaps you would be kind enough to show me the accommodation you have for me.'

'He seems very confident,' I said, when Morice and I were alone.

He smiled ruefully. 'Yes, I've had to listen to him all the way from Croydon. However, he is good. He knows the law and he can use it.'

'That I can believe. I'm glad you found out about this Brooke rogue so quickly.'

256

'I was lucky. Christopher Barker the herald knows him quite well. His land at Wanstead borders one of the Brooke manors. He was able to provide much information about the family history.'

'But not, I imagine, about Brooke's more nefarious activities.'

'No, but it was not difficult to make the necessary connections. By the way, I must apologise for some of the things I said on Saturday.'

'You had every reason to be angry. I'm only glad we have discovered the right person now. Presumably you will be arresting him immediately.'

'I'm afraid it's not that simple. We would have to convince a King's Bench jury.'

'But we have proof – Holbein's notes.'

'Brooke will deny them and he will be supported by his extremely powerful accomplices. They will know we can't produce the artist to back up his testimony.'

'Surely the law is not so stupid!' I stood up and paced across to the window. 'It cannot be that all we have been through was in vain.'

'No, we still have the advantage of surprise. Brooke doesn't know we've discovered him.'

'So what is the plan?'

'I haven't worked that out yet.'

'Well, we don't have much time. Brooke's ruffians are increasingly active.' I told Morice about the latest attacks. 'They're obviously seizing men they can frighten into giving false testimony against the archbishop. If they can bring him down they'll have achieved their objective.'

'I know. And they will also have the support of his grace's enemies in Canterbury. The anti-Cranmer faction among the senior clergy is becoming more confident. You can sense it. They don't have the respect for his grace that they should have and they're beginning to be more open with their criticisms. Germain Gardiner's visits have become more frequent and he always brings letters from his uncle, the bishop. We have tried to intercept this correspondence, so far without success.'

I returned to the table and stood, staring down at Morice. 'Then 'tis becoming a race,' I suggested, 'between those intent on discrediting the archbishop and those determined to expose his grace's enemies. Success will go to those who can present to the king a case that persuades him to take action.'

'His majesty has complete trust in his grace.' Morice seemed remarkably placid.

'His majesty had complete trust in Thomas Cromwell,' I said.

When James returned I prepared to take my leave.

'Dr Legh wants you to stay,' he said. 'He says we need to pool our knowledge if we are to draw up a comprehensive list of potential troublemakers.'

'I am loyal to the archbishop,' I said, 'and I grant that we must do all we can to protect him from subtle schemers and violent foes. Yet I like not this making of lists, dividing all our neighbours into sheep and goats. A man may be uneasy about some of the changes being made in Church and state without being guilty of treason.'

Morice nodded. 'In normal times I would agree with you, Thomas, but these are not normal times. You have seen for yourself the violence of those who oppose us. We are, as his grace has pointed out to you, at war. In war it does not pay to yield a single yard of ground to the enemy. Therefore we have to fight force with force and subtlety with subtlety.'

'In the name of the Gospel?'

Morice sighed. 'Even in the name of the Gospel.'

A heavy step on the stair warned of Legh's approach. He came in and lowered himself on to a chair, which creaked as he did so. 'Right, to business, to business. Sir James we will require paper, pens and ink.'

When these had been supplied, he allocated them to each of us seated round the table.

'We will need two lists,' he said, 'one for clergy and one for the leaders of shire society. Please write down the names of everyone who, in your opinion, merits investigation. Be sure not to omit anyone. If you are in doubt set down the name. My questioning will determine who is innocent and who guilty.'

When we had written down all the names that we could think of, we compared notes and Ralph Morice drew up a master list. It comprised more than twenty parish clergy, gentlemen and townsmen. Legh ran his eyes over the list approvingly. 'This largely agrees with the catalogue of villainy we have already produced,' he said. 'But there are a few more here. Tomorrow I will send for them also. We will make an early start on Saturday. Master Treviot, I look forward to seeing you then.'

Thus dismissed, I made my way home, saddened by the dividing walls now appearing in our rural society but saddened much more by the fact that events were manoeuvring me into the role of informant against county neighbours I had known for years.

During my absence Francis Sturngood had arrived. I explained that he would have two more members in his class.

'I know not what schooling they have had until now,' I said, 'but they are intelligent boys and, I think, apt to learn. The elder, Carl, seems mature for his age. His brother is more excitable, energetic, restless. He may need harder discipline. But I counsel you to be easy on them until you have got to know them. These last days have been very hard for them.'

'I will, Master.' He ran a hand over his thinning hair. 'As for young Master Raphael, I must first discover what he has remembered – or, perhaps, forgotten – since we last met.'

'I'm afraid you may need to give me a taste of the birch on that account. I have been much away and not kept Raffy at his studies. Anyway, let's go and find them.'

The children were in the hall with Adie playing ninepins. An 'alley' had been set up by laying benches on their sides. Within this space the rushes had been cleared to make a smooth surface for the wooden balls to roll on. Adie was helping Annie when her turn came. Together they rolled the ball from halfway along the course. The boys, as usual, were locked in noisy competition. Lizzie sat watching and feeding her baby.

I went over to the players to introduce the teacher. 'This is Master Sturngood. He will be giving lessons to you boys from now on. You will go to him every morning at seven o'clock and study until noon.'

The three reluctant pupils pulled long faces.

The tutor responded with a frown. 'You must start to be men. That means learning the wisdom written down for us by all the best and wisest men who have lived. You are not infants any more. Infants have nurses. Young men have teachers who can open their minds.'

I saw the shadow fall across Adie's face and hastened to introduce her. 'This is Mistress Imray. She is guardian to Carl and Henry. She fills the gap left by their parents – and she does so admirably.' I hoped that my words reassured Adie but sadness remained written across her features. Little Henry went over to her and held her hand. He turned and stuck out his tongue at Sturngood. Dear God, I thought, I have enough conflicts to deal with. I don't need another war in my own household.

The following morning I looked in briefly on the chamber on the top floor that had been set aside as a schoolroom. Everything seemed in order. The boys were seated on their stools, heads bent over hornbooks. Sturngood was moving between them, checking their work and commenting on their progress. I thought I would suggest later that he did not need to be constantly tapping his leg with his birch.

I went in search of Adie and found her in her accustomed kitchen corner, sitting alone and doing nothing. 'Will you walk with me?' I asked. ''Tis a fine morning.'

She rose without a word and we went out, across the stable yard and over the dew-drenched lawn.

'You must not mind Master Sturngood's manner,' I said. 'He is a scholar. That means he understands books better than people.'

'He has his job to do,' she replied expressionlessly.

'I don't want you to think he has taken the boys away from you but he is right that the time has come for them to learn things that you cannot teach them.'

She sighed. 'Then there is nothing more I can do for them.'

'That is not true. Boys are not like blank sheets of paper on which teachers simply print Latin texts and arithmetical sums.'

We were walking on the track that ran from the house to the south gate and had reached the little bridge crossing the stream from which we took our water. It was much swollen after the recent prolonged rains. It had overflowed its banks and tore resentfully at the bridge's stonework, which forced it into a narrow channel. We paused to gaze down into the swirling current.

'Carl and Henry need love. They think of you as their mother. Boys don't stop needing mothers as they become men.'

'Raffy has no mother.'

The words were spoken softly but they still stung. 'I think he also is coming to think of you as a mother.'

'Did he know his real mother?'

'No, she died when he was born.'

'Lizzie told me you were deeply upset by that.'

'Lizzie says many things she shouldn't. But, yes, I thought my world had come to an end. I convinced myself I would never know happiness again. That, of course, was foolish.'

Adie made no reply and for a while the only sound was the angry hiss of the surging water beneath us. At last she said, staring down into the water, 'They'll all three be grown up one day.'

'Of course, and by then you'll be married and have boys of your own to look after – and probably girls, too.'

At that moment her whole body heaved and sobs broke forth from deep inside her. She sagged against the parapet. I grabbed her arm to pull her away but she shook me off. 'Go, go, go,' she cried. 'Leave me alone!'

I ran back to the house and found Lizzie. 'For God's sake, go to Adie!' I shouted. 'She's down by the bridge. I'm worried that—' But Lizzie had already rushed from the room.

I followed as far as the stable yard gate. There I loitered for several minutes looking anxiously towards the trees that lined the stream. At last, to my intense relief, I saw the women coming back, Lizzie supporting Adie with an arm round her waist. Adie was brought indoors and taken to her bed. Ned went to her and later he and Lizzie came to find me in the parlour.

In answer to my enquiry, Ned said, 'I have given her a tiny dose of tincture of opium. Generally I have little liking for it. It has come only recently into England and its efficacy is not proven. However, 'tis something I carry to relieve pain and induce sleep. I find it helps to calm sufferers and makes it easier to examine them in order to get to the root of their problems.'

'And have you determined the root of Adie's problem?' I asked.

Lizzie scowled. 'She fancies herself to be with child.'

'And is she?'

''Tis too early to be certain but I don't think so. In the whore-house, it was always something the younger, inexperienced girls feared. That fear sometimes fired their imaginations.'

'What matters at the moment,' Ned said, 'is what she believes, rather than what is the reality. I can apply all the usual tests and do my best to reassure her, but if she is con-vinced, nothing will dispel the fear until she fails to produce a baby. That, of course, will take several months.'

'A curse on Black Harry and his lecherous rakehells! God grant we come face to face again!'

'I'm almost inclined to say "Amen" to that,' Ned res-ponded, 'but, for now, we have Adie to think of.'

'Can your nostrums keep her calm?'

Ned shook his head. 'A long stupor can be very injurious and, in any case, it will not dispel her fears. Adie will have no peace until she faces her worries and conquers them. The

Bible tells us fear is a demon that can only be cast out by love. The best cure we can administer is to show that we love and appreciate her.'

Lizzie agreed. 'She is convinced that she is worthless. The children adore her and everyone else likes her but she cannot or will not see it.'

I said, 'We must all keep a close watch on her. Meanwhile, I think it is time I wrote to her brother. I'll see if he will come down to visit her. Perhaps we can discover things about her past that may help us to understand her better.'

The next morning it was almost with relief that I set out for Hadbourne to assist with the archbishop's commission.

Chapter 22

The hall had been cleared for the inquiry. A table stood on a raised dais at one end. It was covered by a Turkey carpet and a row of chairs was set behind it. High on the wall above and behind them two large images dominated the room. One was Archbishop Cranmer's coat of arms. The other was a life-like portrait of King Henry, who seemed to survey the proceedings with a fierce gaze. A bench set crosswise halfway down the hall marked off the area where those being examined were to stand. It seemed that Legh had modelled his commission chamber on the royal courts at Westminster Hall, where only men of the law, called 'benchers', were permitted within the hallowed enclosure before the judge's seat. Apart from these, all furniture had been removed. Guards in the archbishop's livery stood at the doors and two more were stationed at either end of the commissioners' table. Several men were already present when I entered, standing in small clusters. It was evident that they were going to have to remain standing until Legh dismissed them. A secretary was arranging papers on the table and indicated the place at one end where I was to sit. Minutes later Legh and his entourage entered and took their places. James was seated next to me and beside the chairman. The other half of the table was occupied by Ralph Morice, two other local JPs and the commission secretary.

Legh began the proceedings with a speech. 'This is an archiepiscopal commission convened under royal charter for the examination of alleged irregularities concerning the preaching and teaching of certain parish clergy within the dioceses of Canterbury and Rochester. When your names are called you will be sworn to give true testimony. You will answer all questions put to you by members of the commission. Anyone we deem to be guilty of holding opinions contrary to those established by the laws of this realm will be sent to Canterbury for further examination by the archbishop's court. The same will apply to anyone perjuring himself or attempting to conceal information from the commission. Those of you who preach or cause to be preached the true doctrine of the English Church by law established and who answer truthfully all questions put to them have absolutely nothing to fear from today's proceedings.'

It immediately became obvious that Legh had skilfully arranged the order of business for maximum effect. The first to face the flight of verbal arrows was Peter Perks, vicar of Sandling Parva, a slight, elderly priest who was already sweating.

The chairman demanded sharply, 'You were for many years sub-prior of the Benedictine house at Laxford, were you not?'

'I was.'

'Speak up, man! Don't mumble!'

'That is correct.'

'You must have been pleased to be offered a benefice after the surrender of your house.'

'Yes, indeed.'

'And you were presented to that benefice by Prebendary Cooke of Canterbury Cathedral.'

'Yes.'

'At that time you swore an oath of loyalty to your diocesan bishop, did you not?'

'Yes.'

'Are you aware that Prebendary Cooke is under investigation for spreading slanderous rumours about the archbishop?'

'Well ... I had heard ...'

'Yes or no!' Legh thundered. 'Do you know that your patron is a sworn and open enemy of his grace?'

'I ... er ... think ...'

'*Think?* I don't want to know what you think! This is your last warning: if you don't give me clear and simple answers to my questions, you'll be in contempt. Do you know your patron is an enemy of the archbishop?'

'Well ... yes.'

Legh addressed himself to the room at large. 'If I had to prise answers from the rest of you in the same way we would be here for days. Well, I won't do it. Any sign of prevarication and you'll be detained, awaiting trial by a higher court. Now, Master Perks, how many times in the last year have you been summoned to Canterbury by your patron?'

The old man was now quivering and dabbing his brow with a kerchief. 'Three, I think ... no, four.'

'And what did you discuss?'

'Well ... er ... many things ...'

'*Master Perks!*'

'Well ... Prebendary Cooke was interested in clergy his grace had licensed to preach in the area.'

'Did he not ask you whether, in your opinion, any of his grace's appointees were guilty of heresy?'

'He was concerned about that, certainly.'

'And what did you tell him?'

'I ... er ... mentioned that John Lanks might, perhaps, be not orthodox on all points of doctrine.'

'And was John Lanks subsequently arrested and taken before the archbishop's court?'

'Yes.'

'And what was the verdict of that court?'

'Not guilty.'

'Louder, please, Master Perks. I want everyone to hear you.'

'Not guilty.'

'Indeed, not guilty of any heretical teaching whatsoever. And why would he be? Do you suppose a man in whom his grace reposed confidence would be a disseminator of damnable heresy?'

'I suppose ... er ... no. Certainly not.'

'So what it comes to is this: you and your generous patron worked together to indict an innocent man of preaching false doctrine. And this was part of a plot to discredit the Archbishop of Canterbury, a godly scholar and pastor who has the love and trust of his majesty.'

'No!' the poor man screamed. 'That was never my intent—'

'Then, pray what was your intention? Have I misunderstood?' Legh glanced to left and right along the table. 'Perhaps my colleagues can fathom how a different conclusion can be drawn from what you have told us.' He paused momentarily.

'No? I thought not. Captain!' he called, 'take this fellow away.'

Peter Perks was hustled, blubbering and protesting, from the room.

After that opening, none of the men being examined was disposed to stand up against such verbal bullying. The commission dealt in brusque and rapid succession with all the other suspects. Rather more than half were dismissed with a stern caution but the remainder were handed over to the guards for transportation to Canterbury. Legh left the rest of us little to do. It was when Simon Belleville was set before us that my interest was particularly aroused. He was a stocky, bristle-haired farmer of yeoman birth whose rise in the first years of the Dissolution had been wing-footed even by the standards of the day. I remember my father telling me that Belleville was one of the first speculators in monastic property to approach him for a loan and that he had doubled his capital many times over in the ensuing years. My father disliked him, often referring to him as 'the man with two popes'; someone who paraded his devotion to traditional religion and had a reputation for generous support of altar gilds and chantries, but who did not allow this to stand in the way of his profiteering from the dismantling of monasticism. Now he was one of the richest men in Kent and one who loved to display his wealth in ambitious building projects. His house at King's Branfield rivalled the mansions of the older shire families – in size, if not in taste, and he had created scarcely less impressive edifices for his two sons. Indeed, their corner of Kent was often jokingly referred to as 'Bellevilleshire', an enclave where the king's writ ran second to their own. He stood before the commission today accused of 'proud words' spoken against the archbishop.

'According to our information,' Legh said, 'you have been

heard to boast on more than one occasion, "I decide what is preached in my churches". Is that correct?'

Belleville made a gesture as though waving the accusation aside. 'If I said that I meant only that I would not tolerate any teaching contrary to that approved by his majesty.'

'Even if that teaching had the endorsement of his majesty's archbishop?'

'Is there any difference between what the king believes and what his grace believes?'

'I will ask the questions,' Legh snapped. 'Confine yourself to simple answers. Have you or have you not challenged the instruction given by priests appointed by his grace of Canterbury?'

'I may have debated one or two points of doctrine ...'

'Indeed?' The chairman smiled. 'Would you be good enough to remind the commission at which university you studied theology?'

Laughter drifted round the hall as the unpopular landowner stood abashed.

'I take it from your silence that you are not qualified to "debate" holy mysteries.' Legh smirked at the man's discomfort. 'Now,' he continued, 'one of the clergy to whom you have given the benefit of your extensive doctrinal knowledge is John Horton, is it not?'

Suddenly, I saw where this line of questioning was leading. I scribbled a note and passed it along to the chairman. He read it, nodded and announced, 'Before we proceed any further with Master Belleville we will take our dinner adjournment. We will resume in one hour.' He led the way from the hall.

In James's parlour the commissioners sat to enjoy the ample meal provided by our host.

Legh said, 'I had intended to adjourn after we had bundled that pompous little demi-king off to jail, but Master Treviot here seems to have other ideas.'

'I'm sorry for disturbing your schedule, Dr Legh,' I said, 'but it may be that there is more at stake here than an argument between Belleville and Horton. You are aware, I'm sure, that Horton is the curate at Branfield Abbots.'

'Of course. The poor man's disappeared. If any ill has befallen him I intend to make Belleville swing for it.'

'Well, the fact is that Horton is not the only one of the archbishop's appointees to go missing.'

'You mean Garrow at Stepton? Yes, we know about him. What's your point?'

'There's also the death of Padman in the mysterious fire at Radlow.' I hurried on before Legh could tell me that he also knew everything about that. 'These events have all taken place in the area dominated by Belleville.'

'Agreed,' Legh said. 'So the sooner we call him to account, the better.'

'Certainly, Doctor. But should we not also be trying to apprehend the gallowsbird directly responsible for these atrocities?'

'Do you know who that is?'

'I have a very strong suspicion and, if I'm right, he has links to those at the very top of the papist conspiracy against the archbishop.'

'Interesting.' Legh pushed his trencher to one side. 'Tell me about your suspicion.'

Briefly, I explained the picture Ralph and I were building up of the connection between Black Harry, Ferdinand Brooke and the leaders of the conspiracy at court. 'If Belleville is another link in the chain,' I concluded, 'he may well be harbouring the gang. He may even know the whereabouts of the missing priests.'

'Well, Master Treviot, I'll have the truth out of him, never fear.'

'With respect, Doctor,' I ventured, 'might it not be wiser to proceed more circumspectly? If we arrest Belleville, his associates will immediately know of it and take fright. They will find some other haven, probably taking their captives with them. We might lose our only chance of running to earth a band of dangerous, fanatical, papist ruffians.'

Legh looked thoughtful. I hurried on. 'But if we can track them down we will earn his majesty's thanks for exposing treachery among his own advisers.'

'So what do you suggest?' Legh asked.

'Let Belleville off with a caution. Then allow me a few words with him in private.'

'To say what?'

'That we have identified all the men involved in a major conspiracy and are about to close in on them. They will all, undoubtedly, hang and he will probably share their fate. At the very least his property will be confiscated by the Crown and he will lose everything he has so painstakingly accumulated. His only hope will be to assist the commission by revealing the whereabouts of the criminals he is shielding.'

'And if your suspicions are wrong?'

'The blame will fall on me and not his grace's commission. Belleville will probably claim that I was pursuing some private grudge against him.'

That satisfied the wily lawyer. He obviously realised that, if successful, my plan would win him considerable favour with the king and that, if it failed, he could deny all involvement.

Saints preserve us, I thought, I'm becoming as subtle as these law men.

After dinner, with James's help, I made the necessary, very simple arrangements. We chose a hay barn for the interview. Ralph Morice insisted on being present, though we agreed he should remain concealed. I waited in the stable yard accompanied by two members of the archiepiscopal guard.

When Belleville came out to collect his horse, I accosted him. 'Please attend on me for a few minutes.'

He raised his voice to protest but the guards took him, one each arm, and steered him into the barn. I followed, closing the door behind me.

'What do you think—'

I ignored the bluster. 'We have a few more questions, which I fancy you would rather answer in private.'

He turned towards the door, now held by the burly guards. 'I have said all I intend to say in there.'

'A pity. I rather hoped you would grasp the opportunity to distance yourself from the man who calls himself "Black Harry", rather than share his gallows. However, if you would prefer to take your chance, you are free to leave.'

I watched him carefully. Everything hinged on his reaction. First of all, he stared at me, eyes widened in surprise. Then he took a step towards the door. Then he thought better of it and turned again. That was when I knew that I was right.

'You are very wise to reconsider,' I said. 'You have got yourself mixed up with a band of traitors. We know about Black Harry, Master Brooke and their connections with foreign agents. You're in a deep hole and the only way to climb out is to tell me everything you know.'

There was still a vestige of resistance in him. 'Who are

these people you're talking about?' he asked warily but not diverting his gaze.

I began to doubt whether I would, after all, be able to break him. I had no evidence to connect him with any crime. It was time to try bluff. 'People who know you well enough,' I replied. 'People who burned down John Padman's house. People ready to swear that you incited them to murder.'

'That's not true!' he shouted. 'I may have complained about Padman's preaching, but I never . . . ' Now he was shaking. He sat quickly on an upturned barrel. 'I had no idea that they would . . . You can't implicate me in that business.'

Time for another lie. 'We have arrested a couple of the villains. I've no doubt that, with a little persuasion, they will reveal the names of everyone involved. *Everyone*.'

'But I'm not involved!' Belleville squealed. 'I only offered them shelter as a favour to a gentleman from London.'

'Ferdinand Brooke?'

He stared at the ground. I guessed that Brooke had sworn him to secrecy and threatened the direst retribution if he broke silence.

'Master Belleville,' I said, 'have you ever seen a man hanged, drawn and quartered?'

He shook his head, then looked up, panic-stricken. 'Master Treviot, you must believe—'

'I will believe you,' I said, 'when you tell me all you know about these men and their plans.'

'Brooke came to see me. A fine-looking gentleman. Expensive clothes. He said he had been sent by his majesty to seek out loyal subjects willing to take part in a secret enterprise.'

'Doubtless you were flattered.'

'He sounded very plausible. He said the leading members of the king's Council were weeding out people who were pouring poison into the king's ear and placing false teachers in many churches.'

I thought, Now we're getting somewhere. I said, 'Did he name these great men?'

'No.'

'Oh, come now . . .'

'On my troth, Master Treviot, he said I didn't need to know.'

That could have been true, although I was not wholly convinced. 'Well,' I said, 'we'll let that pass. For now. The commission will have more questions for you soon. Meanwhile, you'll be given in charge to the captain and taken to jail.'

'No, Master Treviot, please!' He was perspiring freely. He clasped his hands in supplication. 'I see now that the man Brooke was a traitor but it was only a small thing he asked of me. He was looking for somewhere his cut-throat villains could hide.'

At last. I felt a surge of triumph. One more blow on the nail's head and this quaking fellow would deliver Black Harry into our hands. 'So where are these villains?'

Belleville looked around him, as though there might be eavesdroppers at hand. 'Promise you won't let it be known I told you,' he whined.

'You're in no position to demand conditions,' I snapped. 'Where are these traitors hiding?'

'The old convent at Swansford,' he mumbled, almost inaudibly.

'Part of your plunder from the Dissolution.' I could not resist the taunt.

''Tis still as I bought it. I haven't decided what to do with it yet. Perhaps a hospital, school or almshouses.'

'I'm sure you'll find some way to salve your conscience,' I said. 'Now, how many people has Black Harry with him?'

'I'm not sure. I haven't been there.'

'I hope for your sake you can prove that when he comes to trial. You've really no idea how many scoundrels you are succouring?'

'Perhaps half a dozen. Look, you must believe that I'm not privy to their plans. If I'd known what they intended to do—'

'You would have kept your mouth shut and looked forward to reaping your reward, like the grasping, immoral coward you are. Well, you don't deserve it, but I will have a word with Dr Legh and tell him you've been cooperative. Go with these men and wait in the gatehouse until we send for you again.'

When Belleville had been marched away by the guards, Morice and I returned to the hall and had a hurried conversation with Legh.

'It seems your guess was right, Master Treviot,' he said. 'Now we must follow up this information without delay. How far is this Swansford nunnery?'

'Fifteen or sixteen miles,' James said.

'Well, I cannot go. Master Morice and I are fully occupied. You must see to it, Treviot. Go to Swansford and bring in as many of the gang as you can for questioning. How many men will you want?'

I said, 'If you can spare six of his grace's guard, I'll take the same number of my own men.' My calmly reasoned reply concealed my pleasure at the prospect of arresting Black Harry personally.

Legh agreed. 'I'll see that the troops are ready at first light.'

When I went to the gatehouse Belleville looked up anxiously. 'What did he say?'

'He said you could prove your loyalty to his majesty by your silence. Go home. Make no contact whatsoever with Black Harry. Leave the rest to us. If we find the birds have flown when we get to Swansford, we'll know you have warned them.'

The man's relief was pitiable to behold. 'I won't say anything,' he whined. 'I swear it!'

'Be sure you don't. Your life depends on your doing absolutely nothing for the next twenty-four hours. Now, be off with you.'

The commission's business for the day was concluded shortly before dusk. I rode wearily home, too tired to think much about what awaited me on the morrow. Any elation I felt at the prospect of arresting Black Harry had long since evaporated. I certainly felt no pride at my day's work. Not content with becoming a conspirator, I had turned inquisitor.

Such morose thoughts were quickly swept aside when I reached Hemmings. I had scarcely dismounted when Bart came running from the house.

'Saints be praised that you're here, Master Thomas. Come quickly. It's Adie!'

Chapter 23

He hurried me upstairs and we entered the chamber Adie shared with Lizzie. The shutters were closed and the bed curtains drawn on two sides. The light of a single lamp illumined the worried features of a dozen or more people who were gathered round the bed. Adie lay there, eyes closed, the bleached pallor of her face accentuated by the dark hair spread out on the pillow. Ned was kneeling close beside her, applying a damp cloth to her brow, which glistened with sweat. There was scarcely any rise and fall of the bedclothes to indicate the breath of life.

'What's happened?' I demanded.

Lizzie turned and silently beckoned me to follow. She led the way to my chamber.

'She's very sick.' Lizzie's usual composure had deserted her and her cheeks bore the stains of tears.

'So, what is it, a sudden fever?'

'Yes, but there is worse. If it weren't for the boys she'd be dead.'

'Tell me everything.'

''Twas just before noon. Young Carl was looking from the classroom window, bored with his lesson. From there the bridge is just visible. He saw Adie climb on the parapet, then disappear. If he had not acted quickly . . . ' Lizzie dabbed her eyes with a kerchief. 'He yelled to your tutor and rushed downstairs, out of the house, shouting to everyone to follow. When they got to the bridge they saw her a few yards down-stream. Without any hesitation, the two older boys ran along the bank and waded in. The tutor followed. Between them they got her partly out of the water but the weight of her sodden clothes was almost wrenching her from their grasp. Praise God, they were able to hold her till some of the ser-vants came. When I got there I feared we were too late. Adie looked terrible; wet hair straggled over her face, arms hanging down limply. I couldn't see her breathing. The men picked her up and ran back here. Then – I suppose it was the jolt-ing – she suddenly coughed up water. We got her into dry clothes and put her to bed and Ned's been with her ever since. She has a fever and she hasn't moved or spoken – not a murmur.'

'What does Ned say about her?'

'He curses because he doesn't have all his nostrums with him but he says there's nothing he can give her at this stage.'

'That's right.' Neither of us had heard Ned come in. He sighed heavily as he sank into a chair. 'Cool cloths should reduce the fever but we shan't know till then what else ails her.'

'Surely, 'twas the fall into the water . . . '

'No, Thomas, that was, like the fever, a symptom, not a cause. We must try to discern why her humours are so seriously out of balance.'

'Might it be the case that she is with child, as she believes, and that against her will?'

'I think not. She is frantic in mind and half-wishes what she most fears.'

'I don't understand.'

'Few of us do. Only those who have been to the dark, Godless place where life seems too great a burden to be longer borne can know what it is like. We had a brother at Farnfield once who had so great a desire for heaven that he hated this world and everything in it. His confessor tried to make him see that God alone determines our life span and that to wish to shorten it is a sin. His bodily decline and death troubled the community greatly, but, alas, we were unable to prevent him achieving his wish. I still pray for him often. All I can tell you about Adie is that she will recover only when she truly wishes to do so. God be praised, she did not drown, but what matters is that she wanted to. If that desire remains strong within her it will kill her no less assuredly than the water.'

'That must never happen!' I cried. 'We must help her back to her right mind. I'll have someone sit with her all the time ...'

'I've already taken the liberty of organising that,' Ned said. 'I will be told as soon as there is any change in her condition. Tomorrow I will send someone into Tonbridge with a list for the apothecary there. He is reasonably competent and should be able to provide the simples I lack here.'

'And I have already despatched a messenger to bring her brother to Hemmings,' I said. ''Tis even more urgent, now, that he comes to comfort Adie. And to answer certain questions I will have for him about her past. That is where secrets are often locked away.'

Throughout the night I rose several times to visit the sick room but there was never any change in Adie's condition. This was hardly the best preparation for the task I had to perform the following day but I was up long before dawn and, after a final check on Adie, I set off with my chosen escort. Bart had asked to come with me and I could hardly deny him the pleasure of seeing Black Harry arrested. At Hadbourne I collected six of the guards who were encamped in the grounds of James Dewey's house. We set out as the first streaks of light appeared in the sky.

The deserted nunnery of Swansford lay in a dish-shaped hollow. As we gazed down from the wooded hills which rimmed it, the buildings lay submerged in an inland sea of mist. We descended into the grey gloom where the only sound was the drip, drip of moisture from overhead branches.

We stopped at the gate, which was locked and hung with a hand-painted sign warning NO ENTRY TRESPASSERS WILL BE PUNISHED. To reinforce the message, for the benefit of the illiterate, a crude image of a man standing in the pillory was drawn below the lettering. The complete ineffectiveness of Belleville's threat was obvious from the many gaps in the outer wall. It was obvious that locals had helped themselves to supplies of free stone.

The guard captain sent in a couple of his men on foot to spy out the land. They were back after about half an hour.

'Did you see any of the gang?' the captain asked.

'No, Sir,' one of the scouts replied, 'but four horses are tethered inside the inner gate. I reckon the villains are in the eastern block. Most of the conventual buildings are semi-derelict and the chapel has lost its roof.'

'I'll wager old Belleville has sold off the slate for a comfortable profit,' Bart muttered.

'What about escape routes?' the captain asked.

'Apart from the main drive, there's only a track running south to another gate,' the first trooper replied.

'Then here's what we do.' The captain outlined his tactics with calm professionalism. 'We go in on foot, as silently as possible. Master Treviot, if you take your men round to the south side and block that route, we will search the buildings. While we're doing that someone will need to collect the horses and bring them here.' He eyed Bart's empty sleeve. 'Perhaps your friend would like to do that.'

Ignoring Bart's muttered protest, I agreed. 'We don't know how well armed they'll be,' I said.

The captain drew a flintlock handgun from his saddle holster. Having checked its mechanism, he dismounted. 'Don't worry about us, Master Treviot. My lads handle their swords well and we're protected.' He tapped his breastplate. 'We'll also have the advantage of surprise. My hope is we can round them all up inside the building. If any run out of the back they'll find themselves caught between your men and mine. I'll give you a few minutes to get your party in position. When you hear my trumpeter give one long blast on his instrument that will be the signal that we're going in.'

We skirted the buildings at a distance of about a hundred yards. We found the track the guardsman had mentioned and took up position where it entered an overgrown orchard.

'This undergrowth should stop anyone trying to escape us,' I said.

We formed a line between the nearest trees on either side and stared at the wall of mist.

Walt said, 'Anyone running from the house won't see us before it's too late.'

'True,' I replied. 'Of course, we won't see him either.'

He stamped his feet. 'Let's hope for some action. The damp's getting into my bones.'

'You're really keen for a fight, aren't you?'

'After what these cowardly pigs have done I certainly am. Don't you want to settle scores, Master Thomas?'

'I suppose I'd rather leave the fighting to the experts,' I said. 'I don't want any of you to get hurt.'

At that moment the shrill blast of a trumpet pierced the autumn calm.

'No more talking from now on,' I ordered. 'We mustn't give away our position.'

And so we waited, screwing our eyes for any sign of figures emerging from the thinning mist. We waited. And waited.

After what seemed an age, Bart whispered, 'Perhaps they've already gone.'

The same thought had struck me. I felt sure that Belleville would not have warned Black Harry – not after the very real scare I gave him. And yet . . .

There was a loud crash as somewhere a door was thrown open. Then confused shouts.

I drew my dagger and flexed my legs, ready to spring forward.

The clamour ceased. Then there came another sound. Running footsteps. A man broke clear of the mist. Then another.

With a snarl, Walt sprang forward, brandishing a club. He swung the weapon and caught the fellow a blow between the shoulders that sent him sprawling. Walt stood over his victim, club raised, ready for any reaction, but the man stayed where he had fallen.

Meanwhile, the second fugitive reacted quickly. Seeing his companion down, he veered sideways, making for the trees. Long grass and briars were his undoing. He stumbled. Before he could regain his footing, two of my men leaped upon him.

'Keep watching!' I shouted. 'There may be more!'

But no other gang members appeared. After a couple of minutes, I went over to inspect our captives. I hoped I would find myself looking down at Black Harry. I was disappointed. One, a wispy-bearded fellow, lay at Walt's feet, unconscious. The other, a younger man, lay squirming and screaming oaths.

'Tie their hands,' I ordered, 'and bring them along. Let's see what's happening in the building.'

We went in through an open door and entered a kitchen. Following noises coming from beyond, we entered a long, barrel-vaulted room that had obviously been the nuns' refectory. It was bare of all furniture and in the middle some of the guards formed a circle around two men who were sitting on the floor with their hands tied. We dragged our unconscious prisoners in and threw them down alongside their colleagues.

'Well, that wasn't much of a fight,' the captain observed with a smile. 'I thought you said this Black Harry was a fierce opponent.'

I looked at our surly captives. 'But he isn't here,' I said. 'Are you sure you've found all of them?'

'I've got two men searching the place thoroughly but we haven't seen anyone else.'

I went over to one of the villains and prodded him with my boot. 'Where's your leader?' I demanded. 'Where's Harry?'

The man gave a black-toothed grin. 'Miles away. You'll never catch him. He's much too clever for you.'

The man's arrogance set a match to the cannon of my anger. The feelings I had held in check for the last hour exploded within me. I turned to the captain. 'A sword please, if I may.'

With some reluctance he drew his hand-and-a-half blade and passed it to me. I wrapped my fingers round the hilt and felt the weapon's precise balance.

'Master Treviot!' The captain laid a hand on my arm.

'No, don't try to stop me. I've come too far and suffered too much to be balked now by dunghill flies like these. One of them is going to give me the information I want – or remain silent for ever. I walked along the row, prodding each prisoner with the sword's point. 'Which of you cowardly lorrels is going to tell me where Black Harry has gone?'

A stocky man with a scar across one cheek was the first to reply – but not with the answer I wanted.

He glared sullenly. 'Call us cowards, do you? Standing there threatening men who can't fight back.'

'Cowards I call you and cowards you are!' I shouted. 'You murder women and children and peaceable priests.' Images flashed through my mind of good people wantonly, brutally, mercilessly attacked by this fellow – Holbein, his children, van der Goes, and Adie, especially Adie lying now at the point of death. Even with a sword point in his belly, the wretch showed no trace of remorse or even fear. He lay there snarling like a cornered rat, and his arrogance fuelled my rage. For the first time in my life I felt bloodlust – and it tasted good. If it had been Black Harry sprawled on the floor at my mercy I would have thrust the sword through him without a further thought. As it was I leaned forward and the sharp point pierced the leather jerkin.

Now he squealed.

'Master Thomas!'

I heard Walt's anxious voice and waved aside his unspoken protest. Fortunately, my fury had not taken complete possession. The corner of my mind that was still functioning calmly reminded me I wanted information, not vengeance.

'Where is Black Harry?' I lifted the sword and held it, with both hands, about twelve inches above the man's body. 'No? In that case . . .' I brought the sword down. It pierced the flesh of his upper leg, pinning it to the floor.

'Stop!' he screeched, writhing in agony.

'I didn't quite catch your answer.' I tugged the blade free and moved its point to a spot just above the villain's heart.

'I daren't,' he squealed. 'No one betrays Black Harry.'

'You'd rather die for him, then? Very well.'

'Don't!' he cried, 'You can't! You wouldn't! Captain, call the madman off!'

'You're quite right,' I replied. 'Normally I wouldn't kill you. But today I'm not feeling normal. I've been driven out of my wits by a coven of bestial hellhounds who beat to death a young man in Aldgate, and took small children hostage, and left them to starve to death, and murdered their father, and burned down a priest's house, killing everyone in it, ravished a defenceless woman and drove her to take her own life, and committed I know not what other inhuman acts. So, today, yes I would do something that, at any other time, I would regard as beneath contempt. I would kill a defenceless, squirming creature who doesn't deserve the dignity of being called a man.' It was no less than the truth. In those moments I was not myself. I had descended to the level of the men I despised.

'Stop!' he cried. 'In the name of God, I beg you. We only did what the other man paid us to do. It's him you want.'

'Oh, I'll get round to him in good time. For the moment I'm only interested in the whereabouts of the villain who has brought you to within seconds of death.'

My victim rolled on to his side, trying to squirm away from my weapon. I simply moved its point to his throat.

'Harry's taking the prisoners to the man that pays us,' he blurted out.

'And where does he live?'

'Over the river. Essex.'

'Fletcham?'

'Yes!' he cried eagerly.

I stepped back. 'At last!' I returned the sword to its owner. 'At last we have the breakthrough we need.' I realised I was sweating and trembling.

'You know this Fletcham place?' the captain asked.

'Yes. Now if we act quickly, we can haul in all our fish in one net.'

'First we must get these securely locked up.'

We pulled three of the men to their feet.

'What about this fellow?' The captain indicated the wounded man.

'The cut looks worse than it is,' I said. 'We'll tend it when we get back to Hadbourne.'

We collected the horses from Bart, who was very disgruntled at having been excluded from the action.

'You missed little,' I said. 'Black Harry has already gone. But we are on his trail now.'

'Promise me that I'll be there when you find him.'

'I promise you. That is a meeting I would not miss for all the world.'

We tied our captives across their horses and jogged back to Hadbourne, where our prisoners were locked up with the others detained by the commission and awaiting their onward journey to Canterbury.

Morice was eager to know what had happened at Swansford but my only thoughts were now for Adie. My report was brief. 'I'll come back tomorrow,' I promised. 'We have to organise our trip to Fletcham to arrest Black Harry.'

As I made my way homeward with my companions none of us spoke much. I was exhausted and I knew we were all dreading what we might find at Hemmings. And beyond that lay what I earnestly prayed would be the end of this affair.

Chapter 24

I went straight to Adie's room. The inert form on the bed seemed unchanged and a servant was patiently applying damp cloths to her brow.

'How is she?' I asked.

'She still has the great heat, Master, but she sometimes tries to speak – nothing that makes any sense; more like murmuring than talking. Master Longbourne has got her to swallow something and it seems to have eased her.'

'Is that what I can smell?' I had noticed a sickly odour as soon as I entered the chamber.

'Yes, Master, some got spilled on the covers.'

I sat on the bed and took Adie's limp hand in mine. 'Adie, 'tis me, Thomas, Thomas Treviot. How do you fare, my dear?'

Eyelids flickered. Lips slightly parted. But if she wanted to speak she lacked the energy and her face reposed into a calm, devoid of all expression.

I tried to find words for the situation, words that might be more efficacious than Ned's nostrums. The only ones I could voice were, 'Dear Adie, don't leave us. Everyone here loves you.

'Where is Master Longbourne?' I asked, as I stood up.

'In his chamber, Master. He looks fair worn out. He's been here hours and hours. Mistress Lizzie had to drag him away and make him rest.'

I entered Ned's room and saw him stretched on the bed, fully clothed. A candle almost burned down stood on the chest beside him and one hand still held an open book. I turned to leave quietly but, as I did so, Ned stirred.

'Is that you, Thomas?' He struggled into a sitting position. 'Did you find the villains?'

'We found their lair but the archvillain was gone.'

'Slippery as an eel – or perhaps "serpent" would be a better analogy. I've been praying for him.'

'Praying?' I scoffed. 'He merits flaying, not praying.'

'The meanest wretch is not beyond God's mercy – else where would any of us be? Now, I must go and look to Adie.'

I put my hand on his shoulder. 'Sit awhile. We don't want you falling ill as well. What can you tell me of the patient?'

'The next few hours will be crucial. If the fever breaks she will recover. If not . . . ' He shook his head. 'I was able to get powdered Norwegian angelica from the Tonbridge apothecary. He is certainly well skilled; few people know its properties. I'm afraid I made a nuisance of myself in the kitchen. I had to make up some sort of distilling apparatus to make pure water from vapour. That dispels any injurious elements that may have penetrated it. With that I made up angelica water and got Adie to drink some.'

'Was that the sweet odour I noticed in her room?'

'Yes, 'tis the best herb I know for her condition. It grows only on riverbanks and draws out moist humours.' He glanced up with one of his knowing smiles. 'You are more than usually concerned for this young lady.'

'Her plight feeds my anger. I will punish Black Harry for the anguish he inflicts on all his victims, even if I have to hunt him for the rest of my life. But if he should swing and Adie still die I would feel as though he had won.'

Ned stood and stretched his back. 'Well, she is young and strong and that is enormously in her favour. Any simples or other treatments we physicians apply don't really do anything.'

'What do you mean?'

'Merely that they are only aids. The body heals itself – if it wants to.'

'You still think Adie might will herself to die?'

'I think that once the fever has broken she will need another kind of medicine, one that lies well beyond my poor skills. We must all – and you especially – make her want to live. And now, you must excuse me. I have a patient to tend.'

The following morning I returned to Hadbourne. I needed to find Morice before he moved on to Maidstone with Legh's cavalcade. The house was a scene of considerable activity as the clergy of the region came and went to kneel before the fat lawyer and make their formal submission.

'Is everything going well?' I asked, as we sat outside on a bench, enjoying the warmth of an autumn sun.

'Oh, yes. We've packed off a wagonload of troublemakers to Canterbury jail and yesterday in all the churches the clergy either preached on the royal supremacy or read statements affirming it.'

'Legh has proved his worth, then.'

'Certainly. Before he came we were only firing arrows against our enemies. Legh is a cannon by comparison, and has thoroughly breached their fortifications. Several little conspiracies have come to light that we were ignorant of before. Life is going to become very difficult for his grace's enemies in Canterbury when we have compiled all the evidence into a report to set before the king. The guard captain tells me you had quite a productive day at Swansford.'

'Yes, we didn't lay our hands on the leader but as I've thought about it I've come to the conclusion that it is to our advantage that he's still at liberty.'

'What do you mean?'

'Black Harry has gone to Fletcham and he's taken the priests, Horton and Garrow, with him. That can only be for the purpose of extracting confessions of heresy from them. Presumably Brooke, the arch-conspirator, will take charge of the interrogation. With any luck, we can catch them together. We might even be able to gather proof of their own little Inquisition. Connecting Brooke with a gang of convicted felons will strike right at the heart of the conspiracy against his grace.'

'How would you like to proceed?'

'Much as we did at Swansford; an assault by the arch-bishop's armed guard.'

Morice shook his head. 'That could be difficult – perhaps impossible.'

'Why?'

'His grace has no direct authority there. He would have to confer with the Bishop of London.'

'There's no time for such episcopal niceties!' I exclaimed. 'Within a few days, news will reach Fletcham that we've rounded up some of Brooke's criminal henchmen. Then he is sure to run. And I wouldn't take any wagers on the survival of his prisoners. Our only chance of complete success is surprise. We must go to Fletcham tomorrow.'

'Yes, I understand that; I really do.' Morice's brow creased in a deep frown of frustration. 'But I don't have the authority to sanction it, and I know very well what the archbishop's reaction will be. He'll demand time to think about it. Then, because he's a stickler for correct procedure, he'll ask for cooperation from Bishop Bonner, and we know what Bonner's reaction will be.'

'Yes, I was in St Paul's Yard last year when his men raided the bookstalls and went on to smash the presses of printers the bishop suspected of publishing heresy.'

'At the best he'd create delay. At the worst he'd get news to Norfolk or Chapuys that their game was up.'

'So you're saying we can do nothing without his grace's permission and if we wait for his grace's permission we might as well do nothing. That will mean letting Brooke compile his evidence unhindered. It seems to me that someone needs to protect his grace against his grace.'

'It wouldn't be the first time,' Morice muttered.

'Could we not "borrow" some of the archiepiscopal guard for a couple of days?'

'If we did that and the operation failed we'd be in terrible trouble.'

'If we do nothing we're in trouble anyway – *and so is the archbishop*,' I almost shouted. 'You politicians can always find reasons for doing nothing! Mary and all the saints. Does it take a simple merchant to show you what must be done?'

'Let me think! Let me think!' Morice walked a few steps along the terrace and stood staring out towards the orchard. It was several minutes before he came back to where I sat. 'It's all a question of timing,' he said. 'The evidence the commission is collecting is damning. When my report goes to his majesty, he'll understand just how serious the campaign against the archbishop is.'

'And how long will it take you to compile your report?'

'The commission doesn't complete its work for a couple of weeks.'

'Too long,' I said.

'I could do an interim report and show it to his grace. That might persuade him to set his scruples aside and back a raid on Fletcham.'

'When could you do that?'

'By the end of the week . . . perhaps.'

'By which time Norfolk will be laying before the king evidence of the archbishop's support of alleged heretics.'

'That really is the best I can suggest, Thomas.'

'But, Ralph, just think what this business has already cost,' I pleaded. 'A good man has, by now, been brutally murdered in gathering information about Chapuys, Norfolk and Brooke. I won't even mention what I and others I care about have been through in order bring to justice a fanatical killer and his gang. Is all that sacrifice to be wasted? Well, not if I can help it.'

'Then I'm sorry,' Morice said, 'but you may find yourself alone.'

I stood up. 'Then that's the way it will have to be. If it means going against the law – well, that will only prove that law and justice are not the same thing.' I turned to enter the house.

'Just a minute,' Morice called. 'Let me have a word with the captain. It might be possible to do something – unofficially. Wait here.'

It was about half an hour before he returned with the captain.

'I've explained the situation to Captain Trent,' he said.

'I understand you want some professional help with an expedition like yesterday's, Master Treviot.'

'It won't be as easy as yesterday's,' I said. 'The men we're after will probably put up more of a fight.'

'My lads would relish that,' Trent said. 'They were quite disappointed with the Swansford brawl.'

Morice said, 'I'm not very happy about this but I could spare three guards from the commission escort – just for two days.'

'I can detail off three good men,' Trent said.

'Before you agree too readily,' Morice warned, 'I must make it clear that this is unofficial. No one is to wear his grace's livery. They will be acting in a private capacity for Master Treviot. This escapade has nothing to do with the archbishop or me. If anything goes wrong, I know nothing about what you are planning. If anyone is captured or . . . worse, I can't help you. Is that quite understood?'

Trent nodded.

I said, 'Thank you, Ralph. I realise this has put you in a difficult position. We won't let you down.'

Morice departed swiftly, only too anxious to leave any conspiring to us. We arranged that the troopers would come to my house early the following morning, ready for the journey to Gravesend and, thence, across to the Essex shore.

Back at Hemmings I told Walt to assemble all the most able-bodied outdoor estate workers. When they were gathered in the long barn, I addressed them.

'You all know something of the troubles in the county – indeed in the whole country.'

'Aye,' someone called out, 'dear bread and cheap death!'

'Yes, Adam,' I agreed, "tis a hard year and we can only pray for a better one to follow, but I think you are all fairly provided for. No man who works for me goes hungry, unless he wastes his wages. I think I can say that I treat you as well as any master and better than some.'

There was a general murmur of assent.

I continued, 'For my part, I could not want a more able and willing body of men. When I speak of troubles, I don't just mean the terrible weather, the shortages and high prices. England is tearing itself apart with religious strife. I'm sure you would prefer not to be involved in such things, I know I would. But although we don't look for trouble sometimes trouble comes looking for us. It has certainly found me and my friends these last few weeks.'

'How is Mistress Adie?' someone asked.

'Sore sick,' I replied, 'and all because of her handling by evil men.'

'And the bearns?' another voice shouted.

'They've had some frightening experiences but I think they will rise above them. What I have to tell you is that we have the opportunity now to bring to justice the evil rakehells responsible for these and other outrages. Tomorrow I set out for Essex, where, God-willing, we will arrest the leader of this gang, who goes by the name of Black Harry. I would like six volunteers to come with me. It will be dangerous and, for that reason, I would prefer to take unmarried men. I will not press any man and I will not think any the worse of anyone who does not wish to volunteer. Any questions?'

'Will we be armed?'

'Bring knives, clubs and any weapons you feel comfortable with.'

'How many of them will we be up against?'

'I'm not sure but I don't think we will be outnumbered and I plan to take them by surprise.'

'Will there be extra pay?'

'There will be rewards for those who come but I don't want to say anything about that because I only want men who are with me for the right reasons.'

'It'll be like catching rats,' someone said.

'Exactly. That's how I'd like you to think of it. So who wants to come on an expedition to rid the land of vermin?'

Almost every man raised a hand. It took several minutes to make my selection and to pacify the ones who were not chosen but thought they should have been. I assembled my little army and gave instructions for our assembly on the morrow. As I looked round at the familiar faces of men, most of whom I had known for years, I reflected on what I was asking of them and what they were willingly undertaking. Were my feelings, I wondered, those experienced by every commander on the eve of battle – those of mingled pride and fear?

Chapter 25

We set off at first light on Tuesday and reached our destination by midday. Now that I could see Brooke's manor clearly, I realised how small it was. The two-storey house stood on a slight rise at some distance from the tiny hamlet of Fletcham and had, I assumed, begun life as a hunting lodge. It was not the sort of residence where its owner would live for long periods of time but its isolated position suited it ideally for the performance of nefarious activities. I thought again of Adie and the boys shut up here far away from all human contact, hearing only the wind howling across the marsh and the occasional screeching of an owl, as they waited to die.

There was little cover in which to conceal my party. We drew back about a quarter of a mile to a small copse. I sent Cranmer's three guards to reconnoitre on foot the small group of buildings. They were gone more than an hour. They returned with a very thorough report and rather pleased with themselves.

'First of all,' one of them said, 'there's very little cover. There's about fifty yards of open ground all around the main house. The only way to get close is through the stable block. Otherwise we'll have to wait till after dark.'

'There aren't many people about,' another reported. 'I watched from the back and only saw three men come and go.'

A third suggested, 'That was partly because the top man – what's his name?'

'Brooke,' I said.

'Yes, him. Well, he was out hawking. We saw him coming back. He had three men with him and, going by your description, one of them must have been Black Harry. I got close enough to touch him.'

'What?' I gasped in alarm.

'Don't worry, Master Treviot, they didn't see me. There's a ruined cottage over to the east and I was using it for cover when Brooke and the others came past. Just then there was a heavy shower and they pulled in to take shelter. I was afraid they were going to dismount but they just stood in the lee of the building for a couple of minutes. I could hear them talking.'

'Anything useful?' I asked.

'I think they were talking about their prisoners. Black Harry said, "One more session and we'll break the older one." And Brooke came back at him sharply. "See you do," he said. "I go to court tomorrow. Our people there expect results and quickly."'

'Then it seems we've arrived none too soon,' I said. 'Thank God the prisoners are still alive.'

I considered the information we now had and began to

formulate a plan. I gathered everyone around and explained what I had in mind. 'We're not here for a fight. I want to come out of this without casualties. Our two objectives are to capture the leaders and rescue the prisoners. Our best chance of success lies in reducing the odds against us. I suspect that the prisoners are in the stable block. So we need someone to keep a watch on that. Dick, that will be your job. Take up a position from which you can watch all the comings and goings and report back whatever you discover.'

'Then we go in and rescue those poor devils as soon as the coast is clear,' someone suggested.

'No, that will warn the gang too soon. I want to keep the advantage of surprise as long as possible. At the moment Brooke and his men think they're completely secure. The shock of discovering that they're wrong should confuse them. That will be our opportunity. If my idea works, I think we can stun them into coming out to us.' I went over the stages of what was a very simple plan. Then we settled down to wait for the dwindling of the light.

After about an hour Dick reappeared and threw himself down on the grass beside me. 'They've just come to collect the prisoners,' he said.

'From the stable barn?'

'Yes. Poor lambs; they look half-dead already. They're being taken for more torture.'

'After that they'll be brought back,' I said. 'And we'll be waiting for them. Dick, take Walt and Adam to the barn. When our friends come back with the prisoners, you'll know what to do. But do it quietly. Take plenty of rope and cloth to bind and gag them. Report back when that's done.'

The evening was far gone by the time they returned, laughing and very pleased with themselves.

'That was sweet,' Walt said. 'There were two of them. They never knew what hit them.'

'Have you left them well out of sight?'

'Trussed up like pigs for slaughter and covered over with loose straw.'

'What about their prisoners?'

'We untied them and told them to stay well hidden till we got back. We couldn't bring them here, they're too weak. One of 'em collapsed with relief when he saw us. For a moment I feared he'd died on us.'

'Right, we must get back before anyone in the house realises something's wrong. Come along.' I led the way towards the house.

We filed into the darkened stable yard and concealed ourselves between the buildings. By now there were lights showing in two of the ground-floor windows of the main house.

'We know where to find them,' I whispered.

After a few minutes the kitchen door opened. A man peered into the darkness. 'Sam, Will, what's keeping you?' He stepped out into the yard. 'Where are—'

There was a loud thud, followed by a quieter one as he fell.

'Three down,' I said. 'Dick, tie him up and put him with the others. The rest of you come with me.'

We burst into the kitchen. The first person to see us was the cook tending a cauldron over the fire. She let out a piercing scream and dropped her ladle. The three men sitting round the table looked up in alarm and tried to stumble to their feet. They stood no chance. My club-wielding enthusiasts were upon them in an instant. I looked at their faces. Neither Black Harry nor Ferdinand Brooke was here.

'This way!' I called to Bart and ran towards the inner door. I rushed into the small hall. The two men I sought were supping alone, one each side of a long oak table. The noise from the kitchen had given them some warning and they were on their feet. Black Harry drew a long, thin stiletto. Brooke fumbled at his belt, trying to draw his rapier. Walt threw himself at him before he could do so. His grip fastened on Brooke's sword wrist. I knew what that must feel like. Walt spent hours every week wielding heavy hammers to beat iron horseshoes into shape. Black Harry was sharper. His weapon was in his hand as I drew my poignard.

'Come on,' he snarled, bidding me to close in.

We circled each other and I was careful to keep a safe distance. On the other side of the table Walt's strong arms had now encircled Brooke and the two men swayed back and forth like fairground wrestlers. However, I did not dare watch their contest. My eyes were fixed on the tip of Black Harry's vicious stiletto. He waved the weapon to and fro, hissing with animal rage. I ducked beneath the flashing blade; tried to get in a jab with my shorter weapon. He kicked out at me, and I jumped back. As I did so, I saw Brooke break free from Walt's grasp. The courtier leaped sideways, at the same time pushing Walt hard against the wall. There was a nasty noise as his head struck the stonework. Walt slithered to the floor on the far side of the table.

'Help me!' Black Harry cried out.

But Brooke was already running towards the outer door.

'Come on, then,' my assailant shouted. 'Do you want to go the same way as your painter friend?'

Black Harry now had his legs pressed against the table. He glanced across the room as the door closed behind his retreating friend. My eyes followed the direction of his gaze. Stupid! He reached with his left hand for an ale jug and hurled it at my face. Then he lunged again with his dagger. Just in time,

I jumped back out of reach. I overbalanced and fell sprawling among stale rushes. Black Harry turned towards the door and took a couple of steps.

At that moment there was a mighty roar. Walt rose up, gripping the table as he did so and tipping it forward. The massive oak top came away from its trestles. It caught Black Harry sideways on, showering him with trenchers, utensils and food. He fell heavily on the floor beside me. I rolled over. I brought my dagger down on his right wrist. With a squeal he let go of the stiletto. One of Cranmer's guards rushed in, sword in hand.

'Deal with him!' I yelled, as I scrambled to my feet, and ran in pursuit of the fleeing Brooke.

Outside I stopped, my eyes not adjusted to the sudden darkness. I heard running footsteps away to my left, and followed. I found myself in the stable yard and once again paused, ears straining for noise of the fugitive. I could hear nothing above the crashes and shouts still coming from the house. Several figures were in the yard. I ran towards them, calling, 'Did you see a man come—'

At that moment a door to the right burst open. In a clattering flurry of hooves a mounted horse ran into the yard, scattering anyone in its path, and turned towards the gateway. At full gallop Ferdinand Brooke disappeared into the night.

Victors and vanquished were gathered in the wreck of what had been the kitchen. The cook and scullion were crouched, terrified, in a corner, while my men were finishing the work of trussing up their prisoners. Horton and Garrow, the released clergy, had been brought from the stable and were sitting at the table, having their wounds tended.

'Is everyone all right?' I called out.

'Simon, here, has a nasty stab wound,' Dick said. He was by the outside door and crouched over one of the older men, carefully removing his blood-stained shirt.

'Right, you,' I called to the cook, 'hot water and clean cloths quickly. No one else hurt?' I asked.

'A few cuts and bruises,' someone said.

Another added, 'This bunch of poxy knaves had no fight in 'em.'

'Some of 'em's foreigners,' a third called out. 'What d'you expect?'

One of the prisoners responded angrily, 'You meet us equal terms, we show you who's got fight!'

He was greeted with raucous laughter.

'Congratulations,' I said. 'You've done well – better than I dared hope. Unfortunately, we lost the king, but we've got his chief jester.' I pointed to Black Harry. 'He won't be performing any more of his evil tricks.'

'He'll dance well on the gallows,' someone said, to loud laughter.

'You all deserve food and rest,' I said. 'We'll see what's in the larder and after supper you can all go in search of beds. But we still have a few things to do. Throw this lot in the barn and make sure they're tied securely. Walt will organise a rota of men to stand watch through the night. Two of you bring in our horses. Find water and fodder for them. We'll need them fresh for tomorrow. We'll have to make another early start. It'll be a slow journey back. And now, Bart, you and I have a pleasant task to perform.'

I grabbed Black Harry by the collar and pushed him back into the hall. After we had set the table to rights, I forced the prisoner down on a bench, with his hands tied behind him. Bart and I sat opposite.

I began my interrogation. 'You recognise my friend here, don't you?'

He shrugged and shook his head.

'No? Well, he recognises you as the leader of the band of ruffians who beat to death a defenceless young man in Aldgate on the first of September.'

'He must be mistaken.'

'I have other witnesses who can identify you as their abductor – the man who brought them here to this house and left them to die.'

'Women and children imagine strange things.'

'I didn't say they were women and children. Then, of course, there are the two priests, held here as your unwilling guests. I'm sure they will have plenty to tell the King's Bench jury.'

'Lutheran scum!' he muttered.

Bart intervened. 'Stop wriggling, lying varlet! 'Tis all up with you. If you're a man, admit your crimes.'

'Or what? Are you going to take revenge, you pitiable, one-armed loon?'

I put a hand out to restrain Bart, who was obviously struggling to control his emotions, but he responded calmly. 'No, I shan't harm a hair of you. Slitting your throat would give me no pleasure. You wanted to see me swing for your butchery. My delight will come from seeing you at a rope's end.'

Black Harry laughed. 'I shan't hang. I have powerful friends. You've no idea what trouble you're going to be in for today's outrage.'

'Oh, if I were you,' I said, 'I wouldn't rely on the Duke of Norfolk or Ambassador Chapuys to come to your aid. They'll be in a great hurry to disassociate themselves from your murderous career.'

For the first time the villain was shaken. He realised I knew more about his activities than he thought. He glowered sullenly.

'So you see,' I continued, 'there is more than enough evidence to hang you several times over. There's only one thing I require before I deliver you up to justice. You will sign a confession to the Aldgate killing.'

Black Harry sneered. 'And why should I do that? As you say, I'm a dead man anyway.'

There was obvious logic in what he said but I had to do my best to restore Bart's good name without further delay. 'I'm giving you the opportunity to prove that there is still a shred of decency in you.'

'You come here with your crew of heretical cut-throats and dare to talk to me of decency! What is decent about hundreds of souls lured to hell by Luther and his lies? Was your archbishop being decent when he seduced the king into usurping the pope's position as father of the church? If I die it will be as a martyr to Catholic truth. When you die, I will watch you roast in hell.'

I stood up. 'I won't waste any more breath talking with a fanatic. Bart, fetch some of the others and see that this fellow is made as uncomfortable as possible for the night.'

The following morning my strange cavalcade made its way back to Tilbury. We had rigged up horse litters for the two clergy, who were unable to walk or ride. I discovered that they had been strung up by shackles round their wrists for hours at a time until their arms were almost pulled from their sockets. They followed half of my men and were, in turn, followed by our prisoners, all on foot. The rest of my gallant band brought up the rear.

'I'm sorry I couldn't get a confession out of Black Harry,' I said to Bart as we crossed the marshland. 'His guilt will come out when he's convicted but I'm afraid you'll need to stay out of sight till then.'

He shrugged. 'You tried, Master Thomas, but 'tis as you say, useless to argue with fanatics. Their hate drives them.'

'He learned hate in a good school – the Inquisition. He spent years there forcing Jews, Muslims and Lutherans to bow to the pope. I've heard terrible stories brought back from Spain by merchants and mariners. Cruelty has fastened itself so tightly on to his soul that I think not even self-interest can dislodge it.'

On that, I was wrong. Hours later, as the horse ferry was taking us across a grey Thames, Black Harry shuffled his way awkwardly towards me.

'You want me to confess to the Aldgate murder in order to save your friend. Well, if I give you a written confession, perhaps we can do a deal.'

Chapter 26

'I don't think you are in a position to suggest deals,' I said. As I stood in the prow staring at the vessels moored along the Gravesend quay the only thought in my mind was that, within the hour, I would be riding southwards. My single remaining task was to report to Ralph Morice. Then the ordeal of the past weeks would be behind me.

'Wait till you hear what I have to offer,' Black Harry replied.

'I've no interest in your lies and schemes—'

'Your precious archbishop and his friends would, I'm sure, like to get their hands on Master Brooke. He is the pivotal point of all that is planned against Cranmer.'

'Those things are no concern of mine.'

'As you please. But what would your friends say if they knew that you let Brooke slip through your fingers?'

'He can't get very far. As soon as I make my report there will be search parties out looking for him.'

'Do you suppose he hasn't thought of that and made plans to ensure his escape?'

'How will he escape?'

He sneered. 'That is the information I have to sell. I can tell you exactly where you will find him.'

'And why would you do that? Is it that treachery comes as second nature to you?'

'Does not the Bible you set so much store by tell you that 'tis better to be a live dog than a dead lion?'

'So you think to trade your master for your freedom?'

That obviously annoyed him. 'I call no man master,' he snapped. 'If I go free, so does your friend and you capture the one man who links together all the archbishop's enemies. That is for you a good deal.'

'And leave you free to continue your murderous career? I don't think so.'

'Of course, I would have to leave the country. There is still plenty of work to be done in Spain.'

I turned my back on him. Further along the boat Bart was leaning against the rail and looking wistfully out over the estuary. I thought of all he had already suffered and knew how much he and Lizzie longed to get their lives back. A few lines on a sheet of parchment could give them that. Then I thought of Adie, hovering between life and death. Turning again, I said to Black Harry, 'When we land, you will be taken under guard to jail in Canterbury to await your trial for murder.'

His response was an infuriating smile. 'Perhaps.'

'What do you mean?'

'If you won't see sense, somebody will.' He shuffled away.

When we arrived in Kent the party divided. I sent most of my men with Cranmer's guards to convey the prisoners to Canterbury. In order not to slow them down, we hired a wagon in Gravesend to carry the captives and found a local complex of almshouses and hospital where the two priests could be nursed back to health. I set off with two companions to Maidstone, where I hoped to find Ralph Morice. It was not difficult to locate the place where Legh was conducting his inquiries. He had chosen the town's principal inn and commandeered a large ground-floor room for his purposes. Quite a crowd had gathered outside of people eager to know the fate of those being examined.

We arrived during the commission's dinner interval and I was able to locate Morice in the private room where he and his companions were eating. As soon as he saw me at the door, he stood up, excused himself from the company and hurried over.

'Thomas, Lord be praised you're back and in good time. How did you fare?' He took me by the arm and guided me out into the street. 'Let's walk and you can tell me everything.'

As we strolled through the busy town centre, I gave a detailed report of the last two days' activities. Morice listened intently, occasionally asking questions. When I had finished, he grasped my hand warmly. 'Thomas, you have done splendidly! The whole gang rounded up and, I've no doubt, ready to tell all they know in hope of avoiding the gallows.' Then he fell silent and thoughtful.

We had stopped by a market stall selling pressed apple juice and we bought beakers of the sweet liquid.

'You say Black Harry offered to help us apprehend Brooke.'

'Yes, but he would have said anything to save his own skin.'

'Even so, if we could bring in Chapuys' agent – the one man connecting him to Norfolk . . .'

'But the price is too high. To allow this monster to walk free after all the misery and suffering he's been responsible for? Unthinkable.'

'Perhaps.'

The word struck me with almost physical force. Black Harry had used that same word to cast doubt on my allusion to the fate that awaited him. Now I began to see that the villain might have reason for confidence in his bargaining position. To someone like me who had first-hand experience of his vicious career, there could be no doubt the world had to be rid of him. But others who fought in the political arena marked out by compromise and moral variables might see him in a different light.

Morice added, 'I know how you feel about this papist rakehell and I, too, want to see him pay the price for his crimes, not the least of which was his murder of Master Holbein.'

'Then there's no more to be said!' I shouted. Passers-by stared as I lengthened my stride making Morice half-run to keep up. 'I'll listen to no talk of deals. All I want to hear from you is that Black Harry is dangling at a rope's end.'

'No, just stop and think for a moment,' Morice said. 'Our noble German friend gave his life in uncovering a conspiracy against the archbishop and the reformed religion of England. It was he who led us to Ferdinand Brooke. If we allow Brooke to escape, Holbein's sacrifice will have been in vain.'

I struggled with the implications of what he was saying.

'Sweet Jesu, man! You can't honestly think I should have accepted Black Harry's request to negotiate his release!'

'I can see why you did not. He put you in a difficult position. You are a man of principle. He is a reprobate who has lost all understanding of good and evil. Believe me, Thomas, I do share your sense of outrage. His attempt to prey on your concern for your friend, Bart Miller, not to mention his readiness to betray his own nefarious colleague, places him beyond contempt. But—'

'Aye,' I said angrily, 'I knew there would be a "but". "But" is a shovel word with which men bury good deeds and right thinking. I suppose you are going to tell me I should consider the "bigger picture".'

'Yes, I'm afraid I am. That's the picture I have to consider. It's the picture his grace has to consider. He is responsible for preventing England falling back into popery. If you knew the number of times he has had to ... stretch ... his own principles in order to safeguard a greater good, I suppose you might censure him. But, I tell you this, without someone like his grace at the king's elbow, the war against false religion would long since have been lost. It will still be lost if we do not crush his enemies completely.'

We retraced our steps to the inn in total silence.

As we stood on the threshold, I muttered, 'Well, do as you wish. Thank God, I'm not a politician.'

He turned and grasped my hand. 'Thomas, don't let us part like this. You and your men have done an excellent job. 'Tis up to us "mere politicians" to make the best advantage of your achievement. Think about what I've said. I'll discuss the situation with his grace. I'm sure he'll want to thank you personally. I will keep you informed of what he decides.' With that Morice hurried back into the building.

I did think about what he said. In fact, little else occupied my thoughts all the way back to Hemmings. When I arrived, however, other matters pushed Black Harry to the back of my mind. To my intense relief, Adie's condition was improving. The fever had broken. She was taking food and talking with those who came to her room. The most important of her visitors was her brother, Ignatius, who had appeared that very morning.

It was Lizzie who reported all this to me. I found her in the brewhouse where I went to slake my thirst after the journey. She was drawing a jug of ale and we took it through to the parlour. She poured beakers for us both.

'So what do you think of this brother?' I asked.

'Too handsome by half,' was her immediate response.

I laughed. 'Must a man be ugly to gain your approval?'

'Oh, 'tis not his looks I like not. A man may be a popinjay and yet have a heart. This Ignatius is all bound up in himself. He actually told me how inconvenient it was for him to have to come down to Kent. You'd think Adie had got sick to spite him.'

'Yet, he is her brother. We may hope his coming lifts her spirits.'

She sniffed. 'We may hope! Were I his sister, my spirits would be revived by fetching him a box about the ears.'

It was supper time before I had an opportunity to consider Lizzie's judgement of our guest. My friends and I were all gathered round the hall table and I had placed Ignatius on my right. My first impressions certainly supported Lizzie's opinion. Adie's brother was about twenty years of age, yet he had cultivated a short square-cut beard in the latest fashion. His clothes were expensive and, on a chain around his neck, he had a pomander, which he frequently wafted beneath his nose. But it was the large ring he wore on his right hand that, to my expert eye, was most revealing. The stone, a cornelian, was good of colour, but flawed, and the gold was not of high quality.

'A fine ring,' I said. 'Is it a family heirloom?'

'Yes, it was my grandfather's.'

'Was it he who came first to England? The name "Imray" is Flemish, is it not?'

'Yes, we are of an old landed family from near Antwerp.'

'A fine city,' I said.

'You know it?' There was a trace of anxiety in his voice.

'Indeed. I am particularly impressed with that enormous cathedral. The biggest in Europe, is it not?'

'Yes,' he agreed, 'it is a truly magnificent building.'

'So how did your grandfather come to settle in England?'

'That's a sad story,' Ignatius said. 'There was a family feud that ended with my grandfather being cheated out of his inheritance. But there is still a legal battle going on and I am in hopes to recover my hereditary lands, 'ere long.'

Ned said, 'I gather you work for Lord Graves.'

'Well, not so much work for him,' the young man said airily. 'The Graves are distant relatives. His lordship is kindly providing hospitality until I can return to Flanders to take my rightful place there.'

'How like you Leicestershire?' Lizzie asked.

'I like it well. There are several good families among our neighbours.'

He went on to tell a string of stories – many indiscreet – about the leading clans of Leicestershire. 'But they are good-hearted folk,' he concluded. 'I think I may soon find a suitable wife there. That is, if I have time to look. His lordship is much away and he leaves me in charge of the estate.'

The conversation drifted on to such subjects as fashion, hunting and the breeding of horses, on all of which our guest had pronounced opinions. By this time Bart and Lizzie were exchanging conspiratorial smiles and sometimes putting hands to mouths to conceal laughter. When Ignatius boasted of the sums he had won at cards, Bart suggested a game of primero.

At that stage I intervened. 'Excellent idea, but first I must steal our friend away from you. We need to discuss Adie's future.'

I took Ignatius to my parlour and set before him some canary wine in one of my Venetian glasses.

'I am most impressed by your family history,' I said, 'but one thing that puzzles me is how the sister of such a fine gentleman as you finds herself in the position of nurse to the children of a mere artisan.'

He took a long draught of wine and set down his glass with a sigh. 'I'm sorry to have to say that she is responsible for her fall in status. Lord Graves has been very good to us, especially after our father died – worn out by the legal battle over our lands. He arranged a good match for Adriana with the son of a gentleman third in line to an earldom. Any other girl would have been delighted by the opportunity. But not Adriana. She flew into fits of angry tears at the mere mention of her suitor's name. It was all very embarrassing. Naturally, I did what I could to soothe his lordship's anger but he was, very reasonably, upset. He said if she would not have the man he had chosen, he would have nothing more to do with her. As it happened, that painter fellow was in the house to take his lordship's likeness. He offered to give Adriana a home looking after his children and she accepted. She said anywhere would be better than under Lord Graves's roof. It was wickedly ungracious of her.'

I sat back and took a long hard look at the effete young man before me.

'You are an entertaining guest, Master Imray. My problem is filleting out the bones of fact from all the highly coloured flesh of your fictions. Everyone here has become very fond of your sister, and I, for one, do not recognise the picture you have painted of her. Do you think we might start again, so that you can tell me the truth about her and your shared background?'

Chapter 27

Imray covered his obvious shock with bluster. 'Master Treviot, I greatly appreciate your hospitality to me and your care for my sister, but I'll thank you to guard your tongue better.'

I ignored the protest. 'Let us begin with your family origins. Most Flemings who have come to England are cloth weavers – excellent craftsmen, proud of their skill and their independence. They arrived, seeking that freedom to ply their trade that was denied them in their own land. Would I be right in assuming that your grandfather was among their number?'

Imray stared into his glass and made no comment.

I continued. 'I suggest that like others of his honourable calling he, unfortunately, arrived in England at a bad time for independent artisans. The wealthy London cloth merchants were consistently and deliberately extending their control over all sections of the industry. Spinners, weavers and fullers were being forced to work for these clothiers on the terms they set. Many of them went out of business. Was that the fate of your grandfather, or, perhaps, your father?'

'My father was a gentleman attendant on Lord Graves,' Imray responded haughtily.

'Ah, yes, he was resourceful enough to take up another career – as a falconer, I believe.'

'Is that what my sister has told you?'

'It is. Are you suggesting that she was lying?'

The young man's cheeks were flushed as he struggled to retain his dignity. 'She's only a simple woman. She doesn't understand how a noble household operates. Our father was very close to Lord Graves.'

'And looked after his hunting birds.'

'He had a natural talent for falconry. He bought and trained the best birds in Europe. Lord Graves's mews is the finest in England. He even supplied hawks to his majesty.'

'Then why are you ashamed of him?'

'I? Ashamed?' He stood abruptly. 'Sir, you forget yourself!'

'Oh, do sit down,' I said, as patiently as I could. 'It is not my intention to insult you. My only concern is for Adriana's welfare. You want to better yourself and become a fine gentleman. There's nothing wrong with that; though, if you want my advice, I would suggest that putting on airs and graces doesn't create the impression you would like to convey. However, that is your concern. Mine is for Adriana.'

Imray sat down, still sullen. 'In that case I trust you will arrange for her to return to Leicestershire.'

'Certainly, if she wishes to do so – and only if she wishes to do so. Now, I understand you have lost both your parents. When was that?'

'Five years since. They were on a visit to relatives in Flanders. On the way back their ship foundered.'

'I'm sorry. So you were left alone, at the age of fifteen or sixteen, to fend for yourself and your sister. That must have been very hard.'

He nodded. 'We owe everything to Lord Graves. He was like a second father to us. He kept me as his falconer and had Adriana taught with his own daughters. He promised to find a husband for her.'

'But not, I fancy, with a gentleman third in line to an earldom.'

The young man looked down into his glass. 'Well, that might have been a bit of an exaggeration. His lordship urged her to accept one of his tenant farmers whose wife had recently died.'

'How old was this farmer?'

Ignatius shrugged. 'About fifty.'

'I imagine that was a union Adriana did not altogether relish.'

'He's a good man. Adriana would have been well cared for and she could not expect anything better.'

'Perhaps she hoped to find a man more to her liking.'

'It would be a strange world, Master Treviot, in which women chose their husbands! As I said earlier, his lordship was most displeased with her stubbornness.'

'That must have made life difficult for you.'

He nodded enthusiastically, abandoning his image. At last I saw something of his real feelings. 'It was so thoughtless of her, so selfish. After all Lord Graves had done for us. It could have ruined everything – for both of us.'

'You were caught in the middle.'

'Yes, his lordship said I should assert my authority over my sister but she's a proud, malapert little jade, as you may have discovered.'

'How came she to work for Master Holbein?'

''Twas as I said. The painter was come to make portraits for Lord and Lady Graves. He remarked that he needed a nurse for his children and Adriana begged to be allowed to leave with him. His lordship said she could go to the devil for all he cared. And he was right, wasn't he? I gather Holbein is now dead. So Adriana is cast adrift in the world, without any prospects. Shameful!'

'Your sister is currently under my protection.'

'Protection! From what I hear, your care for her has driven her to the sin of suicide.'

'She told you that?'

He evaded the question. 'She didn't need to. I have eyes and ears.'

I was losing patience with this hubristic yonker, whose only concern was his own standing with his patron. 'Then I urge you to use them more carefully. If you do you will realise that she has been battered by cruel fate till she can bear no more. She still grieves for her parents. She has been vilely abused by violent men. She can see no future for herself, save as the bed-fellow of some rural clod old enough to be her father. Her only relative is a brother who regards her as an embarrassment. Life for her seems empty. Can you wonder that she sought to end it?'

Imray's sullen scowl returned. 'And what is there for her here?'

'Friends who will nurse her back to health of body and spirit and help her to find a future that has some prospect of happiness.'

Imray shrugged. 'I see you have some strange ideas about

women, Master Treviot. If you are determined to send me back empty-handed, I suppose I must give way. What am I to tell his lordship?'

'You don't need my advice on that. You are a gifted story-teller. Except that you must be more careful to get your facts right. Antwerp cathedral is not the largest in Europe. In fact, it is smaller than St Paul's. Now, let us rejoin the others and you can demonstrate your skill at primero.'

Later I went to Adie's chamber but she was sleeping. Before I withdrew I left instructions with the servants that Ignatius was not to be readmitted without me being present also.

The stipulation proved unnecessary: young Master Imray departed early the next day without seeking to trouble his sister further. Over the next couple of days Adie rid herself completely of the fever that had racked her body but not of the melancholy that gripped her mind. Bart also lapsed into a sombre mood that contrasted with his usual liveliness. When the men who had escorted our prisoners to Canterbury returned; when all the stories of the Fletcham venture had been told and retold until the hearers tired of them, an air of quiet anxiety settled over Hemmings. We all felt the anti-climax. The days of excitement were over but still the underlying problems remained. Reports arrived of the progress of Legh's commission: of houses ransacked in the search for incriminating material; of jails filling with prisoners; of troops being used to disperse little groups of protesters. There seemed no end to the religious conflicts riving society, no resolution to the underlying problems facing Kent – and the nation. As to the specific questions still disturbing my own mind, I finally decided to seek advice from friends.

Ned and Lizzie joined me in my chamber one morning

when wind and rain were, once again, rattling the casements. I shared with them what I had gleaned from Ignatius about Adie and their family background.

'Small wonder she was driven to a desperate act,' Lizzie said. 'I'll wager if she went with that puffed-up barnyard cock of a brother, she'd soon try again.'

Ned agreed. 'She lacks hope. She doesn't want to go back to Leicestershire. She knows that the respite you have provided can only be temporary. Once there were places where such as she could find solace and even a purpose in life.'

'The nunneries?'

'Aye. And now they have gone, there remains only one estate she can embrace – marriage.'

'And her treatment at the hands of Black Harry's gang will make it hard for her to yield herself to a husband's demands,' Lizzie said.

'So what can we do?' I asked.

'Continue showing her kindness,' Ned suggested. ''Tis a slow cure but one that ...'

At that Lizzie glared at us. 'Men! All you think of is *doing*! As though some wise words or generous actions will change her. What Adie needs is to *be* somebody; to know that she has it within her to perform a role in life; to believe that she matters to at least someone. *Think!*' she almost shouted. 'When is she happiest?'

'When she's with the children,' I said.

'Right! And she knows that children grow up. One day they will no longer need her. And then what can she live for? Who can she live for? What you may not have noticed,' Lizzie went on, 'is that we women live for others. We give ourselves to people who need us. Take away that sense of being needed and what remains?'

After a long silence, I said diffidently, 'So what we should do is find what she is good at and provide opportunities for her to ... do it.'

'That would make a start,' Lizzie agreed, 'until she discovers the person for whom she would be willing to do anything.'

'As you do for Bart,' I said hurriedly, diverting the conversation from the channel Lizzie was digging for it. 'And that brings me to the other problem I have on my mind. The strain of all this business on Bart is, I think, beginning to tell.'

Lizzie said, 'He feels he has suffered long enough. He managed to keep his spirits up until your raid on Fletcham, by persuading himself that, once you'd caught Black Harry, his troubles would be over. Now it seems he still has to wait to clear his name.'

'Perhaps that's my fault,' I said.

'Why do you say that?'

I told her about Black Harry's offer and my rejection of it. 'The thought of helping that bestial, blood-soaked monster to go free ... Well, it just seemed utterly wrong. Now I'm not so sure. If I'd agreed to do a deal, Bart would probably, by now, have gone to the magistrates with Black Harry's confession and would no longer be a wanted man.'

Lizzie received the news in shocked silence. She sat at the table, head in hands. At last she muttered, 'Bart will get free of this burden sometime, won't he?'

'Oh, yes, certainly,' I replied, with all the conviction I could muster, 'as soon as Black Harry is brought to trial.'

'That could be quite a while yet, couldn't it?' she asked.

'Yes.'

'Then I wish you hadn't told me,' she said miserably.

'You think I was wrong?'

At that she flared up. 'God in heaven, yes! Of course I

think you were wrong. I don't know how you could deliberately prolong Bart's agony. Don't you think he's suffered enough? But that's between you and your conscience. All you've done by telling me is make me a partner in your stupid cruelty. Do you expect me to say, "That's all right, Thomas, you did the right thing"? Now I've got to share your problem. What am I supposed to do? Tell Bart you've let him down? You know how much he respects you. He would be shattered. Or do you want me to keep the truth from him, to deceive him in order to keep your guilty secret?'

Ned tried to calm the atmosphere. 'Lizzie, Thomas didn't have a simple choice between right and wrong. He had to choose, on the spur of the moment, which course of action was less wrong than the other.'

'I might have known you'd take his side,' she snapped.

''Tis no question of taking sides. I know not what I would have done in his position. What I do know is that we all have a responsibility to support Bart until this terrible charge against him is dropped and the real villain is brought to justice.'

Lizzie showed no sign of being mollified. Neither of my problems had been resolved by this discussion. It was as well that I was not left for long to brood on them. Next morning a troop of the archbishop's guards arrived to escort me to Croydon for another meeting with Cranmer.

I decided to take Bart with me. I am not sure why. It may be that I half-intended, as we travelled, to explain my rejection of Black Harry's deal. Or, perhaps, I hoped he might learn something about the larger issues at stake and see his own problem in their light. In the event, my motivation was of little consequence. As we rode, I did not raise the Aldgate affair and events in Croydon would push it into the background.

As soon as we arrived at the palace we went in to dinner. The great hall was very full and the reason soon became apparent. Cranmer's high table was filled with distinguished guests, all of whom had obviously brought attendants with them. From my vantage point at the bottom end of one of the lower tables I saw the archbishop surrounded by several senior clerics, as well as gentlemen whose costly court clothes indicated their importance. At a distance I recognised only one of these notables but that one was highly significant. If Anthony Denny had left the touring royal court for talks with the archbishop, those talks must be of the utmost importance. Some of England's grandees of church and state had come together to discuss matters of high politics. Like it or not, I was to be caught up in their deliberations.

Chapter 28

During the course of that day and the next morning Bart and I made conversation with several of our fellow guests. Among the more obvious common concerns was the situation in the capital. The plague was apparently showing no sign of abating. Opinion differed as to whether the death toll was rising or falling, though all agreed that this visitation was the longest in living memory. The king and court were still keeping their distance. The Westminster law courts remained closed, and the jails overcrowded as a result of the backlog of cases waiting to be heard. The beginning of the legal term, already transferred from Michaelmas to All Saints Day had once again been postponed to 12 November and it had been decided to hold sittings in St Albans. Those obliged to remain in the stricken City were running short of food because farmers and wagoners were unwilling to risk contagion.

Preachers, of course, were unrestrained in identifying the cause of the visitation. Some declared it God's curse on a nation that had cut itself adrift from Catholic Christendom, while others were equally certain that divine wrath was being vented on a disobedient land still clinging to the vestiges of popery.

Political news was largely taken up with rumours of imminent war with France – the first military adventure in a quarter of a century. King Henry, it was confidently asserted, would be following his friend, the Emperor, in lighting more human bonfires of heretics. Those who claimed to have knowledge of the inner workings of the royal court spoke of the emergence of bitterly opposed factions – 'Catholic' and 'Protestant' – the latter being a new word imported from Germany. There was much debate about who would be the next powerful minister to follow Wolsey, More and Cromwell to disgrace and death. Some said it would be Bishop Gardiner. Others prophesied the imminent fall of Cranmer. Most observers seemed to be agreed that the present meeting at Croydon was a gathering of Protestant leaders to plan their political strategy.

The next day I was told to wait with others in an anteroom for my summons before the archbishop and his colleagues. That summons came in mid-morning. I entered the library to see eight men sitting around a long table. A vacant space was pointed out to me and I obediently took my place. Ralph Morice sat at Cranmer's left hand, and was taking notes. He addressed me very formally.

'Master Thomas Treviot, goldsmith of London, you are here to provide information to this committee and to answer any questions we may put to you. You will regard everything said within these walls as spoken in confidence and you will now take an oath to that effect.'

An attendant handed me a Bible and, with one hand upon it, I swore myself to secrecy.

Cranmer spoke. 'My Lord (he inclined his head to the thin-lipped, thin-faced man on his right, who, as I later discovered, was the Earl of Hertford – brother-in-law to the king and uncle to the young heir to the throne), gentlemen, I have already intimated to you the ways in which we are indebted to Master Treviot. It would be no exaggeration to say that without his tenacious pursuit of a dangerous gang of subversive seditionists we would not now be in a position to tear up by the roots the papist plot we have been considering. I have commanded his presence because he has had close contact with the seditionists and is in an excellent position to answer any questions we may wish to ask about them. But first I have a pleasant duty to perform.'

He nodded to Morice, who silently slid a sheet of paper across the table. I read the few lines written in a scrawling hand:

I, Henry Walden, sometimes known as 'Black Harry', do
solemnly confess that on 1 September in this year, 1543,
I did feloniously enter the house of Johannes Holbein,
King's Painter, in the Aldgate ward of London, and did
there assault and kill a servant of the said Johannes
Holbein, to the disturbance of the king's peace. I now
repent me of this deed and affirm that I alone deserve
such punishment as the king's justice may impose. And
further I acknowledge that the attribution of this
felonious deed to any other than myself has no
foundation in fact. Signed by me of my own free will, this
23 day of October in the year 1543.
Henry Walden

'I thank Your Grace,' I said. 'This will relieve an innocent man of a great burden.'

I was, indeed, delighted for Bart and Lizzie. This was what they – and I – had wanted all along. If I did not feel overwhelmed with joy and relief it was because a question nagged at me: what price had been paid?

Hertford began the questioning. 'Master Treviot, this Walden fellow has given his word to help us apprehend his superiors in the plot. How reliable do you think he is?'

'My Lord, I think him very unreliable.'

There was a murmur round the table and I was aware of many pairs of eyes fastened upon me.

'Let me explain,' I continued. 'The Black Harry I first encountered seemed to me nothing more nor less than a violent, unprincipled hellhound, ready to commit any abomination in return for money. More than that, he was a man so devoid of humanity that he actually enjoyed inflicting pain and suffering, quite apart from any financial advantage it might bring him. Later, when I spoke to him, I slightly revised my opinion. Now he seemed to be a fanatic, driven by loyalty to papal religion and obsessed by hatred of heretics. I knew he had been a servant of the Inquisition in Spain, so I readily believed him when he told me he would willingly die for his faith. Yet, within hours, I was obliged to change my opinion yet again, when he offered to betray his colleagues in order to save his own skin.'

Hertford leaned forward with a stare that was disconcertingly intense. 'Would you say that his latest change of tactics is motivated solely by self-preservation or by something more subtle?'

'I'm not quite sure I understand Your Lordship.'

Hertford explained. 'Walden claims he can help us to

329

apprehend Ferdinand Brooke, who, as you already know, is the vital link between English conspirators and foreign papists. Do you think he's simply playing for time? He knows that there are other plots afoot against those of us who favour the Gospel. He might hope to defer his own execution until such plots come to fruition and his friends can engineer his release.'

'Surely, My Lord, he is merely showing himself to be a menial of the Devil, who, as Scripture assures us, is the father of lies.' The speaker was a cleric sitting at the extreme right of the table.

Cranmer said, 'What Prebendary Ridley reminds us is undeniably true, but it helps us little in the present instance. We know our enemies are working with frantic haste to make a case against us to his majesty. It behoves us to act with equal despatch.'

'We have letters from Bishop Gardiner to his nephew urging him to undermine the archbishop's authority in Canterbury,' someone said. 'Surely that's all we need without having to trust in rakehells and assassins.'

'And Dr London is under investigation in the Fleet for perjuring himself in court with false accusations against his grace,' another voice added.

Ridley said, 'All this is true but we must not be complaisant. I say we should use every weapon God places in our hands.'

At this point Anthony Denny introduced another thought. 'There's more at stake here than foiling the intrigues of our own enemies. England is about to be dragged into a disastrous war with the Empire against France. His majesty is enthusiastic for it. He will hear nothing said against his friend, the Emperor. If we could apprehend Brooke and expose his nefarious dealings with the imperial ambassador, we could open the king's eyes to what is really going on. I believe any risk is worth taking if it can draw us back from the brink of war.'

Cranmer smiled wistfully across the table. 'You see, Master Treviot, how divided we are. Is there any guidance you can give us?'

I almost had to pinch myself to make sure I was not dreaming. Was I really sitting here with some of the greatest men in the land, discussing issues of war and peace? Choosing my words with extreme care, I said, 'May I know what you have promised Black Harry in return for his cooperation?'

Cranmer replied. 'That he will be placed on the first available ship leaving England and no further action will be taken against him as long as he remains abroad. If, however, he should at any time return, he would be fully accountable in the king's court for all his crimes.'

'In that case I would suggest that you keep him in very close custody until you have Brooke safely under lock and key. And then honour your promise. Broadly, I am in agreement with Prebendary Ridley. Use this wretch for your own ends if you can but, if he fails you, show no mercy.'

'I'm afraid he's already thought of that,' Morice explained. 'I have had three long sessions with him and he is not prepared to trust us. He says, "When you've got your man, what is to stop you going back on your word and delivering me to the hangman?" What he is asking is that he accompanies us when we go to arrest Brooke and that, as soon as he has pointed Brooke out to us, we let him go.'

'In that case,' I said, 'you should wash your hands of him. I've been close enough to this rogue to recognise the smell of trickery.'

In the silence that followed there was much exchanging of glances round the table. Eventually, Cranmer said, 'Master Treviot, thank you for your help. We are much indebted to you.' I was dismissed.

I had no chance for a private word with Bart before dinner, which we again took in the hall. Then, as soon as we rose from the table, I saw Morice leave his place at the archbishop's side and stride down the hall towards us. Outside in the courtyard he shook my hand.

'Thank you, Thomas. Your contribution was invaluable.'

'Did you manage to reach a decision?' I asked. 'There seemed to be a marked difference of opinion among you.'

'Yes. It wasn't easy, but I think we got there in the end. I need to explain it to you.' He glanced meaningfully at Bart and only continued after I had sent him to fetch the horses. 'There are two things I must tell you. The first is that, after much debate, and not without some reluctance, we have resolved to accept Walden's offer to lead us to Brooke.'

'You know my opinion on that.'

'Indeed, but the court party has a different perspective. Hertford and Denny were adamant that we must grasp every opportunity to lay our hands on Brooke.'

'Then I wish you every success. What was the other thing you had to tell me?'

'That is more difficult, and I hope you will not take it amiss. Believe me, I did stress – very strongly – that you had already done much more than we had a right to expect of you.'

I stared at his care-furrowed face. 'I imagine I'm not going to like this.'

He nodded. 'I fear not. It was just that you have had such close dealings with Black Harry.'

'Go on.'

'They're asking you to come with us when we go to apprehend Brooke in case he tries any more trickery.'

'Asking?' I said.

Morice avoided my gaze. 'You know what I mean.'

'And when will this take place?'

'That is yet to be determined. Now the decision has been
made I must go back for more talks with the prisoner.'

'God's blood! What have we come to when high policy is
made by one of the foulest villains ever to be lodged in an
English jail?'

'Nevertheless . . .' Morice shrugged. 'I am told to request
you to remain at Hemmings while we complete our plans.
When the time comes we will despatch a fast courier to
summon you.'

'Well, I will not be at Hemmings for a couple of days,' I said
brusquely. 'I have a vital engagement elsewhere.'

As soon as Bart reappeared with the horses I bade Morice
a brief farewell, mounted and led the way down the long
drive.

When we turned on to the highway, Bart said, 'Master
Thomas, we are going the wrong way. This is the London road.'

I unfastened my purse and took from it Black Harry's confession. Without a word, I handed it to him to read.

Chapter 29

Bart must have read the brief confession three or four times. So intent was he that he was almost unseated when his horse stumbled in a pothole. At last he held the paper to his lips and kissed it.

'Where did this come from?' he asked.

'Friends in high places.'

'Thank you, Master Thomas, thank you. I don't know how you did it, but thank you.'

'You'd better give it to me for safe keeping,' I said. 'Did Lizzie not say anything about how I might come by it?'

He returned the confession, with a last, lingering look. 'Lizzie? No. What does she know of it?'

'Nothing,' I lied, as I carefully folded it and replaced it in my purse. 'I simply mentioned that I was going to try to get Black Harry to write this without any more delay. I told her not to raise your hopes, just in case.'

'Is that why we're heading for London?' he asked.

'I thought you'd want to deliver this to the magistrate without delay.'

'Most certainly.' Bart uttered a long sigh. 'No more hiding!'

'It's been a long time. I'm delighted it's all over.'

'Not quite *all* over, is it, Master Thomas?'

'What do you mean?'

'Well, that meeting back there at the palace. All those important people. There's something big in the air, isn't there?'

'I'm not in a position to say. I've been sworn to secrecy.'

'Ah, then it *is* something big. Everyone I spoke to was guessing about it. Some reckoned they knew what was afoot.'

'Oh, and what did these well-informed experts say?'

'There's much talk of plots and conspiracies.'

'What sort of plots and conspiracies?'

'Some say the pope and the Emperor want to drag England into war with France and some of the king's council want a league with the Lutheran princes to prevent it. There's murmuring about a revolt of the bishops against religious change. I even heard someone claim he had it on good authority that the Earl of Hertford was planning to depose the king and take over the government in the name of Prince Edward, his nephew.'

'Well,' I responded, 'I'm happy to tell you that you can ignore all those alarming ideas. They say more about common fears and anxieties than about the real state of political affairs.'

'But there must be some reason for all these bishops and councillors and courtiers meeting in secret well away from the royal court.'

'There are certainly matters of concern that some of his majesty's closest advisers want to discuss.'

'Why weren't the Duke of Norfolk and the Bishop of Winchester at the meeting? Is there a plot against them?'

I laughed. 'Oh, Bart, you do love intrigues! Cranmer is an archbishop, not an arch-rebel. And if such revolutionary ideas were being discussed at Croydon Palace, I certainly would not have been invited to share in them.'

Bart was obviously not convinced. 'Well,' he said, 'something's going on – or, if it isn't, people think it is, and that's just as bad.'

With that I could not disagree.

We rode straight through the City to Aldgate and asked our way to the house of James Corridge, the magistrate.

''Ere, I know you! Stop! Hold, I say!' We had almost reached our destination, when a bulky figure lurched out of a doorway and stood in our path. Constable Pett.

'You've led me a merry dance, Bart Miller. Come now to give yourself up, have you?' He took hold of the bridle of Bart's horse.

'Unhand my mare,' Bart shouted, 'or you'll feel my whip-stock across your face.'

Pett leered up at him, 'Oh, no, my fine fellow. You'll not get out of my clutches a second time.'

Bart raised his crop and I said hurriedly, 'If I were you, I'd do as he says. We are peacefully on our way to the coroner's house with a confession.'

Pett released his grip. 'Brought him to his senses have you, Master? Well, it's not before time. Hand me the confession.'

'Get out of the way, oaf,' I said. 'Our business is with Master Corridge and no one else.'

Pett grunted. 'Follow me, then, but if there's any trickery ...'

I spurred my gelding into a trot and the fat constable had

to run to keep up. When we reached the house he knocked loudly as Bart and I dismounted. To the servant who opened the door he said, 'Tell your master I've brought in the murderer, Miller.'

The magistrate received us in the small room he used as his office. 'Master Treviot, I'm right glad to see you again. Is it true what the constable says; have you brought your man to confess the crime of murder?'

'I very much doubt whether Constable Pett can ever be relied on to speak the truth,' I said. 'Here is a document that will explain all.' I handed him Black Harry's confession.

Corridge read it with raised eyebrows. 'This certainly changes things, Master Treviot. May I ask how you came by this confession?'

'It was written in the Archbishop of Canterbury's jail and passed on to me by his grace himself. The assassin now awaits his trial for several crimes in the court of King's Bench, which, as I'm sure you know, will be in session at St Albans in a couple of weeks' time.'

'Then the matter is out of my hands,' Corridge said, 'and I'm not sorry for it.'

Pett thrust himself forward. 'What's all this, then? What knavery is here, Master Corridge?'

The magistrate scowled at him. 'Only the knavery you bring with you! Had you done your job and set up the hue and cry when the crime was committed we might have apprehended the real murderer long since.'

'Aye,' I added, 'and prevented other killings, too.' To Corridge I said, ''Tis not for me to tell you your business but in my opinion your ward is ill served by this bragging tosspot. I have evidence that he abuses his office. If you choose to look into his conduct I will happily tell you what I know.'

Pett mumbled and muttered his protest but no one was listening.

Corridge said, 'I am obliged to you, Master Treviot. I have purposed for some time to set in hand just such an investigation. If I need any information I will certainly call upon you.'

'Please do. Now, before I go, may I ask you to make a copy of this confession for your records? We will need to keep the original in case it is required in a higher court.'

'Of course. I will do it myself. Unfortunately, I have recently lost my clerk to the pestilence.'

When he had written a duplicate and I had endorsed it, Bart and I took our leave. As we closed the door behind us, we heard the sound of angry raised voices within.

We spent the night at Goldsmith's Row and set off back to Hemmings the next morning.

A heartening sight met us as we entered the hall. Lizzie was seated by the fire busily knitting and Adie squatted close by, sewing a patch on one of the children's items of clothing. But what was a relief to see was that the women were chatting and laughing together.

'What is amusing you two?' I asked as I warmed my hands at the heat from the burning logs.

'Women talk,' Lizzie replied. 'You're excluded.'

'That's a pity,' I said. 'We have news that might be of interest to you.'

'Really? And what's that?'

'Bart has something to show you.'

Without a word, Lizzie's husband handed her Black Harry's confession. She read it through quickly, then jumped up from her stool, letting wool and needles fall to the floor. She threw her arms round Bart and the two hugged ecstatically.

338

After several moments Lizzie disentangled herself. 'Come upstairs and tell me all about it and I'll give you a better welcome,' she said to her husband.

When they had left I took my place on Lizzie's stool.

'What was all that about?' Adie asked.

I explained how Morice had extracted a confession from Black Harry.

'What marvellous news,' she responded. 'It is good to see them so happy.'

'And 'tis good to hear you laughing,' I said. 'How are you now?'

Immediately, the old pensive look returned. 'I thank you, Master Thomas. I think I am as well as I can be.'

'A strange answer. Come walk with me and explain it more fully.'

We linked arms and I led her out on to the lawn.

'I should not loiter long,' she said. 'The boys will be back from their lessons soon.'

'Then they will have to wait. I want to assure myself that you are fully recovered and that we shall have no more jumping into streams.'

She lowered her head. 'I've caused everyone a lot of trouble.'

'No trouble that we have not gladly accepted.'

'You are all so good to me. I haven't known such care since . . . '

'Since your parents died?'

She nodded.

'We've all known loss – mothers, fathers, brothers, sisters, wives, close friends. Why, even Ned – or perhaps I should say, especially Ned – has known heartbreak.' I told her briefly about Ned and Jed and their close relationship. 'The poor

339

man lost, first of all, his secure and meaningful life in the abbey, then the one person who meant everything to him. But, when you look at him, do you see a picture of brooding sadness?'

'No.'

'No. That's because he looks forward. He once told me that life is like a book with many chapters. As one closes, another opens. We are, of course, free to simply turn back the pages, trying to relive the earlier chapters, but the new ones have their own delights and fascinations and we should start on them fearlessly.'

We were approaching the bridge. Adie's steps became slower but I urged her forward. 'I found that a very hard lesson to learn. When my Jane died I had no interest in turning the pages of my life. I could not think that I would find anything written there that could be of interest to me. For over a year I cared not whether I lived or died.'

'What happened to change you?'

'Someone else turned the page for me. But that's a long story.'

We had reached the bridge and I deliberately stopped. As we leaned against the parapet, I said, 'This is solemn talk. Tell me what you and Lizzie were laughing about when Bart and I arrived.'

'I was asking her about her earlier life.'

'In the brothel?'

'Yes. She has so many funny stories to tell about it. I imagined it must have been a terrible time but she didn't let it affect her. She's an amazing woman.'

'Life in the Stews was hard. It still is for women locked into that existence. Fortunately for Lizzie, Bart came along and she found ...'

'A new chapter?'

'Yes.'

'They are very much in love,' she said wistfully. 'I asked her how that could be.'

'I don't see what you mean.'

Adie stared down into the water. 'Well, letting lots of men do things to her that she didn't want. How could she ever find pleasure in those things with Bart?'

'Only she can answer that but I suppose ... Well, have you heard men speak of the philosophers' stone?'

'No, what is it?'

''Tis something that can change any other metal – copper, lead, iron, or anything else – into gold.'

She looked up with wide eyes.

'I'd like some of that.'

I laughed. 'Oh, 'tis only a legend – at least, I hope so. If anyone ever found this amazing mineral, I would be out of business. Would you buy gold if you could make your own? Well, I sometimes think that perhaps love is a kind of philosophers' stone. It can transform bad experience into something beautiful and precious.'

She looked down again into the swirling water and sighed deeply. 'I think love must be just as rare as this miraculous stone.'

'Perhaps it is not as good an example as I thought. People do find it – people like Lizzie.'

There was a long silence and I wondered whether I should mention what was in my mind. At last I said, 'Ignatius told me about your mother and father. It was a wretched thing to happen to you – and you little more than a child.'

She made no answer.

'But 'tis an old chapter. Let it float away on the stream.' I took hold of her shoulders and gently turned her round. 'Turn your back on tragedy. Just as Lizzie turned her back on the whorehouse and Ned turned his back on the monastery and I turned my back on wedded life.'

'Have you found your philosophers' stone?' she asked.

'No, but the important thing is that I believe in it. So I go on looking.'

She smiled at me. 'Then I hope you find it, Master Treviot.'

'And I hope you find it, Mistress Imray.'

We both laughed.

That was the moment a servant came running across the lawn. 'Master Thomas, Master Thomas, there's a messenger come from the archbishop! He says 'tis urgent!'

Chapter 30

The expected summons was brief and to the point. I was to present myself as early as possible at the ferry stage at Gravesend on Thursday 28 October, two days hence, with whatever hand weapons I could muster. There I would place myself under the authority of the captain of the archiepiscopal guard.

It would be an exaggeration to record that the message filled me with foreboding. But I certainly had a strong sense of dread. The policy that Cranmer and his friends had adopted was, in my opinion, dangerously faulty. I did not believe for a moment that Black Harry could be trusted. And I did not want to be personally involved in any kind of military confrontation. Warfare was for the sons of noblemen and gentlemen, who seriously believed that there was honour in it, and for poor wretches unable to avoid being forcibly drafted into an army. The injunction to arm myself was alarming. It was one thing to be inveigled into this expedition because of my 'close dealings' with Walden. To be expected to fight was quite another.

I took a bunch of keys from my chamber coffer and went to the room at the top of the house where we stored damaged furniture and other items that were temporarily out of use but which we did not want to throw away. In a corner stood an old chest that had lain undisturbed since my father's day. I unlocked it and the scent of lavender assailed my nostrils as I lifted the lid. I rummaged among old clothes, fragments of tapestry, bent candlesticks and broken rushlight holders. What I sought lay at the bottom wrapped in cloth.

I carried it back to my chamber and removed the coverings. The rapier, I saw, was in good condition. The blade bore no hint of rust and gleamed in the light from the window. I had acquired it some ten years before from a customer who was having difficulty paying a debt. I was then a young man indulging glamorous dreams of military prowess and hoping to impress girls with my skill in fencing. My father was furious at such foolish extravagance. Honest merchants had better things to do, he scolded, than ape their betters by swaggering around with swords. As I looked at it now I realised I had forgotten what a fine piece of workmanship it was. The blade was Toledo steel and the foundry mark showed up clearly. The hilt had been fitted by one of the best London armourers in Coleman Street. I weighed it in my hand. The balance was perfect. But the thought of using it in anger was abhorrent.

The concern was shared by other members of the household. When I was observed harnessing the rapier to my belt, questions were asked. Questions I could not answer. Bart said if I was going to a fight he wanted to come, too. Walt and one or two others asked if I wanted their support. I turned down such offers. It was bad enough that I had to set out on this foolhardy venture. There was no reason to involve anyone else. Yet, much as I made light of it, there was no ignoring the real anxiety that permeated Hemmings.

On Thursday I was up before dawn. When I went into the stable yard Walt was already brushing down Golding, my grey horse.

'Are you sure you want no company, Master Thomas?' he asked, as he fitted the bit into the gelding's mouth.

'Quite sure, thank you. Please assure everyone that there's no need for alarm. I expect to be back tomorrow, or Saturday at the latest.'

'God go with you,' he called as I rode out of the gate.

I muttered an 'Amen' under my breath.

I was at Gravesend in less than a couple of hours. An extraordinary scene met me at the quayside. It was as though the contingent of a royal army were preparing to embark for a foreign war. There were horses and men everywhere. Some were already crossing the estuary on the ferry boats and other craft that had been commandeered. I threaded my way through the throng and eventually found Morice in conversation with the guard captain.

He turned to greet me. 'Ah, there you are, Thomas. Good.'

'This is an enormous turnout,' I said. 'How many men have you got here?'

'We want to be absolutely sure of our man,' he replied. 'You, yourself, impressed upon us how slippery Black Harry is.'

'Where exactly are we going?'

'"Exactly"? I'm not sure. Our guide is keeping the details very much to himself.'

'I can't help repeating myself,' I said, lowering my voice.

'This is madness. You're seriously letting this knave lead all these men on a wild horse chase? All he's interested in is giving you the slip.'

'He won't do that. He's in that wagon over there, securely bound and well guarded.'

'Even so, I like it not. Have you no idea where we're bound?'

'His story is that Brooke has a small ship on an inlet further along the coast.'

'Supposing that to be true, why hasn't he gone already?'

'Apparently, his craft can only get away on a high tide. Black Harry called for an almanac and calculated that this afternoon will be the first opportunity for Brooke to escape the country.'

'This stretch of coast is shredded with channels, is it not?'

'Yes, but few are navigable by larger vessels and the sands are treacherous. That limits his choice. If he did manage to slip away we have a galleass patrolling further offshore to give chase.'

'Since you've made such elaborate preparations, I can't see why you need me.'

'Black Harry says he'll only give directions to you.'

'Black Harry! Black Harry! Black Harry! Who's in charge of this expedition?'

Morice frowned. 'Thomas, you've made your feelings clear. What you have to remember is how much is hanging on the success of today's events. If we capture Brooke ... well, I don't need to tell you again what that would mean. Our friends at court have persuaded his grace that no opportunity should be lost, however slight. That's why we've mobilised this large force. Now, if you'll excuse me, I must get the wagon loaded.'

*

By the time everyone had been transported to the Essex bank the morning was far spent. When we set off inland, Morice instructed me to ride behind the wagon. Black Harry obviously regarded my presence as a petty triumph. As I took up my position, he leered at me and nodded. I did my best to ignore him.

When we reached a crossroads the prisoner stood abruptly and called out, 'Stop.' He made a great show of looking all around. Then he called out, 'Master Treviot, if you please.'

I drew alongside the wagon.

He smirked. 'How pleasant to be together again, Master Treviot. Do you not admire my retinue?'

'Just give us the directions,' I muttered.

'Directions? Well, let me see. I think we'll go . . . right.'

This play-acting was repeated every time we came to a junction or fork in the road. Black Harry gave the impression that he was making up the route as he went along. I became increasingly convinced he was deliberately leading us nowhere, just for the perverted pleasure of wasting our time and causing us maximum discomfort. A chill wind was blowing in off the German Sea across the marsh and we were all huddling into our cloaks as much as we could. As we meandered, apparently aimlessly, across the barren landscape the troops became increasingly restive. After a couple of hours my patience snapped. I spurred my horse, rode to the head of column and drew level with Morice and the guard captain.

'This is utterly futile,' I said. 'Can't you see what he's doing? He intends to keep us on the move until 'tis dark and we are miles from anywhere.'

The captain agreed. 'We don't have provisions for an overnight camp. If we don't get to wherever it is we're supposed to be going in the next half-hour or so, we'll have to

347

turn back. This fellow's simply making fools of us – or perhaps he's hoping to escape somehow under cover of darkness.'

Morice scowled, and I could well imagine the question that was going through his mind: how was he going to explain this fiasco when he returned to Croydon? 'I'm afraid you're right,' he said. 'Turn the column round, Captain, and we'll retrace our steps as fast as we can.'

The captain called halt and rode back past the ranks of his men.

When Black Harry realised what was happening he called out, 'Stop! What are you doing?'

'We've had enough of your game, Master Walden,' Morice replied. 'We're heading for home and, by the saints, I'd make you walk, if that wouldn't hold us up.'

'You can't do that now,' Black Harry cried. 'We're nearly there.'

'Save your breath,' I called out. 'We've had enough of your lies.'

'No! No!' the prisoner shouted. 'I'm telling the truth! See those trees up ahead? Just beyond, the road slopes down to the creek where Brooke's ship lies.' For the first time, he seemed genuinely agitated. The braggadocio had gone. He was almost pleading.

I found this sudden change more worrying than his former arrogance. What was he planning now? I wondered.

Morice, however, was still eager to be convinced. He stopped by the wagon. 'The other side of that copse, you say?'

'Yes, that's right. You'll see.'

'Very well, we'll ride as far as the trees – and no further.'

As Morice trotted after the captain to have his order countermanded, I caught him up. 'Just a moment, I don't like this,' I said. 'I know this fellow. He's up to something.'

'Well, we'll soon see. Three or four minutes and we'll look for this ship of his.'

'Might it not be better,' I suggested, 'to send a couple of scouts ahead to look for Brooke's vessel?'

'I don't want to keep everyone standing still in this wind. Another quarter of a mile and we can shelter among the trees, rest the horses and then start back.'

I had to admit there was a certain amount of sense in that. The clump of leaning, wind-blown oaks was the only visible cover to be seen. It would be good to dismount for a few minutes and stretch our limbs. When we turned round we would, at least, have the wind at our backs.

Morice told the captain what he had decided and the captain passed on to his men the welcome news that they could have a short break.

While the column reorganised itself, I scrutinised the figure in the wagon. He was standing and closely watching what was going on. Was he calculating something? Perhaps he was concocting yet another story to keep us on the move and to maintain the illusion that it was he who was in command.

I edged Golding up to the side of the wagon. I looked at the prisoner and satisfied myself that his bonds were tight. 'Keep a close watch on this fellow,' I said to his guards. 'Whatever he says to you, don't believe him. Better still, make sure he keeps his mouth shut.'

The wagon jolted as we resumed our march.

The clump of trees lay to the left of the road and was obviously thicker than it looked at a distance. It was circular in shape and the ground within rose up to form a large mound. It was obviously a prominent and ancient landmark. In time past, I guessed, it had been a sacred grove where our pagan ancestors had once worshipped their fearsome deities. Please

God, no such malign spirits still haunted this windswept terrain.

We turned aside from the road and the order was given to dismount. The men stretched and stamped or sprawled on the ground, while their horses thankfully cropped the sparse grass. I did not immediately join my resting companions. I was anxious to test Black Harry's assertion that we were near journey's end. I rode on and emerged from the trees. After a few more paces the ground began to slope away before me. I found myself looking down on a wide creek. In the middle of it was a narrow eyot. Moored in its lee was a sleek, two-masted ship.

So the villain was telling the truth, I thought to myself.

No sooner had I thought it than I was aware of shouts and screams behind me. I turned Golding's head and cantered back along the track. The copse was now alive with struggling men and the sound of clashing steel. Instantly, Black Harry's plan became obvious. He had led us into an ambush.

Chapter 31

The scene was one of total confusion. It was obvious that our men had been surprised by attackers rushing down the wooded slope. Some were fighting on foot. Others were desperately trying to remount. My immediate impression was that there were not many assailants – probably fewer than half our number. But they had the temporary advantage of surprise. There was no time to consider how I might help. I simply rushed into the melee, wildly slashing with my sword from side to side. Before me the guard captain had his back against a tree and was feverishly defending himself against two of the raiders. I thrust the point of my rapier into the neck of one man and saw him drop to the ground, howling with pain. The captain made short work of the other.

'The wagon!' he shouted. 'Get to the wagon!'

I wheeled Golding around and pushed my way past groups of struggling men to the edge of the copse, where we had left our prisoner. One of the guards was slumped over the rail. Another lay on the floor of the wagon in an ominous pool of blood. One of the attackers was bent over Black Harry, sawing at his bonds with a knife. My blade caught him a blow in the upper arm and he dropped his weapon. Cursing loudly, Black Harry kept on struggling with the ropes.

The captain emerged from among the trees, having regained his horse. He leaned from the saddle and grasped the rein of the draught horse. He pulled on it and the animal ambled forward, the wagon lurching behind it. Some thirty yards further on, he released his hold. 'Guard that son of a she-devil!' he shouted. 'I'll be damned if he's going to escape us!' He turned back towards the fighting.

I prodded Black Harry's would-be liberator with my rapier.

'Get down!' I shouted.

He turned to face me, his swarthy face glaring hate. 'Heretic pig!' he yelled, and stooped to regain his knife.

I was filled with passion of an intensity I had never felt before. It was a mixture of anger and elation. I think that, at that moment, I felt invincible. With all my force I thrust the weapon into his upper chest and felt it jar on bone. The man staggered and fell backwards out of the cart. He struggled to his feet and limped awkwardly away.

I jumped up and checked the prisoner's bonds. As I did so, I said, 'You've really sealed your fate now.'

He sneered. 'It was sealed already. Better to die fighting than on a gallows.'

I turned my attention to the two guardsmen. The one on the wagon floor made no sound as I turned him on to his back. The reason was immediately obvious. His clothes were soaked in blood issuing from a dagger thrust to the heart that had penetrated cloak, jerkin and shirt.

'All you have achieved today,' I said to Black Harry, 'is the waste of yet more lives.'

'Heretic lives are worthless. As for my people, they die as martyrs.'

I turned my attention to the other trooper, carefully lifting him from the rail and placing him on the wagon bench. There was no obvious sign of blood and he groaned as I moved him. He blinked his eyes open and put a hand to his head.

'Here, drink this,' I said, putting a flask of ale to his lips.

'Oh, something hit me,' he murmured.

I picked up his helmet. 'I reckon this saved you.'

He stared blearily down at the body. 'Is that Jake? Is he dead?'

'I'm afraid so.'

'Poor Jake. His wife's just had her first bearn,' he said, his speech still slightly slurred. He rubbed his eyes. 'We were ambushed.'

'That's right. And it was planned by our friend here.'

'Whoreson churl.' He drew his dagger. 'Let's slit his poxy throat now and have done with it.'

I laid a restraining hand on his wrist. 'Few things would give me greater pleasure, but one of them would be seeing him writhing on the gallows. Let's tidy up here a bit.'

Between us we moved Jake's body to one side and covered it as decently as we could with his cloak.

By now the sounds of the skirmish were dying down. Looking back along the road I saw the captain's men emerging from the trees pushing prisoners before them or helping wounded colleagues to walk.

I jumped down from the wagon as Morice and the captain rode up. 'What are our losses?' I asked.

'Could be worse,' the captain replied. 'Two dead, three badly wounded. One of them probably won't survive unless we can get him to a surgeon.'

'Three dead,' I said, indicating the body in the wagon. 'What about the attackers?'

'Four back there, dead or dying. The crows and foxes can have them for all I care. And we have six prisoners.'

'Did any of them get away?' I asked.

Morice said, 'I spotted a couple limping off in that direction.' He pointed towards the creek.

'Then may I suggest we find them?'

'Devil take them!' the captain scoffed. 'I'll not waste any more time on them.'

'The reason I suggest it is that Black Harry was telling the truth about the ship. It's in an inlet about a mile along there. That probably means Brooke is on board. We might be able to take him. That would give us something to show for all our effort – and sacrifice. If some of his men have escaped us we ought to try to stop them giving the warning.'

'I agree,' Morice said. 'Captain, could you spare a few men for a search party? It should be easy to spot any escapees. There's very little cover in this bleak landscape.'

The captain muttered something under his breath but rode off to organise the search.

Morice turned to me. 'Show me this ship.'

I noticed that he had tucked his left hand inside his doublet.

'You're hurt,' I said, as I mounted the grey.

'Broken arm, I think,' he replied. 'Some barbarian wielding a heavy staff. It gives me yet another reason for catching Brooke.'

We rode to the vantage point. The light was fading but it was easy to spot the barque, because lamps had been lit aboard.

'Brooke is there. I'm sure of it,' Morice said. 'But how do we get to him? We have to stop him. We can't just sit here and watch his ship slip away to sea.'

'How long to full tide?' I asked.

'About an hour. He won't wait beyond that, whether his accomplice reaches the ship or not. Oh, Jesu, this has all been devilishly well planned.'

'But how?'

'Letters smuggled in and out of prison. Easy if you have money.'

'Well, I'm damned if I'll let them get away with it. I think there might be a way for us to capture the ship. Do you speak Spanish?'

'A little,' he replied.

'That's all we would need. Let's find the captain.'

When we had rejoined the remnants of our little army, I explained my makeshift plan. 'It would need half a dozen of your fit men and we'd have to take Black Harry along to support our illusion.'

At that moment the silence of the marsh was split by the roar of a ship's cannon.

'That must be the signal that they're about to leave,' Morice said. 'Hurry.'

The captain detailed six of his men and I quickly briefed them. They removed their helmets and wrapped cloaks round them to conceal their breastplates. We collected Black Harry from the wagon and untied his legs but not his hands. Pushing him ahead of us, we moved quickly in the direction of the creek.

355

When we reached the water's edge, I said to Morice, 'Time for your best Spanish.'

Cupping his hands round his mouth he called out, '*Este es Harry. ¡Vengo pronto!*'

The response from the ship was immediate. '*¡Llegando!*'

Moments later we heard the sound of creaking oars as the ship's boat crossed the short expanse of water.

'You'd better wait here, Ralph,' I said. 'This is no job for a one-armed man. We'll signal as soon as we've got control of the barque.'

'Is there nothing else I can do?' he asked.

'Yes,' I said. 'Pray.'

The boat nosed up to the bank. We could see that it held two oarsmen. One of them called out. I pushed Black Harry forward, so that they could recognise him. My dagger was pressed firmly against his neck.

'One word and it will be your last,' I whispered.

'*Te tomaste tu tiempo,*' one of the boatmen called as he swung the craft broadside on to the land.

In the next instant hands grabbed him and his companion, yanked them out and silenced them.

We took our places in the boat and rowed towards the ship. I held my blade tight against Black Harry's windpipe.

Someone was holding a lamp over the side to show us where the boarding net was hanging down. My men scrambled up, two at a time. I pushed Black Harry and sent him sprawling in the bottom of the boat. 'Don't go away,' I said, as I reached for the net and hauled myself up.

On the deck it was apparent that we had achieved almost complete surprise. Two of Brooke's men were grappling with my guards but three others were being securely held.

'What do we do with them?' someone asked.

I thought quickly. 'Oh, put them in the boat!'

'Suppose they try to escape?'

'Bring the oars up. They'll not get far without them.' I turned away to give other orders. 'Search the ship. Round up everyone you can find. I'm going to look for Brooke.'

I strode across to the aft cabin. I was about to push the door when it opened. Ferdinand Brooke, alarmed by the commotion, stood there, sword in hand. Lamplight glinted on his gold chain and beringed fingers. It even caught glints from the gilt thread of his stylish doublet.

I drew my own weapon. 'It's finished, Brooke,' I said. 'We have command of your ship. Drop your weapon.'

He remained motionless. 'I think not.' He smiled, revealing gleaming teeth. 'I've yet to meet a mere merchant who knew one end of a fine blade from the other.' He made three or four rapid and professional-looking passes.

I backed away, fending off his blade with my own. 'Don't be a fool,' I shouted. 'You can't escape.'

'Then I'll send one more heretic to hell first.' He glared at me and I knew I was facing not a man, not even an expert swordsman. The gloating creature before me embodied hatred and fanaticism.

I retreated, trying to keep my wits sharp and not dulled by fear. Occasionally, my weapon made contact with his, deflecting the advancing point from my body. But more often he avoided contact and lunged at me. I felt a stab of pain in my left shoulder. Then, another in my right thigh. I could do nothing but continue stepping backwards, keeping my eye fixed on the needle-sharp point of his rapier. I came to a sudden halt, my back against the mainmast. With a wide grin, Brooke thrust at my chest. Only a quick sidestep enabled me to avoid a blow that must have been fatal. His point buried itself in the wood. With an inept lunge I managed to pierce his upper sword arm.

He winced. Then laughed. 'A lucky strike, master merchant. *En garde.*'

He came at me again and I felt a searing pain in my abdomen. The shock of it made me drop my sword. I staggered back, clutching a hand to the wound. Brooke closed in for the kill.

'Don't ... match ... yourself ... against ... your ... betters,' he recited, emphasising each word with a prod of his sword. He was playing with me, like a barn cat with a cornered mouse.

Mistake. One of my men came behind him and felled him with a single dagger thrust.

I staggered to the mast and managed to remain upright by propping myself against it.

'Are you hurt bad, Master Treviot?' my deliverer asked anxiously.

I shook my head. 'How are the others?'

'No problems. We have the crew safe – all shut up below, save for three we've put in the boat. Best let me look at that wound of yours.'

He helped me to the cabin and sat me in a chair. With difficulty, I pulled off my outer clothes and shirt. I looked down. There was a lot of blood trickling from a gash just below my ribs. My attendant made a bundle of the shirt and pressed it hard against the wound. 'That'll staunch the flow till we get you ashore and have it properly bound.'

At that moment I was aware of movement. I heard the faint creaking of timbers. There was shouting out on the deck. Another guard burst in.

'We're under way!' he cried. 'Drifting on the ebb tide!'

Chapter 32

Still holding the cloth to my wound, I hobbled out on deck.
The ship was, indeed, moving, and at what seemed alarming
speed. From what could be seen in the gloom, we were drifting,
slightly sideways on, down a narrow channel between mud
flats and marsh.

'Fetch the ship's captain,' I ordered. 'He's the only one who
can help. Make him understand that he's in command of the
barque and can use whatever men he needs. But watch them
all like hawks.'

I returned to my chair in the cabin, my body throbbing
with pain. I heard the clamour outside as the prisoners were
released. Orders were shouted in Spanish and running feet
hastened to carry out the captain's instructions.

It seemed an age before anyone came in to tell me what was
happening. Eventually, one of the archbishop's guards entered –
a no-nonsense, authoritative man in his forties.

'Let's have a good look at your wound,' he said brusquely.

'First tell me what's going on. In God's name, how came we to be adrift?'

'The rogues we put in the boat.' He brought the lamp closer to examine the wound. 'They cut the mooring ropes.'

'Ropes?' I was puzzled. 'Were we not anchored?'

'Sit still!' he snapped. 'I can't untie these rags if you're wriggling. No, the anchor was already inboard. The ship was ready for a quick getaway, only held by fore and aft ropes.'

'How are things now?' I demanded. 'Is the ship well in hand? We must make a landfall somewhere on our own coast. Make sure the captain steers us into a good haven. Can you get him to understand that?'

'At the moment he's understanding what he chooses to understand.'

'Don't let him try to take us out to sea.'

'We won't. Right now he's more worried about steering us through the shallows. This is a treacherous bit of coast. He's got a linesman out there taking readings every couple of minutes.'

He removed the pad of soaked rags. 'Hmm, we need more cloth – lots of it.'

'Try that.' I pointed to a low locker fixed to one of the walls, which served as both a seat and storage space.

He opened it. 'Very nice,' he muttered, pulling out various garments. 'Master Brooke's costly finery. Well, he won't be needing it now.' From the pile of highly coloured silks and velvets, he extracted some cambric shirts and began tearing them into strips. He sent one of his colleagues in search of water and, when a bucket had arrived, he gently washed down the skin around the hole in my body. 'What we have to do,' he said, 'is close this up as much as we can, then bind it as tight as you can bear.'

'You seem very expert.'

'I've watched many field surgeons at work.'

'Is it very bad? Am I likely to ...'

'Die? That you'll have to ask a priest.'

Strong fingers pinched the edges of the wound. Fresh padding was applied.

'Hold that, while I bind it,' my 'doctor' ordered. He wound long strips of cloth round my stomach so firmly that I could take only shallow breaths.

'I suppose Black Harry and his companions will get clean away,' I muttered disconsolately.

'I don't fancy their chances in the dark – not in all this mud and marsh.' He helped me into a clean shirt.

'Pray God you're right,' I said. ' If that murderous hellhound slips through our fingers after all we've been through ... Our men must be feeling very dejected.'

'I've seen troops with better morale. No one likes losing friends in battle but when you can't see the point of the battle ... When you're just obeying orders because they're orders ...'

'I'm afraid I've led you all into a real mess and we've nothing to show for it.'

'No one blames you, Master Treviot. Most of us know you were caught up in this against your will. Please God, you'll live to laugh at this fiasco. Right, that's you patched up. Keep as still as you can. Don't waste whatever strength you've got. You'll need it when we get ashore – if we get ashore.' With those comforting words he departed.

The next few hours seemed like days. I had nothing to do but try to keep my mind off the pain. I thought back over the events of the last two months. Should I have done anything different? Every single event had been like a link in a chain pulling me inevitably towards the situation in which I found myself now. Could I have broken any of those links or was I the victim of inexorable fate? Strange that a respectable London merchant should end his days on a foreign ship wallowing through turgid waters off the east coast of England. I thought of my prim brothers of the Worshipful Goldsmiths' Company. My unconventional passing would make a fine topic of conversation in our hall on Foster Lane. I imagined the solemn, nodding heads and the wiseacres who would claim they had always known young Treviot would come to a bad end. I laughed. That was a mistake: I yelped loudly as arrows of pain pierced my torso.

It may have been the very weirdness of my plight that prompted me to be almost detached from it. I was like an observer at some inns of court play, intrigued by the action, yet aware that at the end of the performance I would return to humdrum reality. But this time I was not in the audience. When the last line had been spoken, my drama would be ended. That made me think of those I was leaving behind. I was glad that there was only Raffy to be concerned about. I hoped Adie would stay as long as she was needed. As for the future of Treviots, the Goldsmiths' Company would take care of everything, either winding the business up or ensuring that Raffy was trained to take over eventually. It would be sad not to see him grow up. I prayed he would have the strength to survive the loss of his only parent – his only relative, in fact. My friends would, I knew, do all they could to help him. Bart, Lizzie, Ned – they would each have their unique stores of wisdom to share – if Raffy was humble enough to listen. I pictured their faces; tried to remain focused on them; tried to stop them being engulfed in the ocean of throbbing, unending pain. It was a losing battle. The only reality was the agony. My only desire was for it to stop.

My gaze went frequently to the window's night-blackened glass. The dark seemed like the pain – unending, unyielding. I longed for the light that would reveal where we were.

Suddenly, my little world erupted into chaos. It lurched sideways. Things were thrown off the table. My chair shot forward with such force that I was almost thrown out. I heard shouts and running feet on deck. With an immense effort, I got to my feet and hobbled to the door.

'What's happening?' I shouted to the men who were rushing to and fro.

I had to repeat the question a couple of times before someone answered, 'We've run aground!'

I made my way to the rail and peered into the darkness. A stretch of estuarial water lay between wide banks but slowly I was able to make out the shapes of sand bars. We had obviously fallen foul of one of these obstructions. The ship was leaning at a slight angle. Its stern was still in the water but the bow was held firmly. On the upper deck a furious captain was screaming abuse at his crew, some of whom were aloft, furling sails. My men could only stand around and watch the confusion.

One of them pointed to the captain. 'He's one of those leaders who blame everyone else when things go wrong. I reckon he'd have slit the helmsman's throat if we hadn't taken his weapons off him.'

Someone else said, 'He's angry because the boat's gone. He could have used it to tow us out into the channel. Now he's got to wait until the tide floats us off.'

'How long will that be?' I asked.

"Twill be on the turn shortly but I reckon it'll be a good couple of hours before there's enough depth.'

The ship gave a sudden lurch. I fell hard against the rail and screamed in pain. A couple of troopers grabbed me and supported me back to the cabin. They stayed to keep me company. The men's chatter was a welcome distraction. After a while someone brought food – salt fish and apples. I could not face it, but did drink a little ale. Occasionally, one of my companions went outside to check on the state of the tide. Another found an hourglass and the guards fell to gambling on how soon we would be afloat. They asked me to mind the money and turn the glass. It was good of them; they only did it to distract me from my sufferings. Eventually the familiar motion of the ship signalled that we were afloat again. It was now daylight. The captain ordered more sail and we were soon making good progress before an offshore wind. But the day's excitements were not over.

The next development began with excited shouting on deck: 'A sail! A sail!'

One of my companions hurried in to report. 'A king's ship about a mile away. We're trying to hail her.'

'Let me see,' I said.

He helped me from the cabin and steadied me against the barque's motion. Out to seaward stood a low-lying, four-masted craft. She carried little sail but was being propelled towards us at some speed by oarsmen.

'A galleass,' I said. 'Master Morice told me he had such a craft patrolling this water. Can this be it?'

'More like 'tis inward bound for the Gillingham dockyard,' my companion replied.

'Well, she seems interested in us. She's closing rapidly.'

At that moment we saw a puff of smoke issue from the

ship's bow. It was followed by a splash and huge plume of water not far off our port beam.

'She means to intercept,' I said. 'Have the captain haul in all sail. We don't want to attract more cannon fire.'

I allowed myself to be led back to the cabin.

A while later I heard the bump of a boat against our hull and the sound of men scrambling up the boarding net. An English voice shouted a string of orders. Shortly afterwards the owner of that voice entered the cabin.

'Charles Benson, Master of his majesty's ship, *Anne Gallant*,' he announced.

I saw a tall, beardless, ruddy-faced officer with a friendly smile.

'Thomas Treviot of the Worshipful Company of Goldsmiths,' I replied.

He laughed. 'Well, Master Treviot, you appear to have taken a Spanish prize. I'll warrant that's a first in the history of your guild. 'Tis certainly a first in my naval experience.'

'It all happened by accident,' I said.

He laughed again. 'That is a story I cannot wait to hear. But they tell me you are badly wounded.'

'Fatally, I suspect.'

'We can't let our heroes die that easy, Master Treviot. We've a barber surgeon aboard. Good man. He's brought many "fatally" wounded sailors back to life. We'll get you across to the *Anne* and let him have a look at you.'

He went off to give the necessary orders and, shortly afterwards, I was taken out on deck and laid on a plank. To this I was securely lashed. Then four sailors hoisted me up. The galleass had, by now, been grappled to our ship, so that my bearers were able to pass me across the short gap. Directed by the attentive Benson, the sailors were as gentle as they could be but the movements of the two ships in the water and against each other inevitably caused jarring. Every jolt was a fresh torment and each stung worse than the last. Before the manoeuvre was completed my world went black.

When I drifted into consciousness I was lying, stripped naked, on a table with a gaunt, bald man bending over me. He was working at my wound with various instruments and his probing sent spasms of pain through my body. I wanted to writhe and twist in response but could not move. At first I believed I was still strapped down. Then I realised I was being held by four muscular sailors. When I wanted to cry out I was thwarted by something pressing on my tongue. Only later did I realise that a cloth wedge had been securely fixed between my teeth. Never in my life have I felt more panic than at that moment. I was in pain, totally immobile, with a stranger doing things to my body that I could not see.

I know not how long I lay there. There must have been periods when I lapsed back into unconsciousness. Eventually, I was aware that the surgeon was no longer tending me, that my limbs were not restrained and that I could speak. Now a sheet covered my body. The surgeon was cleaning his implements.

'How bad is it?' I asked weakly.

He looked down at me, unsmiling, businesslike. ''Tis bad, but you might live. You will know in four or five days.'

'Where are you taking me?' I asked.

'Gillingham Water.' He closed his chest and set it on the floor. He removed his bloodstained apron and brushed himself down with his hands. He turned towards the door and it seemed that he was about to leave me ignorant of my immediate prospects. Then he seemed to think better of his reticence.

'They'll finish you off ashore, in the sailors' hospital,' he said. 'I've cleaned the wound but not closed it. 'Tis not the cutting of tissue that kills, but foreign matter lodged in the wound. I've poulticed you with turpentine and oil of roses bound with egg. That will protect the wound and give you some relief. The surgeon at Gillingham will re-examine the wound. Please God, it won't be festering, in which case he will close it up.'

With the help of a sailor, I got back into my clothes. The small cabin where the ship's doctor operated reeked of many unpleasant odours and I was glad to stagger on deck. Someone found me a chair and, seated in a corner out of the way of those working the ship, I was able to watch as the *Anne Gallant* crossed the estuary to the Kent shore, heading towards the dockyard.

After a while Charles Benson strode up. 'How are you feeling now?' he asked.

'Terrible. Unfortunately, your surgeon says there's a risk that I might live.'

The ship's master gave another of his ready laughs. 'Billy Bonesaw ain't the cheerfulest of souls but he's one of the best barber surgeons in the navy. Now' – he lounged against the rail – 'tell me what you've been up to this last couple of days. I've gathered bits and pieces from some of the archbishop's men but I'm sure you can give me a clearer picture.'

I described everything that had happened since we left Gravesend.

Benson listened intently. 'That is the most amazing story I've ever heard,' he declared, when I had finished.

'What happens now?' I asked.

'We're taking the prize into Gillingham. She's a trim craft.

I reckon the navy will make good use of her. We'll deliver you to the hospital.'

'What about my guards?'

'I guess they'll report back to the archbishop. He and the politicians can take it from there. Saints be praised, that's not my job.'

'Nor mine,' I said, and profoundly hoped that my involvement was, indeed, over.

Chapter 33

Later that day, Saturday 30 October, we docked in Gillingham Water and I was conveyed ashore to the sailors'
hospital. For the first time in three days I was able to lie down
in a bed. It was only a narrow truckle bed but to my
exhausted body it felt luxurious. For twenty-four hours I
drifted between sleep and waking. Billy Bonesaw's ministra-
tions eased the throbbing in my abdomen but the respite was
of short duration. The next day the chief naval surgeon
decided that the wound could be closed. That meant more
probing, a final cleaning with vinegar and then the appli-
cation of needle and silk thread. There being nothing more
the medical men could do for me, they were eager to send me
home. I despatched a message to Hemmings and on Wednesday Walt brought my coach to Gillingham. He had
removed the seats and arranged a mattress on the floor so

that I might be as comfortable as possible for the short journey. By evening I was in my own bed and actually beginning
to believe that I might recover.

Everyone wanted to welcome me back and hear an
account of my 'adventure' but Ned placed himself in charge
of the patient and ensured my rest was not disturbed. I felt as
weak as a newborn baby and the soreness in my belly abated
almost imperceptibly slowly. Ned brought me regular
nourishing broths but, apart from his visits, I spent most of
the next couple of days in a state between waking and
sleeping.

Sometime late on Friday morning I was dragged from slum-
ber by lashing rain rattling the casement. At least that was my
first impression. Suddenly I realised the window was open.
Worse than that, a figure was climbing in. The man's jerkin
was wet from the rain and his riding boots were thickly caked
in mud. He jumped with a feline movement and landed softly.
He walked to the foot of the bed. As his face came into the
light I gasped in alarm. Black Harry!

I tried to cry out but words would not come.

I felt his weight as he sat on the edge of the bed.

He turned on me that appalling smile that revealed arrogance, contempt and cruelty. 'Master Treviot, I'll wager you
thought never to see me again. Yet here we are having our
final meeting.'

'So I'm to be added to your long list of cowardly murders.'

'Cowardly?'

'Aye, you specialise in women and children. Now you add
a sick man to your score.'

'I don't choose the people who stand in my path, who try
to obstruct my mission.'

'Oh, let us have no rich-embroidered nonsense about

"missions" and "sacred causes". You're a blood-soaked ribald, who kills for the love of it. If you really think you are serving some higher cause, you deceive no one but yourself.'

He drew his poignard and tested its edge against the palm of his left hand. 'You're not a religious man, Master Treviot, or you could not make such ignorant comments. If you knew anything of the just God I follow, you would weep for the thousands of souls condemned to hell for embracing false religion.'

'I like not the sound of that god.'

He ignored my comment. 'I wish you could have seen some of the cringing wretches in the cells of Valladolid: Moham-medans and Jews who pretended conversion to the Catholic faith; misbegotten Lutherans who brazenly defied ancient truth. When we brought them to the edge of death, when they looked beyond it and saw the lurid flames of the pit, why, they shed tears of gratitude because we had revealed these things to them. You do not see into that other world. You do not know what endless torment awaits you. That is why men like me are needed. Men who are not obsessed with the things of this world. Men who have the courage to force the wilfully blind to see reality.'

'I've heard enough of your twisted religiosity. Do what you came here to do. Then we will see which one of us ends up in hell.'

But there was no stopping him. 'If only you could witness the souls being led to perdition by that Satan-hound, Arch-bishop Cranmer, you would know that he must be stopped.'

'You won't achieve that. There are good men determined to foil you.'

'The archbishop's time will come, I assure you. And now yours has come.' He pulled back the bedclothes and placed

371

the point of his dagger against my stomach. I felt its sharpness even through the thick dressing covering my wound.

Strangely, I felt no fear. If I closed my eyes it was not to escape the reality of death. It was simply that I did not want my assassin's leering face to be the last thing I saw in this world.

'Why, Thomas, whatever have you been doing, throwing the bedding about like this?' Ned set down his tray of nostrums beside the bed.

'Have a care, Ned!' I cried. 'He's in here somewhere and he's armed.'

'Who's here?' He glanced round the room.

'Black Harry! He came in through the window.'

Ned walked across the room. 'Well, he was considerate enough to close it behind him.'

'But I saw him – quite clearly, I heard him. I felt him.'

'You dreamed him, Thomas. That's quite common in people recovering from the kind of shock that your body has had. When I was in the monastery—'

'No, Ned! He *was* here. *Really*. He must still be in the house.'

'I'll tell the servants to make a thorough search,' Ned said. 'But now, let's have a look at your dressing. It will need changing, I expect.'

I sat up to help him remove the cloth bindings. He stooped to peer at the wound. He stroked his beard. 'This is very good,' he said. 'Remarkably good.' He gently fingered the wound. 'How does this feel today?'

'Much less painful than yesterday,' I replied.

'Excellent. Excellent. Well, we'll bind it again, just for a few days more.'

*

The following morning I had another visitation. The first I knew of it was when Adie and Lizzie burst in. They seemed flustered. Lizzie bustled around the room, tidying and straightening things, while Adie helped me into a sitting position and smoothed the covers.

'Why all the fuss?' I demanded.

'Important visitor!' Lizzie muttered, moving my heavy chair from the table to the bedside. 'Ned's delaying him as best he can, but he'll be up directly.'

'Who?' I shouted – and the result was an immediate stab of pain in my abdomen.

'The archbishop,' Adie whispered in my ear. 'In person.'

No sooner had she said the word than the door opened and Thomas Cranmer entered with his usual solemn gait. He was closely followed by Ralph Morice, who carried his left arm in a sling. The women made curtsies and withdrew silently.

The archbishop took the seat provided for him. He reached out to the coverlet and laid his hand on mine. 'Master Treviot, it is so good to see you. We have been very concerned about you. It was an immense relief when news came from Gillingham of your safe arrival there. As soon as we heard that you were returned to your home, we decided to come to thank you in person for all your help.'

'Your Grace does me great honour,' I replied, 'but I fear you have nothing to thank me for. I was supposed to help you apprehend Ferdinand Brooke. All I did was get him killed.'

Morice, standing behind the archbishop, said, 'It would have been better to bring the traitor to justice – publicly, in the king's law court – but we found several papers among his belongings on the ship that make his appalling crimes quite clear.'

373

Cranmer said, 'I am on my way to Westminster for Council business. It will be my duty to lay this information before my colleagues. I could not pass by the opportunity to make this diversion to satisfy myself that you were recovering from your ordeal. I feel responsible for all you have suffered.'

'It was an honour to be of service to Your—'

Cranmer raised a hand to silence me. 'Thomas Treviot, you are not a courtier and you are, therefore, spared the necessity for flattery.'

'Is this wretched business really over?' I asked.

'Almost, please God,' Morice said. 'Our enemies are, as we hear, thrown into some confusion. Yesterday another of Bishop Gardiner's messengers was arrested in Canterbury. The letters we confiscated carried instructions to cease their harrying of his grace.'

Cranmer smiled. 'My Lord of Winchester is confident that he can, himself, do all the necessary harrying. Now, we dare not stay long; his majesty is returning briefly to Whitehall from Ampthill in order to consult me before the Council meeting. It would be most useful to hear everything you learned about Master Brooke and his plans aboard his ship.'

I gave a detailed account of all that had taken place a week before. As I spoke, it was as though I were describing the strange adventures of some other man at some other, long-distant time.

When I finished, I said, 'Your Grace, I'm equally anxious to hear what happened to the men you sent into Essex. May I ask Master Morice what happened after we left him and his companions on the shore?'

'An uncomfortable night is the short answer,' Ralph said ruefully. 'We heard your attack on the barque and expected

374

the boat to return. We waited for news and were startled to realise that the ship was under sail. By then it was too late for our return journey, so we camped among the trees. At first light we put our dead and wounded on the wagon. Our prisoners were trussed up and tied across the spare horses. Thus we made our slow progress back to Tilbury.'

'I'm so sorry my stupidity enabled Black Harry to escape,' I said.

'Oh, but he didn't,' Morice replied. 'Before we left, the guard captain ordered a last search of the area to make sure none of the Spaniards were skulking in the vicinity. One of our more sharp-eyed men spotted the boat, beached higher up the creek. We sent a group of horsemen to investigate and they came upon Black Harry and his friends, soaked through, and shivering with cold. That meant more prisoners to be watched and slowed us down further but we managed to get all of them back to Gravesend, where we packed them into the jail.'

'How did Black Harry escape again?' I asked.

'Black Harry? Escape? Not he. We had had more than enough of his tricks and prevarications. A special court was summoned. That evil scoundrel was tried and straightway executed.'

'Executed?' I gasped. 'You're sure?'

'I went to witness it myself. Like you, I was well aware of Master Walden's capacity for getting out of tight corners. He was quite unrepentant to the very end. In fact he screamed abuse and railed like a madman. He even had the gall to threaten his grace from the scaffold.'

'The archbishop's time will come,' I muttered.

'Aye, those were his very words.' Morice looked puzzled. 'Has someone else already reported the hanging to you?'

'No matter,' I said. 'When was the execution?'

'Noon, yesterday. Thomas, are you all right? Is the pain worse? You look suddenly ... Shall I fetch your apothecary?'

My heart was thumping and my head had fallen back against the cushions. 'Don't be alarmed,' I said, recovering quickly. 'Just a twinge in the wound. It happens from time to time.'

'Then we must not tire you further,' the archbishop said, rising. 'I bid you farewell and assure you of my prayers for a complete recovery.'

Morice stayed momentarily after Cranmer had left the room. 'You might remember his grace in your prayers,' he said. 'We are not completely in the clear yet. Gardiner and Norfolk may be desperate enough to try anything.'

A short while afterwards Lizzie, Bart, Ned and Adie crowded into the room.

'Well,' Lizzie demanded, 'what did your distinguished visitor have to say?'

'He enquired after my health.'

'And?'

'He thanked me for my help.'

Lizzie treated me to her familiar pout. 'I should think so too. If he really knew what you ... what all of us have been through ...'

'Ralph Morice told me Black Harry is dead.'

All four of them cheered, though Ned crossed himself.

'It really is over, then,' Bart said.

'I think so.'

'Well, there's a couple of months none of us will ever want to see again,' Ned said. 'I think I'll away to the kitchen and brew something special to celebrate.' He sidled out of the room.

Bart sat down on the bed. 'We can really start thinking

about business again. There's several customers we need to make contact with. They'll want to know when we plan to reopen the shop.'

'Bart, let the poor man rest,' Lizzie said.

'We have to start—'

'Bart!' Lizzie threw him a knowing glance from the other side of the bed.

'Oh ... er ... yes. Well. I suppose that can wait a bit.'

He stood up and his wife almost pushed him out of the room.

Adie turned to leave also but, from the doorway, Lizzie said, 'Keep the patient company for a while.'

I patted the bed and Adie sat demurely.

'You're looking much better,' she said. 'You had us really worried. We were afraid you might ...'

'Die?'

'Yes.'

'There was a time when I thought I was going to die.'

'Were you afraid?'

'Strangely, no. Just annoyed that I wouldn't be able to do things I very much wanted to do.'

'What sort of things?'

I put a hand behind her neck and pulled her face down to mine. Hurriedly, hungrily, clumsily, I kissed her.

She drew back, gazing at me with wide eyes. She looked as surprised as I felt. For a long moment I stared at her, cursing my impulsiveness, hoping I had not upset her, regretting – yet not regretting. Then Adie smiled and, very gently, she kissed me back.

Epilogue

November 1543
(The exact date is unknown)

The Archbishop of Canterbury and his secretary sat facing each other in the canopied area of the archiepiscopal barge. Even on a morning such as this when the river, swollen with autumn rain, was running swiftly and the oarsmen had to dig deep to counteract the pull towards the City, it took no more than five minutes to cross from Lambeth Palace to White-hall. Neither man spoke during the brief journey. Each was fully occupied with his own thoughts.

Ralph Morice tried to imagine exactly what would happen when they reached the Council chamber. Who would be present? Who would take charge? What – exactly – would they say? He looked at Cranmer, resting placidly against the cushions, eyes closed. Trying to radiate a calm he did not feel? Praying? Knowing his master as he did, Morice could well believe that the archbishop was interceding for his enemies.

The six rowers lifted their oars and the barge gently nudged the staging of Whitehall Stairs. Attendants reached out to pull the boat sideways on to the landing stage and make fast the mooring ropes.

With a scarcely perceptible sigh, Cranmer stood, stepped forward and accepted a hand to help him on to the stairs. He climbed the few steps. Morice followed. They made their way between the sprawl of buildings that flanked the river, crossed the Sermon Court, where preachers approved by the king pronounced official doctrine, and so reached the broad stone stairs leading to the Council antechamber.

A motley collection of some twenty or so men occupied this sparsely furnished room – lawyers, liveried retainers of great men, merchants, clergy and any others with petitions or appeals to present to the Privy Council and prepared to wait hours, or, if necessary, days for their lordships to grant them a hearing. They relieved their boredom in various ways. Some gossiped in small groups. Some lounged against the wall reading books or checking through papers, rehearsing the evidence they intended to present when their names were called. Two men sat in a window embrasure playing at dice.

At the far end was the large arched doorway to the Council chamber. Before it stood a royal guardsman, halberd in hand and beside him, at a small table, the petitioners' clerk. Cranmer walked steadily forward. What should have happened; what always happened was that the guard tapped on the door, which was opened from within by an attendant who, recognising the archbishop, stood aside to allow him to join his conciliar colleagues.

This time the guard did not move. When Cranmer stepped closer, he brought his halberd to a horizontal position, silently barring the portal. Morice turned angrily to the clerk.

'What means this?' he demanded. 'Have his grace admitted immediately.'

'I'm sorry, Master Morice.' The clerk's embarrassment was obvious. 'We have orders. His grace is not to be received till sent for.' Scowling, Morice turned back to the archbishop.

'This, then, is to be the way of it,' Cranmer sighed. 'Condemned unheard.'

'We'll see about that!' Without waiting for the archbishop's consent, Morice strode from the room.

Cranmer calmly walked across to the fireplace and engaged in conversation with the group of men warming themselves there.

Within half an hour the secretary was back. After a brief word with the archbishop, he went across to the clerk's desk and, without comment, handed over a slip of paper. The official jumped to his feet, tapped on the door beside him and passed the note to someone inside. After a brief pause the door opened. The attendant approached Cranmer and bowed. 'If Your Grace will be good enough, the Council will see you now.' At the door Morice said, 'God save Your Grace.' Cranmer smiled and entered the chamber.

The tense atmosphere was immediately apparent. At the head of the table the portly figure of Lord Chancellor Thomas Audley was in the presidential chair. Beside him Bishop Gardiner sat, his hand resting on a pile of papers. Opposite him was the Duke of Norfolk. Among others present Cranmer scrutinised Sir Thomas Wriothesley who, as royal secretary, enjoyed something of the power once held by Cromwell; the Venerable Lord Russell, whose one good eye was fixed on the newcomer; and Edward Seymour. These were the men who counted. The others, Cranmer knew, would follow their lead.

What had they decided? From glances being exchanged across the table it was clear that discussion had been tense and not unanimous. Cranmer tried to gauge who had taken the initiative. Who was looking confident? Who had gained control?

He stepped forward. 'My apologies, My Lords.' He smiled. 'I was somewhat delayed.' He moved towards one of the empty seats.

Gardiner leaned across for a quiet word with the president. Audley nodded and said, 'Your Grace, before you take your place you should hear something we have agreed earlier.'

Cranmer inclined his head, still smiling. 'As Your Lordship wishes.'

All eyes were fixed on the archbishop. Some showed anger. Others nervousness. Audley glanced to his left. 'My Lord Bishop, since you have presented your case so eloquently perhaps you will declare the Council's will.'

Gardiner looked far from pleased. He shuffled his papers. He cleared his throat. 'Thomas Cranmer, Archbishop of Canterbury,' he announced solemnly, 'it has come to the attention of his gracious majesty's Council that you and others – encouraged, supported and set on by you – have infected the whole realm with heresy.'

'Tell me what erroneous doctrine I am guilty of spreading,' Cranmer said quietly.

Gardiner extracted a sheet from his pile. 'Here is evidence that you said of the mass—'

'We are not here to argue doctrine,' Norfolk interrupted. 'We'll not listen to your damnable, foreign ideas. You'll not spread your Lutheran poison here. You will be handed over to the Captain of the Guard. He will convey you to the Tower of London. It is there that you will be examined – and condemned.'

Several heads nodded. Other councillors, including Gardiner, looked displeased at the outburst.

Cranmer moved to the bottom of the table which was untenanted. 'My Lords, I am truly sorry that you compel me to appeal directly to the king's majesty.'

'Too late for that!' Norfolk snapped. 'Your evil influence over him has come to an end.' He stood and began to saunter down the room, his eyes gleaming with triumph and hatred. 'You are under arrest.'

Cranmer stood his ground. He opened the palm of his right hand and held its contents for all to see. 'I think you all know this ring,' he said calmly. 'It is his gracious majesty's token. Last evening he summoned me to his presence and entrusted it to me. "If my councillors lay anything to your charge," he said, "show them this ring. Inform them that I have taken the matter into my own hands and tell them to meddle with it no further".'

After a moment of stunned silence pandemonium broke out.

''Sblood! I warned you this would happen!' Russell bellowed.

'This was your doing, Norfolk,' Wriothesley whimpered. 'You know I wanted none of it.'

'Who's for the Tower now?' Seymour wagged a finger at Gardiner.

Audley banged the table, demanding silence. 'We must to his majesty straight and seek pardon for our presumption.'

Everyone rushed for the door.

The last man to leave the chamber was Cranmer. He placed the ring back in his purse, with a long sigh and a short prayer: 'Father, forgive them. They know not what they do.'

The failure to destroy the Primate of All England had taken fewer than three minutes.

Historical Note

Readers of historical fiction have a right to know where the history ends and the fiction begins. *The Traitor's Mark* is closely based on real events. At the heart of the story there are two mysteries, two events that have never been fully explained. In the autumn of 1543, the greatest portrait painter of the age, Hans Holbein, died. Where, when and how are questions that have never been answered. Karel van Mander, the Belgian poet and painter, asserted that Holbein fell victim to plague, but he was writing sixty years after the event and was not even born when Holbein disappeared. His explanation certainly cannot be accepted without question. The other happening was the Prebendaries Plot, a sinister attempt to have Archbishop Thomas Cranmer, England's leading churchman, indicted for heresy and burned at the stake (or, at the very least, unfrocked). Had it succeeded, it would have stopped the English

Reformation in its tracks. Who were the conspirators and how close did they come to drastically changing the nation's history?

These were the major 'headline-grabbing' events of that appalling autumn of 1543, when ungathered crops lay rotting in the sodden fields, plague flourished in the humid air and closed London down, gangs of desperate men wandered the country and, to cap it all, religious conflict split communities into rival camps.

In *The Traitor's Mark* I have interwoven these two momentous mysterious events to create a tapestry of plausibilities. The adventures in which Thomas Treviot and his friends became entangled did not happen – but they could have. Many real life men and women were caught up in intrigues, crimes and brutalities similar to those I have invented.

The following participants in the imaginary drama were real-life characters:

Hans Holbein, Jnr, the King's Painter
Thomas Cranmer, Archbishop of Canterbury
Ralph Morice, his Secretary
Thomas Howard, Duke of Norfolk
Stephen Gardiner, Bishop of Winchester
Edward Seymour, Earl of Hertford
Anthony Denny, Groom of the Stool
Dr William Butts, Royal Physician
Sir Thomas Moyle, MP and Chancellor of the Court of
  Augmentations
Dr Thomas Legh, jurist and diplomat
John Marbeck, composer and Member of the Chapel Royal
Richard Turner, a Reformist Preacher
Jan van de Goes, a Flemish Goldsmith

About the Author

D.K. Wilson is an acclaimed historian and expert on the Tudor period, and author of several fictional mysteries. He lives in Devon.